Did You Like the Ravioli Tonight?

Emmy's Story, Part 4

by
Kenneth Lee McGee

To Paul,
Thank you for the hundreds of hours playing basketball, wiffle ball, football, ping pong and those amazing table hockey games. I hope you add this to your little collection of books.

I want to offer a special thanks to Sue Midlock for creating the cover. She has the ability to take my confusing suggestions and turn them into amazing covers.

I would like to thank Denise and Stephanie again for their support and for sharing their knowledge and opinions. Without their help, this series of books would not have been possible. I would also like to thank Liz, Sue and others for reading my books.

I will forever be indebted to the people of WriteOn Joliet without whose knowledge I would have never learned the skills necessary to become the writer I am today. You can't imagine how clueless I was in the beginning.

I want to thank the people from my church who have graciously allowed me to include fragments of their lives as inspirations.

I want to thank my wife Sheila for her suggestions. Several of which I have used. Some were off the wall and made me laugh, but she's getting better... and more critical.

Chapter One

Heavy wet snow continued to fall as Emmy Colasanti crawled along with the other drivers in the early Monday morning traffic. She scanned the FM stations while on her ten mile commute from South Hampshire to Melrose Grove and her job at Robertson Industries. *This music sucks. Doesn't any station play decent music anymore?* She sat at a red light and reached over to the glovebox. She pulled out the Fridays At Five CD *Hero For Hire* and slid it into the recently installed CD player.

Suddenly, the driver in the car behind her leaned on his horn.

"What?" Emmy looked in the rearview mirror.

The driver blasted his horn again.

Emmy looked up at the green light. "Sorry." She waved at the car behind her and raced through the light at a snail's pace as the wheels struggled for traction.

"In a boy's mind as the lights go out." She sang along as the title track played. "Gonna fight fire. Gonna save the girl. I'm a hero for hire."

Despite the heavy traffic on her commute to work, Emmy had reasons to smile. Her boyfriend, Kenny Colwell, had just returned home from California where he and his partners in the band, Fridays At Five, had been recording their new project for the last month. She would see him this evening after work. Not only that, but she and her former boyfriend, Tony Bertucci, mended their broken friendship. He and her best friend, Kristen Keasling, even went to church with her the previous morning in South Bend. She offered a prayer of thanks as she drove into work. She slammed on her brakes as the car in front of her stopped suddenly, yet again.

"I hate this blasted traffic." She pounded on the steering wheel and cringed as her horn blared. *It's days like this that make me wish I could work from home.* Finally, traffic eased, and Emmy made it to work five minutes early. She parked the car and glanced up at the top of the fifteen-story glass and steel building as she walked to the entrance. *I wonder if we'll really get six inches of snow today.* She dashed into one of the elevators just before the door closed.

Mr. Oliver, her office supervisor, had just hung up his coat when Emmy skipped into the office suite. He ran a hand through his thinning, gray hair and grinned as he listened to her singing a song.

"Emmy, you sound so happy today, especially for a Monday. Care to tell me why?"

"Oh, Mr. Oliver, everything is absolutely wonderful today." Her blue eyes sparkled as she took off her coat and tossed it at the coat rack next to her desk.

Mr. Oliver shook his head. "How do you always manage to get your coat to stay on the hook?"

She shrugged and said, "It's all in the wrist. Anyway, Kenny got home late last night. I haven't seen him yet, but I will after work today." She smiled at Mr. Oliver, sighed and said, "I've missed him so much. Oh, and Tony was in a car accident Friday and had to go to the hospital. Isn't life wonderful?"

Mr. Oliver tilted his head and arched his bushy eyebrows. "You're happy that Tony is in the hospital?"

"What?" She landed back in reality with a thud. "Oh, that's not the reason I am so happy. Well, it is in a way. Kenny came home. Not because of the accident, but because of what happened after. He was flying home to see me and got hit by a truck when he was going shopping. The truck totaled his car because of the ice, but the band is home for now."

Emmy waved her hands around, talked too fast and didn't make any sense whatsoever.

"Slow down, Emmy. Come and have a seat in my office, and you can tell me all about your weekend."

Emmy followed Mr. Oliver into his floor-to-ceiling glass office and sat facing him.

"Now take a deep breath and tell me what happened, please."

"Okay, it all started Friday night. I wanted to see this band, The Notable Exceptions, because they are one of Kenny's favorites. I've seen them before, and I know P.J. He's the lead singer, and he plays guitar, too. Anyway, Richard wanted to take me to dinner, but I didn't want to go, so he came to the club with me." She still talked a mile-a-minute and waved her hands around and confused Mr. Oliver as much as ever. "I listened to the band. Oh, I saw my friends, Barry and Linda, so we shared their table, and I danced with Barry because Linda's feet hurt. Richard ordered the food. He was drinking beer, but that's besides the point. He took me home..."

Mr. Oliver tilted his head and still looked confused.

"Richard took me home, not Barry and Linda. I made some coffee while he picked out a movie. I sat on the couch with him, but I don't even remember what movie. Oh, I don't know if I should tell you this part."

"You know that anything you tell me in confidence stays right here, Emily." He reached across the desk, grabbed her hands, and held them still. "Now finish your story."

She looked down at their hands. She tried to move her hands, but Mr. Oliver held onto them tightly. "Yes, sir. Okay, I'll tell you." She talked slower now. "Richard and I were watching a movie, and he kissed me and sorta made a pass at me. He became pretty aggressive, and I tried to get away. All of a sudden the phone rang, and it was Mama, Tony's mother. Everyone calls her Mama."

"So I've heard." He let go of her hands.

She immediately began talking faster and waving her hands around. "She left a message that Tony had been in a wreck and an ambulance took him to the hospital. I threw Richard out, and told him I never wanted to see him again and not to ever call me again. I should have listened to Kristen because she warned me about him. I never wanted to be anything more than his friend, but I guess he wanted more." She blushed as she got embarrassed. "Then I called Mama. She told me what she knew, and then I called Kristen. Saturday morning I emailed Kenny to let him know what happened, and we drove to South Bend to see Tony. Not me and Kenny, because he was still in LA at the time, but I took Kristen and Mama to South Bend."

Mr. Oliver rubbed his forehead as he tried to make sense of Emmy's story.

9

"He's banged up, but he'll be all right. Kristen met John, who is Tony's roommate, at the hospital, and they are gonna fall in love, I just know it. She thinks he's a hunk." Emmy took a breath, sighed and said, "And that is why I am so happy today."

"I'm very happy for you, Emmy." He was still a bit confused, but Emmy smiled with joy, and that thrilled him.

"Thank you, Mr. Oliver."

Everyone in the office soon knew of Emmy's adventurous weekend.

The hours flew by. She locked up all the files and checked her desk. She tossed several letters in the outbox and looked at the clock. "Wow, it's after five already. I wish all days went by this fast."

She knocked on Mr. Oliver's door and entered. "I'm going to take off now unless you need anything else."

"Go ahead. I will be leaving in a few minutes myself."

"Good night, Mr. Oliver."

"Good night, Emmy. See you tomorrow."

Emmy noticed a car parked in the street as she pulled into her driveway. She saw Richard Demarco waiting on the front sidewalk and grimaced as she thought, *Why are you here? I told you to stay away.* Emmy was determined not to have a confrontation with him. She didn't want anything to spoil her relationship with Kenny Colwell, or her renewed friendship with Tony Bertucci. She slammed on the brakes of the red 1993 Honda Civic, threw the transmission into park and opened the door.

She kept her voice calm and under control as she stomped toward him. "What are you doing here, Richard?"

"Hi, Emmy, I wanted to talk to you for a minute. Can I come in?"

"Not a chance! Why are you even here? Did you not understand what I told you on Friday?"

"Emmy, I promise I won't try to kiss you, or even touch you." He held up a hand.

"I know you won't because I won't let you come near me. You can't come in the house."

"Can I talk to you at least?" he pleaded.

10

"All right, but just for a minute. I'm expecting someone."

Richard didn't move closer as she walked up the front steps. He remained on the front sidewalk with his hands in the pockets of his black trench coat and a fedora covering his graying hair. "Have you gotten back together with Tony? Is he all right?"

"He's going to be fine, and we are friends again, not that it's any of your business." Emmy looked to her right as an icicle fell from the roof gutter and shattered on the frozen ground.

"I suppose that means we are just going to be friends then."

"Hmmmph! I doubt it. I could be a friend, but you showed me that you're not interested in being my friend. You just want to get me in bed, and I can guarantee that ain't gonna happen. Not in this universe. I'm sorry, but that's the way it has to be."

"Is there anything I can do to regain your trust? I'd really like to be your friend. I have enough enemies already," he joked.

"You could move back to Kansas," Emmy said with a straight face. *I'm not falling for your charm again.*

"I do have a few friends who are women."

I find that hard to believe. She rolled her eyes. "If I thought for one second you could keep our relationship platonic, maybe we could still see each other for lunch at work occasionally. But friends? No way in hell are we ever going to be friends."

"Okay, I thought I would make sure you were all right."

"I'm doing great. Goodbye, Richard. Have a nice life," Emmy said sternly as she walked into the house. She watched from inside the front door as Richard walked toward his car. She grinned as he slipped on the snow and landed on his butt. *Shoot! Are you hurt?* She opened the door, but before she stepped outside, Richard rose to his feet, brushed off the snow and with head held high, marched to his car, got in and drove away. *I'm sorry for laughing at you, but that did look funny.*

She felt an icy blast of air as she closed the door. *I hope we don't get all that snow. At least not before Kenny gets home.* She sprinted up the stairs two at a time to her bedroom, ripped off her skirt and top and sat on the bed and struggled to shed her pantyhose. *I wish I never had to wear these things. I hate them with a passion.* She found woolen socks, put on a pair of jeans and

11

a sweatshirt. She was coming down the stairs when she heard the back door open. She stopped to listen and heard footsteps.

"Emmy! Where are you? I let myself in."

"Be right there!" She flew down the stairs, slid around the corner on the hardwood floor and darted into the kitchen where Kenny Colwell met her. She held out her arms and he picked her up and hugged her.

"Hey, Emmy, how are you? How was your weekend? Is Tony okay? Sit on the counter, and tell me everything."

He helped her jump up on the counter.

"Oh, Kenny, I'm so glad you're home. I missed you so much!" She kissed him all over his face. "I'm going to kiss you all night long."

"I missed you, too." He kissed her and ran a hand through her curly dark hair. "You got it trimmed."

"Do you like it? Is it too short?"

"It's still pretty long. It's way past your shoulders."

"I have to tell you what happened..." She began to tell him about the weekend as fast as she could possibly speak.

"Slow down, Em. Start with the phone call you got from Mama, okay?"

Emmy took a deep breath and calmed down. "I should start with earlier Friday. I went to see The Notable Exceptions with Richard Demarco from work. We ran into Barry and Linda at the club and sat at a table with them. Richard wanted to leave, so he brought me home. I let him come in—big mistake." She waved her hands in the air. "We were sitting on the couch in the TV room, and he tried to kiss me. He actually did kiss me. Against my will." She kept bouncing up and down on the countertop. "The phone rang, and it was Mama. She left a message that Tony had been in an accident and was in the hospital. I told Richard to leave and called Mama."

"Is Tony all right?"

"He broke his arm and has some bruises and scrapes, but he's okay." She paused and wasn't sure what to say next.

"Who is this Richard guy?"

"It's a long story..."

12

"I've got all the time in the world," Kenny said as he grinned. He put his hands on the counter on either side of her. He leaned forward and kissed her again.

She wrapped her arms around his neck and held on tight. They kissed until they ran out of breath.

"I like that," Kenny said.

"Me, too." She kissed him one more time. "Okay, he's the guy who used to deliver the mail, but he got a job in Kansas and just got back a short time ago. I met him in the elevator, and we ate dinner and lunch."

Kenny laughed as she waved her hands all around.

"He's older and used to be married, but I don't think he is now. Kristen and Barry think he looks old enough to be my father because he has some gray hair. I thought he was nice, but he tried to kiss me, and I told him I never wanted to see him again. He was here when I got home from work today, but I didn't let him in. I told him to go away and never call me or see me again. Kristen was right about him." Emmy paused for breath.

Kenny smiled at Emmy. "Oh, I missed you so much. I could listen to you all night long. You can tell me more about this guy later. I'm glad Tony is all right."

"He'll be fine. Did I mention that we met his roommate? His name is John Randolph, and he likes Kristen. Kristen thinks he's a hunk, and they are in love. They may not know it yet, but they are."

"You are so funny, Em. Didn't Tony try to set you up with him before?"

"Yeah, but I wasn't interested. Now it's a good thing."

Kenny kissed her again, and she responded by kissing him for as long as she could breathe.

"Are you hungry?" Kenny asked. "Should we go somewhere, or eat here?"

"Let's eat here, so I can tell you about everything that has happened since you've been in LA. Did you see Becky at all?"

"Yes, I did. I ate dinner with her and her whole family twice, but we never went out by ourselves."

"It would be okay if you did. I know you're still friends."

13

"What do you have for dinner?" Kenny opened the fridge. "I see you have the ingredients for a salad. I can make that."

"I bought stuff to make Reuben sandwiches. Do you like those?"

"Yeah, I do. Do you have real corned beef or the canned version?"

"I bought the real stuff at the deli. It's almost St. Patrick's Day, so I thought I would fix some Irish food. I bought soda bread and even found a green sweater at Kohl's to wear to work."

"Ah! You need a new jumper with the fierce weather we been havin'." Kenny used his approximation of an Irish accent.

"What?" Emmy squinted her eyes.

"A sweater is called a jumper in Ireland. Ah, never mind."

Such a dork. Emmy shook her head. "You still have a few days to work on being Irish."

They both worked on getting dinner ready and ate in the TV room while watching *Father Of The Bride* on DVD.

"Have you ever seen the original version?" Kenny asked.

She held a finger up as she chewed on her Reuben sandwich. "Yes, but I like this version better. Steve Martin is perfect for this role and the actress playing is daughter is adorable. I love her hair."

"She sorta reminds me of you except your hair is longer."

"Yeah, and I'm better at basketball than her. She dribbles and shoots like a girl."

"Duh!" Kenny held out his hands.

"You know what I mean." Emmy poked him in the side.

While they ate, Emmy told him everything that happened lately.

"It's already eleven." Kenny checked the time later. "I need to run, Em."

She kissed him. "Wouldn't you rather stay here?"

"Yes, but I can't. I'll see you tomorrow."

Emmy grabbed her coat and followed him to his car alongside the house. "It's still snowing. The roads might be treacherous with all this fierce weather we been having. Maybe you should stay."

"Are you making fun of my accent?" Kenny used his arm to clear some snow from the top of his car and flung it at Emmy.

"Hey! Stop that!" She jumped back and then scooped up some snow, pressed it into a snowball and threw it at him.

He ducked. "Missed me!" He laughed just as she launched a second one.

"Got you with that one," she squealed.

Kenny lunged at her and grabbed her coat before she could escape. He put his arms around her and lifted her onto the front fender of his car. He put his hands on her shoulders and rubbed his nose against hers.

Emmy grinned and asked, "Is that an Irish kiss?"

"It's the way Eskimos kiss."

"I'm not an Eskimo." She pressed her lips to his.

"Em, I can't stay," he said after breaking off the kiss.

"Please be careful going home."

She helped him clean off the three inches of snow from his car.

"See you tomorrow," Kenny said.

She waved as he started to back out of the drive. Then she reached down, formed a large snowball and threw it at his car.

He ducked as the snowball hit the windshield.

Emmy laughed. *You are a dork, but I still love you. Even if you have funny ears.*

Chapter Two

After work on Wednesday, Emmy rushed home, ate a quick supper, and then ran upstairs to get ready for the evening teen service. She called Kristen. "Hey, Kristen, got a minute to talk?" Emmy asked as she found a clean pair of jeans.

"Sure. What's up? Aren't you going to church tonight?"

"Yes, but I'm scared to death." She put the phone on speaker mode as she changed clothes. "I promised to talk to the teens tonight, and now I'm not sure I can go through with it."

"I remember you telling me about that. To be honest, I was shocked that you would agree." Kristen paused. "Is Kenny there? Can he hear me?"

"No, he's at the studio, but you are on speaker."

"You can do it, Emmy. Just say a prayer and let God help you. That's what you're always telling me."

"Thanks, Krissy. I gotta run. I just hope I don't puke in front of everyone."

"Yuck! You are so gross sometimes. You're worse than the guys. Call me later and let me know how it went."

"I will."

As she drove over to the Crest Ridge United Nazarene Church, Emmy sang along to her Fridays At Five CDs. She had talked to Kenny earlier. The band would be in the new Steward Music Group recording studio until nine or ten that night. She arrived at the church with time to spare and saw Chase Hillman, the worship team leader, in his office in the music suite.

"Hey, Emmy. How are you tonight?"

"I'm doing fine, Chase."

"Are you really?" he asked with a grin. "You look a bit pale. Almost as pale as me."

"I'm scared to death." Emmy hung up her coat. " How is your daughter? Is she feeling better?"

"Jada's doing much better. We took her to the doctor Monday. He thought it was just a cold. Her fever is gone, and she's eating again."

"That's great. It's so sad when little ones are sick. I'll be back in a few minutes."

Chase checked his watch. "We have plenty of time, Emmy."

She made her way to the small chapel down the hall from the music suite and took a few moments to pray. Chase would help Emmy lead the song service, and she was going to share some of her life story to the teens since Youth Pastor Brian Riley out of town. She felt nervous, but trusted in the Lord to guide her.

"Ready to run through the songs?" Chase asked as she walked back into his office.

"I'm as ready as I'll ever be."

Chase smiled at her. "You can do this, Emmy. I know you can."

"I'm glad you think so," she said as she smiled nervously.

Chase led her upstairs and into the recently remodeled teen center.

Emmy noticed the name on the wall. "Cross Fire Youth Center. That's kinda original."

"Pastor Brian came up with the name," Chase informed her.

He introduced her to the band composed of teenage musicians, and they practiced for twenty minutes. Emmy knew all the words to the songs by heart. The group worked out the arrangements and transitions between songs. Emmy knew all the hand signals, so the band could follow her if she decided to change anything. They finished practicing and made time for a quick prayer. High school and college kids filled the room. She watched some of the guys flirting with a couple of new girls. The kids were still milling around and socializing as Chase stepped up to the mic.

"Okay, everyone grab a seat. We're ready to start. It's good to see some new faces in the crowd."

The kids found seats, and the noise level dropped. Chase opened with a short prayer. As soon as he finished, the band began to play. They opened with an uptempo song that nearly all the kids knew.

"It's good to see such a large crowd," Emmy said. "Please join in and let's sing our praises to the Lord."

Emmy led them as they stood and sang along. When she

17

sang something, changed in Emmy. Normally shy and quiet, Emmy opened up when she sang to the teens. She smiled and danced as she sang. The band paused for a moment after the third song to allow Emmy to talk to the kids.

"Okay, now this is a new song—kinda. It's actually a song that a friend of mine wrote for his band. I helped a little with some of the lyrics, and it really fits. We didn't write it originally to be about God, but with a few changes, it is now about God and our love for Him. Anyway, it's called 'I Will Be True To You,' and the words are on the screen if you need them."

Emmy shouldn't have been surprised that the kids already knew the lyrics. Most of the kids loved Fridays At Five songs. The band, comprised of local SoHam musicians, was one of the hottest rock acts in the world. The few minor changes in the lyrics were easy to remember. Emmy made a circle with her hand to keep the band playing through the chorus an extra time because the kids really got into it. She smiled at the guys in the band, who treated Emmy like a fellow teenager. The fifth song, a familiar, worshipful song called "Amazed," prepared the kids for the more serious part of the service.

Chase took over and led the kids in a session of prayer as they prayed for anyone with a need. The spirit of these teenagers amazed Emmy. For ten minutes Chase led the teens as they prayed. After taking up a collection, Chase introduced Emmy. Not that she needed an introduction—almost everyone knew her.

"Hi, like Pastor Chase said I'm Emmy Colasanti, and I'm a relatively new believer in Christ." She paused and took a deep breath. "I don't mind admitting that I'm frightened to be up here. Scared to death actually."

"Don't be scared. We won't bite," one of the guys shouted.

"Thanks, I needed that," she said and then giggled. "I've lived in SoHam all my life, and I realize this is Crest Ridge, so please don't hold that against me."

The kids grinned and some laughed out loud. She spoke openly and honestly about her life. She didn't hold back as she shared stories of her childhood growing up in SoHam.

"I moved out of my parents house before I was eighteen. I

18

graduated from Roosevelt, got a full-time job, found an apartment and thought I knew it all. Needless to say, I didn't. I used to fight and argue with my mother all the time. She tried to control my life, and I didn't appreciate that." Emmy saw several heads nodding. "I can tell there are some of you who feel the same way. I hate to admit it, but I still don't have a great relationship with my parents. I'm trying, but it's not easy. I pray about it, and for them, every day.

"I'll tell you about the night I accepted Jesus. My... uh... friend Tony and I had struggled in our relationship, and I had been praying for him. I opened my Bible, which I hadn't read in years," she confessed. "And I read John 3:16 and part of I Corinthians. I felt the Holy Spirit compelling me to pray so I did. I knelt by my bed and prayed for Jesus to forgive me. He did! The next morning I came to this church and talked to Lynette. She explained what had happened to me 'cause I didn't have a clue."

She witnessed to the kids about how Jesus changed her life. She even talked about sex.

"I'm not sure if I should mention this." She looked at Pastor Chase.

He nodded and said, "You can talk about whatever God leads you to."

"Even sex?" Emmy bit her lip as she asked.

The kids laughed.

"It's a subject we should discuss," Chase said then shrugged. *I hope you know what you're doing.*

She saw a few faces in the crowd that might have known her, or her sister Diane, from their high school days. "Okay. I haven't always been exactly an angel. I did a few things that Daddy would have grounded me for had he known. I wasn't too wild, but I wasn't perfect. I'm thankful that even before I became a Christian, I had decided to wait until I got married to have sex. It hasn't always been easy, and I know people do make mistakes and slip up. Jesus is there for us if we do. We need to confess our sins and trust in Him to guide us..." She continued for a few more minutes.

"I hope I have made some sense to you. I know it's not easy, but I try to read my Bible and pray every day. Sometimes I pray while in the shower, but I don't think God minds." She

19

blushed. "I think He understands."

Chase took over after she finished. He prayed for Emmy and the teens, and asked if anyone would like to pray for salvation. Two young girls came forward, and then three young men knelt at the edge of the platform which served as their altar. Several other young people came forward to pray with them.

Emmy apologized, "I'm sorry, Chase. I should have asked you for permission before I mentioned sex."

He put an arm around her shoulders. "You talked about it because the Holy Spirit guided you. Look!" He pointed to the kids who were still praying. "I think you did the right thing. The kids respect you for your honesty."

One of the girls sought Emmy out after the service ended.

"Hi, Emmy. My name is Yolanda Garcia."

"Hi, Yolanda. I'm Emmy." Emmy noticed Yolanda's dark brown eyes, hoop earrings and slight trace of acne.

"I really appreciated what you told us tonight. I mean about sex. I had a boyfriend, and he wanted me to sleep with him. I refused, and he broke up with me."

"I'm sorry, Yolanda. It's not easy to be young and in love."

"I'm not sorry I broke up with him, and now I know that I don't have to feel alone. There are other girls who feel the same way. So many of the girls I know in school are already having sex."

"You don't have to follow the crowd. I learned that in high school." Emmy asked, "Are you from SoHam?"

"I grew up in Mexico City and moved here a year ago. I have been going to St. John's since I came to South Hampshire because it's close to where I live. I heard about this church, and I thought I would come here. I'm glad I did. Tonight I felt like I needed to pray. I guess I always thought that just going to church would be enough to get by, but now I know better. Thank you for taking the time to talk to us. I feel like you care about us."

"I do care for the teens, Yolanda. I know how difficult high school can be. I've been through it."

"You weren't a believer back then, right?" Yolanda asked.

"No, I wasn't a Christian then, so I tried to fit in with the popular kids, but I couldn't do some of the things they would. I know all about the peer pressure to have sex. I kinda got caught up in the wrong crowd for a while. If you ever need to talk, or anything, just call me. Do you have a cell phone?"

"It's in my coat. I'll grab it."

Yolanda retrieved her cell phone, and Emmy gave Yolanda her number.

"I really like to listen to you sing, Emmy. You have such a beautiful voice, and you really understand how to get through to us."

"Thanks, but I just try to allow the Holy Spirit guide me. I don't try to do anything on my own. I'm not smart enough to do that," Emmy said with a grin.

Emmy and Yolanda laughed, and then Emmy hugged her. One of the teens wandered around the room taking pictures. She took one of Yolanda and Emmy together as they smiled for the camera.

Chapter Three

"How did it go, Em?" Kenny asked as he stopped by her house a few minutes after nine. "Have you eaten yet?"

"Not yet. I just got home." She opened the fridge and pulled out the leftover Chinese from yesterday.

"So? How was it?" Kenny grabbed two plates from the cabinet.

She opened the white cardboard containers. "Better than I thought. I had butterflies in my stomach, but I didn't puke in front of them."

"That's good."

"I talked about sex and some kids got saved."

Kenny's eyes opened wide. "Really?"

Emmy blushed. "They didn't get saved because I mentioned sex."

"You can tell me about it while we eat."

They nuked their food in the microwave, sat on the couch in the TV room and ate while Emmy explained.

"I wish I had been there to see Pastor Chase's reaction." Kenny put his arm around her. "God uses all kinds of things to lead people to Him."

"I talked about growing up and some of the things I did in high school, but I didn't get real specific about my sex life."

Kenny tilted his head and stared at her.

"What?" she asked as she chewed on some steamed broccoli.

"Do you have a sex life?" Kenny asked as he grinned.

"No! Unless kissing counts." She smacked his arm. *God doesn't remember the other stuff.*

"You are so amazing, Em." He turned her face to his and kissed her.

"Stop that."

"Why? Did you promise not to kiss me tonight?" Kenny asked.

"No, but I want to eat before my chop suey gets cold. I might let you kiss me later after I finish studying."

Kenny turned on the television, and Emmy did some reading for her night class while she balanced a plate of food on her lap. Kenny headed home as the *Late Show with David Letterman* started.

Emmy had just gotten to sleep around midnight when the phone rang.

"Hello."

She listened and then dropped the phone. She lay on her back in bed and began to sob.

Emmy's eyes were bloodshot, like she hadn't slept at all, and her hair pointed in every direction. She arrived at work three hours late the next morning dressed in jeans and a sweatshirt. She wore a pair of old tennis shoes without any socks. She didn't even have on a coat. She saw Mr. Oliver sitting at his desk, so she walked into his office.

"I'm sorry I'm late, Mr. Oliver."

He jumped up and came around his desk. "Are you all right, Emmy? We've been so worried about you." Mr. Oliver knew something was terribly wrong because Emmy had never come to work in jeans or a sweatshirt.

"No, I'm not." She shook her head and started crying.

"Sit down, dear."

She stopped crying, sat down, put her elbows on her knees and put her chin in her hands. "My dad had a heart attack last night and is at St. Bart's hospital. I spent the night at the hospital and came straight to work."

"Emmy, you shouldn't be here." He patted her back. "You should be at the hospital with your family."

She looked up and used her sweatshirt sleeve to wipe her face and dry her tears. "I didn't want to let the team down. You need my help today. Mom told me to go home, and she would call if she wanted me to come back to the hospital."

"Emmy, we will survive without you today. You should be with your mother."

"But what about the project?"

"I'm sure the men will find the right files," Mr. Oliver said.

23

He finally convinced her to go back to the hospital.

"May I please call Mr. Robertson? He might want to know about Daddy."

"Of course you can, Emmy. You should take the whole day off. I'll call his office for you."

"That's all right, Mr. Oliver, I'll call him." She called Mr. Robertson's private number, and the founder and owner of the company answered on the second ring. "I'm sorry to bother you, Mr. Robertson, but I need to talk to you in person. Something terrible has happened."

"Emmy, you can come right over." He always made time for her if he possibly could. He buzzed his secretary and said, "Something has happened to upset Emmy Colasanti. Would you see if you can learn what happened, please?"

"I'll get right on it," Mrs. Moneywell said.

Emmy arrived at the company headquarters, parked in a visitor's spot, jumped out of the car and dodged several people as she ran inside. A member of the security team escorted her upstairs. He opened the door to Mr. Robertson's office and Emmy scooted past him.

Mrs. Moneywell told her, "Go right in, honey. He is waiting for you."

Emmy walked into his office and stood next to him. She tried not to, but she started crying. Mr. Robertson put his arm around her and let her cry.

"I have never seen you so upset. It must be very serious for something to upset you this much. Tell me, please."

"My dad had a heart attack last night. He's old, and I'm afraid he is going to die."

Mr. Robertson put his hand on her shoulder. "I'm so sorry to hear that. I think you should be with your family." He walked quickly over to the door, opened it and called to his secretary, "Mrs. Moneywell, please cancel everything for the rest of the day. I will be taking Miss Colasanti to the hospital."

"Yes, sir. Walter Oliver just called, and he filled me in on everything he could. I thought you might want to do that, so I have already started to reschedule your appointments. Your car will be waiting downstairs. If you get Emmy's keys, I will make arrangements for someone to drive her car home."

"You think of everything." Mr. Robertson smiled.

"I try my best, sir," she answered with pride.

Mr. Robertson took Emmy downstairs, and his driver took them both to St. Bart's. On the way Emmy told Mr. Robertson everything that happened since she last talked to him.

"I'm glad Kenny is home, and I'm pleased that you and Tony are friends again. I don't really know Richard Demarco, but it sounds as if he tried to take advantage of you. I will not stand for that. I will take care of the matter for you."

"Oh, please, Mr. Robertson, don't fire him. It's just as much my fault as his. Please don't do anything."

"I doubt that it was your fault at all, Emmy, but I will respect your wishes as long as nothing else happens. I will look into his background more carefully though."

They arrived at the hospital, and Mr. Robertson instructed Roscoe to grab some lunch, but to stay close. Emmy hurried over to the elevators, and she and Mr. Robertson headed up to the cardiac intensive care unit. She stopped at the nurse's station.

"I'm Emmy Colasanti, and my father is in the CICU."

"There's still no change, Emmy."

"Has the doctor been in to see him?"

"About fifteen minutes ago, dear. He talked to your mother and filled her in on his condition. She's in the waiting area if you want to see her."

"Thanks."

"You're welcome, Emmy. I said a prayer for your father. I think he's going to be all right."

Mr. Robertson stayed with Emmy and her mom for the rest of the afternoon. It had been years since he had seen Emmy's mother and father.

"Emmy, I want you to take the rest of the week off. Next week, too, if you need. I will let Mr. Oliver know to get a temp for the next couple of weeks. As for tonight, my driver and car will be at your disposal. This is his cell number. I will take a cab home."

Emmy shook her head. "Mr. Robertson I can't..."

25

He placed his hands on her shoulders and gently squeezed. "Emmy, I am your boss. I am not giving you a choice in the matter."

"Yes, sir. Thank you, Mr. Robertson." Emmy gave him a hug, and he hugged her back.

He turned to face her mother. "Good night, Patricia. Raymond is in good hands. I'm sure he will be all right. Please have Emmy call me if you need anything, anything at all, anytime."

"Thank you, Bill. I appreciate everything you've done for Emily. She loves her job. I know we've had our differences in the past," Mom said. *I hope you still don't hold a grudge for what Raymond did. He won't ever apologize for saying your company would go bankrupt in a year. He's as stubborn as a mule.*

"We've all made mistakes. This is more important."

Emmy found the chapel downstairs and knelt to pray. She spent ten minutes in prayer for her father and other people she knew in need. Later, the nurses convinced Mrs. Colasanti to go home for the night. Emmy called the driver, and he took them home. Emmy decided to spend the night with Mom.

Emmy walked into her old bedroom. "You got rid of the old wallpaper and this is new carpeting."

Mom stood in the doorway. "We've made some changes in the last four years."

Wow! It's already been four years since I moved out. Emmy realized. "You got a new bedroom set. I can sleep in here."

That plan changed when Diane and Craig arrived later that night with five-week-old Carson. Diane made the trip so her father could see his grandson. She would hate herself if she didn't make the effort to be there and something tragic happened to her father.

Shortly after Diane arrived, Kenny called Emmy's cell phone. "Emmy, I'm sorry, but we've been in the studio all day. I just got home and Mom told me about your father. Are you all right? Is he going to be okay? How much do you know at this point?"

"He's still in the hospital, but he's stable, and the doctors assure us that he will be all right. I'm staying at Mom's tonight."

26

"How is your mother doing? This must have been quite a shock to her."

"She's okay. I'm sorry I didn't call you, but I was just so busy."

"It's okay, Em. I understand. Will you be able to sleep all right? Do you want me to come over?"

"I'll be okay. Maybe we can have breakfast tomorrow. Mr. Robertson practically ordered me to stay home for the next couple weeks."

"That sounds like him. He's a good man."

"Do you know him?"

"Kinda. My parents have known him for a long time. Dad went to school with him. If you want, I'll take you and your mother to the hospital in the morning."

"Okay, thanks. Diane and Carson are here, too. Craig came with them, and they're staying here tonight."

"Where are you going to sleep?" Kenny asked. "There isn't room for all of you."

"I guess I'll crash on the couch."

"I have some extra blankets," Mom said. "Too bad that couch doesn't fold out into a bed. It's not very comfortable."

"Em," Kenny said slowly, "Why don't you stay over here tonight? You can stay in the house if you want, and I'll stay in the carriage house."

"Oh. I don't know if I should. Mom might not like it..."

"What won't I like, Emily?" Mom heard Emmy's part of the conversation.

"Kenny offered to let me stay there tonight, and he will take us to the hospital in the morning. I'm not sure I should."

"It would be easier if you did. At least you would have a bed to sleep in. You should go ahead, Emmy."

"Will you be all right if I do?" Emmy asked. *This is different. You are actually encouraging me to sleep at Kenny's.*

"I will be fine. Diane and Carson will keep my mind off of your father."

"Okay. As long as you promise to call me if anything changes."

"I will call you if I hear anything from the hospital." Mom kissed Emmy's cheek and then walked to the living room and took Carson from Diane.

"Kenny, are you still there?"

"Yes, Em, and I heard everything. Come over whenever you're ready. I'm sure you will want to see Diane and Carson for a while."

Emmy whispered to him, "I want to stay in the carriage house with you tonight. I need you to hold me and be there with me."

"Okay, baby." *I wonder if her mother knows about the futon?*

Emmy checked her purse. "I don't have my key. I gave all my keys to Mrs. Moneywell."

"I'll leave the door unlocked for you," Kenny said.

Emmy visited with Diane and Carson for a time while Craig sat on the couch and watched TV without talking to anyone.

"I should go and let you guys get to bed," Emmy said to Diane. "Craig is yawning and you look tired."

"See you tomorrow, Em. Say hi to Kenny for me."

Emmy walked through the alley, staying in the tire tracks in the packed down snow and over to the Colwell's carriage house. She climbed the stairs and walked into the apartment. Kenny heard her enter. He spun around in his desk chair, stood up and held out his arms. She shivered and sobbed as he held her close.

He rubbed her back and sides. "It's all right, baby, just let it all out. It's been a rough week for you."

"I don't know what I'll do if Daddy dies. I do love him even though we haven't always gotten along."

"I know you do, Em. Do you need some water, or something to eat? Have you eaten anything today?"

"No, I didn't feel hungry."

"You need to eat something, Em. I could fix you some soup or a sandwich. Soup would warm you up. You are still shivering."

"I guess I am kinda hungry."

"Sit on the futon."

She sat on the futon while he grabbed a blanket from the

28

closet. "Wrap up in this and I'll run in the house and fix you some chicken noodle soup and a turkey sandwich. You can eat as much as you want."

"Thanks, Kenny."

He came back five minutes later with a plastic bag of groceries. "We didn't have any turkey. Will ham be all right? I grabbed some crackers and chicken noodle soup. Just take a minute to fix."

Three minutes later he set the soup, crackers and a sandwich on the small table.

"Eat as much as you can."

She finished everything and drank a bottle of water. "I feel better now."

"Would you like dessert? I have some Ben & Jerry's in my fridge."

"What flavor?" she asked as she walked over to the old couch and sat down.

He opened his small fridge. "Let me see. There's Cherry Garcia and Chocolate Fudge Brownie."

"Definitely Cherry Garcia. That's my favorite."

Kenny grabbed a spoon and brought the ice cream over to the couch. "Is it all right if we share?"

"I might let you eat some of it."

Ten minutes later, Kenny tossed the empty carton in the trash.

"Are you ready to lay down and get some sleep, Em?"

"I just realized something."

"What's that?"

"Duh! I don't have any pajamas. I really don't want to sleep in my clothes."

"You could wear..." Kenny looked through his dresser. "I don't think I have any shorts that would fit. I could run in the house and see if Mom has any old pajamas."

"What? No way! I'm not gonna wear your mother's clothes." Emmy jumped up and checked through his dresser drawer. She pulled out a t-shirt and an old pair of gym shorts with an elastic waistband. "Can I borrow these? The t-shirt will be long

29

enough on me and these shorts might just stay up."

"Yeah, I guess so."

"Will you please add another blanket to the futon while I get ready for bed? A pillow, too." Emmy kissed his cheek.

"Whatever you need, Em." *Maybe I should tell Mom you're staying out here.*

She came out of the bathroom a few minutes later and tossed the shorts to Kenny. "Too big. They won't stay up."

He looked at the t-shirt and then at her legs. "So what are you wearing?"

Emmy grinned.

"Never mind. I don't want to know."

She slipped under the blankets on the futon. "You have to stay on top of the covers." She curled up in a ball and patted the spot behind her. "Hold me close and cuddle with me."

Kenny lay next to Emmy on the futon until she fell asleep. He kissed her cheek and moved to the old couch where they shared their first kiss and slept there.

Chapter Four

Emmy slept on her stomach while Kenny showered and dressed in the morning. He walked out of the bathroom and used a towel to dry his hair. He smiled as he looked at Emmy. *You are taking up the whole futon, Em.*

She finally opened her eyes around nine.

"Morning, sleepy girl. Are you hungry?"

Emmy stretched her arms over her head and yawned, "I'm starving. What time is it?"

"It's a few minutes after nine. If you want, I can go in the house and start breakfast while you shower and get ready."

"Okay. Can you make pancakes for me?"

"I imagine so. I'll add blueberries if Mom has any." Kenny sat on the edge of the futon. He leaned over and kissed her cheek.

"Do I still have some clean clothes over here?" Emmy asked. "I can't remember. So much on my mind."

"Look in the top drawer of the dresser. I think you might have a change of clothes in there for emergencies. I'll start breakfast. Come on over to the house when you're ready." He pointed to a coat hanging up by the door. "Make sure you wear a coat. It might be a little big, but it's better than nothing.

"Thank you, Kenny." She reached out her arms. "You can't kiss me because I have morning breath."

Kenny hugged her, kissed her cheek and headed to the main house.

Emmy dumped her emergency bag of clothes on the futon. *Underwear, socks, deodorant, toothbrush. So far, so good. Oooh, this must be for the summer.* She picked up a t-shirt and shorts. *I guess I'll have to wear my jeans.* She looked in the dresser and found one of Kenny's sweatshirts to wear. She showered and dressed. *I should call the office.*

"Mr. Oliver, I wanted to tell you how Daddy is doing. He's stable and starting to get cranky, so I know he's doing better. I know Mr. Robertson told me to take next week off, but I'm going to come in Monday to make sure everything is all right."

"You don't have to do that, Emmy. We will be all right. I've

31

got a temp coming on Monday," Mr. Oliver said.

"I'll feel better if I at least come in for a few hours on Monday."

"Okay. Call me if anything changes. Have a good weekend."

Emmy ended the call and headed into the house. She hung Kenny's coat on a hook by the back door. Mr. and Mrs. Colwell were in the kitchen with Kenny.

"Emmy, I'm so sorry about your father, but I'm sure he will be all right. It will just take some time," Mrs. Colwell said as she gave her a big hug.

"Thanks, Mrs. Colwell. I have been praying for Daddy, and I'm sure God will answer my prayers. I hope His will is the same as mine."

Kenny grinned at her. "Nice sweatshirt."

She poked his side. "All I had in that bag was this t-shirt." She lifted the sweatshirt.

Emmy and Kenny ate breakfast and then walked over to her parents' house. Craig let them in. "Diane took your Mom and Carson to the hospital already, Emmy."

"Why? Did the hospital call? Did something happen? Mom should have called me."

"Chill, Emmy." Craig backed away and held up his hands. "Not as far as I know. They got up early and left without eating. Diane said they would stop and get McDonald's on the way."

"Thanks, Craig," Emmy said. "By the way, Carson is absolutely adorable."

"Thanks, I think so, too."

Kenny drove Emmy over to St. Bart's, they parked in the deck and took the elevator to the third floor.

"Good morning, Kenny. Thanks for bringing Emmy up to the hospital," Mrs. Colasanti said.

"No problem. Mom and Dad send their best wishes, and they want you to know they are praying for Mr. Colasanti."

"Thank you. I appreciate that."

Diane walked up to Kenny with Carson in her arms. "Would you like to hold Carson?"

Kenny shook his hands. "He's too small. I might drop him."

"You better not drop my grandson," Mr. Colasanti said.

"Daddy, are you feeling better?" Emmy rushed to his bedside.

"I'm all right. I need to go home. The food sucks and I need a beer."

"You can't have a beer, Raymond!" Mrs. Colasanti yelled.

"Emmy, sneak me in a beer, okay?"

"No, Daddy. You have to do what the doctors say."

"They never said I couldn't have a beer."

Diane shook her head. "You can't have any beer. Get over it."

Kenny checked the clock. "I should go, Em. I have to meet the guys at the studio at noon."

"Thanks for the ride, Kenny, and for last night," Emmy said.

"Promise me you will call if anything changes. I know it will be good news, so call me when you can."

"I will, Kenny."

He hugged and kissed her as Mom and Diane watched.

I wonder what you guys did last night? Diane grinned.

Emmy noticed the grin on Diane's face as Kenny left. "We didn't do anything."

"If you say so," Diane smirked. "I'm going to run Carson home so Craig can take care of him. Can I bring you anything, Mom?"

"Bring me something for lunch. I'm not going to eat hospital food."

Diane ran Carson back to the house so Craig could take care of him. Two hours later, she returned to St. Bart's.

"Where's my lunch? I'm starving," Patricia complained.

Diane handed her a bag from Darby's. "Here. It's still warm."

Emmy called Kenny. "I'm going to spend the night here. That way Mom and Diane can go home and get some rest."

"Do you want me to come up? I could keep you company overnight."

33

"No, you don't need to do that. I'll be all right."

"I'll talk to you later, Em," Kenny said.

"Hey, Diane, could you run me home? I don't want to be here all day if I'm going to spend the night."

"Yeah, I could do that." Diane rolled her eyes but agreed.

Diane pulled into the driveway and Emmy pointed. "Look! There's my car. I totally forgot about it. I left it at the corporate office. I bet I know how it got back." She rushed inside and called Mr. Robertson's office. "Thank you for getting my car back to me, Mrs. Moneywell."

"You're welcome, dear. How is your father doing?"

"He's complaining, so I know he's getting better."

"I will inform Mr. Robertson."

"Thanks again. I'll keep you updated."

Kristen called Emmy later that Friday after her last class at North Park College and asked about her father.

"He's doing better. He's whining about wanting a beer. I miss you. I haven't seen you all week."

"We talked on the phone, Em."

"Can you come over to the house?"

"Okay, I'll be there soon. We should do dinner."

Later, Kristen walked in the back door. Emmy saw her and ran to hug her best friend.

"How is your dad really doing, Emmy?"

"He's getting better, but the doctors are telling us he will be there for at least a week, maybe even longer. They're concerned about pneumonia, so he still can't come home. I'm planning to spend the night there."

"I called Mama and told her."

"Thanks. Are you hungry, Kristen?"

"I could eat."

"Let's go out for Mexican."

"Where is Kenny? I know he came home?"

"He's at the studio with the band. He took me to the hospital this morning."

Kristen didn't say anything, but she realized Emmy most

likely spent the night with him.

Emmy showered and got ready while Kristen cleaned up the kitchen.

"I'm ready, Kristen!" Emmy hollered as she flew down the stairs. She stepped into the kitchen and saw Kristen at the sink. "You didn't have to clean up my mess. I would have gotten around to it eventually."

"You've got more important things on your mind, Em."

Emmy hugged Kristen. "You're the best friend anyone could ever have. I love you so much, but you really need to use soap when you wash the dishes."

"I love you, too, Em, and I did use some soap. The suds just disappeared. Let's walk to the restaurant. It's not far, and the fresh air will be good for us."

They sat in a booth and placed their drink order. Emmy surprised Kristen by ordering a margarita.

"I think I need one tonight, Kristen. Maybe even two."

"Just be careful, Em. You haven't had any alcohol in quite a while."

The sound of her cell phone ringing interrupted their conversation. "It's Kenny. I should talk to him."

"I'm home now, Em."

"Good. I miss you. I need you to take care of me. You know how to make me feel so good." She tried to whisper so Kristen couldn't hear, but Kristen heard Emmy's remark.

"It's all right, Em. Just be careful." Kristen scooped some more salsa onto her chip.

"I didn't mean it like that. He slept on the couch."

Emmy finished her first drink before the food arrived. She requested a second and finished that while they ate. Kristen limited herself to one. Emmy had ordered a burrito, beans and rice to eat and surprised Kristen by finishing everything. Then Emmy wanted another margarita.

"Emmy, are you sure you should be drinking another margarita? That will be your third one."

"No, I'm not sure, but God will forgive me this one time. I know it." *My third one? I must have lost track.*

35

Emmy looked around the restaurant as she and Kristen were leaving. She saw Richard Demarco at a table with another woman.

"Kristen, do you see that guy in the booth with the blue shirt sitting with a woman? She's got short dark hair."

"Yeah, the guy drinking a beer."

"That's Richard Demarco!"

"For real?"

"That's him. He sure hasn't wasted any time finding someone else to have dinner with," Emmy said sarcastically.

"I'm going to go over to him and create a scene that he won't soon forget. I'm going to pretend I am his lover. I'll tell him I'm pregnant and demand that he marry me immediately."

Emmy held onto Kristen and wouldn't let her go. "No, Kristen, that will only embarrass me more."

Kristen told her, "I know someone who will take care of him for you. Just say the word, and he's gone."

Emmy looked at Kristen and didn't know if she meant it or not.

"Some of my cousins are rather shady characters, remember, and you have met Uncle Carmen."

Emmy pulled Kristen out the door before Richard spotted them. She laughed as Kristen pointed her finger back at the window where Richard sat and "blew him away." Emmy hadn't laughed so hard in some time as she and Kristen staggered arm in arm toward home.

"Emmy, really!? Three margaritas? Did you ever drink three margaritas before? Or three beers, or that much wine?" Kristen asked.

"Not that I can remember. Why?" Emmy asked as she nearly ran into a tree.

"Because you are drunk, Emmy Colasanti. That is why."

"I'm not drunk, Kristen. I've never been drunk in my life."

"You are now, sweetie. If a cop pulls us over you will get a WWI."

"What's a WIWWI... whatever?" Emmy asked as she dodged around the tree as though it was moving.

"A WWI, Emmy—Walking While Intoxicated."

"You're making that up aren't you, Kristen?"

"No, I'm not! Now sit down with me for a while until you are sober enough to walk home."

Emmy sat with Kristen on a bench, put a hand to Kristen's cheek and looked into her eyes. "Have I ever told you how pretty you are, Krissy?"

"Yes, Emmy, many times."

"I wish I looked as pretty as you." Emmy touched Kristen's nose tenderly. "Have I ever told you how much I love you?"

"Yes, you have, sweetie." *You are really plastered, and you're acting so weird.*

Emmy lowered her finger to Kristen's mouth. "Have I ever... I don't feel so good now. I think I'm going to..."

Kristen scrambled to get out of the way as Emmy got sick to her stomach.

Kristen pinched her nose. "Do you feel better now, Em?"

"I've never done that before."

Oooh! Gross! That smells horrible. "It's because you haven't had any alcohol for quite some time, and the margaritas and all that Mexican food was too much for you to handle. You'll be fine in a few minutes." *I hope.*

Emmy sat with her head by her knees as Kristen massaged her back and shoulders. Kristen managed to get Emmy home without any further incident. Once inside, Emmy lay down on the living room couch and fell asleep. Kristen woke her up later so she could go to bed.

"I have to go to the hospital to see Daddy. He's probably waiting up for me."

Kristen said, "I'm sure he's not waiting up for you, Em. I'm sure he's sleeping."

"What if he's not? I should at least call him."

"You can't call his room this late at night."

"I don't feel so good, and I have to pee real bad."

Kristen got out of the way just in time as Emmy ran to the bathroom.

Kristen decided to stay overnight with her. Neither one of

them noticed someone had left Emmy a message on her phone.

Emmy felt like crap the next morning. She rolled out of bed, knelt beside it with her head resting on her comforter and asked for forgiveness for what she had done the night before. Then she prayed for her father, Tony and Kristen. Kristen listened to Emmy from the hall. Emmy finished her prayer and jumped up. She wanted to see if Kristen was awake so she ran out of her room and immediately collided with Kristen.

"Oh, Kristen. Are you all right? I wanted to see if you were awake."

"I'm fine, Emmy. I'm used to you running into me. That's how we met, remember? You ran into the restroom at school and right into my arms."

"I remember. I was running from Todd Delaney. Are you hungry?"

"I could use some breakfast. What have you got?"

Emmy grabbed her jeans and slipped into them. "I thought we could have cottage cheese and maybe a piece of fruit."

"Are you on a diet or something?"

"Not really a diet, but I need to lose a few pounds."

Kristen looked at Emmy like she had gone bonkers.

"Emmy Colasanti! You don't need to lose any weight. You don't even weigh a hundred pounds. If Mama heard you say that she would paddle your butt. Is there something you aren't telling me?"

"Not really. You wouldn't tell Mama would you?"

"Emmy!"

"My jeans are tighter now for some reason. See." Emmy tried to slip her hand down her jeans.

"You goof. Those are the same jeans you have been wearing since you were fifteen. You might be a couple pounds heavier now, but I don't think you need to worry about getting fat." Kristen poked Emmy in the stomach.

"All right, then how about bacon and eggs for breakfast?"

"That's more like it."

Emmy and Kristen headed to the kitchen, and Emmy

38

started cooking breakfast as Kristen watched.

"I told Tony I would call him this morning to make sure he is all right."

"What time do you have to call him?" Emmy asked.

"Eight thirty. What time is it?" Kristen asked.

"It's only seven forty-five. We've got time."

Emmy saw a light blinking on her phone.

"Hey! There's a message. It might be about Daddy."

She listened to the message. "It's from Tony," she whispered.

"Hey, Emmy. I'm feeling better and wanted to talk to you. I guess you're out somewhere. I'll try again tomorrow. Kristen is supposed to call me in the morning. Take care, Emmy."

Emmy looked at Kristen, "Should I call him to let him know what's going on."

"Of course. He's still one of your best friends, and you do love each other."

Emmy made a face at Kristen. "I'm not going to tell him. He has enough stuff going on at school already. I don't want to bother him with this. Promise me you won't say anything when you talk to him."

"No, I won't promise. He should know."

"Please, Krissy! Don't tell him. He will probably rush home, and I don't want to deal with that."

"Because Kenny's here, right?"

Emmy bit her lip as she nodded her head.

"All right, I won't say anything, but if your father gets worse, you have to tell Tony, okay?"

"That's so reassuring," Emmy said sarcastically. "But I will if Daddy gets worse."

Emmy and Kristen sat at the kitchen table to eat their breakfast. Kristen waited for Emmy to pray before they started. They talked about school and work as they ate. Emmy told Kristen about church and how she talked to the teen group.

"Who would ever believe that shy little Emmy Colasanti could ever get up in front of a group of kids and make a speech?"

"You know it's not like making a speech, Kristen. I pray

39

and let the Spirit lead me."

"I think I understand, Emmy. Oh, look. I need to call Tony."

"Remember, Kristen. Don't say anything about my dad. Tony has enough on his mind already. He doesn't need to be worrying about Daddy."

"I still think you should tell him."

"Kristen. You promised you wouldn't."

"All right. I'll keep my promise."

Before Kristen could call Tony, Emmy ran to the bathroom and lost her breakfast. Kristen went into the bathroom to check on her.

"Have you been getting sick in the morning a lot, Em?" Kristen asked.

"Just this past couple weeks. Why?"

Kristen thought about how Emmy told her about her jeans being tighter. "Are you pregnant? Have you been trying to get pregnant because of what your doctor told you?"

Emmy looked at Kristen and whispered, "No," but nothing else as she bit her lip. "You need to call Tony now."

"You aren't supposed to drink alcohol if you're pregnant, Em. Doctors aren't always right, either."

"Really, I didn't know that."

Kristen couldn't tell if she was admitting to being pregnant or not.

Kristen called Tony, and she and Emmy talked to him for an hour. After the accident, Tony decided to stay on campus during spring break—not having a car made that decision unavoidable. Since he wouldn't be involved with spring football, Tony had more free time. He decided not to use his final year of eligibility and enter the NFL draft. He still worked out everyday because of the NFL tryouts. After saying goodbye to Tony, Emmy and Kristen showered and headed to the hospital.

Emmy and Kristen exited the elevator and a nurse waved to get their attention. "Ms. Colasanti, I have good news. Your father was moved to a private room on the eighth floor a little while ago. Room 8030."

"Really? That's great. Thanks."

40

"You're welcome."

Emmy pulled Kristen back into the elevator and stabbed the button for the eighth floor. The door opened and Emmy and Kristen scurried to her father's room.

"Good, you're here. I need some beer."

"Daddy, I'm not bringing you any beer. You finished your food, so you must be feeling better."

"I feel great. I don't have pneumonia." He coughed and struggled to breathe.

Emmy called Kenny's cell phone.

"Hey, Em, what's up? I just pulled into the parking deck."

"Daddy's up on the eighth floor now. Room 8030."

Kenny met Emmy in the new room. Kristen listened to their conversation.

"Emmy, did you get the utility bills paid? What about groceries?"

"I mailed the checks on Tuesday." She straightened his collar. "You need a new shirt. The collar is worn."

Kenny couldn't see the collar. "Will you order me some, Em. You know my size."

"Okay, but I will use your credit card."

Oh, my God! You guys are acting like you're married. Kristen thought.

The conversation dwindled. Emmy checked the time and asked Kristen, "Would you wait outside for a minute, please? Kenny and I want to talk to Daddy for a second."

"Sure, Em, I'll be outside in the hall. Take your time." Kristen walked out of the room and waited. *So you don't want me in the room, huh? Are you going to tell your father that you're having a baby? Are you trying to give him another heart attack?*

Emmy sat in a chair next to the bed and held her father's hand. He squeezed her hand gently. Kenny stood behind her with his hands on her shoulders.

"Daddy, you know I love you, right?"

He nodded his head in response.

"I need you to do something for me, okay. I would like you to promise me that you will stop drinking as much as you have

41

been. I don't expect you to stop completely, like the doctors recommend, but you can cut back. I pray for you everyday. I pray for Mom, too, and your relationship. I don't want to be too pushy, but I want you to know that I care." She kissed his forehead tenderly. "I've gotta go. I'll see you tomorrow after church. Love you, Daddy."

Emmy waved goodbye and Kenny held her hand as they left the room. She found Kristen by the nurse's station.

"What should we do now, and where should we go?" Kristen asked Emmy.

"Are you guys hungry? We could grab something to eat," Kenny suggested.

"I'm starving. We skipped lunch," Emmy said.

"That's fine with me as long as it's not Mexican. Are you sure your stomach can handle food?" Kristen smiled as she asked Emmy.

"I'm all right now, but, please, no more Mexican food for a while. How about Darby's?"

"Sounds good to me. At least they don't serve alcohol there."

"Are you gonna be on my case for last night?" Emmy sounded hurt.

"No, I know last night was just one of those things. It's not like you're an alcoholic like your dad."

Emmy looked at Kristen, and, for the first time in her life, realized how Kristen viewed her father.

"Oh, Emmy, I'm sorry. I didn't mean that."

"It's all right, Kristen. You are right. I've never wanted to face the truth before, but I need to now. Daddy has to understand that he needs help."

The three of them grabbed a bite to eat at Darby's. Emmy surprised Kristen by having a garden salad.

Emmy explained, "I need to start eating healthier."

Kristen looked at Emmy, and then at Kenny, who was rubbing Emmy's back tenderly. *What is going on with you guys? Did you elope and forget to tell anyone?*

They returned to Emmy's house.

42

"Are you gonna stay here tonight, Kristen, or do you need to get home?"

"Do you want me to stay, Em? I can if you want. Is Kenny gonna stay?"

"Not tonight. He's going home because he needs to be at his church in the morning. Would you stay with me, Krissy? I feel better when you are here."

"Of course I'll stay. It's a good thing I always keep an overnight bag in the car."

Kristen listened as Emmy and Kenny talked quietly. She observed Kenny touching Emmy's belly several times as they talked. He kissed her quickly and left.

You guys are definitely hiding something. Kristen knew.

Emmy went to church in the morning and stopped by the hospital afterward for a quick visit with her father. She stayed for an hour before heading home. Mom and Diane were at the hospital and convinced Emmy to go home because she looked ill herself.

Emmy got back to the house and saw Kristen in the kitchen.

"Did you eat anything yet?" Kristen asked as she searched through the fridge.

"I couldn't eat anything this morning."

"Did you throw up again?" Kristen frowned as she asked.

"Yes."

"I haven't had lunch. What should we eat?" Kristen asked. *Do you think you can keep something down? You need to eat for the baby's sake.*

"There's not much in the fridge..."

"I know. Let's go see Mama. She always has something to eat," Kristen suggested.

"Okay. We should call her first to let her know we're coming."

"We can call her on the way. She should be home, but if she's not, I know where the spare key is hidden. We can raid the fridge. It will be fun."

They headed over to Mama's, and Kristen called ahead.

43

Mama answered after she checked the caller ID.

"Hello, honey. I've been thinking about you. When are you gonna come and see me?"

"Actually, Mama, Emmy and I are on our way over right now. We're hungry. Do you have anything to eat?"

"I might be able to feed you girls. What would you like?"

"Anything! As long as it's homemade. We'll be there soon."

Kristen and Emmy walked in the back door. Mama stood by the stove making a pot of spaghetti. She turned to see the girls and gave them both a big hug. Mama noticed that Emmy seemed even thinner than before, but she didn't say anything.

"How is your father doing, Emmy? Is he going to come home soon?"

Emmy frowned at Kristen. "He is doing a lot better, and he should be able to come home this week. How did you know, as if I need to ask?"

"Now, don't be mad at Kristen. She told me that you didn't want Tony to know so I haven't told him. I say a prayer for your father every morning."

"Thanks for not telling Tony. He's got enough things on his mind already."

"Tony is a smart young man, Emmy. He can handle more than you might think. I hope you girls are hungry enough to eat all this spaghetti. You will have to take anything that's left home with you, Emmy."

They sat at the kitchen table to eat. Emmy and Kristen visited with Mama until five o'clock.

"We need to go, Mama. Thanks for lunch and the leftover spaghetti."

"You're welcome, honey. You can always come over here and see me even if you're not hungry, you know," Mama said as she hugged her. "Kristen, you say hi to your mother for me. Tell her to call me on Tuesday, and let me know what time she wants to go see Carmen."

"I will. Thanks for lunch, Mama."

Emmy and Kristen headed back to Emmy's house.

"I have to get back to my dorm," Kristen said. "I've got to

44

finish reading for class."

"I feel so much better since you came to see me. I don't know what I would do without you. I love you so much."

"I know you do, Em, and I love you, too. I know Jesus loves us both, and maybe he drank a margarita once, too."

"I feel so stupid for having too much to drink Friday night. I don't know why I did that."

"It's kinda funny now, Emmy. You acted so goofy when you were plastered."

"I was not plastered," Emmy insisted.

"Yes you were, Em, or do you always pass out on the couch like that."

"Kristen, remind me to never drink that much again. Saturday morning I fell to my knees and prayed for forgiveness. I asked God for the strength to never do that again, and I am trusting in Him to protect me from that."

She hugged Kristen until Kristen told her, "Emmy, I can't breathe."

Emmy smiled and let loose.

On Sunday night Diane and Craig packed for the trip back to Toledo. Just before Diane left, Emmy called.

"I'm so glad you came, Diane."

"We can't stay any longer. Craig needs to get back."

"I know that you haven't gotten along with Mom and Dad."

"Ya think!" Diane laughed. "We still don't get along, Em, but I had to come to let Dad see Carson. I'm glad that you are close enough to keep an eye on them."

"You don't have to live in Toledo," Emmy said.

"Craig won't move back to SoHam. His family is in Ohio. He's got a better job now. He might even get a promotion and a raise." *If he doesn't get fired.*

"Does Mom know you are going home today?"

"I told her yesterday that we needed to get back."

"What did she say?" Emmy asked.

"Just the usual complaining about us living in Toledo. You know she never lets go of anything. She will be bugging us as long

45

as she lives. It's who she is."

"Don't say it like that, Diane."

"Sorry, I didn't mean anything."

"You be careful on the way home. Take care of Carson. He is adorable."

"I will. You take care of yourself. I couldn't help noticing you look like you've lost more weight. Have you?"

"Maybe a little. I can't eat anything in the morning without getting sick."

Diane remembered how she felt when she was first pregnant. "You should see a doctor. Say hi to Tony for me and Kenny, too."

"I will."

Chapter Five

Despite feeling nauseous Monday morning, Emmy decided to go in to the office to keep her promise.

Mr. Oliver was standing by her desk when she arrived. "How is your father doing, Emmy?"

"He's doing better, and they moved him out of intensive care Saturday morning. I think it's a miracle."

"I'm glad to hear that. We were all concerned. You do know you can take the week off if you need?"

"I know, but I thought I would come in today and make sure everything is all right." She smiled at the temp as she approached.

"We are not totally dependent on you, Emmy. Close, but not totally. Ms. Widomski has helped us out before." Ms. Widomski handed Mr. Oliver a file and then adjusted the lapel of her gray pantsuit.

"Hi, Paulina. Thanks for coming in."

"No problem, Emmy. I'm sorry to hear about your father. I hope he improves real soon." Ms. Widomski pushed her glasses back up her nose and headed back the desk she was using temporarily.

"Oh, before I forget, Mr. Robertson asked to see you in his office promptly at eleven o'clock," Mr. Oliver told Emmy.

Emmy's eyes opened wide as she asked, "Do you have any idea why Mr. Robertson needs to see me?"

"I think everything will be all right. You shouldn't worry," Mr. Oliver said as he opened the file.

Shoot! That is going to make me worry even more. Emmy bit her lip.

"I updated him about your father."

"Thank you, Mr. Oliver. I'll see if Paulina has any questions."

She sensed the guys treating her differently today, but couldn't be positive. *Something weird is going on, but I'm not sure what, and it doesn't seem to be about Daddy.* She kept glancing at the clock and couldn't concentrate on even the simplest task.

47

Mr. Oliver called her into his office at ten thirty. "You don't need to worry about us. Paulina will be here all week if we need her. We will get by. You take as much time to be with your family as you need."

"Okay, Mr. Oliver. Thank you."

He checked his Bulova watch. "You should be leaving. You don't want to keep Mr. Robertson waiting."

"I'll leave now."

She felt apprehensive as she drove to Mr. Robertson's office. She didn't know why since he always treated her with kindness and consideration. Suddenly a thought popped into her head. *Is Mr. Robertson going to fire me because of my youth and inexperience. Paulina can do my job even better than me.* She hoped not, but she said a quick prayer just in case.

Emmy parked in a visitor space and trudged into the building. Security cleared her and she took the elevator upstairs. She entered Mr. Robertson's office.

"Hi, Mrs. Moneywell. I'm here," Emmy said without making eye contact.

"He's expecting you, Emmy. You can go right in." Mrs. Moneywell pointed and then a comical smile appeared on her face for barely a split second.

Emmy's legs shook, her knees weakened and her heart raced as she entered his office. She kept her eyes on the floor as she walked over to his desk. She looked up and noticed Mr. Robertson talking on the phone. He motioned for her to sit. She sat on the front edge of one of the large leather chairs. She bit her lip as she noticed several photographs on the wall to her left of Mr. Robertson with his family. *That's Brady and Bennett and their mother.* She squirmed in the chair and rubbed her hands together. *I feel like a kid in the principal's office.*

Mr. Robertson ended his phone call quickly. "How is your father doing, Emmy? I heard they moved him out of intensive care. That is a good sign."

"Yes, he's doing so much better. Kristen and I were able to spend time with him on Saturday when they moved him, and I went back yesterday. I'm going to spend the night at the hospital if he needs me to."

"Did you forget my instructions about taking this week off to be with your family? Mr. Oliver has a temp filling in for now." Mr. Robertson removed his reading glasses, placed them on the desk and then pinched the bridge of his nose.

"I'm sorry, sir. I thought I should be here today to make sure everything was all right."

He waved a hand and then looked at her.

Oh, crap! This is where he tells me I'm fired. She bit her lip hard enough to hurt.

Instead he asked, "Did you let Tony know about your father?"

She tilted her head. *What does that have to do with my job? Please, just tell me if I'm fired. I won't cry until I get outside.* "No, I didn't want to bother him. He's busy with classes and everything. Did I tell you about his accident at school?"

"No, you didn't mention that to me. I don't mean to pry into your personal life, but you do realize that he cares a great deal about you, right?" he said as he straightened a stack of folders in front of him.

"Yes, I know. I took Mama and Kristen Keasling to South Bend so they could see him. I guess I wanted to see him, too, and make sure he was okay. We talked and I think our relationship is better now." Emmy giggled nervously and then said, "I have this terrible habit of yelling and screaming at him and saying the most awful things to him. You wouldn't believe the words that come out of my mouth when I get mad."

Mr. Robertson smiled. "I admit I use some improper words at times." He stood and pressed a button on his phone. "Now, please."

Emmy heard the office door open behind her, but didn't turn around. *That's probably security here to escort me off the premises. I've seen that in movies.* She closed her eyes.

"Hi, Emmy," Tony Bertucci said while he walked into the room. *I hope you're happy to see me.*

Emmy bounced up and turned around. "What are you doing here?"

49

Tony looked at Emmy and then at Mr. Robertson. "Just happened to be in town."

"You are not. Why are you really here?" She put her hands on her hips.

Mr. Robertson walked quietly out of his office and told Mrs. Moneywell, "I know I really don't have to tell you..."

"I will not put any calls through until instructed otherwise." She smiled at her boss. "You really are a sentimental old softy."

He smiled at her and whispered, "Mrs. Moneywell, if one word of that ever gets out, you are fired."

She smiled and saluted him. "Yes, sir!"

Back in the office, neither Emmy nor Tony moved for a few seconds. Then Tony took a step toward her.

"When did you get here? Why are you here? What the hell is going on?" Emmy took two steps toward Tony. "Don't you have classes?"

Tony quickly closed the gap, put his hands on her shoulders and looked down into her sparkling, blue eyes. "Why didn't you tell me about your father?"

"I didn't want you to worry and miss school or anything." Emmy whispered as she rested her head against his chest and began to cry.

He held her close, but remembered not to squeeze her too tightly. "Emmy, don't you know that you are more important to me than anything. School, football, anything." He wiped the tears off of her face with his hand.

Emmy backed up and said, "I know I'm not, but that's sweet of you to say so." She glanced at his arm. "Does it still hurt? Does the cast itch?"

"Doesn't hurt, but it itches and maybe not more than football," Tony said. "Tell me about your father and this Richard guy."

"How do you know about him?"

"Don't be mad."

Emmy waved a hand. "Kristen told you, huh?"

"She knew you wouldn't."

Emmy told Tony about Richard and what happened.

50

"I'm so sorry. I felt so confused, and I didn't think we would ever be friends again. Kenny was in LA at the time, so I spent some time with Richard. Just lunch. Nothing big. I won't make a mistake like that again."

"It's not your fault, Emmy," Tony said. *If I ever run into that jerk, I will break his jaw.*

"Tony, how did you know about my dad?"

"Mr. Robertson happened to be in South Bend over the weekend, and he talked to me. He told me about your dad. He asked me to come to his office Monday morning. He talked to Coach Theismann and cleared the way for me to be gone for a few days."

They spent the next few minutes talking to each other before they were ready to leave. They walked out of the office to see Mrs. Moneywell smiling at them from behind her desk. "Would you like to see Mr. Robertson now?"

"If he's not busy," Emmy replied.

"I'll inform him you are ready to see him."

He appeared in a matter of seconds.

"Is everything better now?"

They both answered, "Yes."

Mr. Robertson looked at them and said, "Take what has happened recently and learn from it. We all make mistakes and stumble. The people who get back up and learn from their mistakes and failures are the ones who grow stronger and succeed. Take Tony to the office and show him off, and then take the rest of the week off as I instructed." He pointed a finger at her. "Your job will be waiting for you when you get back, and I expect you to work even smarter and more efficiently when you return. Got that, young lady?"

"Yes, sir!"

Emmy wrapped her arms around Mr. Robertson and hugged him. Tony shook his hand. Mr. Robertson watched them leave. He thought Tony would pick her up and carry her on his shoulder because of the way they teased each other. He turned to his secretary and said sternly, "Not one word, Mrs. Moneywell, not a single word."

51

"Old softy," she whispered as she smiled at the best boss in the world.

Back at her office, Emmy introduced Tony to the guys. They gathered around and shook his hand.

"We're all football fans and enjoy watching you play, but you better be nice to her or else you will have to answer to us."

"That's right. We don't care how big you are. You better treat Emmy right."

It felt as if she had five new fathers, or maybe uncles, now. Mr. Oliver being the only one left from when she started working on the team. Even Ethan Hanks worked out of a different office now.

"Are you hungry?" Emmy asked as she drove home. "Forget it. Stupid question. How about Chinese for lunch?"

"Sounds good to me."

Emmy called in the order, and they picked it up on the way. They got to her house and as soon as Emmy put the Chinese carryout on the kitchen table, Tony hugged her.

Why did you do that? Emmy backed up after Tony released her. "When do you have to be back at school?"

"On Wednesday. I'd like to go to the hospital with you to see your father. Is that okay?"

"Sure, it's all right. He has always liked you. I think it would be good for him to see you."

They stared at each other for a moment before Emmy mentioned, "You do know that Kenny is home, right?"

"I wasn't sure until Kristen told me. Will he be upset if I go with you to see your dad?"

"No, why would he be?"

"No reason, I guess. I just want to make sure."

"Let's eat the Chinese before it gets cold."

They sat at the kitchen table and talked about school and Emmy's job. After a moment of silence Tony blurted out, "I miss you so much when I'm at school, Em. I wish we could be together all the time. I want to spend my nights with you."

Emmy froze with a forkful of rice halfway to her mouth. She didn't say anything.

Oh, no! I've really blown it now, Tony thought as he saw the look on her face. "I guess I shouldn't have said that. I'm sorry, Em. I guess you and Kenny are really together for good now. I'm sorry for saying what I did."

Emmy looked at Tony and whispered softly, "I love you, Tony. I really do, but it's different now. I think you know it, too. We are special friends. That's all we can be right now."

Tony looked at her and nodded, "I guess you're right. I'm sorry for hurting you."

"We do have a special relationship. I get mad at you and yell and scream, and you get mad at me, but you almost never raise your voice back at me. You get my blood boiling at times. I used to picture us as an older married couple, and we would always be fighting. I guess I assumed all marriages were like my parents' relationship. It's different with Kenny. Probably because his parents are so different. They never yell at each other. They have a way of working things out by talking to each other."

"It's funny, Em. You used to yell at me and you used some language that would get my mouth washed out with soap if Mama ever heard me talk like that."

"I know. I'm trying to watch my mouth now, but it's not always easy. Mom and Dad still swear at each other. I grew up hearing that language all my life."

Tony grinned at her. She grinned back.

"What are you thinking about?"

"Where do you think our relationship would be today if I had gone ahead and done what you wanted?" he asked and then took a bite of fried rice.

"You mean if we made love?"

"Yeah, I wonder if we would still be together. We might even have a kid already."

"I guess I was pretty willing back then. It always amazed me that you possessed the strength to say no. I remember that I would get so frustrated with you."

"Well, we can't change the past. I know you are different now because of your new faith in God."

"Yes, but there are some things about me that are still the

53

same," Emmy said and then giggled wickedly. "Let's finish the Chinese, so we can go to the hospital."

After she finished eating, Emmy called Kenny, "Hi, how are you this fine day?"

"Okay, how are you. Are you at work?" Kenny asked while tuning his guitar.

"I'm home now. I went to the office this morning and surprised Mr. Oliver. He told me they will be all right without me this week. Oh, I went to see Mr. Robertson. We talked for a few minutes, and then Tony walked into the room."

"He did. Did you know he would be there?"

"No, it was a total surprise. We talked, and I apologized for the way I yelled at him. He came home with me, and we picked up some Chinese takeout. We're going to see Daddy in a few minutes." Emmy whispered into the phone, "Is that all right?"

"Of course it is. I'm happy that you guys can be friends. Maybe we can go to dinner tonight. We're only working until six today because Jeff and Frances are celebrating a birthday. Maybe Kristen can go with us."

"I'll call and see if she's busy. I gotta go. I love you."

"Love you, too, Em. Talk to you later."

Tony heard Emmy's part of the conversation. "Ready for St. Bart's?"

She nodded.

Emmy took Tony to see her father. They spent an hour at the hospital, and then Emmy took Tony home so he could see Mama. She called Kristen, and they made plans to meet at The Hungry Lion for dinner.

Kristen and Tony were already at a booth when Kenny and Emmy arrived at seven.

"Hey, guys. How long have you been here?" Emmy asked as she sat down while Kenny and Tony shook hands.

"About twenty minutes. We got here a little early so I could talk to my favorite cousin," Kristen said. She didn't mention that she wanted to ask Tony if he knew anything about Emmy being pregnant.

"How's school going? It's almost over, right?" Kenny asked

as he slipped in next to Emmy.

"Just a couple more months to go. How have you been? You guys are working on the next CD, right?" Tony asked as he picked up a menu.

"Yeah, we recorded in LA for a month, but we're going to finish it here at home. This is the first time I've been home this long since our first tour." Kenny smiled at Emmy and kissed her.

Kristen elbowed Tony in the ribs. *See? I told you they act like they're married.*

Tony rubbed his side. "Why did you do that?"

Kristen frowned.

"Did you guys order yet?" Emmy asked as she flipped through the menu.

"We ordered some Texas fries, but figured we would wait for you guys. Do you know what you want, Em?"

"I'm gonna have a house salad and maybe eat some of Kenny's fries. You are gonna order fries, aren't you?" Emmy grinned at Kenny.

"Absolutely! Anything else I should order?"

"Please don't order anything with bacon on it. Lately the smell of bacon in the morning has been making me nauseous."

Kristen looked at Tony. *See? I told you so.*

They ordered and spent over an hour at their booth. Kristen was too afraid to come right out and ask Emmy what she really wanted to.

As they were leaving, Emmy asked Tony, "How are you getting back to school? Do you need a ride?"

"I'm going to take the bus. Thanks for the offer though, Em. You need to stay in town so you can be close to your father."

Kristen slugged Tony in his side.

"Ow! Why'd you do that?" Tony took a step back. "My ribs are going to be bruised from you hitting me all night."

"Did you have to remind her that her father is in the hospital?"

Tony looked at Emmy, "Sorry, Em."

"It's all right. He's getting better and might be able to come home later this week."

55

"That's good to hear."

They said their goodbyes and headed out. When Tony and Kristen got in the car, she smacked his arm.

"Now what did I do?"

"You didn't ask Emmy about... you know."

"I can't just blurt it out. Especially not with Kenny sitting next to her. What would I say? 'Hey, Emmy, are you knocked up?' Why didn't you ask her?"

"I did before, remember?" Kristen frowned at him.

"And she said no. Why do you even think she's pregnant?"

"Just little things. Like morning sickness. Not liking the smell of bacon. You know she loves bacon. I saw Kenny rubbing her belly, and they chased me out of the room so they could talk to her father. Alone! Her jeans are tighter. What else could it be?"

"I think you're imagining things," Tony said as he rubbed his arm.

"She has spent a lot of time in his apartment. They stay overnight with each other."

Tony grinned. "Well, if you're right, we will know in a few months."

Kristen looked at him with scorn. "Men! I hate all you guys. Now take me home, and don't you dare say a word about this to anyone."

"You know Mama would be able to tell if Emmy is expecting. Did she say anything?"

"Not yet, but I think she suspects it like me."

Kenny took Emmy home and they sat on the couch in the TV room. Emmy rested her head against his shoulder.

"Are you going to be at the studio all day tomorrow?"

"Tomorrow might be a long day. We might be working a little late. There's this one song that we want to finish up. If I can get out of there in time, I'll go with you to the hospital."

"You don't need to. I think I'll go see Daddy in the morning. I've got class tomorrow night, and I still need to study for a couple hours."

They sat on the couch and cuddled until eleven.

"I'm gonna go, Em." He stood up while Emmy remained on

56

the couch. She moved to her knees and lifted her arms for a hug.

He hugged her. "I'll call you in the afternoon. I know it's a bit frustrating that we can't spend more time together right now. Between the hours in the studio and your busy schedule, there just aren't many hours left."

"There are always the overnight hours," Emmy whispered as she stood up.

He held her close, and their bodies betrayed their desires.

"I want to, Em."

"Me, too, but if you stay, then neither one of us will get any sleep at all." She kissed him quickly and then pulled him out of the room.

They paused for a moment in the hallway, standing at the bottom of the stairs. They could either go upstairs, or on into the kitchen. Kenny lifted her up and put her on the first step of the staircase.

Her heart raced. "Are we going upstairs, Kenny?"

He looked into her eyes. He kissed her. She wrapped her arms around his neck and let her body melt into his.

"I've gotta go. I don't want to, but I should."

Her shoulders sagged. "I know. I wish you could stay, but I understand. Will you call me tomorrow?"

"I will. I promise." He kissed her once more before he headed home.

The next afternoon Kenny called from the studio's control room. "Em, we're gonna be stuck here until probably ten or eleven."

"That's all right. Are you gonna come over afterward? I'll be back from class by then."

"I'd love to, but I really shouldn't."

"Are you afraid that you might not want to go home if you do?"

"Yes. Well, not exactly afraid, but..."

"I know. You're afraid I will drag you upstairs and rip off your clothes and have my way with you."

"Have you been watching TV, Em?"

"I've been studying in the TV room, and I turned on the Lifetime Channel. That's what happened in this movie." She muted the sound.

They both laughed.

"Maybe you should watch some cartoons, Em. That might take your mind off of romance."

"You're probably right. Will you at least call me when you get done?"

"I can do that."

She giggled then said, "Maybe we can have phone sex."

"Em," he said slowly. "No more Lifetime movies for you."

Later that night, Kenny called as he drove home from the studio with bad news.

"We didn't finish that one track. Tomorrow is going to be another long day. It looks like I won't be able to go to church with you. Sorry."

"That's all right. You guys do what you have to. I'll go by myself. Oh, since Daddy is doing better, I'm gonna go in to the office for a few hours on Thursday morning."

"I'll call you tomorrow, Em."

She giggled for a few seconds. "Since we're not gonna see each other tomorrow, can we have phone sex now?"

"Sure!" Kenny grinned. "Do you know how to go about that?"

"No, don't you?"

"Not the foggiest idea. I'm a dorky rock star, remember?"

"True. So true. Maybe we can pretend to kiss over the phone."

"Yeah, I don't think that's gonna work for me, Em. I like to kiss your lips for real."

"Yeah. It wouldn't be the same."

"Night, Em"

"Night, Kenny boy."

He shook his head. "I know you're watching *The Waltons*."

Chapter Six

After working a half day on Thursday, Emmy visited her father in the hospital. When she arrived, he was sleeping. She didn't want to leave without talking to him, so she waited. He woke up and smiled at her.

She held his hand. "Your hand feels cold. How are you feeling today? Did Mom come to see you this morning?"

"She stopped by, but we started arguing. I told her to get out so I could sleep."

Emmy didn't know whether she should be upset or pleased, "Well, that means you are getting better. Have you seen the doctor today?"

"Yeah, he said I might be discharged on the weekend. He wouldn't make a commitment though. I need to get out of here. This place is full of sick people, and I need a drink," he said.

"Daddy, you can't..."

"I was joking, sweetheart. I know I have to be more careful now. But I wasn't kidding about all the sick people in here."

She smiled. "I haven't heard you trying to be funny for so long. You used to make me laugh when I was a little girl."

"I guess somewhere along the way, your mother and I stopped seeing the humor in life."

"You can still find it if you try."

"I guess we've stopped trying. That happens to people when they get old."

"You're not that old. At least compared to Grandma Isabel," Emmy said. "I gotta run. I'm meeting Kristen."

She kissed him on the cheek, said goodbye and rushed over to North Park College to meet Kristen for an early dinner. Emmy walked quickly through the familiar campus. All of her classes were now at North Park. She had finished up her night classes and received her two-year degree from Paul Frank Junior College last December. Emmy didn't attend the graduation ceremony because she didn't consider herself finished with college yet. Kristen would receive her degree at the end of the semester.

Kristen stood on the steps of Jordan Dining Hall with two

friends as she waited for Emmy. She spotted Emmy coming and waved.

"Hi, Emmy. Did you have a good day at work, and how is your father doing?"

"I stopped by to see him after work, and he's doing better." Emmy held the door open for Kristen and they entered the warm building. "He and Mom argued, so I know he's feeling better. He's still weak, but he's resting more comfortably. He might be able to come home Saturday. I think Mom is worn out though."

"What about work?" Kristen asked. "I thought you were taking the week off."

"I stopped at the office to see how everything was going. Paulina is still there, so I left after lunch," Emmy said. "I like Thursdays because they go by so fast."

"What time do you need to be at the church?" Kristen asked as she handed Emmy a tray.

"Six thirty. We've got plenty of time. Anything new here at school?"

"Nothing major. Except I was talking to Lainey Novicki, I mean Coyle, and she's pregnant."

"Wow. That sure didn't take long. They haven't been married a year yet."

"It only takes one time to get pregnant, Em."

Emmy ignored her statement. "Have you heard from any of the other Roosevelt alums who graduated last year?"

They picked out their food, Kristen paid, and they found an empty table.

"I get emails from Annie O'Dell and Diana Ahronson once in a while."

"Is Diana still engaged to Damon Barclay?" Emmy asked.

"Yeah, the wedding is set for June fifteenth. It's a Saturday, and the wedding and reception are at the Barclay home. It will be the social event of the year."

"Maybe my invitation got lost in the mail."

"Oh, Emmy. I didn't know."

"It's all right. I was never really a friend like you are."

"We weren't really friends until I got to North Park. If you

60

went to school here full-time, you would be her friend, too."

Some of Kristen's college friends stopped to say hi to Kristen, but they ignored Emmy making her feel invisible. Even though she took classes at North Park, she felt a little out of place. After her friends left, Kristen looked at Emmy. "Don't mind them, Emmy. They can be a bit snobbish at times. Just so you know, you are still my best friend."

"I hope we are always best friends, Krissy."

"We will be."

They finished dinner and Emmy asked, "Wanna go to practice with me? You might have fun."

"Are you going to make me sing?" Kristen asked. "I like to sing, but I'm not as talented as you."

"You don't have to sing, but you are as good as any of the singers who will be there."

"I'll go if we can get some ice cream afterward."

"So, I have to bribe you, huh? All right, we can stop for ice cream after practice. I'll drive."

Kristen had been curious about Emmy's church and the difference it made in her life. They arrived at the church, and Emmy introduced Kristen to everyone.

"Hi, Chase. This is someone I dragged in off the street," Emmy said and then giggled.

Kristen's jaw dropped. Chase looked at Emmy and shook his head. He was already used to Emmy's quirky sense of humor.

"All right, this is my best friend, Kristen Keasling. Kristen, this is Chase Hillman. He's the worship leader, so I guess he's my boss at church."

"It's nice to meet you, Kristen. Emmy has told me about you. I hear you are a singer, also."

Kristen gave Emmy a hard look. "I'm not as gifted as Emmy. I only came with her to listen."

"Well, you're welcome to listen, and if you want to sing along, you're welcome to do that, too."

Emmy introduced Kristen to everyone else, but Kristen couldn't remember all their names. She sat in the middle of the sanctuary and listened as the worship team went through their songs. After hearing the two older background singers, Kristen relaxed. She could sing as well, if not better, than either of them. She listened to Emmy and was impressed by how confident Emmy sounded as she sang. At times Emmy closed her eyes and sang to God alone.

"How did we sound?" Emmy asked later.

"You guys are really good. Except for that one singer, of course." *I don't think she ever sang on key. Some of the notes she hit sounded like fingernails on a chalkboard.*

"I know who you mean. She tries so hard, but she just doesn't hear her part."

"Ready for ice cream?" Kristen asked.

"First I need to help Chase in the music room. Give me a few minutes, or else you can come with me."

"No big hurry. Take your time, Em."

Emmy returned in fifteen minutes with Chase and four other guys from the band. Kristen tried to remember their names but couldn't.

"These guys want ice cream, too," Emmy said. "I told them they could go with us, but they have to buy."

"That sounds good to me. I eat a lot of ice cream though. Hope you guys brought enough money." Kristen smiled at the guys.

"How much ice cream can two girls eat?" Chase asked.

Emmy introduced the guys again. Hank Lysenko played bass. John Patterson played acoustic guitar. Steve Van Zant played lead guitar. His name sounded familiar to Kristen.

He grinned. "I'm not that Stevie Van Zandt."

"He plays for Springsteen, right?" Kristen asked.

"Yeah, but I think he spells his name differently."

All of these guys looked to be in their forties, or fifties, at least. The other guy looked much younger. Emmy introduced him last.

"This is our drummer. He's only been playing for a couple years, but he is so good."

"Hi, Kristen. I'm Skip Mason. Emmy is exaggerating a bit. I'm still learning."

"You sounded pretty good to me, Skip."

"Worship music is usually pretty easy to play. Most of the songs are in four/four time."

"Let's go before the ice cream melts." Chase hurried them out of the building. "I need to get home and see my girls."

The group headed over to Sonny's, just down the road. Emmy and Kristen ordered hot fudge sundaes and Hank, the oldest member of the team, paid for them. He had been playing bass at the church for over twenty years. Emmy and Kristen thanked him and found a table big enough for the whole group. After everyone was sitting down, Chase prayed, and they began chatting away as they ate. Kristen sat back and listened. The guys appeared to be really close friends despite their different backgrounds and ages. They accepted Emmy and treated her like one of the guys. Emmy appreciated this because Kenny wouldn't have any reason to be jealous. She kept her romantic relationship with him a secret from the guys in the band, and the whole church as well. Chase knew she was friends with Kenny, but he thought Tony might be her boyfriend.

"Are you still in college, Kristen?" Skip asked. *I wonder if you have a boyfriend. I don't think Emmy does. She's cute, but you are a number ten without doubt.*

"Yes, I'm graduating after this semester. I'll be looking for a job and a place to live. Until I find a place, I'll probably live at home."

"Are you from SoHam?" Skip's eyes betrayed his interest in Kristen.

"I've lived here most of my life, but we did live in West Bartlett for a time." Kristen smiled at Skip, but didn't want to encourage him.

"Did you commute to North Park?" Skip tried to keep Kristen engaged in his conversation.

"No, I lived on campus. I'm rather used to living away from home now." *You should eat your cone before the ice cream melts. I can't believe you're hitting on me. You aren't ugly, but those acne scars kinda turn me off.*

Emmy heard this and an idea popped into her head, but she

63

didn't say anything about it.

Kristen licked some fudge off her spoon and turned her attention to the other men. "You guys sound really good as a band. Have you ever thought of making a CD?"

"The subject has come up before," Steve replied. "We need someone who knows what they're doing to produce it though. We could do it ourselves, but a real producer would be better. We figure if we're gonna do it, we want it to be the best it possibly can."

"I know someone who might be able to help," Emmy said.

"If you're thinking of who I think you are, Emmy, don't even go there. He's much too busy," Kristen said.

Emmy whispered, "Don't be silly. He's sitting at home doing nothing."

Hank, Steve and John were talking to each other and weren't listening to Emmy and Kristen.

"Aren't they recording a new CD now?" Chase realized who Emmy meant.

"Yeah, but he's not busy 24/7. He has some time off. I'm going to call him right now."

The other guys didn't realize who Emmy meant and assumed she was joking when she pulled out her cell phone. She dialed Kenny's number, and, after a couple of rings, he answered.

"Hi, Emmy. What are you up to? Is practice over? Are you home already? How's your father?"

"Geez! You accuse me of talking fast. He's doing much better. I know you're still working on your CD. Is that still going okay?"

The guys listened to Emmy without knowing who was on the other end.

"We're ahead of schedule. All the basic tracks are finished. I have to add some guitars, do the vocals, then mix and master it. We're hoping to release it in August. How is the church band doing? Did you convince Kristen to sing with them yet?"

"As a matter of fact, I'm with them right now. Kristen is with me, too."

"Tell Kristen hello for me."

Emmy turned to Kristen. "He says hi." She talked to Kenny again. "What would you say if I told you the guys were looking to record some songs for a CD. Just live stuff at the church."

"That sounds like a great idea, Emmy. We used to record a lot of our practices."

Emmy shook her head. "No, they want to record a real CD."

"Oh, sorry. I misunderstood. Have they thought about who they want to produce it?"

"I mentioned you, and Kristen told me not to bother you because of how busy you are." Emmy bumped into Kristen as she changed positions in the booth.

"Hey! be careful, Em."

Emmy sat with her feet tucked under her now.

"I'm not that busy. I'd love to gain more experience as a producer. When do they want to do it?"

"We don't have a time picked out yet."

"How about July? I'll be in town for the Fourth and on vacation after that until the tour starts. Maybe we can set something up."

"Are you sure? What about your CD? I don't want to take away your free time."

"Emmy Colasanti! How long have we known each other? You should know me better than to think I would turn down a chance to hang out with you. Don't worry about our CD. By July it will be almost done, and it will be good for me to take a step away. Let's work on the details and set it up. We can record it using the Steward Music truck. I can have Will Consoli work on the technical stuff."

"I'll tell them. Talk to you later." She turned away so the guys couldn't hear and whispered, "I love you."

"Love you, too, Em."

Emmy hung up and looked at the guys. "That was my friend Kenny. He'll do it in July."

The guys stared blankly at Emmy. Hank slurped up the last of his chocolate shake.

Kristen said, "She means Kenny Colwell from Fridays At

65

Five. He's an old friend."

"For real? You gotta be kidding. You're joking right?" Skip Mason reacted first.

Emmy grinned as she replied, "No, he's going to be here for that big show on the Fourth of July, and then on vacation until September. He even said he will let us use his remote truck to do the actual recording. His record company's truck, I mean."

"This is so amazing, Emmy," Skip said. "It would be so cool to meet him. I've never met a celebrity before."

"Isn't there something in the Bible about the faith of a jar of mustard or something?" Emmy asked. "Something in Matthew, I think."

"Close, Emmy, close, but we get your point. Too often we try to put limits on what God can do for us. We can't begin to fathom the power He possesses," Chase said.

Emmy knew exactly what Matthew 17:20 said, but she tried not to sound preachy to these guys. Kristen looked at her best friend with awe and new respect.

Chapter Seven

On the Saturday before Easter, Emmy went through the house with a dust rag, picked up anything out of place, did her laundry and cleaned the bathrooms. After that she sat down to read a book, but soon lost interest. She turned on the TV, but nothing appealed to her. She decided to call Kristen.

"Hey, Krissy, what are you doing later? I'm bored and want to get out of the house." She lay on the couch in the TV room with her feet on the back of it.

"Oh, Em, I'm sorry but I've got to finish a paper this afternoon, and I've got a date tonight." Kristen scrolled through her laptop reading what she had written.

"With who?"

"Do you remember Joaquim Rafael from Brazil?"

"Is he the model who is absolutely gorgeous? The one with the silky long hair and dark gorgeous eyes and the great bod? I don't remember him."

"You're a goof. He's back in town for the weekend. He called and wants to take me to dinner."

"Can I go with? I promise I won't flirt with him too much." Emmy crossed her fingers.

"No way! I know how much you like him, and crossing your fingers doesn't count."

"He is absolutely gorgeous and so sexy," Emmy said as she laughed.

"What are you laughing at?"

Emmy sat up. "I was just picturing him in a suit like the last time I saw him."

"And why is that funny? I think he looks sophisticated in a suit."

"Oh, he does. He's like the most glamorous man I've ever seen. I'm imagining Joaquim taking me to dinner in his suit and me dressed the way I am right now."

Kristen rolled her eyes. "All right, the suspense is killing me, Em. Exactly what are you wearing now. Should I guess? I bet you're wearing a t-shirt and shorts."

Emmy giggled and said, "Not even close."

"Please tell me you are wearing something."

"Well, I'm not naked!" Emmy exclaimed.

"Tell me what are you wearing so I can finish this paper."

"I'm wearing one of Kenny's stretched-out, old sweatshirts and some sweatpants that have rips at the knees and a hole in a certain spot."

"I'm not even going to ask where the hole might be," Kristen said. "I hope you don't wear them in public."

"I wore them when I went for a run. No one saw me. Can I please go with you? I'll change clothes and maybe even take a shower."

"I'm hanging up now..."

"Wait! I'm only joking. You're just going out for dinner, right?"

"Unfortunately, yeah," Kristen said.

"Well, have fun, but be careful."

"I'm sorry, Em."

"No you're not, and I don't blame you one bit. See if you can get a picture of him. I'll take it to work and put in on my desk and tell the guys that he's my new boyfriend."

"Bye, Em. You're so goofy."

Emmy decided to try Kenny and caught him at the studio.

"I'm bored. Can we do something?"

"I'm gonna be here for a few hours. Why don't you come over here and hang out? After we're done we'll go somewhere."

"Okay, Ill be there soon."

Emmy headed over to the Steward Music Group building. Kenny met her in the lobby and took her to Studio Three. She joined the band as they worked on a tune.

"Hi, Emmy," Jeff Rawlings said as he set his bass in a stand and reached out to hug her. "It's good to see you."

Dave Persching played a short drum solo and then stood up. "I bet you can't play that, Emmy."

"Pffft! That was easy. Piece of cake."

Dave walked over, hugged her and then handed her his sticks.

68

She walked over to his kit and sat on his throne. "This is like sitting in a recliner. Are you getting too old to use a regular seat?" she teased. "I can't reach the pedals."

Dave grinned and said, "The throne is set up high enough for me. Not for a small child."

She stuck out her tongue.

Jeremy Lenhart entered the studio.

"Jeremy!" Emmy squealed. She set the sticks on the snare drum and ran over to hug Jeremy.

"Hello, princess. How have you been? Have you practiced your keyboard lately?"

"I try to practice once a week, but I'll never be as good as you."

Emmy spent ten minutes talking to the guys who made up Fridays At Five.

"Maybe you should hang out in the control room with Will while we work on this track," Kenny said.

"Okay, I won't ruin anything, will I?"

"What do you mean?" Kenny tilted his head.

"I mean if I talk to Will or ask him some questions."

"You can talk to Will all you want." Kenny laughed.

"What's so funny?"

"He will talk your ears off. You won't be able to ask any questions. He will tell you everything you'd ever want to know about the recording process. He'll show you what every knob, fader, slider, button and meter do on the board."

Three hours later, Kenny and the band called it a night. Kenny joined Emmy in the control room and asked, "How did it go?"

Emmy laughed then said, "You were right. I only asked one question 'Where is the bathroom?'"

"Are you hungry? Wanna grab something to eat?"

"I'm starving. Can we go to Darby's, please?"

"Oh, I don't know... I don't really like the food there... what about..."

"Oh, stop trying to tease me. I know Darby's is your favorite restaurant on the planet."

They made a quick stop at Kenny's apartment in the carriage house. Kenny left his car and Emmy drove over to Darby's. They ordered and sat in their favorite booth.

"Are you singing with the worship team in the morning, Em?" Kenny asked as he took a bite of his chili cheese dog.

"Yeah, we practiced for over two hours Thursday. We're doing this kinda new song 'Shout To The Lord.' The guys struggled with it a bit."

"I know that song. I like it."

"Can you play it?" Emmy tried to sneak one of Kenny's onion rings, but he swatted her hand away.

"Sure, it's easy enough. Why?"

"Why don't you come to church with me tomorrow and show the guys how to play it?"

"Oh, I don't want to intrude. I'm sure they know how to play it." *I would never do that, Em. They would think I have a big ego.*

"Don't be silly. The guys would love to have you show them some new licks. They wouldn't resent it at all. I know it's Easter, and you probably want to go to church with your parents."

"Actually, they are with Grandma. I was going to have to go by myself."

"Then how about it? I'll make dinner for us."

"You're not going to Mama Bertucci's for dinner? I know you aren't going to your parents' house."

"She's going to go to Carmen's house."

"All right. It's a deal, but I'd rather not intrude on your practice or anything. I'll go and sit in the sanctuary."

She grabbed an onion ring before he could stop her. "Okay, but someday I want you to meet the guys in the worship band, all right?"

"One of these days, but not tomorrow. The timing isn't right."

Kenny picked Emmy up in the morning. She wore one of her best dresses and looked fabulous—Kenny told her so after he kissed her. They arrived at church early and saw Pastor Ausland.

"Good morning, Emmy. How are you on this glorious day?"

"I'm doing great," Emmy replied as she hugged him. "This is my friend, Kenny Colwell."

"It's a pleasure to meet you. I'm Pastor Herb. You are the singer and guitar player, right? Emmy has talked about you." He shook hands with Kenny.

Kenny chuckled and said, "She does that sometimes."

"I assure you, she had nothing but compliments about you."

"I can say the same about you, Pastor Herb. She has remarked about how you have the whole Bible memorized."

"She is exaggerating a bit. I'll let you guys go. I'm sure Emmy wants to have time to practice. I'll talk to you later." Pastor Herb patted Kenny on the back, and then greeted more people.

Emmy decided to tease Kenny. She took him to where one of the senior adult Sunday School classes met and introduced him to the teacher. She giggled and hurried off to the music room where the guys were already going over the songs. Kenny entered the classroom, looked at the people in their comfortable chairs and chuckled. He knew Emmy didn't go to this class. *You are gonna get it later, Emmy.* He thought, as he smiled. He didn't see a single person who looked younger than sixty. Kenny enjoyed the lesson and even took part in the discussion about Peter's denial. No one paid him any undo attention, but after class they all welcomed him. Some of them looked at him and thought they recognized him, but assumed he just looked familiar for some reason.

"Hello, I'm Bob Cartwright," one of the men said as he shook Kenny's hand.

"Hello, Mr. Cartwright. I'm Kenneth Colwell. I enjoyed the class today."

"It's nice to see you here, and I want you to know that you are always welcome. Do you live in the area?"

"I live in SoHam, so it's not far away."

"Are you still in college, or are you older than that? I can't always tell."

"I'm not in college anymore."

"What do you do for a living?"

71

Kenny wondered how he should answer. "I play guitar and sing a little."

"I see. That's a tough way to make a living. Are you talented? Maybe you could try out for the band here. We have a good group of musicians, and we have this new young singer who has a beautiful voice. I can't remember her name..." He tugged on his ear as he tried to remember her name. "Anyway, I think she's in high school and is pretty as a picture."

"I'll think about it, sir. Is that young girl singing today by any chance?" Kenny felt bad as soon as he asked. He certainly didn't intend to deceive this man.

"Probably. I thinks she sings every week. Maybe one of the younger guys can point her out to you. We have a lot of younger people who attend church here. There are even some classes for the younger adults."

"I might have to check them out next time."

Kenny noticed an older lady walking over toward them. She stopped and Mr. Cartwright introduced her. "This is my wife Rosa."

"Hello, Mrs. Cartwright. My name is Kenneth Colwell."

She offered her hand, so Kenny shook it.

"It's a pleasure to meet you, Kenneth. Should I call you Kenneth, or do you prefer Kenny?"" She smiled at Kenny, and then led her husband away. She looked back and whispered, "I won't tell anyone, and my husband thinks rock music ended when The Beatles broke up."

Kenny laughed. He made his way into the sanctuary and many of the people smiled at him. A lot of the men shook his hand. Some of the people recognized him, others didn't. He saw where the teens sat and moved to the opposite side if the large sanctuary. He certainly didn't want to be a distraction during the Easter service.

Just before the service started, he saw Emmy and pointed to a couple of empty chairs.

"I'll join you after the song service is over. Did everything go all right in class?" She tried to keep a straight face, but started to giggle.

"Yes, I really enjoyed the discussion, and you're gonna get it later."

"That could be fun. Are you gonna punish me for being bad?"

"Geez, Emmy, we're in church."

"I gotta go before Pastor Chase yells at me." She kissed his cheek, and then took off.

"Do a good job, Em. I'll say a prayer for you."

The service started, and Kenny looked out over the mass of worshipers. He could usually make an accurate guess of the size of a crowd. He estimated today's crowd at over a thousand people. He stood and sang along as the worship band played. He caught Emmy's eye and she smiled at him. Later, he listened as she sang "Shout To The Lord." He thought back to the day he first met her and his heart was warmed by the memory of how she had grown from a shy little girl to a beautiful *shy* young lady. After the band finished, Pastor Paul Jefferson stepped to the front of the platform. He made a few announcements and they took up an offering for mission work. The church set a goal of raising $10,000. Emmy slipped into the seat next to Kenny, and he took her hand in his.

"You sounded fantastic, Em."

"Really? I can't ever tell."

Senior Pastor Herb Ausland stood from his place in the front row and smiled at the congregation. He looked around and saw many familiar faces. He took a moment to look at the many visitors and wondered how he would be able to greet all of them after the service. He closed his eyes and bowed his head as he began to pray. After his prayer Pastor Ausland began his message with scripture.

"This, my friends, is from II Corinthians 8:9. 'For you know the grace of our Lord Jesus Christ, that though he was rich, yet for your sake he became poor, so that you through his poverty might become rich.'"

He spoke to the congregation for a few minutes, then used another passage.

"I'm using the NIV and this is from the gospel of Luke 24:1-12. 'On the first day of the week, very early in the morning,

73

the women took the spices they had prepared and went to the tomb. They found the stone rolled away from the tomb, but when they entered, they did not find the body of the Lord Jesus. While they were wondering about this, suddenly two men in clothes that gleamed like lightning stood beside them. In their fright the women bowed down with their faces to the ground, but the men said to them, "Why do you look for the living among the dead? He is not here; he has risen!"

Emmy looked at Kenny and smiled. As Pastor Ausland continued, she whispered, "Didn't I tell you he knows the whole Bible."

Pastor Herb used another scripture passage before he ended his message. "I would like to use I Corinthians 15:1-8 as my final scripture reference today. 'Now, brothers and sisters, I want to remind you of the gospel I preached to you, which you received and on which you have taken your stand. By this gospel you are saved, if you hold firmly to the word I preached to you. Otherwise, you have believed in vain.

For what I received I passed on to you as of first importance: that Christ died for our sins according to the Scriptures, that he was buried, that he was raised on the third day according to the Scriptures, and that he appeared to Cephas, and then to the Twelve. After that, he appeared to more than five hundred of the brothers and sisters at the same time, most of whom are still living, though some have fallen asleep. Then he appeared to James, then to all the apostles, and last of all he appeared to me also, as to one abnormally born.'"

Pastor Ausland made his final points, then the congregation stood as he prayed. He opened the altar and invited anyone who needed to pray to come forward. He watched as several people made their way to the front. The rest of the ministerial staff and others from the congregation come to the front to pray with those in need. After the session of prayer at the altar ended, the congregation began leaving.

As Emmy and Kenny headed toward an exit, he saw Mr. Cartwright and his wife again. He wondered what he must think as he saw him with Emmy. He didn't have a chance to talk to him though as some of the teenagers surrounded him. He took time to talk to them and felt embarrassed as he signed a few autographs. Most of the crowd had left by the time Kenny and Emmy finally were able to get away. They saw Pastor Ausland as he talked to the church treasurer, Ron Smith, and his wife, who Emmy knew as Aunt Doris.

Ron explained to Pastor Ausland about the mission offering. "We counted it twice just to be sure. It added up to over $10,000, with one more check to add to the total. I had to look at it three times before I realized the last check was written for $10,000. I looked at the name, but I don't know the person," Ron said then mentioned the name on the check.

"I believe I know the man who wrote the check." Pastor Ausland smiled. "I'll talk to him if he's still here. Isn't God great?"

"Yes, Pastor. Sometimes we forget that He is in control and can do things we cannot imagine."

Pastor Herb saw Emmy and Kenny getting ready to leave and walked over to talk to them.

"Emmy, you sounded like an angel today." He smiled and patted her arm. "I want to thank you for what you do for the church."

"I just try to sing a little," Emmy said without a trace of insincerity.

Pastor Ausland smiled at Kenny and shook his hand. "I know you are a member of another church, so I won't try to pry you away from them. However, if you are ever interested in talking to our teens one day, you would be welcome. I saw how they surrounded you once they realized you were here."

"I would be honored, Pastor Herb. Emmy and I have sung to the teen group at my church in the past." He reached for her hand. "Did you know she has written some songs? She is the one you should ask to talk to the teens."

"I believe she has done that at least once. If I remember correctly, at least two young teens who gave their life to Christ that evening. It's amazing what can be accomplished when people follow what the Holy Spirit leads them to do." Pastor Herb patted Kenny on the back and smiled. "Thank you for being here today and for having a giving heart for missions. I will keep you and your band in my prayers."

"Thank you, Pastor Herb." Kenny realized he knew about his check.

On the way home Emmy was quiet but then suddenly asked, "What did Pastor Herb mean about you having a heart for missions?"

Kenny looked at Emmy and answered, "I'm not sure. He probably meant someone else."

"He will pray for you and the guys. He spends a lot of time in prayer."

"I could tell, Em. He is an amazing man, but then he does take direction from someone pretty special."

Chapter Eight

Mr. Oliver opened the cafeteria door for Emmy.

"Thank you, Mr. Oliver. It's good to know that chivalry is still alive."

"What? Oh, right. I guess I open doors instinctively."

They picked up a light lunch at the counter, and Emmy looked for an empty table. She spotted one against the windows and waited for Mr. Oliver to pay. The lunch was a reward for Emmy's help in finishing a new project.

"There's a table over there." Then she spotted Richard Demarco with a woman. Luckily, he had his back to Emmy. She turned around and headed in the opposite direction. "I think we should sit over here. The sun's too bright by the windows."

Emmy's destructive relationship with Richard Demarco had ended the previous month. After Emmy rejected his advances the night of Tony's accident, his interest in her dwindled. At first Emmy thought he really liked her as a person, but now felt his sole interest was in trying to seduce her. She ate her lunch with Mr. Oliver, but her mind, and her eyes, wandered to Richard. She alternately hated him for trying to take advantage of her and liked him for his charming personality.

A couple of days later, Emmy bumped into Richard as she arrived for work. They talked briefly, and he treated her respectfully and didn't try to flirt with her.

In the elevator Richard asked, "Would you like to meet for lunch again sometime to talk?"

Not in this lifetime, you creep, Emmy thought, but she waited a few seconds before replying, "I don't think that would be a good idea, Richard. I know we will probably see each other from time to time, but I don't think I should have lunch with you, at least not at this time. Maybe sometime in the future, but not yet."

Richard thought, and hoped, they could still have a relationship, but he realized Emmy loved her boyfriend and that things would never work out between them the way he envisioned it—he wanted to sleep with her. He regretted not having a chance to even make-out with her. He chuckled about how she would not let him touch her when he kissed her. He wondered, *Could it be possible? Could she actually be a virgin? Nah, she couldn't possibly be, not as pretty and sexy as she is.*

Emmy naively thought maybe she and Richard could be friends, and only friends. After awhile she realized it would be in her best interest never to see Richard again. In an office building as big as where she worked, she hoped to avoid him.

Emmy did see him again, though. Over the next two weeks, they met several times in the building and talked to one another. Richard used his experience and charms on her again. He worked slowly to regain her trust. Emmy didn't tell Kenny or Kristen about talking to Richard at work because she knew they would both tell her to stay away from him. Her stubbornness wouldn't let her listen to their advice.

One day Richard met Emmy quite by accident on the way to the cafeteria. He waited for twenty minutes to run into her accidentally. He put her at ease and convinced her to sit with him as they ate a quick lunch. He regaled her with humorous stories about his latest project. He decided to take a chance.

"Would you be interested in dinner Friday night? I've been invited out to dinner with a couple from the apartment complex. They made reservations for four, and I need someone to go with me. It wouldn't be like a real date, and we would be with another couple."

She coughed as she almost choked on her Coke. "I'm not sure it would be a good idea, Richard."

"I understand your hesitancy, Emmy, but I assure you it would just be dinner between friends and nothing more."

Emmy thought about the invitation for a moment. "I don't think so, Richard."

"I understand. I don't deserve your trust after what I tried. Would you be willing to have dinner if you brought a friend along? I'm sure we can change the reservation to five people."

"If you're willing to do that, why don't you go to dinner by yourself, and your friends? Make the reservation for three."

"Good point. I'm not sure why. I suppose I am so used to having someone with me." Richard laughed at himself.

Emmy laughed along with Richard. She tried to remember if Kenny planned to be busy at the studio that evening and remembered that he would be working late all week. They talked about work as they ate.

"How is your father doing?" Emmy asked during a lull in the conversation. "I remember he was in the hospital."

"You remember that?" Richard was genuinely surprised.

"Yeah, I remember. How is he doing?"

"He's out of the hospital, but still undergoing treatment."

"My father suffered a heart attack last month," Emmy said as her lip quivered.

Richard didn't say anything for a few seconds. "I'm sorry to hear that. Is he … all right?"

"He's getting better, but he has another issue to deal with."

"What's that?" Richard asked as he looked around the cafeteria.

Should I even mention this? Emmy wondered. *I don't want Richard to think that I'm trying to be friends.* She bit her lip, but then answered, "Daddy is an alcoholic."

Richard snapped his eyes back to Emmy. "I'm sorry to hear that." He clenched his hand into a fist under the table. *I never would have guessed. I can certainly sympathize with you. My old man has been a drunk all his life.*

I shouldn't have mentioned anything about Daddy. I've got to go before I start crying. I don't want to cry in front of Richard. "I need to get back to the office," Emmy said and then carried her tray to the trash receptacle.

Richard followed her. "I'm really sorry about your father."

She dumped her trash, set her tray down, and then faced him. *Lord, what should I do?* She prayed silently. *Maybe I could use this to witness to him.*

"If we have dinner, we could talk about our fathers," Richard whispered.

"All right. I will go, but only because Kenny will be working late and there will be another couple with us."

79

Richard managed not to let his surprise show. "I'll pick you up at seven."

"I think it would be best if I meet you there, Richard."

"All right. If that is better for you. Will you let me pay for dinner at least?"

"Yes, you can pay for dinner. I'll make sure I order something expensive."

"That sounds fair. You can order the most expensive bottle of wine they have."

"I don't think I will drink any wine, but you can if you want."

Emmy arrived at McBride's Irish Pub on Friday. She saw Richard walking inside. *This place doesn't take reservations. You lied to me, Richard. I should just leave. You're such a jerk.* She stopped and stood still. *Wait a second. I think this is what Jesus would want us to do. We can't only witness to people that we like or approve of. We have to witness to the needy and boy is Richard needy.* She decided to stay. She went inside, and Richard introduced her to his friends.

"This is Emmy Colasanti. She works for the same company as I do in a different office. This is Wesley and Roberta Ruben. They live in the apartment across the hall."

"It's a pleasure to meet you, Emmy," Roberta said. "Do you live in SoHam?" *Richard, are you crazy? She's young enough to be your daughter.*

"Yes, I've lived here my whole life. Have you lived here long? You have a bit of an accent." Emmy asked trying to get Roberta to talk about herself. That way Emmy didn't have to share any details about her personal life.

"Wesley and I moved here from Seattle about a year ago."

Emmy's plan worked to perfection as Richard, Wesley and Roberta spent most of dinner talking about living in Seattle and their own lives. Wesley immediately realized Richard's only interest in Emmy—sex. He wondered why Richard would be after such a petite girl who didn't even look old enough to order a beer. Emmy and Richard stuck to bottled water to drink even though

80

Wesley and Roberta ordered a bottle of wine. Richard craved a beer, but for now he stuck to water simply to impress Emmy.

Wesley finally realized that he and Roberta were dominating the conversation. "Would you tell us more about yourself, Emmy? I'm sorry we've been talking about Seattle so much."

Finally, I get a chance to tell you about Jesus.

Emmy didn't want to share much her personal life, but she did tell them about her church and her faith. Now Wesley realized why Richard was after Emmy.

Richard, you dirty devil, Wesley thought. *This girl is probably a virgin and you want the challenge of deflowering her.* Wesley stared at Emmy while she listened to Richard and Roberta talking. *Personally, I don't think she would be worth all the effort. She's so petite, but she is pretty.*

Roberta stole glances at Wesley as she talked to Richard. *I wonder if Wesley even has a clue that Richard and I have been seeing each other. He can be so oblivious to things.*

Emmy mentioned her classes at North Park College. Wesley and Roberta listened politely, but as soon as Emmy paused, they started talking about their alma mater, Oregon State University. Emmy managed to keep the Rubens talking about their college experiences until it was time to leave.

Richard walked Emmy to her car after they said good night to the Rubens. As Emmy opened her car door, he asked, "Would you let me come over for a short visit?"

"I don't think that is a good idea. You might try to kiss me again, and I don't want to ruin my relationship with Kenny."

"I promise I will behave like a gentleman."

"Sorry. Not buying that." She got in the car and closed the door. *Do you think I'm stupid?*

"No, I really mean it this time. I won't make the same mistake as before."

She rolled the window down halfway. "Do you swear you will behave?"

He put a hand on the window. "Yes, Emmy. I promise I won't try anything. I will even stop by the store and buy a carton of ice cream as a peace offering. What flavor do you like the best?"

Emmy thought about it. "All right, but you can't stay long. I like about any flavor, but if I have to choose one... Vanilla Fudge Twirl!"

"I will pick up the ice cream and meet you at your house. Do you have coffee at home? I could pick some up."

"I have coffee. You can buy the ice cream."

She naively thought she would use the time to witness to him about her faith. She had the coffee made by the time he arrived.

"I didn't see any Chocolate Fudge Twirl, so I bought plain chocolate instead."

"That's all right. It's still ice cream." She didn't bother to explain he looked for the wrong flavor. "How do you take your coffee? I forgot."

"Black is fine. Where are your bowls and silverware?" He opened the wrong cabinet.

She took two bowls from the cabinet and opened the silverware drawer. She poured the coffee as he filled two bowls with ice cream. They sat in the dining room on opposite sides of the table. Emmy didn't want to give him an opportunity to kiss her. Richard tried to charm her as usual, but Emmy kept her guard up.

Crap! He swore to himself. *This isn't going the way I hoped. I've got to be patient. I can't make the same mistake I made the last time.*

They finished their ice cream and the coffee, and Emmy talked about church.

"You would always be welcome to come to a service."

"That's very kind of you, Emmy. I'll see what I can do."

Richard realized his efforts were not working, so he told her good night and left. He knew that he didn't want to just be Emmy's friend and going back to her church did not interest him in the least. He decided not to call her again. After all, he knew plenty of other women who found him very attractive—plenty of women with looser morals. Yet, he loved a challenge and hated to admit to a defeat.

Chapter Nine

On Saturday, April twentieth, the day of the NFL draft, the Chicago Bears selected Tony Bertucci from Notre Dame with their first round pick. Tony and John Randolph watched the ESPN telecast with some of their teammates in the lobby of Dillon Hall. When they heard Tony's name, they stood up and yelled. They all tried to slap Tony on the back. Tony dreamed about playing for the Bears like he dreamed about playing for Notre Dame.

After several minutes of celebrating, John pulled Tony away from the crowd. "Congratulations, big guy. Your wish has come true."

"Thanks, John. I should call home," Tony said as he high-fived his roommate.

"Good idea," John said.

Tony walked around the corner and down the hall so he could hear better. Then he called home. "Guess what, Mama?"

"I don't know. Are you going to tell me? I know this is the draft day. Emmy called earlier and told me that. Did you get picked by a team already?"

"I did! I'm going to be playing for the Chicago Bears. Isn't that great? I've always dreamed about playing middle linebacker for them just like Dick Butkus and Mike Singletary."

"I'm very proud of you, son. I'll be even more proud when I see you graduate. Are you making sure you get all your papers written and whatever else you have to do?"

"Yes, Mama. I make sure I do all my homework before I go out to play," Tony teased.

"Oh, stop teasing me. I'm so glad that you won't have to move to another city. I was so worried about that. I had a bad dream that you might end up playing for some city in Canada or somewhere like Seattle."

"There aren't any teams in Canada, Mama."

"There are hockey teams there, right?"

"Yes, and two baseball teams."

"I thought they played football in Canada."

"That's a different league, Mama."

"Well, don't ever play in that league. It's much too cold in Canada, and I would never get to see you."

After he finished talking to his mother, Tony decided to call Emmy's cell phone.

"Did you hear?" Tony asked, but then held the phone away from his ear.

Emmy screamed, "The Bears! It's a dream come true. This means I will be able to see your games without traveling as far."

"And in the first round," Tony added.

"I guess the experts got it right for once. Maybe if you're good enough, they might put out a poster like the ones in your bedroom."

"If they do, would you want one?"

"Absolutely! I want one so I can throw darts at it."

"Very funny, Em."

"Where are you? What are you doing?" Emmy asked.

Tony explained.

"Are there any girls hanging around?" Emmy asked.

He shook his head. "Nope! Just the guys."

"Okay, thanks for calling. You better get back to your friends. Call me sometime."

Early in the second round the dream got better as the Bears chose John Randolph. Tony and John high-fived each other.

"We're going to be teammates again," Tony said. "That is if we make the team."

"It looks like I will be moving to Illinois," John said.

"Sorry, roomie. I know you've always been a Browns fan. Are you disappointed about going to the Bears?"

"Not really. I think the Bears have a better chance of going to the Super Bowl. The Browns may never get to the Super Bowl."

"That's my goal. I want to win a Super Bowl."

"Just one?" John grinned.

"I meant one per year." Tony high-fived him again.

On the way back to their room John realized. "I'll have to find an apartment before training camp."

"Hey! We've got an extra room," Tony said as he punched John's shoulder. "You gotta stay with us until you find a place."

"Do you think Mama will let me stay?"

"She would be mad at you if you didn't. I better warn you, though. She will try to fatten you up. She'll make all kinds of fattening stuff. Lots of pasta. Homemade pies. You name it."

"I suppose I could force myself to eat her cooking."

John Randolph grew up in Defiance, Ohio, in a middle class family. His father taught at the local high school and his mother worked as a nurse at the hospital. John's two older brothers, Kirk and Keith, played football in college. They never had a chance to play professionally, though. They were both married now with regular jobs and families to support. John appreciated his opportunity with the Bears and planned to make the most of it.

Tony called Kristen's cell phone while she was at Emmy's house. "Did you hear? John got drafted by the Bears in the second round. Isn't that great?"

"You guys will be teammates again. Is he with you?"

"Yeah, do you wanna talk to him?" Tony asked.

"Sure."

"Then call his cell phone. Why should I let you use all my minutes?"

"Because I'm your favorite cousin, and you love me. Now put him on the phone," Kristen ordered.

"You'll owe me."

"Just put him on the phone."

Kristen talked to John until her battery almost died.

"Emmy, isn't it great? They will both be playing for the Bears. Tony won't have to move away, and John will be moving here." Kristen's eyes glowed as brightly as her hair.

"That will work out for you, but Kenny will be on tour when football season starts. That kinda sucks."

Kristen said, "We can go to the games together."

"But the games are on Sunday," Emmy said.

"Yeah, so. They're in the afternoon."

"Yeah, but we would need to leave by like ten o'clock to get there in time. I would have to miss church."

"Are you worried that the church won't survive if you aren't there?" Kristen made a valid point without even realizing it.

85

"I guess I can miss church a few times to see his games. They will get by without me. They survived without me before."

Kristen grabbed a belt loop of Emmy's jeans. "Are your jeans still getting tighter? Are you putting on weight? These look pretty tight to me."

"These are new jeans and they fit just right. Why are you asking?"

Kristen didn't answer, and Emmy finally figured it out.

"Oh, for crying out loud. You think I'm pregnant, don't you?"

"Well, you did have morning sickness, and you said your jeans were getting tight, and Kenny was rubbing your belly. You kicked me out of your father's hospital room so you and Kenny could talk to him. I thought you were telling him about the baby."

"What baby? There is no baby. I'm not pregnant, Kristen, and that's all I'm saying about it."

"Are you absolutely positive?"

Emmy glared at Kristen. "Do I have to pee on a stick?"

"Did you do that already? What did it say?"

"It said I need to smack you," Emmy said.

"I'm so relieved. I thought for sure you were expecting," Kristen said, then waited for Emmy to reply.

She didn't.

"I'm sorry. Are you still my friend?" Kristen touched Emmy's belly.

"For cripes' sake. Are you trying to feel the baby?" Emmy pushed her hand away. "Yes, I'm still your friend. I still love you."

A few days later contract negotiations began. Tony enlisted a team of attorneys put together by Mr. Robertson. It took a week of negotiating to finalize the deal. Tony signed a multiyear deal that paid him more money than he ever dreamed. John signed a multiyear deal, also.

Mr. Robertson set Tony and John up with his financial advisor. Both young men were mature enough to realize that football would be only a short term career, and they would not always be making this much money.

Chapter Ten

Tony Bertucci placed his completed test on the professor's desk and glanced at the clock. It was two thirty in the afternoon on Friday, the tenth of May. He had just finished his *final* final exam at the University of Notre Dame. He took a few minutes to reflect on the past three years of classes and studying. He never regretted his choice of college because of the opportunity to play football and the academics. He earned a college degree that would serve him long after his days of playing football ended.

John turned around from his desk as the dorm room door opened. "How did it go?"

"Better than I hoped. I'm confidant I did well." Tony sat on his bed and leaned against the wall.

"Are going to celebrate tonight?" John asked. "I know you talked to Brenda this morning."

"I did talk to her, but I told her I couldn't go anywhere. We can go out for dinner, or eat at the dining hall. Your choice."

"The dining hall is convenient, and the food's all right. We might as well eat there since we only have a week or so left to enjoy their food."

Mama called Emmy the next morning, "Hi, dear, how are you? Are you feeling better?"

"Yes, I'm fine, Mama. Have you been talking to Kristen?"

"Not in the last week. You know Tony is graduating, right?"

"Yes, hasn't the time flown by. It seems like he left for college last week."

"Do you have plans for next weekend? If not, I'd like for you to take me to South Bend for the ceremonies. Would you be willing to do that for me? I'd drive myself, but you know I don't like to drive to unfamiliar places."

"As far as I know, I don't have anything planned other than going to church on Sunday. I suppose it won't kill me if I miss one Sunday. I'll call Kenny to be sure, but otherwise, I'll take you. Is Kristen going?"

"I'm not sure if she and Derrick are planning to go to the

ceremony. It's early on Sunday."

"I'll let you know by tomorrow night, Mama."

"Thank you, dear. Have you been eating all right?" Mama asked.

"Yes, Mama. I've been eating, but I haven't gained any weight."

Kenny and the guys in the band were taking the entire weekend off from recording. The guys needed to spend some time with their families. Kenny came over to see Emmy just before noon. He pulled into the long driveway, parked in front of the garage and saw Emmy working in the yard.

She waved. "I'm over here."

"Hey, Em, you look so good. I want to kiss you all over."

Emmy wore cut-off jean shorts and an old sweatshirt with the sleeves cut off above her elbow. A red bandana held her hair in a ponytail. Smudges of dirt and sweat, from clearing out the bushes on the side of the garage, lined her face.

"You must really love me if you want to kiss me when I look like this." She trimmed an overgrown branch and then set the clippers down.

"I suppose I do." Kenny kissed her. "How did you scrape your elbow? You know it's still bleeding, right?"

"On these... darn... weeds and wild bushes." Emmy wiped off the blood on her shorts.

"And how did you get this bruise?"

"I hit my thigh on the door and it hurts. Will you rub it for me?"

"With pleasure." Kenny started to rub her thigh.

"Wait." She grabbed his hand. "You better stop. Kristen might see you."

Kenny glanced around. "Is she here? Her car's not here."

"No, but she might drop by. I didn't tell you, but three weeks ago," Emmy said, paused and waved a hand. "Whenever it was draft day for the NFL, Kristen came over, and she asked me again if I was pregnant. She saw you rubbing my belly and assumed I was expecting."

Kenny put his hands on her shoulders. He looked very

serious. "You know sooner or later you are going to have to tell her about the baby. You are starting to show. Are you sure you should be out here working in the yard like this? Shouldn't you be inside sipping lemonade with your feet up on the couch."

Emmy lifted the sweatshirt and let Kenny see her belly. "Am I really starting to show? I didn't think you could tell as long as I wear loose-fitting clothes. I am a little tired from working out here. Maybe I should go inside. Will you run a warm bath for me? I want to soak in a sea of bubbles for an hour."

"Whatever you want, precious."

Emmy grinned and quickly put a hand on her belly.

"What is it? Are you all right?" Kenny asked.

"I just felt him kick. Put your hand here. Can you feel that?"

He placed his hand on the spot. "Yes, I can feel him moving."

"I think he's going to be a drummer because he's always moving his hands and feet."

"Maybe he will be a singer like his parents."

Kenny leaned down and kissed her belly. She smiled and put her hands on his head.

"Oh, wait. I think it was just gas," Emmy said and then shrugged.

They both laughed.

"Does she really think you're pregnant? Are you teasing?" Kenny asked as he pulled a few weeds.

"She really thinks I'm pregnant. I told her there was no baby on the way. I even offered to pee on a stick to prove it to her, but I didn't say anything else. I'm not sure if she believes me."

"Do you really want to soak in a bubble bath?"

"I would love to, but we don't have time. Maybe tonight. Right now I'll take a quick shower and be ready in ten minutes."

"Take your time, Em. We don't have to be at Jeff's until two. At least that's when Frances said they planned to eat."

Jeff and Frances Rawlings purchased a large three-story house shortly after their wedding in 1997. Five years of restoration would soon be over. Frances grew up in the Timberline Heights neighborhood and wanted to stay there to raise a large family. Two years after suffering a miscarriage, they tried again to start their family.

Emmy got ready, and she and Kenny walked the few blocks to where Jeff and Frances lived. Jeff saw them coming up the front sidewalk.

"Hi, guys. I'm glad to see you walked over here instead of wasting gas."

"Hi, Jeff," Emmy said. "It's only a few blocks and it's such a nice day. I was working in the yard like you are."

"I'm trying to get all these bushes trimmed to please the boss."

A little later, Jeff fired up the grill, cooked some burgers and they sat outside on the deck to eat.

"Would you like another burger, Kenny?" Frances asked. "There are three left."

"I think I have room for another," he answered. "I love the cucumbers like this."

Emmy took another bite of the cucumbers. "So do I. I don't often have the time to fix them. I know you have to soak them in vinegar and you added fresh tomatoes and onions. I should find a recipe."

Frances smiled and said, "I'll email you a copy of my recipe. It doesn't take as long as you might think."

Two hours later, as Kenny and Emmy were walking back to her house, Emmy asked, "Would it be all right if I take Mama Bertucci to South Bend next weekend? Tony is graduating, and she doesn't want to drive by herself."

"Just the two of you? Aren't Kristen and Derrick going?"

"I'm not sure. They might be coming on Sunday."

"It's all right with me if you go. Since we took this weekend off, we will probably be busy all next weekend."

"Thanks, Kenny, I wouldn't go if you didn't agree."

"I appreciate you asking, but you know you don't have to."

"Doesn't it say somewhere in the Bible that a wife is supposed to obey her husband? I guess I was just getting a jump on that."

"Is that a proposal?"

Emmy smacked his arm and told him, "No way! I'm never going to propose to a man. If he wants me, he will have to ask me the old fashioned way—in an email." She giggled and took off running. Kenny shook his head and ran after her. He caught her and they walked together.

"Kenny, do you ever regret not going to college for more than one year?" Emmy asked.

"Not really. I know how much it means to you, but I always knew I wanted to be a musician."

"You could always work on a degree after the band slows down. I know the guys won't always want to be on the road. They will want to start having kids eventually."

"I have thought about that, but I'll have to wait and see."

"Kristen will be graduating, too. It doesn't seem possible."

"Why? She's smart enough to earn a degree," Kenny said.

Emmy poked his side. "I know that. It just seems to have all gone so fast. I feel like we were just in high school and now most of my old friends will be out of college."

Kenny thought, *I would have paid for you to go to North Park, or wherever.*

Emmy looked at him. "I know what you're thinking and don't even say a word. Sure, I would like to be finished, too, but I'm not sorry."

"I'm proud of you, Em. Not many kids would work as hard as you have to get through college."

Later that evening, Kenny opened the fridge. "Hey, Em. I'm gonna make myself a sandwich. You want one?"

"No, thanks, I'm still full from this afternoon."

"Are you sure? You're eating for two now, remember?"

"Okay, make me one, but make sure you put pickles on it," she said and then giggled.

They relaxed and sat out on the deck enjoying the spring weather. They decided to go for a walk and spent an hour walking around the neighborhood. It was almost dark when they returned.

"What are we gonna do tomorrow, Em?"

"I'm singing tomorrow. Are you going to your own church,

or do you want to come with me?"

"I promised Mom I would go with them. We can get together in the afternoon. What about going somewhere for the afternoon? A park or something."

"Is it supposed to be nice like today?"

"Who knows? You know how unpredictable the weather is this time of year."

He woke up the next morning to the sound of rain against the windows of the carriage house apartment. It rained all morning, so Emmy went over to Kenny's after church. They ate lunch with his parents, and then spent the afternoon in the carriage house working on a new song.

"How about these chords, Em?" Kenny played a chord sequence on his guitar.

"Is that a D or an E at the end?" She asked as she played a keyboard.

"It goes A, G, Bm, A/C#, and then D." He played the chords for her.

"I like it."

Kenny worked on the music while Emmy plopped down on the old couch with a legal-size pad of paper. "It's still raining. I was hoping we would be able to do something outside today."

"We could still go out, Em. You won't melt."

"Very funny. I can't wait for summer."

"I'm going to use some of the lyrics we tried for that other tune."

By suppertime, they had a new song.

"You can sing it the next time we play for the teen group," Kenny said. *Who knows? Maybe someday it will be on your very own CD, Em.*

Kenny and the guys kept busy in the studio all week. Emmy stayed busy with work and church. They did have dinner Friday night at Ciao Bella. Kenny brought her back to her house after dinner.

"I need to put my entree in the fridge, and then I'm gonna

run upstairs and change." She made room in the fridge for her country rigatoni while Kenny made himself comfortable in the TV room. He kicked off his shoes and sat on the couch with his feet on the ottoman.

She ran upstairs and slipped into some comfortable pajama pants and a sweatshirt. She came downstairs and joined Kenny in the TV room. She set some magazines on the floor to make room for herself and leaned against him. "Do you want to watch something, or are we just gonna cuddle?"

"Can't we do both?" He put his arms around her and pulled her close.

"This feels good. We don't need to watch TV."

"What time are you leaving tomorrow?" Kenny asked.

"Mama wants me there by eight. She wants to get to South Bend early." She put her feet next to his and they were quiet for a moment. "Are you even a little tiny bit jealous of my friendship with Tony?"

"I'm not jealous of you guys being friends."

"Does that mean you're jealous that we used to date?"

"I don't think jealous is the right word."

"I never did this with Tony." She pulled his arms around her waist. "I'll admit that at one time I would have."

"I'm glad you didn't, Em." He pressed his nose into her hair. "Are you still using that strawberry shampoo?"

"Yes, do you like it?"

"I do, but isn't it for kids?" he teased.

She kicked his leg. "I like it, and I use a conditioner, too."

They cuddled for a moment without saying anything.

"I suppose you have every right to be jealous of my relationship with Becky."

"Because you guys were lovers?" she whispered. "I won't ever hold that against you. You guys were in love, so it wasn't a casual thing."

"I never told you, but it complicated our relationship."

"How? Move your feet and lay on your side."

"Like this?"

"Yes, that's better. We can cuddle more." She turned and lay

93

on her side next to him. She put a hand on his chest.

"Once she realized she wasn't going to be with me forever..."

"Did you ask her to marry you? You never told me that."

"I didn't propose, Em, but we kinda hinted at it. Anyway, after it happened..."

"The sex?"

"No! After she realized she couldn't be married to a man who wouldn't be there all the time, she felt really guilty about what we did."

"Didn't she like making love with you?"

"Emmy!"

She grinned. "Did you do it wrong?"

"You're gonna get it."

She grabbed his hands so he couldn't tickle her.

"I know she probably liked it. I know I..."

"Em, can we talk about something else?" He sat up and edged away from her.

She giggled and then said, "You mean something that won't get you all excited."

He stood up. "I need to go."

She sat up and patted a spot next to her. "I'm sorry. I'll behave now, and I won't ever mention sex again."

"It's not easy, you know. It's just human nature to do things that feel good." He sat down.

"I know that now. I always think of that verse in Philippians that says we can do everything through his strength. I could never sing at church or write songs without God's strength."

"And sometimes we need His strength to not do something. Does that make sense?"

"Yes. Without His strength, we would be upstairs in bed."

He looked at her and shook his head.

"What?" she smiled. "I didn't say sex."

Chapter Eleven

Early on Saturday morning Emmy drove over to pick up Mama for the trip to South Bend. She walked in the back door and hollered, "Mama, I'm here. Where are you?"

"I'm in the living room, dear."

Oh, I can smell chocolate chip cookies. Emmy noticed some freshly-baked cookies on the counter, grabbed one and took a bite. *Oh, these are so good.* She grabbed another cookie and made her way to the living room. She found Mama looking at the family pictures. "I hope it's okay that I took a couple cookies."

"We need to save a few for Tony." Mama looked at Emmy and smiled. "Just think. All three of my children now have college degrees. Heather and Marco are going to be doctors, and Tony is going to achieve his dream of playing football. Marco isn't a medical doctor like Heather. He has worked hard in college and gotten his degrees faster than most people."

"And Tony will have a good education to fall back on after football," Emmy added.

"Peter would be so proud of his kids," Mama said as she looked at a photo of him.

"You should be proud, too, Mama. You've done a great job."

Mama sighed. "Sometimes I wonder if I really have."

Emmy assumed she was thinking about Marco.

"Are you ready to go?" Emmy asked.

"Yes, I'm all packed. Would you carry my suitcase to the car for me, dear. I need to make sure the house is locked, and I'll be right there."

Three hours later Emmy and Mama arrived at Heather's apartment. Heather and Tony greeted them. Tony hugged his mother, then held his arms open for Emmy.

"Before I hug you I want to make sure you are really graduating. Do you have any proof?"

"I have a cap and gown. Is that enough proof?"

"Anybody can go out and buy those," Emmy said.

Tony grabbed her before she could get away and hugged

95

her. "I'll have plenty of proof tomorrow, okay?"

Mama took everyone out to dinner at Callaghan Brothers Bar and Grill to celebrate. Even Alex got home in time to go along.

"Hey, Emmy, you wanna go for a walk?" Tony asked as they left the restaurant.

"Sure, but if I get tired, you will have to give me a piggyback ride." Emmy tried to jump on his back, but he stopped her. "Where are we gonna walk?"

"Depends. Where are you staying tonight?" he asked.

"I'm staying at Heather's. I claimed the couch. Why?"

"Just wondered." Tony grinned.

I can't stay with you. Emmy teased, "Do you have a better offer?"

"Not really. Since you're staying at Heather's, we should walk that way. We could walk over to the river if you want, or to the hospital."

"I've been to the hospital. You do mean Memorial Hospital, right?"

"Yeah. Heather's place is kinda between here and the river."

"But then you will have to walk all the way back up to Dillon Hall. That's a long way."

"It's only a couple of miles if even that far."

They spent an hour walking around before they returned to Alex and Heather's apartment.

Marco and his wife Nancy arrived after dinner. Alex picked them up at the airport and took them to the hotel.

On May nineteenth, Tony graduated from Notre Dame with a degree in management consulting from the Mendoza School of Business. The weather cooperated for the ceremony in Notre Dame stadium with sunny skies and temperatures in the seventies. Mama beamed with pride as she watched her youngest son get ready for the ceremony.

"Let me fix that tie for you." Mama adjusted his tie and stepped back. "You look so handsome in your suit."

Emmy grinned and said, "Yeah! You don't even look like a creep."

96

"You will pay later, Emmy," Tony said as someone knocked on the door.

Heather opened it and smiled. "You guys made it."

Derrick and Kristen stepped inside.

Emmy rushed over. "Kristen! I'm so glad to see you. I didn't think you were going to make it. Derrick, I'm happy to see you, too. Give me a hug."

Derrick hugged Emmy tightly.

"Kristen, did you come just so you could see John again?" Emmy asked.

"No! I wanted to see Tony."

"Kristen!"

"Okay, maybe I wanted to see John, too."

"Did you guys just come for the day, or are you staying overnight?" Emmy asked.

"Derrick wanted to drive back tonight, but I convinced him to stay. We were lucky that we found a hotel room. Most of the places are booked solid."

"I crashed on Heather's couch last night."

"You could stay with us," Kristen said.

Emmy looked at Derrick. "I don't know if I could share a room with him."

"Yeah, I can understand that. It's bad enough that I have to live in the same house with him," Kristen said.

"Keep it up, little sister. I might make you sleep in the car."

"He's bluffing. Daddy would disown him if he did that." Kristen made a face at her brother. "Let's get your stuff and put it in the room as soon as we can check in."

Heather made sure everyone received a ticket to get into the stadium. The ceremony lasted for over two hours, and it was noon before everyone returned to Heather's place. They ate lunch and headed over to the Joyce Center for the Mendoza School of Business commencement ceremony. After that ceremony, Tony finally felt like a graduate. John Randolph graduated with the same degree and his family made the trip from Ohio to celebrate as well. Very early in the year John reserved three suites at the Inn at Saint Mary's for his family. He planned ahead. After the ceremony at the

97

Joyce Center, John and Tony found their families and introduced everyone. Kristen met John's parents, Jerry and Evalyn, and also his brothers, Kirk and Keith, and their spouses. Tony and John reserved a banquet room at the Carriage House restaurant for seven o'clock that evening. They treated everyone to dinner.

John asked Tony, "Can we afford to feed sixteen people at this place? It's a lot more expensive than ordering pizzas."

Tony laughed. "I thought about pizzas, but Heather threatened to end my pro football career before it started."

At the restaurant Tony smiled at Emmy and Kristen. "How come you guys changed into dresses?"

"Mama told us we should dress up for dinner," Emmy replied. "I didn't want to, but I changed just to please her."

"You look very elegant, Kristen."

"Hey!" Emmy poked him in the side. "What about me?"

Tony grinned as he looked up and down Emmy's dress.

"Stop staring at my legs, you creep."

"I'm not staring at anything." *You do look really nice, Em.*

John finally had a moment of privacy with Kristen and smiled. "Hi, I didn't know if you would be here today or not. It sure is good to see you again."

"It's nice to see you, too, John. Oh, this is my brother Derrick. He's in law school now, but he played tennis for the Arizona Wildcats."

The guys shook hands, and John introduced his brothers to Derrick. Soon all the guys were talking about sports while all the ladies chatted about family. They celebrated for two hours before breaking up the party. The Randolphs went back to their suites at the Inn at Saint Mary's. They would head back to Ohio early in the morning. Mama went back to the apartment with Heather while Alex dropped Marco and Nancy off at the Fairfield Inn. Emmy and Kristen stayed with Tony, John and Derrick to celebrate some more. They decided to take a walk around campus. Tony pointed out the various buildings to the girls and Derrick.

"This is Dillon Hall, of course. That building right next to it is South Dining Hall."

"How convenient for you guys to have a dining hall right

next to your dorm," Kristen teased.

Emmy looked at the building and commented, "It looks sorta Gothic or even medieval."

As they passed the north side of Dillon Hall, Emmy pointed. "Look! There's a ship carved on the building. It looks like a Viking ship or something."

"It's got something to do with St. Olaf. He was Norwegian like Knute Rockne. You have heard of him?" Tony asked.

"Of course," Emmy answered. "He's the guy who built the stadium."

The guys laughed, and Tony told her. "He didn't actually build it, but he was responsible for it being built. He's probably the most famous coach in the history of Notre Dame football. Probably all of college football."

"I know," Emmy said as she rolled her eyes. "I've seen the movie where President Reagan played George Gipper."

"George Gipp! Not Gipper."

"Then why do they always say 'win one for the Gipper' and not 'win one for the Gipp,' huh?" Emmy asked as she stuck out her tongue at Tony.

Tony started to grab Emmy, but she ran away.

Kristen yelled at her, "Stop it. You're wearing a dress. You're not a tomboy anymore."

Tony caught Emmy and instead of throwing her over his shoulder the way he used to do, he tugged on her hair. Every time they passed a building Emmy asked the name.

"That's the law school and that's Cushing Hall for engineering." They kept walking and passed another large building.

"What's that one?" Emmy asked.

"That's DeBartolo Hall. It's mostly classrooms," John said.

Derrick added, "Dad knows Mr. DeBartolo—well, he met him once. He started this huge construction company that built shopping malls and stuff."

"The family owns the 49ers, too. They used to at least. I'm not sure if they still do," Tony mentioned.

They kept walking, enjoying the sun and a gentle breeze.

Emmy looked to her left at the stadium. Tony pointed out the Mendoza School of Business.

"I spent a lot of time in there," John said. "Tony would have too if he ever went to class."

Tony and John walked with the girls, and Derrick, over to their room at the Fairfield Inn.

"We'll see you in the morning at Heather's. Get there early if you want breakfast."

Mama got up early in the morning and made breakfast for Heather and Alex. Tony and John said goodbye to John's parents, and then ambled over to Heather's. They wandered in as if they could smell Mama's cooking from their dorm. Derrick, Kristen and Emmy arrived last and Mama offered to make breakfast for them.

"I'm sorry we're late, Mama, but Emmy wouldn't wake up."

"Me! You're the one who wouldn't get out of bed, Kristen."

"It's all right, girls. We have plenty of time. What do you want to eat?"

"Do I smell biscuits and gravy?" Emmy asked.

"No, I made eggs and bacon for everyone. I suppose you want biscuits and gravy."

"I don't have the right ingredients, Mama," Heather said.

Mama said, "You can have eggs and bacon or cereal."

"We're out of eggs, too." Heather shrugged. "Sorry, girls, but Tony and John cleaned out the fridge. I guess the early bird gets the egg and not the worm."

"Cereal is my favorite." Emmy sounded like a little kid. "Can I have Frosted Flakes?"

"Sorry, Emmy, but I have cereal for grownups. There is oatmeal and shredded wheat."

"Do you have any ice cream?"

"You can't have ice cream for breakfast, Emmy." Tony scolded and Emmy pouted. "I'm not giving in just because you're going to pout like a child. No ice cream for breakfast."

"Fine! I'll starve then." Emmy stuck out her lip.

Kristen tried to grab it. "Stop that. Try acting like a grownup for a change."

100

"Okay by me. You can starve, Em," Tony said.

Emmy could not get Tony to cave. "Fine. Where's the shredded cardboard."

Everyone laughed at Emmy, so she made a childish face at them.

After breakfast, Mama chased everyone out of the apartment—she wanted to rest. Heather, Alex, Marco and Nancy visited some friends they knew in town. The younger kids decided to take another tour of campus. This time they took John's car and were gone for three hours.

They returned in time for lunch. Emmy helped Mama with the preparations so they could have a family lunch together. Mama made cilantro chicken and Emmy made a huge garden salad. Heather made everything else.

Mama explained, "We're having a large lunch because this is all I'm cooking for the day. After this you are all on your own if you get hungry."

"Everything smells delicious, Mama," Tony said.

Kristen offered to help in the kitchen, but Mama knew about Kristen's limited cooking ability and shooed her out.

"Kristen, you can help set the table. Ask Heather where everything is. Maybe you can pry John away from Tony and Derrick and he can help you. First let me give you a hug, honey. It is so good to see you. I meant to ask you yesterday, but I forgot, did you cut your hair? It looks very nice."

"I got it trimmed a little."

"I love your curls."

"Sometimes I wish I didn't have such curly hair. It makes me look like Shirley Temple or someone."

Emmy changed clothes and wore a dress for lunch. Kristen fixed a couple braids in her hair the way Tony liked it. She looked like a princess to Tony, and he couldn't take his eyes off of her. Emmy used the bathroom, and, when she came out, Tony stood in the hallway waiting for her. Tony took her in his arms and kissed her all over her face and neck.

"Tony, what are you doing? Stop it, please." She tried to push him away without success.

Just then Heather walked out of her bedroom and saw Tony and Emmy. She assumed Emmy willingly let Tony kiss her.

"Excuse me, guys. I need to get past."

Tony held Emmy close so Heather could get past. He started kissing her again and this time she responded.

Meanwhile, Mama announced, "Lunch is ready. Everybody grab a chair and sit down. Emmy, will you say grace?" Mama looked around for Emmy, but didn't see her. "Kristen, will you find Emmy, please?"

Kristen stopped when she saw Emmy and Tony in the hallway. She approached cautiously and whispered, "What are you guys doing? Emmy, lunch is ready, and Mama wants you to say grace." She poked Tony in his side, "Stop kissing her and let her go before I hurt you."

Tony released Emmy and looked at Kristen, who stood with her hands on her hips and a frown on her face. Emmy's face turned red. Her heart pounded. She was breathing as if she just ran a hundred yard dash.

"Emmy, come on. Lunch is ready," Kristen repeated.

Emmy looked at Kristen, then up at Tony. She bit her lip, then turned and headed to the dining room table where everyone waited patiently. Kristen looked at Tony and smacked his arm.

"What was that for?" he asked.

"For where you had your hands." She smacked him again, even harder. "What do you think you were doing with her. Don't you know she loves Kenny Colwell, and they are going to have a baby together," Kristen scolded.

"What?" Tony asked slowly. "Are you teasing me, or what?"

"Come with me and don't say a word to anyone about the baby. Do you hear me?" Kristen glared at him.

"I won't say anything. I promise. It's all my fault. I started kissing her and wouldn't let her go. Emmy didn't do anything wrong."

"She already did!"

Tony and Kristen joined everyone and Emmy offered thanks for the meal and the time together.

After lunch John took Kristen to a movie. Heather and Mama took Marco and Nancy to the airport. They had to catch a flight into Chicago, and then home to Baltimore. Alex and Derrick decided to find a bar to kill some time. Emmy and Tony realized they were alone in the apartment.

"I'm sorry for what I did earlier, Em. I saw you in the hall and you looked so pretty in your dress and with your hair braided like that. I lost control and had to kiss you. I forgot you're going to be having a baby."

Emmy stared at him. "You've been talking to Kristen, haven't you?"

"Yes, is it true? Are you and Kenny having a baby? I'm happy for you if you are."

Though tempted to tell Tony she was pregnant, she didn't. "I'm not pregnant, Tony. I can't make Kristen understand though."

I'm so glad to hear that. Tony exhaled. *Not that I could do anything if it were true.*

Emmy asked, "What are you thinking?"

"We could fool her and pretend you are... expecting."

"I don't think we should. She would hate me if I teased her about that."

"It would serve her right in a way."

"No!" Emmy said adamantly. "Do not tease her about this."

Tony nodded his head.

"How would you like to walk over to my dorm? It's so nice outside."

Emmy looked up at him. "I suppose we can."

"Brenda isn't here. She left for home already."

"Okay, let's go."

Emmy loved the feel of the sunshine and the light breeze on her face. Their hands brushed against each other at times as they walked through the beautiful campus. Tony felt sentimental because of how much playing football for Notre Dame meant to him. They reached his dorm and went up to his room. Tony had packed everything the day before. Tony would ride back with Derrick in the van. Kristen would catch a ride with Emmy and Mama. Emmy looked around the room for the last time. She felt

103

mixed emotions as she pictured Tony in this room with Brenda. To Tony this room had been home for three years. This was where he met John Randolph, who became his best friend. Emmy turned to face Tony. He bent down to kiss her, but she moved back.

"Please, don't do that." She sat on John's bed as Tony sat on his. "I know this is where it happened, Tony, but I want to have a better memory than that. I want to be able to think of this room differently."

Tony didn't know how to respond, so he leaned back against the wall and closed his eyes. His thoughts drifted back to the first time he took Emmy to his house. They played in the snow, and he knew he might never love another girl the way he loved her.

Emmy whispered, "I love you, Tony. I want us to be friends forever."

"I love you, too, Emmy. I'll do anything to make you happy, anything."

She moved and sat next to him. "There is one thing I want you to do more than anything else. It's the most important thing you could ever do."

"Tell me, Em."

"I want you to give your heart to Jesus like I have done."

"While we're in bed?"

"We're not *in* bed." Emmy giggled despite the seriousness of the moment. "Maybe on the bed like this would not be the best way to ask Jesus into your life, but I bet if you did, he would forgive you anyway. Let's get off the bed and kneel beside it." Emmy looked into his eyes.

Tony looked at the opposite wall. *This is kinda weird, but something tells me that it's the right thing to do.* He turned his eyes to Emmy. "Okay, Emmy, but I don't know what to say. Is there a specific prayer you have to say?"

"There is not a specific prayer you have to repeat, but there is something specific you need to ask for. You need to ask God to forgive you of your sins."

"You mean like going to confession."

"Kind of, but you are not talking to a priest. You are talking directly to God. You need to ask Him for forgiveness, and ask Him

104

to enter your heart and be your personal Savior. Do you understand that Jesus died on the cross for our sins?"

"Yes, of course."

"Okay, I will pray first, and then we can pray together. I will guide you through."

Emmy prayed as they held hands.

"Okay, Tony, now let's pray together. You can repeat what I say, or say it in your own words, it doesn't matter. The important thing is that you are sincere and really mean what you say. If you are, then God will forgive you of your sins and accept you as his child."

"I'm ready, Emmy."

Emmy prayed again, but Tony didn't have to repeat her words. He prayed these words, "Dear Jesus, I know I am a sinner and don't deserve your grace and love, but I know Emmy believes in you and now I do, too. Please come into my life and change my heart."

They continued to pray for each other and their friendship together. When they finished, they held each other close.

"Why didn't I cry like you are, Em?"

"I guess not everyone cries. It's not the emotion that saves you. I think that as long as you are sincere, Jesus will forgive you. You were sincere, right?"

"Yes. I feel different, and kinda at peace." He wiped the tears off of Emmy's face. "I'm really sorry for what I did earlier. I shouldn't have kissed you like that." He sighed. "I've make a lot of mistakes in my life."

"We all have, Tony. None of us are perfect, and we never will be. But we are covered by God's grace."

He stood up and helped Emmy rise.

Emmy touched his arm. "We should get back to the apartment before they send out a search party."

He laughed. "I doubt that anybody even misses us, Em. John and Kristen certainly don't."

Everyone else had returned by the time Tony and Emmy walked in the door.

Mama noticed their happy expressions. "What have you

105

two been doing?"

They believed Mama was upset with them, so they both stammered, "Nothing," much as a child would say.

Mama shook her head and whispered to Kristen, "They are both such bad liars. Look at their faces. They are glowing. Something has happened."

Kristen looked at Emmy, and then at Tony. She wasn't sure how she felt. She always wanted Emmy and Tony to be together, but she knew how much Kenny and Emmy loved each other. She believed without a doubt that Emmy was expecting, and, if she became involved with Tony, everything would be ruined.

Mama asked them again, "Well, are you gonna answer me?"

Emmy smiled at Tony and grabbed his hand. "We were praying, and Tony accepted Jesus as his Savior just like I did."

In spite of her deep faith in the Catholic church, Mama knew this was an important step for Tony and Emmy both, so she held them both in her arms. "I love you both very much."

"We know, Mama. We love you so much, too."

Kristen sighed with relief. *At least they weren't fooling around.*

Later, Emmy and Tony spent time talking to Mama in the living room.

"This applies to both of you no matter who you might be with in a relationship. You have to communicate with each other. Not just small talk about 'how was your day,' but real communication and trust. You must have absolute confidence in each other. After what has happened your faith has been severely tested. What's past is past, and you have forgiven each other for your mistakes. Over time you will begin to forget. You are still both very young and have, God willing, a long life ahead of you. Emmy, right now you are friends, and I'm so happy to see that. If that changes in the future, well, I'll be happy about that, too. If it doesn't, and you remain just friends, I will love you just as much."

"We will try, Mama," Emmy said.

Tony got up, walked into the kitchen and opened the fridge.

"Are you hungry again?" Kristen rolled her eyes. "Could

you grab me a water, please?"

Tony handed Kristen a bottle of water. "Anything else, your highness?"

"That will be all for now."

"Tony, I need a minute of your time," Heather said. "Alex and I need to get to the hospital."

Tony closed the fridge after grabbing an apple. "Thank you for putting up with me. I've raided your fridge a thousand times."

"I didn't mind." Heather hugged Tony. "I don't often tell you, but it's been good to have my little brother with me for three years."

Tony lifted Heather off of her feet as they hugged. "I'll miss you, Heather, and you, too, Alex."

"Put me down before you hurt yourself," Heather said.

"We'll talk to you soon, Tony." Alex shook hands. He and Heather left for work.

John walked into the kitchen. "Kristen, would you come out to the deck with me, please?"

"Of course," she said.

Emmy wandered into the kitchen and saw Tony eating his apple. "Any of those left?"

Tony pointed to the fridge.

"You're a big help," Emmy said.

Meanwhile, John took Kristen's hand. "I need to leave for home soon, and I wanted to talk to you before I left." *I love your eyes.* He gazed into them.

"I wouldn't have let you leave without saying goodbye." Kristen put her hand on his arm.

"The truth is I don't want to say goodbye. I mean I have to say it now because I'm leaving, but I don't want to say goodbye permanently. Know what I mean?"

Should I let you off easy, or should I pretend I don't know what you mean? Kristen looked up at John and smiled. "I think I understand. I don't want to say goodbye either. You will be coming to the Chicagoland area to live. I hope you can find a place in SoHam or close by."

"I don't think I'll even look anywhere else."

107

Emmy took a bite of her apple and then stared out the door to the deck. "Hey, what are John and Krissy doing?"

"What do you think? They're saying goodbye."

"Why? He's coming to SoHam soon, isn't he?"

"Not for a few days," Tony said.

John took Kristen in his arms. "I will miss you even though we haven't known each other all that long."

"I will miss you, too. Are you going to kiss me?"

"Just try and stop me," John said with a grin.

"Look! They're kissing!" Emmy squealed.

Tony took a bite of apple and then frowned. "Emmy, let them have some privacy. Would you want everyone watching when you kiss Kenny?"

"I wouldn't mind." She scooted back over to the counter beside Tony. "They're coming back inside."

John opened the door for Kristen and they glanced toward Tony and Emmy. Emmy teased Kristen by making kissing noises at her.

"Grow up, Em." Kristen rolled her eyes.

Later, Tony, John and Derrick took the van over to Dillon Hall and made quick work of loading it. Tony sold most of what he had in the room, so the van was filled mostly with clothes and some books and CDs. They loaded John's remaining possessions into his old pickup truck. John was heading home to Ohio, but would be coming to SoHam soon to visit. He wanted to find an apartment so he could be near a certain girl that he liked.

"Well, John, it's been a slice," Tony said.

"I couldn't have asked for a better roommate. I'll see you in about a week. You're sure Mama won't mind if I crash with you until I find a place."

"She would be upset if you didn't."

They slapped each other on the back, and John hit the road. Tony and Derrick drove over to Heather's place to meet Emmy, Kristen and Mama.

"Are you ready to travel?" Derrick asked Kristen. "I need to get home."

"We're about ready. Emmy's still getting dressed."

108

"What do you mean?" Derrick asked.

"She took a shower because she went out for a run. She said something about getting in shape for training camp and took off before I could stop her."

"She said something earlier about wanting to be in shape to run with John and me," Tony said as Emmy walked out of the bedroom and joined them.

"She will probably keep up out of sheer stubbornness," Mama said.

"Don't you guys understand?" Kristen mentioned excitedly. "She can't be running with you guys. Certainly not in her condition."

"What are you talking about, Kristen?" Mama asked.

Kristen looked around at everyone, then blurted out, "She's going to have a baby! She's pregnant, and Kenny Colwell is the father."

No one said a word for what felt like an eternity. Mama looked at Kristen, and then at Emmy. Derrick looked at Emmy, and then at Kristen. Tony looked at Kristen, but didn't say anything.

"Way to go, Kristen." Derrick frowned and then shook his head.

Tony grinned. Mama saw the look on his face.

"What is going on? Kristen, why are you saying that Emmy is pregnant? And why are you grinning?" Mama asked Tony. "This is very serious."

Emmy moved in front of Kristen. "Krissy, I love you and please understand. I am not pregnant, have never been pregnant and don't plan to become pregnant in the near future. I know I exhibited some symptoms of pregnancy—morning sickness, tight-fitting jeans—other things that made it seem like I was pregnant, but I'm not. I caught a stomach bug that caused my morning sickness. It made my belly swell a little bit..."

"You're not going to have a baby?" Kristen asked softly. "You're sure? Did you pee on a stick?"

"No, I didn't need to." *There are a couple of reasons why.* Emmy hugged Kristen and whispered in her ear why she knew she couldn't be expecting.

"Really? But I thought you guys..." Kristen didn't finish that thought in front of the guys. Instead she said something that embarrassed Emmy just as much. "Last week?"

Emmy blushed because the guys could hear. "Yes, last week. I know I'm not very regular."

Tony and Derrick got the picture.

"Now, is all that cleared up?" Mama asked and everyone nodded their head. "Emmy, are you about ready? I want to get home before dark."

"I'm ready, Mama. We can leave anytime you want."

Tony knew he would return to watch football games at some point in the future, but for now, it was goodbye. As they left, Tony took a look at Touchdown Jesus. This time he saw it in a different light.

Chapter Twelve

After not having a clue what she wanted to major in at the beginning of her freshman year, Kristen graduated from North Park College with a bachelor's degree in business management and marketing. She knew she didn't want to be a teacher, or an attorney like her brother. She knew she wanted a degree that she could use to find a career unlike some of her friends who chose majors in areas such as Philosophy and Gender, and Women's Studies. She always laughed at her roommate Tess who majored in Classical Civilizations. Tess told Kristen that she wasn't looking for a job, but a husband. Since Derrick was going into law and not interested in working for his father's company, Kristen decided that she might—at least until she found a husband.

Kristen's parents planned a graduation party at their home. She asked them one day as they sat on the couch in the family room, "Why don't we make it a combined party for Tony and me? We have so much more room here than Mama has at her house."

Mrs. Keasling set her *Fashion* magazine down and looked up at Kristen. "We thought about that but didn't know if you would want to share your party with Tony."

"I wouldn't mind at all. It would be so much easier on Mama if we do it here."

"I'll call Mama and see if the eighth will work for them."

And so it became a huge combined graduation party for both Kristen and Tony.

The Keaslings rented a large tent for the backyard, and Kristen arranged to have one of her favorite local bands, The Notable Exceptions, playing by the pool house. Many of Kristen's and Tony's friends made it to the party including Derrick and his new girlfriend, Lisa Shinaver. Even some of Tony's teammates, who lived close enough, made it to the party—including John Randolph. John had been staying at the Bertucci house while he looked for an apartment. Kenny Colwell made Emmy's day by bringing her to the party. When they first arrived, some of the people stopped and stared as they recognized him. He even got on stage and played with the band. He convinced Paul Joseph, the leader of the band who everyone called P.J., to ask Emmy and Kristen to get on stage with the band to sing a few songs for the crowd. The girls did such a good job singing that the band decided to offer them jobs singing background vocals. When Emmy wasn't on stage, she danced with Tony, since Kenny was playing with the band. Kristen danced with them and even pried Tony away from Emmy for a dance.

"What is it like to be a Christian?" Kristen asked. "I know Emmy has such a peace about her now. How are you doing?"

"I am doing fine," Tony answered. "I go to church with Emmy every Sunday I can, and she takes me to her Bible group. I'm kinda lost there, since the only time I've ever read the Bible was for a religion class, but the other people are very understanding and helpful."

"Emmy doesn't try to push me into religion or anything, but I know she prays for me. I heard her once when she didn't know I was there."

"She loves you, Kristen, and wants you to have the same peace that we have."

Kristen grinned as she said, "She told me that you guys were in bed when she talked to you about Jesus."

"You know it wasn't like that. We knelt by my bed."

"She told me all the details. If I ever do that, I think I will cry like a baby."

"I guess I'm wired differently. Being a macho guy and all."

Kristen poked him in his arm. "You guys are really serious about this."

"We are, Kristen. It's not merely a phase we're going through. Accepting Christ doesn't make us perfect people or anything. We will still make mistakes and suffer through hard times, but we have a peace that helps us get through." He paused then added, "I think I really started to think about the whole Jesus thing after Emmy sent me that letter. At first, I didn't understand anything, but then I kept reading it and I felt something in my heart. I didn't know what it was at the time, but I do now."

"What was it?"

112

"I believe it was the Holy Spirit preparing my heart for the day..."

"The day you guys were in bed," Kristen teased again.

"She should have never told you that."

"It does make for a good story."

Tony and Kristen continued to talk about his new faith as Emmy watched. She said a quick silent prayer thanking God for her two best friends.

She smiled at Kenny. "Thank you so much for bringing me today. I really appreciate it."

"I'm pleased that you invited me. I'm always happy to see my best girl. Did you have a good time at the graduation?"

"If you mean Tony's, yes, I did. You're teasing me."

"Of course. I was so happy when you called and told me he gave his heart to Jesus. I was a bit surprised it happened in bed."

Emmy smacked his arm and reminded him, "We were kneeling next to his bed. We weren't in bed, and you've got no room to talk about being in bed."

"It just goes to show that you don't have to be in church to find God. I wish I could have been there when Kristen told everyone you were pregnant. What did Mama say?"

"Not much. I think for once we caught her by surprise, and she didn't know what to think."

Emmy placed her hands on his shoulders and he held her close as they danced.

"Is the CD finished?"

"We are still working on two tracks. We think it needs some more background vocals. Wanna help us out?"

"You want me to sing on your CD! Are you nuts?"

"Yes, but that's beside the point," he said. "There is a part that you could add. Why not help us out? We might even pay you."

"If I do it, you have to take me to Darby's. I'd rather do that than just be paid for it."

"We can pay you, and I'll take you to Darby's. How's that for a deal?"

"Deal!" Emmy shook his hand, and then kissed him.

Several of Kristen's friends from North Park made it to the

party. Mace Franklin and his fiancee, Erin Bezick, waited in the line for the buffet table on the large deck behind the house. They graduated the previous year and would be getting married in a few weeks. Annie O'Dell and Matt Sullivan, who also graduated last year, stood behind them. Annie O'Dell would be the maid of honor for Mace and Erin's wedding.

"Can you believe how much food is here?" Mace asked Matt.

"That doesn't mean you have to eat all of it, Mace Franklin," Erin said.

"I'll save some for the other guests, honey."

"Hey, Mace. The rest of us want to eat, too," Annie said as she poked him in the back.

"Don't worry, Annie. I'll leave a few scraps for you."

"That's what I'm afraid of," Annie replied.

"Come on. I don't eat that much."

"I've seen you eat before, and it's not a pretty sight."

"I can't help it if I have a high metabolism."

"Metabolism my eye! You just like to stuff yourself," Annie teased.

"Will you two knock it off and behave?" Matt laughed.

Christopher and Randy Braun showed up a few minutes later.

Randy Braun graduated one year ahead of Kristen and Emmy as the valedictorian of his Roosevelt High class. Despite a rough start to college, because of alcohol, he earned his bachelor's degree in mathematics from North Park. He entered into the graduate studies program with a goal of teaching at the college level, preferably at North Park. Randy lost interest in his church after high school. He began attending the same church as Emmy and Tony in his last year of college. He gave Emmy credit for bringing him back from the brink of alcoholism, but Emmy refused to take credit. She knew the Holy Spirit convicted Randy, and he answered God's call for his life. He and Emmy were good friends who often attended church functions together when Kenny was on tour. They had even kissed. Fortunately, they both agreed it was like kissing a sibling. Since then their friendship had strengthened.

"Hey, Christopher. Aren't you a father yet? What's taking so long?" Mace asked.

"I guess she isn't ready to leave the womb and face people like you," Christopher said.

Erin and Annie laughed at Mace.

"I saw Victoria at the store last week. She looks like she's ready to pop any day now," Annie mentioned to Christopher.

"She's a week overdue, and she's getting real cranky. I hope the baby comes soon."

Emmy and Kristen talked quietly as they strolled over to the buffet tables. Kenny trailed along behind them. They waited patiently in line behind several other guests until Annie O'Dell saw them.

"Kristen, why are you waiting? You should be in front of the line. It's your party after all."

"It's all right, Annie. I had some food earlier. Emmy and I are getting more food for John and Tony. They're too afraid to go through the line again. They eat like horses."

"They're big guys. They need to eat a lot. Are they getting anxious for training camp to start?" Matt asked.

Kristen answered, "They're working out a few hours everyday. Doing a lot of running together."

"I'm running with them," Emmy said.

Matt moved up in line but everyone else stood still.

"She's trying to at least," Kristen teased.

"I keep up with them for a mile or so, but that's all I need to do. I just want to stay in shape."

"For what, Emmy? You look great."

"Thanks, Annie. You look fantastic, too. How are things going for Matt?"

"He's doing better. It was such a shock when he found his father. He's taking over the business with help from Mike Bushell and his Uncle Denis."

"A heart attack, right?"

"Yeah, they did an autopsy, and that's what they learned."

"How are your father and grandpa doing?" Emmy asked.

"Daddy is doing great. He's going to work on the police

115

force for two more years, and then retire. He and Elisabeth are building a house on the farm. Grandpa enjoys retirement. He claims he doesn't miss Roosevelt High at all. We go fishing a lot, and we take Keyshon with us."

"Keyshon is Mace's brother. He has Down syndrome and is the sweetest kid," Emmy explained as she held Kenny's hand. "It's good to see you, Annie."

"You, too, Emmy."

"Annie, when you see Principal O'Dell, I mean your grandfather, please tell him I said hi. He always encouraged me to keep after my dream," Kenny said.

"I will, Kenny. Just so you know, I always give him a copy of your CDs. He actually likes rock music."

Emmy said a quick prayer for Annie and Matt. He recently lost his father. Emmy realized that praying had become automatic for her. Not as a matter of routine, but she prayed immediately when she sensed a need.

"Emmy, you don't have to say a prayer every time you get a plate of food," Kristen teased.

"I was saying a prayer for Annie and Matt."

"Oh, I'm sorry I interrupted. I hope he's doing okay. He looks sad to me."

"It's probably just stress. I'm sure that running the Hungry Lion takes a lot of his time. We better get this food over to the guys before they starve."

The caterers kept filling the buffet table all day. Even Tony and John had enough to eat. Guests came and went all afternoon and evening. The band finished playing, so Derrick turned on the outdoor speakers. Kristen and Emmy stayed together—as if joined at the hip. Kenny hung out with the guys, and they talked about sports.

"What are you girls doing?" Mama asked later as she caught Emmy and Kristen in the kitchen.

"Nothing, Mama. We're filling these balloons for the kids."

"You mean for you and Kristen."

Emmy and Kristen giggled as they prepared water balloons to throw at Tony and John.

116

"Will you help us?"

"Oh, all right." Mama answered with a little bit of glee in her voice. "You know they will get you back."

"We know. That's why we changed clothes and put on shorts and tank tops. We didn't want our dresses to get ruined."

"Water wouldn't ruin our dresses, Kristen. You do wash yours, right?"

"Sorta."

"One of these days you have to learn how to do laundry, Kristen Keasling. I swear. You are such a pampered princess."

Emmy and Kristen stockpiled their water bombs and prepared a strategy. Ten minutes later the attack began. Kristen and Emmy isolated the targets and coordinated their surprise assault. At Kristen's signal Emmy launched the bombs. Several of them reached the targets. Unfortunately an innocent bystander was hit as well—Kenny Colwell. Kristen and Emmy retreated to a secure location. They ran and hid behind Mama.

Tony and John recovered from the surprise attack and began planning a counter assault. Kenny joined forces with them.

"You two started this so I won't let you hide behind me." Mama pulled Emmy and Kristen out from behind her. "Go out there and let the boys have some fun, too."

"But Mama..."

"No buts about it. You know they will get you sooner or later. The water will cool you off. It must be ninety degrees outside."

"Come on, Emmy. We can hide by the pool house," Kristen suggested.

"Let's stay close together and use some of the guests as cover."

"Good idea. The guys won't attack if we are around innocent bystanders."

It sounded like a good plan to Kristen and Emmy, but it didn't work out that way. As soon as Kristen and Emmy left the deck, water balloons pelted them from all sides. John, Tony and Kenny found an extra bag of balloons and recruited allies to help in the assault. Derrick, Mace and Matt joined the guys to help win the

117

fight. Emmy and Kristen ran to the pool house and hid inside. They peeked out the glass doors but didn't see any sign of John or Tony. All of a sudden Emmy and Kristen heard a loud voice.

Tony announced, as if he was the leader of a SWAT team, "You have two minutes to lay down your weapons and come out and surrender, or we're coming in after you."

"What should we do, Kristen?" Emmy asked.

"I'm sure they think we'll go out the side door. Let's surprise them and go out the pool door."

"Okay. I'm ready to make a run for it."

Kristen and Emmy charged out the door facing the pool. Six water balloons hit them immediately.

"So much for that idea."

"Okay! You win. We surrender," Kristen yelled as she noticed a garden hose. Emmy saw the hose and nodded to Kristen.

"We give up. Come and claim your prize."

Tony and John moved forward cautiously. Kenny and the other guys hung back in case it was a trap. When Tony and John came into range, the girls opened fire with the hose hitting both guys. Derrick and Mace retreated out of range. Kenny moved forward to help his wounded comrades. Emmy and Kristen advanced to see if the guys would surrender. Suddenly the two casualties sprang into action. They captured Kristen and Emmy and carried them on their shoulders. By now the other guests were watching the battle—and laughing so hard their sides hurt.

"What should we do with these guerrilla fighters, John?" Tony asked.

"I say we toss them in the pool for starting this uprising."

"Let's think about this for a moment. If we treat them with compassion, they might become more docile and never attack us again."

"On the other hand, I say we go for the kill. Toss them into the pool and be done with them."

"If we set you down, will you promise not to attack us again?" Tony asked the girls.

"We promise," Emmy answered.

"Scout's honor?" John asked.

118

"Yes. On our Girl Scout's honor. We promise not to attack." Kristen looked John straight in the eyes.

Emmy looked at Kristen and whispered, "We were never Girl Scouts."

"I know, and Tony knows, too. So... we don't have any code of honor to break."

"You're sneaky sometimes, Krissy."

Tony and John released their prisoners. They stood facing each other like two armies trying to decide what the other would do next. Tension filled the air as the opposing sides looked each other in the eye—probing for a weakness. There was a hushed atmosphere as the crowd anticipated the next move.

Suddenly, the girls turned and sprinted for the hose, but reinforcements, Derrick and Mace, thwarted them. The girls tried to escape in another direction, but Kenny and Matt blocked the way along with some innocent bystanders. This left the girls with only one option—a frontal assault on the main line—John and Tony. They whispered "good luck" to each other and went for it. The crowd groaned as John and Tony captured the two guerrilla fighters again. This time John and Tony punished the girls quickly and severely—they tossed them into the pool. They acted with compassion and offered an outstretched hand of peace to their foes. The girls tried to prolong the fight by pulling John and Tony into the pool, but the guys anticipated this sneaky attack and released the girls so they fell back in the pool to the delight of the guests watching. Kenny helped Kristen and Emmy climb out of the pool.

"You guys win. We surrender for real this time."

"Are you sure?" Tony asked suspiciously.

"Yes, we have accomplished our goal. We have cooled off."

Tony hugged Emmy and John hugged Kristen, and they were all soaked but happy.

Emmy turned to Kenny and smiled. "Did you have fun, Kenny? You look like you're as wet as me."

"I'm soaked, but it feels good."

Kristen, John and Tony walked back to the deck, and Emmy pulled Kenny around the side of the pool house.

"I'm glad you're here," Emmy said as they kissed.

119

"Yeah, so you could get me with water balloons."

Emmy giggled and then said, "That was fun, but now my underwear is soaking wet."

"Didn't you put on a bathing suit like Kristen did?"

"No! She didn't tell me she changed into a bathing suit. Wait til I see her."

"You are something else, Em."

"Do you still love me even if I'm goofy?"

"Always."

Eventually, all the guests left except for immediate family. Heather took Mama home shortly after eight. Kristen convinced John to spend the night at the house—in a spare bedroom, of course. Not necessarily their idea, but Kristen's parents insisted. Tony realized he didn't have a way home since he rode with John. Kenny and Emmy offered to give Tony a ride home. They drove past Emmy's neighborhood and Tony wondered why, but then he realized.

Duh! Kenny is going to spend the night at her house. I should have known that.

Kenny pulled into the driveway, and Tony hopped out of the back seat. "Thanks for the ride, guys. I appreciate it."

"No problem. Congratulations again on the graduation thing. We'll have to gang up on Emmy and Kristen again sometime," Kenny said.

"Why? You guys had as much fun as Krissy and I did."

"Just because it's so much fun," Kenny teased her.

"Good night, Tony. Seriously, I enjoyed dancing with you," Emmy said. "And getting you with the water balloons, too."

"Good night, guys. See you later."

They got back to Emmy's and she ran upstairs. She got ready for bed and came back downstairs.

"It's so late, why don't you stay here tonight? There are two empty rooms upstairs, and I don't think anyone will care."

"Are you sure, Emmy? What would your friends from church say?" Kenny asked with a smile on his face.

"I think they would understand."

Emmy's smile convinced him to stay.

"Do you promise not to attack me in the night?" Kenny asked.

"Don't you want me to?" Emmy sounded disappointed.

"I was talking about water balloons, Em. I know there are some left," Kenny replied.

Emmy bit her lip and felt embarrassed. "Oh, sorry. I guess I was thinking about something else."

Kenny kissed Emmy, and she went upstairs to bed. He locked the doors. He waited for a few minutes before he headed upstairs to the spare bedroom.

Chapter Thirteen

Kenny woke up early, got dressed, headed downstairs and started making breakfast. Emmy came downstairs a few minutes later, still in her pajamas.

"Good morning, Em. Did you sleep well?" Kenny asked. *Nice hair!*

"Yes, but I wish I didn't have to get up so early. This is one of those days where I could stay in bed all morning."

"You would feel guilty if you missed church." He tried to smooth her hair down without much success.

"I know." Emmy looked at him and bit her lip. "Kenny?"

He turned down the heat on the eggs, and then looked at her. "What, baby?"

"Does it bother you that Tony goes to church with me? He usually picks me up and we go together."

Just then Tony pulled into the driveway—a bit earlier than normal.

"It doesn't bother me, Em. I've been thinking and praying about it, and I wonder if now would be the time to switch churches. Maybe I should start going to Crest Ridge with you. I've been going to Faith Bible all my life. Maybe I need to switch. I told you before that, if we were married, I would go with you to your church."

"I would like that." Emmy smiled as she hugged Kenny, then put her arms around his neck and kissed him.

Tony walked in the unlocked back door and saw them kissing. He noticed Emmy was still wearing her pajamas.

"Oh, sorry, guys. I guess I should have knocked." *Shoot! Kenny is going to think I always walk in without knocking. I did today because I could see you guys.*

"It's okay. I was just kissing him. Kenny is thinking about changing churches and coming over to Crest Ridge with me... with us."

"That would be fantastic. It would be good to have someone there I know." *Oooh! Is that how your hair looks every morning? That's kinda scary.*

122

"You know other people there," Emmy said.

"I didn't mean it like that. I know lots of people there now. Everyone is so friendly for such a big church. I meant that I've known Kenny for longer than the other people."

"Why are you so early?" Emmy asked. "I haven't even showered or anything."

"I thought you needed to be there early for practice."

"Oh, crap!" Emmy swore, and then put her hand over her mouth. "I totally forgot. Give me ten minutes, and I'll be ready." She ran out of the kitchen and up the stairs.

Kenny looked at the scrambled eggs on the stove, then at Tony. "Well, do you want some breakfast? I'll split these with you."

"Sure," Tony answered as he sat down. "I can always eat."

Emmy made it downstairs in fifteen minutes. "Sorry it took so long. I tried to do something with my hair, but it's a disaster."

"Maybe you should get it cut, Em. You've talked about it before."

"I might have to do something with it. Are you gonna get ready and join us today?"

"I can't today, but I will soon. I promised Ronnie Rojas I would listen to his teen band. They're playing in the service today for the first time."

"Are you gonna come back over this afternoon?" Emmy asked.

"It won't be until after lunch. Ronnie promised the band I would eat with them. I'll see you as soon as I can."

Paul Joseph, from The Notable Exceptions, called Kristen the morning after the party with an opportunity. Kristen responded. "You got to be kidding me."

"No, we're serious about you and Emmy singing with us. It sounded great and obviously would attract more guys to the shows."

"Why do you say that?" Kristen naively asked.

Paul chuckled and said, "Duh, have you ever like looked in the mirror. You are so gorgeous and your little friend is cute, too."

"You know Emmy would hit you if she heard you call her 'my little friend', right?"

"Believe me, I'm fully aware of that. I've known Emmy longer than you. Did I ever tell you that I auditioned to be part of Fridays At Five?"

"I didn't know that."

"The circumstances just didn't work out," P.J. said.

Kristen called Emmy in the afternoon, and they talked about the offer.

"I really enjoy singing at church, but I haven't thought about singing for a real band in a long time. Other than with Kenny," she said and then grinned.

"I've never sang in front of people other than at the party, and that really doesn't count. We were just goofing around."

"It could be fun," Emmy said. "We do have more time on our hands since you're finished with school, and I'm not taking any classes this summer."

"It's easier for you because you've sung in front of big crowds before with Kenny," Kristen said.

"If you don't want to do it, that's fine with me. I enjoy singing at church."

Kristen thought about it for a while. "I'll give it a shot if you will, Emmy."

"Sure. Why not?" Emmy answered. "It's not like it's going to be forever."

They met the band at lead singer Paul Joseph's house later that evening. Kenny went with them since he wasn't busy and knew where P.J. lived. The band rehearsed in the basement. The guys jammed on some cover tunes to warm up. Emmy and Kristen knew most of the cover songs in the band's set list already, so they sang along. The band did some original songs as well. P.J., the lead singer, thought that one of their new songs would be perfect for Emmy to sing the lead vocal. Emmy tried it, and the band thought she sounded great. Emmy had a distinctive and immediately recognizable vulnerable quality to her voice.

Three hours later, P.J. told the girls, "Our next gig is on the fifteenth. It's a small venue that would be the perfect place for your first show. I will have to talk to the other guys to see how much we can pay you. How about it?"

Emmy looked at Kristen. "They're gonna pay us."

"We'll give it a shot!" the girls answered simultaneously.

The band, including Emmy and Kristen, but not Kenny, practiced every night for the rest of the week, and the night of the gig approached quickly. The band staged a dress rehearsal in P.J.'s basement on the fourteenth in front of friends, including Kenny Colwell. Emmy and Kristen made it through with flying colors, and Emmy sang her solo without a hitch.

Finally, the night of the gig arrived. The band would play from nine to midnight at a local venue. They expected probably three hundred people to show up for the gig—including Tony and John. Kenny didn't plan to go because he figured he would be a distraction.

Kristen came over to Emmy's house before the show.

"What do you think we should wear, Kristen? I heard a couple of guys commenting about the dresses we wore at the party."

"Emmy, we can't wear dresses. We have to dance around too much." Kristen checked Emmy's closet. *Is this all you have? You need to buy some new clothes, Em.*

"I know that. I'm not totally naïve. How do these jeans look? I could wear this top and layer this over it."

"That top makes you look like a dork. Find a different one that doesn't look so weird and fits better."

"Does it really make me look like a dork?"

"I'm sorry. You don't look like a dork, but that top is just not right." Kristen took a deep breath. "Sorry, I'm nervous about tonight."

"You will be fine. Once we get on stage and the band starts playing, you'll forget all about being nervous."

Kristen looked in the dresser for other tops for Emmy. She pulled out four before she found one she liked. "Try this one, Em. It's the best one."

125

Emmy and Kristen spent an hour trying on different outfits trying to decide what to wear. They decided to take several tops along so they could change between sets. Tony and John picked them up and drove them to venue.

"Could you bring a limo the next time, Tony?" Emmy asked. "We want to arrive like stars."

Tony bowed. "Certainly, your highness. Whatever you desire."

The band opened up with a fast song that got the over-twenty-one crowd in a party mood right away. Emmy and Kristen danced and sang on several of the songs. During one song Emmy and P.J. sang a duet. After the first set, Emmy and Kristen joined Tony and John at their table.

"Well, what do you think? How did we sound?" Emmy took a sip of Tony's beer and smiled at him, fishing for a compliment.

"The band sounds great, and one of the singers is really amazing."

"Which singer do you mean?" Emmy asked.

John grinned. *You just set yourself up for this, Emmy.*

"Kristen, of course, she sounds fantastic and looks so pretty, too," Tony said to get a reaction from Emmy.

"What about me? Didn't I sound good?" Emmy frowned at Tony.

Tony pretended to be surprised. "Oh, were you singing, too, Emmy?"

"Fine, no kisses for you tonight if that's your answer." Emmy stuck out her tongue. "Not that I would let you kiss me."

"You were the best part of the show, Em. I really liked the duet you and P.J. sang."

"Really? I wasn't sure about that song because I have to get so close to P.J., and he puts his hand on my hip. Do you think Kenny will get mad if he sees that?"

"Probably not as long as you don't have to kiss him in front of everybody."

"I can't kiss him. He's married."

The girls returned to the stage for the second set. In the

middle of the set, Emmy and Kristen sang the lead on a song. The song went over big with the crowd, and they got a lot of applause and some whistling from the guys in the crowd. Emmy and Kristen used a lot of energy to entertain the crowd but enjoyed the energy they got back, especially from the guys who hollered after every song now. The second set finished with an up-tempo party song.

Emmy's solo would be the third song of the last set.

"Oh, Kristen, I'm worried about my song. What if I screw it up? What if I forget the words and stand there like an idiot? At church we have the big screens, but we don't have anything here."

"Emmy, if you forget the words all you have to do is stand there and smile at all the guys. Bite your lip like you always do, and they will go nuts just watching you. You could start singing 'Happy Birthday' and get a reaction from the crowd."

"Yeah, I would get a reaction all right. They would start throwing things at me."

"Just pretend you're that actress singing to the president like we saw on that clip on the Internet." Kristen started to sing "Happy Birthday" to Emmy as she imitated Madolyn Masters.

"Oooh, Kristen, you are too sexy."

They laughed and Emmy forgot all about being nervous.

During the last set Emmy sang her song, and the crowd gave her a loud ovation led by Tony and John. The band finished with an encore of the second set closer. Emmy and Kristen danced and jumped all around and the crowd really enjoyed watching them. After the gig, the band needed to break down their gear and load-out.

"Tony, would you and John be willing to help the guys break down the gear and load it up?" Kristen asked. "They could use a couple of big strong men to help them."

Emmy said, "Yeah, if you guys know where they could find a couple of hunks, that would help."

"Maybe I should load you out to the truck, Emmy," Tony said.

Tony and John helped the band with their gear, and, with the assistance of two other guys, the work was soon completed. P.J. approached Tony and John with a pen and a piece of paper.

127

"Hey, Tony, I hate to bother you, but could I get you and John to sign our set list for us? I'm a big fan of Irish football and the Bears, too."

"Sure, P.J."

Tony and John didn't expect to be recognized or have anyone ask for autographs.

"Maybe I can score some Bear tickets for you and the band."

"Yeah, that would be great."

A few minutes later, Emmy and Kristen finally took some time to sit down with the guys.

"Well, what do you think? Did you like the show or not?" Emmy looked back and forth at Tony and John.

"Emmy, don't bother asking these guys. We'll never get a straight answer out of them," Kristen said as she smiled at John. *You better say I sounded great if you want a kiss later.*

John told Kristen, "I thought you sounded great, and you certainly looked fantastic, especially in the last set."

"That's sweet of you, honey, but you think the garbage disposal sounds great, too."

Emmy laughed at Kristen teasing John.

Tony smiled at Emmy. "Since you are a star now. Can I have your autograph, please?"

"Sure, but it will cost you," Emmy said and then giggled.

Tony winked at John and asked, "What's it going to cost me?"

"A kiss," Emmy said as a joke.

"A kiss! If that's what you charge everybody for an autograph, you are retired as of right now. No guys are going to be kissing my girl for an autograph."

Kristen looked at Emmy and Tony as they carried on. *What are you doing, Em? Are you changing your mind again? Are you getting tired of Kenny? You're flirting with Tony and you don't even realize it.*

Emmy got serious for a moment. "Do you think we danced around too much? Would it be better if we just stood there and sang?"

128

Tony thought about it. "You didn't do a lot of dancing in the last set except for that encore. Every guy in the crowd loved the way you and Kristen jumped and danced around during that song. I don't think you should just stand there and sing. You guys get into the songs and need to dance around. That really gets the crowd energized."

"We kinda got carried away during that last song, didn't we? We will be more careful in the future."

"Emmy, you looked and sounded like an angel during your solo."

She blushed. "Thanks, Tony." She didn't mention she was thinking about Kenny the whole time.

"What's the name of that song?"

"It's called 'I Will Be True To You' and Kenny wrote most of it with help from the other guys in Fridays At Five. Some of the words are mine."

"It's a beautiful song, Em."

Tony and John dropped the girls off at Emmy's house so Kristen could spend the night with Emmy.

"I'll see you in the morning, Emmy. It's Sunday remember."

Tony told Emmy good night as John kissed Kristen. Tony took John to his house for the night.

"Kristen, would you go to church with me tomorrow?" Emmy made sure the bed in Diane's old room had clean sheets.

"Yes, I will, Emmy. For some reason I have had the feeling lately that I should go with you and check it out. We used to go to church sometimes when Derrick and I were kids, but I haven't been in a long time."

In the morning Tony stopped by to pick up Emmy. "Good morning, ladies. I hope you're enjoying this beautiful day. I asked John to come with us but he went to mass with Mama instead."

"Kristen is coming with us," Emmy said as he grabbed the last donut.

"That's great."

"At least he is going to mass," Kristen replied.

Many of Emmy's friends at Crest Ridge United Nazarene

129

greeted Kristen and made her feel welcome. Kristen used to imagine people who went to church as being like the 'old people with frowns on their faces all the time who were never allowed to have any fun' that she remembered as a child. She knew that Tony and Emmy still behaved like the same loving friends as they had always been, but with something extra added in—like a bowl of Breyers vanilla ice cream with chocolate sauce on top. Kristen sat with Tony during the worship service and listened as Emmy sang with the worship band. Kristen sang along to the words on the screens. Kristen noticed that when some men took up the offering, Tony put a check in the plate.

Emmy joined Kristen and Tony after the band finished.

"The worship band sounds fantastic, Em," Kristen whispered.

"Thanks, Chase is really good at picking out just the right songs," Emmy replied.

Tony frowned. "Sssh! Be quiet. Pastor Herb will get after you if you aren't quiet."

Kristen looked at Emmy.

"He's teasing, Krissy. Don't pay any attention to him." Emmy grinned at Tony and her eyes sparkled. "Let's just ignore him, and he'll leave us alone."

Dr. Ausland started his message with a prayer and Kristen listened closely. She felt something tugging on her heart but didn't know why. Dr. Ausland preached on First Corinthians and talked about love. Kristen thought he was talking directly to her with a gentle spirit and a heart of love. After he finished, he paused. He prayed quietly and asked the people to bow their heads and close their eyes. He let the people know that if they felt the need to pray, he would pray with them. Emmy felt a tug on her arm. She opened her eyes, looked at Kristen and saw tears running down Kristen's cheeks.

"Emmy, I need to do what he is talking about. What do I do?"

"Come with me, Kristen. I'll show you."

Emmy took Kristen by the hand and led her to the altar in the front of the church where they both knelt down. Emmy began

130

praying with Kristen and soon some other women joined them. Lynette and Aunt Doris prayed for Kristen. Dr. Ausland came over and began talking to Kristen. He instructed her, and Kristen prayed and accepted Jesus. Emmy hugged Kristen after she finished praying. Tears flowed like the Mississippi River during a spring flood. Even Tony had tears in his eyes as he hugged his favorite cousin.

Emmy looked at Tony smiled and said, "Now you start bawling like a baby. You're such a goof."

"Sorry, I couldn't help it."

They went out for dinner with a few other people from church. During their conversation Emmy heard someone mention that Emmy and Kristen seemed almost like sisters.

"Kristen, I have an idea. Listen to this, and let me know what you think. I have so much room in the house, and since we didn't have a chance to be roommates at North Park, how would you feel about moving in with me?"

"Are you sure, Emmy?"

"Yes! I would love to share the house with you. Please say yes."

It only took Kristen a few seconds to decide.

"Oh, Emmy. I'd love to share the house with you."

They jumped up and down as they hugged each other.

"Let's go to your house and pack up all your clothes. You can move in right away."

"Wait!" Tony said seriously. "We'll have to rent a moving van if we want to move all of Kristen's clothes.

Emmy poked him in the ribs. "You're such a dork."

Kristen moved in with Emmy, and they became roommates for the first time ever. Emmy had been thinking about moving back to an apartment or a smaller house since Diane moved out. She had even been thinking of moving into the carriage house. Now that wouldn't be necessary. Emmy enjoyed having her best friend with her all the time. Kristen applied for, and got a job working for Robertson Industries. She worked in the same building as Emmy, and they arranged to see each other for lunch almost everyday.

131

Kristen joined Emmy and Tony on Wednesday nights for the Bible study and went to church with them on Sunday mornings. They even learned to share the upstairs bathroom.

Emmy found Kristen sitting in the dark in the TV room one night watching an old version of *Pride and Prejudice* starring Sir Laurence Olivier and Greer Garson.

"I didn't know you liked to watch these old movies, Kristen."

"I like watching them sometimes, but I always end up crying like a baby."

"So do I, but we can't tell the guys or else they will make fun of us."

"It will be our secret."

One morning Emmy came downstairs and saw Kristen throwing something in the garbage can.

"What happened? Did you burn something again?" Emmy asked.

Kristen sighed and slumped down onto a kitchen chair. "I give up. I'm never going to learn how to cook."

Emmy giggled and asked, "What was it this time?"

"Instant oatmeal." Kristen pointed at the box on the counter. "Go ahead and laugh at me. I don't care."

"We could buy those packets. All you have to do is add water and stick the bowl in the microwave."

"You can buy oatmeal like that?" Kristen asked. "Since when?"

"Have you ever been in a grocery store?" Emmy shook her head.

"I've been past the Sainsbury's," Kristen said. "I've even been inside a few times, but I never bought anything."

Emmy rolled her eyes. "You're coming with me this Saturday. It will be a new experience for you."

"Do they have clothes at the grocery store?" Kristen asked with a straight face.

John began spending most evenings at the house since

Kristen was there now. Tony tagged along at times, and Emmy didn't mind. Emmy and Tony weren't normally alone except when John and Kristen needed to have some quality time together. Emmy made sure Kenny didn't object. He didn't mind because he and the band were busy finishing up details for the new CD and the tour that would follow its release.

Emmy told Kristen one Sunday afternoon, "It was so funny listening to Tony ask Mama if he could eat dinner with us. He sounded like a ten-year-old kid asking to spend the night at his friend's house."

"Even though Tony is a grown man, he still respects Mama enough to seek her approval, or her permission at least," Kristen replied.

"It's still funny."

"Em, I haven't seen Kenny all week. Did you guys have a fight or something?"

"No, he's just been busy with the band," Emmy said. *Come to think of it, he hasn't been here since you moved in, Krissy.*

Chapter Fourteen

"Emmy, come and take a look, please" Kristen waved her hand and motioned for Emmy to join her.

"Are there many people out there?" Emmy walked up to the curtain at the front of the stage and peeked out. "Holy cow! The place is almost full."

"Have you ever sang in front of this many people, Em?" Kristen asked. "I'm kind of nervous about it."

"You will get over it. It's not any different than singing in front of twenty or thirty friends."

"Why is it that I don't believe a word of that?" Kristen asked.

The Notable Exceptions played a Fourth of July gig in front of a capacity crowd. They opened the show in South Hampshire Memorial Stadium for Fridays At Five. Emmy and Kristen got to sing and dance in front of some of their friends.

After the show, Emmy and Kristen met up with Barry and Linda Newton.

"I can't believe how good you guys are. I've heard these guys plenty of times before, but you and Kristen make the show so much better. Can I please have your autograph, Miss Colasanti?" Barry asked only half-jokingly.

"I'm sorry, but I don't give autographs to rowdy fans like you." Emmy laughed at him. *Barry, you can be such a nerd at times. You don't need my autograph. You have my friendship.*

"The crowd went totally nuts on the last song, and I really liked the one you sang with P.J. Does Kenny gets jealous of him singing with you?" Barry raised his eyebrows.

Emmy said, "Kenny knows P.J. is married and would never jeopardize his marriage. It's just an act for the crowd."

Tony saw Emmy talking to Barry and Linda and came over to hug her and say hello to their old friends.

"Emmy, you did a great job. That was your best set ever."

"Thanks, Tony. I sure liked singing in front of all those people even if they weren't here to see us."

Fridays At Five were the reason over 30,000 fans packed

into the stadium. Kenny made sure The Notable Exceptions opened the show. He even paid for their set to be recorded and filmed. Emmy's all-access pass enabled her to go backstage and mingle with the crowd. Emmy along with Tony, Kristen and John had backstage passes so they could join Kenny, Andy Walker and the rest of the band in their dressing room before they went on stage. Emmy hugged and kissed Kenny as if she hadn't seen him in forever. Kenny shook hands with Tony.

"I'm sorry I haven't seen you all week. I've been busy at work and practicing with the band for this show. I did email you," Emmy said as she hung onto Kenny's arm.

"It's all right, Em. I know you have other priorities now."

Emmy let go of his arm. *What is that supposed to mean? Other priorities. You better not be jealous of Tony coming around.*

Kenny shook hands with John and smiled at Kristen. "Hello, Kristen, it's good to see you again. You, too, John. Are you guys getting anxious for training camp to start?"

"Yeah, but we need to train harder. Emmy has been running with us, and she can keep up. If we can't drop her..."

"You know I only keep up for a mile. Quit teasing me," Emmy said.

Andy came over after he finished talking to the promoter. "Hi, cuz. How have you been? Did you lose my email address and my phone number?"

Emmy hugged him and quietly said, "I'm sorry I haven't been very good lately at keeping in touch. I thought you might be mad at me for going to church with Tony instead of Kenny."

"Nonsense! I could never be mad at you and besides," he whispered in her ear, "I know you still love Kenny. If he had a normal career, you guys would be married by now."

Emmy looked up at Andy and said softly, "We almost eloped during the holidays last year when we were in Florida with Grandma. Please don't tell anyone. We never said a word to a soul."

"Your secret is safe with me, cuz," Andy told her before heading over to talk to another group of music execs.

Emmy stood close to Kenny and held his hand. She didn't

often get to see her friend in his setting as a famous rock star.

Kenny whispered to Emmy, "I need to talk to Kristen for a minute."

"Okay. I'll hang out with Tony." *Why do you need to talk to Krissy? Are you spying on me? Is she telling you how often Tony comes over?*

Kenny walked over to Kristen and said, "Emmy told me about your new faith. I think that's great. How is everything going with that?"

"It's going great. I'm still learning stuff, but I know that Jesus is with me and guiding me. I know you're a Christian, too."

"Yes, I am. I grew up going to church and got saved as a teenager, but just last year I gave my life completely to Him." He waved at Frankie Hanna. "I know most people would think being a Christian and a musician aren't very compatible, but my faith keeps me grounded and sane."

"I noticed there is always a Bible verse on your emails."

"Shameful of me, but maybe some good will come of it."

Kenny smiled at Emmy as she and Tony were goofing around.

Kristen asked, "Have you heard from Becky at all lately?"

If Kenny was surprised by her question, he didn't let it show. "Yes, we usually email each other once or twice a month. She is back home with her parents. I did see her a couple of times out in LA. She thought about flying into town to see the show, but something came up. I better see what Emmy is up to before she and Tony start fighting."

"I'll talk to you later." Kristen laughed as she saw Tony pull on Emmy's ponytail.

"Stop that!" Emmy hollered.

"What's going on with you two?" Kenny asked as he watched Emmy poke Tony in the stomach.

"He was teasing me," Emmy said. "Ow! That hurt."

"You shouldn't hit people, brat."

"Creep!"

"He always teases you. What's special about that?" Kenny wondered.

136

"Nothing, I suppose."

After a moment, Kenny asked Emmy, "Are you ready to sing for another band tonight? They really need some help."

"I would be honored to sing with you guys. I even prayed for the chance to sing onstage with you. Is it wrong to pray selfishly like that?"

"Emmy, I don't think you have ever done a selfish thing in your life."

"Kenny, you're so sweet, but you know that's not true."

"I know, but you are the most unselfish person I know. Just to let you know, I checked with Will, and he listened to the recordings. He said everything turned out great. You sounded fantastic tonight."

"Before I forget, P.J. wanted me to be sure and thank you for getting this gig for them. He is very grateful for the way you have supported his band over the years. I told him I would give you a kiss from him. No wait, not a kiss from him, but by him, no..."

"I know what you are trying to say, Emmy. Just give me the kiss and be quiet."

Emmy kissed Kenny and hugged him tightly. They visited with all their friends until almost time for them to perform.

After the second band finished their set, the crowd noise grew in anticipation of the main headliners coming out to play. The Fridays, as the guys on the crew were called, prided themselves on quick stage changes. Most of the stage was already set on the backline, but the previous band's gear needed to be removed and a few finishing touches made before Ralph Glissman, the tour manager, and Tim Perino, the stage manager, gave a thumbs up. Total time—under twenty minutes. Ralph nodded to Andy Walker who made eye contact with Frankie Hanna. The stage went totally black and the crowd roared. Frankie led the guys onto the stage as he had been doing from the beginning. Emmy felt goosebumps on her arms as the opening music played. Kenny made sure that Emmy, Kristen, Tony and John received passes to be on stage during the show. Everyone, except Emmy, watched the special lighting and stage effects in awe. Emmy pretended to be used to it.

137

About halfway through the show, the stage lights dimmed and Kenny stood alone in a spotlight. He looked to the side of the stage and saw Emmy. For a few seconds he traveled back in time. He thought about the shy fourteen-year-old girl who sang like an angel, even then. Just as before, he introduced Emmy as the band's first singer and number one fan. She sang "Storms" and Kenny didn't let her leave the stage. She sang with the guys for the rest of the show. Kenny knew just how to keep the show building until at the end, the crowd went totally crazy for the hometown heroes.

After all their years of success, almost everybody in the world thought of them as famous rock stars now. But to Emmy, he would always be Kenny Colwell, her neighborhood friend—the boy who held her hand when she crossed the street on her first day at Roosevelt High—the boy she practiced with in his garage—and the boy she almost married. She remembered that he was also the first person to reveal to her that God had a purpose for her life.

After the show, Emmy and her friends spent more time with Kenny and the band.

Emmy whispered to Kenny as they stood close together, "Are you tired of staying with your parents while you're in town?"

"Not really. I spend most of my time at the studio and sleep in the apartment. Why?" Kenny asked, and then it dawned on him. *You want me to propose, huh?*

"I thought you might come and visit Kristen and me sometime. You haven't been around much since she moved in. Are you embarrassed because she thought I was pregnant?"

"I guess that's part of it, Em. I have been busy with the band, but that's not the whole reason. I guess I just didn't want Kristen to think I spent every night with you when I'm home. I guess I went a little overboard, huh?"

Emmy nodded. "You know we have an extra room upstairs where you could crash if you didn't want to sleep in the basement."

"Would Kristen be all right with that?"

Kristen overheard the conversation. "I don't mind. You can crash in the spare room. I know how much Emmy enjoys it when you are home."

"Okay, maybe we can work out a time. I'll talk to you later,

Em, but I've got to talk to some other people right now."

"Call me when you get home, okay?" Emmy hugged Kenny. Then he left to mingle with some other fans.

Tony and John took Emmy and Kristen back to their house.

"Are you guys gonna hang around?" Emmy asked. "If you are, should I make a pizza or something. You're probably starving."

"Don't you have to work in the morning, Kristen?" John asked.

"We both do, but you can stay. I'm too wound up to fall asleep," Kristen said.

Tony checked the freezer. "Hey, Em, you've got two Home Run Inn pizzas. Can we make them?"

"What? One for each of you guys?" Emmy slipped in front of Tony. "Will you guys share? I'm hungry, too."

"Yeah, I'll let you have a slice of mine," Tony said.

"What a pig!" Emmy said as she turned on the oven.

They sat in the TV room to eat and watched a movie until Kristen took John's hand and led him into the living room.

"Do you want another slice, Em?"

"No, two was enough for me." She leaned her back against his shoulder and stretched her legs out.

"You don't mind if I eat the rest, huh?"

"Go ahead." She crossed her arms over her chest. *Kenny, I don't understand why you are jealous of Tony hanging around. He's just a friend now.*

Thirty minutes later Tony nudged Emmy. "Wake up, Em. You need to get to bed."

She opened her eyes. "Did you really wake me up to tell me to go to sleep?"

"Uh, yeah."

"Creep!"

Chapter Fifteen

Emmy and Kristen reluctantly crawled out of their beds on Friday and made it to work. They kept busy right up until five o'clock even though most of the employees had taken Friday off to extend their holiday. Emmy met Kristen at her office, and they headed home.

"I don't know how your day went, but mine sucked," Emmy complained. "I didn't even have time for lunch. The phone kept ringing all day, and I needed to plan a trip for next month."

"I managed to grab a fifteen minute lunch, but my day was hectic, too," Kristen said.

They walked out to the car and Emmy asked, "Can we stop and pick up some Chinese for dinner? I don't feel like cooking."

"That's fine with me. We have a menu in the glovebox. What would you like?"

"Fried rice and sweet and sour chicken, please."

Kristen chose chicken chop suey, called in the order, and they picked it up on their way home.

"Shoot! Look at the time. I gotta get going." Emmy shoveled a last mouthful of fried rice into her mouth. "Kristen, are you coming to practice with me tonight?"

"If you give me a minute to change, I'll go. I don't want to wear this outfit."

"I'm not going to change. I like to wear dresses more now."

"When I first met you, Emmy, you were still a tomboy. You hated to wear dresses or skirts."

"I didn't hate to wear them. I felt more comfortable in jeans. Tomboy?" Emmy tilted her head. "Definitely. I think a part of me still is. Like the water balloon fight at your party."

"I wonder if anyone caught that on video? I'd love to see it. Everyone seemed to be watching us and laughing so hard. I heard Mama laugh every time we hit Tony."

"I think some of the other guests envied us because we were able to cool off." Emmy grinned as she remembered how good it felt to be in the pool. "My only regret is that I didn't have a bikini on like someone I know. You stinker."

"Well, it's not like we planned to do that ahead of time."

They finished eating. Kristen changed clothes, and they headed over to the church. Because of the holiday on Thursday the worship team shifted practice to Friday.

"Hi, guys. How is everyone tonight?" Emmy asked.

"Just peachy, Emmy. How are you guys on this lovely evening?" Steve smiled as he played a riff on his guitar.

"Okay. Why are you so cheerful, Steve?" Emmy asked the lead guitar player for the praise band.

"Actually, I don't know whether or not I should be so cheerful. Mrs. Ceranzo informed Chase earlier this week that she won't be able to sing for the worship team any more."

Emmy couldn't help but smile. Mrs. Ceranzo was the weakest singer in the group and really shouldn't have been on the platform in the first place. Emmy thought this would be the perfect time to ask Kristen to fill in for the night.

"That's really a shame. Did she say why?"

Steve shrugged. "Something about her hips hurting her too much."

Later, Emmy saw Chase in his office. "I heard about Mrs. Ceranzo. I hope she feels better soon."

Chase grinned. "Just between you and me and the walls, there's nothing wrong with her physically. Her husband convinced her to stop singing because he knew she didn't fit in with the group any more. She was all right when we only sang hymns, but her voice is just not right for the contemporary worship songs we do now."

"We are losing singers right and left. Silvia Fredkin left and now we're down to just you and me."

"I think we need to have an open audition and see who else might be interested. We've experienced trouble recruiting singers in the past because of how often and long we rehearse. Not a lot of people are willing to spend the time."

Emmy smiled and her eyes sparkled. "God will find a replacement for Mrs. Ceranzo soon, I'm sure."

"Emmy! I know you well enough to realize that you've got someone in mind already."

141

Emmy put her hands behind her back and twisted back and forth. "Well, it so happens that Kristen is here, and she is a very good soprano singer. Just the person to fill the vacant spot. We just have to convince her somehow."

"Are you going to put her on a good old fashioned Catholic guilt trip?"

"If I have to," Emmy said as she grinned.

"You can be so devious and mischievous at times, Emmy."

"I know. If you think I'm naughty now, you should have known me when I was in high school. I was really wicked. You should pray for me, Chase. Pray for me a lot," Emmy said and then giggled, as she ran to find Kristen. Chase shook his head.

Emmy explained the situation to Kristen. "We really need someone to sing soprano. Will you help us out?"

Kristen took a few seconds to decide. "All right. I'll sing harmony with you."

Emmy's mouth opened. "You will for real? That's awesome."

"Don't get too excited, Em. Pastor Chase might not think I'm good enough."

Emmy re-introduced Kristen to the guys in the group. They were down to seven members. The five musicians and Emmy and Kristen.

Some of the guys from the teen worship band would practice with them, but they wouldn't be on the platform on Sunday mornings. They were gaining valuable experience, though, and one day would take over from the older guys. Bobby O'Connor would split practice time with Skip Mason on the drums tonight.

"I'll introduce you to the tech guys later, Kristen. Without them we wouldn't be able to lead worship."

"Where are they anyway?" Kristen asked.

"Up there." Emmy pointed to a balcony in the rear of the sanctuary

"If you want to take a minute to run upstairs go ahead, Emmy. I have to run through a couple new songs with only the band," Chase said.

"Thanks, Chase. We'll be back in a few minutes."

142

Emmy led Kristen out of the sanctuary, around the corner and into a room off to the side. Emmy scrambled up a steep ladder and Kristen reluctantly followed. Kristen shook her head as Emmy climbed. She would have to talk with her later.

"Hi, guys. I want to introduce my friend, Kristen Keasling. She's going to sing with us tonight."

Everyone shouted "hello" to Kristen.

"This is Mary Lawson. She runs the screens and the computers for us. She has two young boys and works part-time here at the church."

"Hi, Kristen. It's nice to meet you."

"Thanks, Mary." Kristen glanced at the three monitors and a rack of other gear. *I wonder what all that stuff is for.*

"This is Yvonne Hillman, Chase's wife."

"Hi, Kristen. We met last week."

"Yes, I remember."

"Yvonne is the producer. She makes sure everything runs smoothly and according to the plan."

"It's pretty easy. These guys are very good at their jobs," Yvonne said.

Emmy pulled Kristen over a few feet. "This old guy runs the sound board. He knows what every single button on this monster does. Bruce, what happens if I touch this button?"

"Emmy! Don't touch that. That's the self-destruct button. We'll all be blown to bits if you touch it."

Kristen knew he was kidding, but wondered why Emmy referred to Bruce as an old man since he looked like a college-age kid.

"Kristen, this is our resident sound geek, Bruce Sutherland. Bruce, Kristen Keasling."

Bruce shook hands with Kristen. She noticed a wedding band on his finger.

"What about me?"

"I haven't forgotten you, Jeff." Emmy walked over to where he sat. "I saved the best for last."

Jeff stood up and hugged Emmy. Kristen guessed his age to be probably close to sixty.

143

"This is Kristen. She's going to sing, so make sure you light her good side."

"I don't think she has a bad side, Emmy. Hello, Kristen. I'm Jeff Morrissey."

"Jeff programs the light board for us when we practice. That way all he has to do on Sunday is push this button." Emmy pushed a button and the whole place went black.

The musicians stopped playing.

"Hey! What happened?" Chase hollered.

Jeff waited a few seconds before hitting the correct button to restore the lights.

Emmy giggled. "Oops! I'm sorry, Jeff. I guess I shouldn't touch your toy."

"It's okay, Emmy. No harm done." He knew she had purposely pushed the blackout button.

"We need to get back downstairs. See you guys later." Emmy grabbed Kristen's hand and pulled her back to the ladder.

Kristen stood at the top and looked down. "This can't be the only way up there, Em. I saw a door behind Jeff."

"That's the easy way up here." Emmy scrambled down the metal stairs. "There are classrooms on the second floor in that part of the building and there's a normal stairway. That door opens onto a storage room and then the hallway."

"Then why on earth did we climb this steep ladder?" Kristen asked as she cautiously climbed down.

"Because it's fun. I like to climb the ladder."

Kristen reached the bottom and said, "You're wearing a dress, Emmy."

"Duh. I wouldn't climb up like that in front of a guy."

"That's good to know."

"I'm still part tomboy."

"Maybe you should make sure the tomboy part of you wears jeans."

They entered the sanctuary and Chase waved at Emmy.

"I think he's ready for us." Emmy hurried to the platform, but Kristen took her time. "Come on, Krissy. Don't be nervous. You can do this."

I'm glad you have so much confidence in me, Em. I'm kinda scared. Kristen twisted her hair around her fingers.

They started the first song, and Kristen recognized it immediately. Emmy had been singing it at the house all week. Emmy knew two weeks in advance which songs they would use so she would play the CD and sing along. Kristen picked up her part right away. They rehearsed the five songs for Sunday, and then kept playing simply because they enjoyed it. Practice ended at eight thirty and Emmy and Kristen hung around to talk to some of the guys. Some of the guys needed to get home but most of the younger guys hung around. Yvonne left to round up her daughters from the child care room.

"You fit in just right, Kristen. Have you and Emmy sung together before?" Bruce asked.

Skip Mason moved close to Kristen, hoping for a chance to flirt with her.

"We've been singing with a group over the summer. Ever hear of The Notable Exceptions?" Kristen asked.

"I have," Bobby O'Connor, the young drummer, shouted. " I saw them open for Fridays At Five yesterday at the stadium. Did you guys go to the show? Don't tell me you got to go backstage since you're a friend of his."

"We were there," Emmy said modestly.

"Yeah, you could say it like that," Kristen said as she smiled at Skip.

"Wait a second." Bobby's eyes widened. "Are you telling me that you guys were the cute singers I saw on stage?"

Kristen nodded.

"My friends and I ended up at the other end of the field from the stage, so I wasn't close enough to get a real good look."

"Since you saw the show, you must have heard Emmy sing with Fridays," Skip told Bobby.

"No way! I didn't even make the connection." Bobby grinned at Emmy and then turned around. "Hey, you guys! Did you know Emmy is a rock star?"

"I'm not a rock star. Kenny and I are old friends. We grew up together. His parents live three doors down from mine. I used to

145

sing with them back in the old days."

"Emmy, you and Kenny are more than just old friends. Are you trying to keep it a secret?" Kristen asked when no one else could hear.

Emmy whispered, "We don't need to tell everyone."

"How old are you, Emmy?"

"Bobby! You shouldn't ask a lady her age," Bruce scolded him.

"Sorry, Emmy, but aren't you just a kid like me?"

"I'll be twenty-two on Monday just like her." Emmy pointed at Kristen. "She's much older than me."

Kristen glared at Emmy. "At least I act my age." *Why are you telling them how old I am, anyway?*

"I never would have guessed. I thought you might even be younger than me. You still look like teenagers to me. Both of you."

Skip took this moment to take Kristen's hand. "I think you're much too pretty to be a teenager. I think you're absolutely gorgeous."

"That's sweet of you, Skip." Kristen jerked her hand away.

"Would you like to go out for dinner sometime?"

Despite all of her experience with men, Kristen didn't see this coming. "I don't want to hurt your feelings, Skip, but I'm in an exclusive relationship." She moved back a step before Skip had an opportunity to kiss her. If that had even been on his mind.

"Too bad. If you ever break up with whoever, I'm interested."

"I'll keep that in mind," Kristen said as she joined the other people.

Bobby and Emmy were still talking. "I never thought you could be twenty-two, Emmy. That's really old."

Chapter Sixteen

On Sunday morning Kristen sang with the worship team for the first time. Though nervous at first, as they started singing, the nervousness vanished. Emmy smiled at her and helped her feel at ease. After church, Emmy saw Kenny talking to Tony and Chase. She ran over and stood in front of Tony with her back to him. Tony put his hands on her shoulders.

"I didn't know you would be here, Kenny. Why didn't you tell me?"

"I should have, Em, but I thought it might make you and Kristen nervous. You both sounded fantastic by the way. I wanted to hear what you guys sound like before next week, so I have an idea of how you should sound on the CD."

"That's right. We're recording the next two Sundays. I can't wait. It will be so much fun."

"Have you guys got plans for dinner?" Kenny asked.

"I'm making taco salad, and Tony is going to pick up some potato salad and chicken strips from the store on the way home. Wanna join us?" Emmy hoped that Kenny would join her for lunch, so he and Kristen could begin to feel more at ease with each other. Emmy knew that, although he hadn't said anything, Kenny had been a little upset with Kristen because she told everyone that Emmy was pregnant.

Kenny nodded. "Sure. If you don't mind."

"I think we will have a little bit for you," Emmy teased as she looked over her shoulder at Tony. "Would you and Yvonne like to join us, Pastor Chase? I'm sure we will have enough food. Even with Tony there."

Tony forgot he was still in church and swatted Emmy's bottom without thinking. She jumped and her eyes opened wide.

Oh, shoot! I didn't mean to do that, Emmy. Tony turned red.

Chase noticed as he answered, "Thanks, Emmy, but Yvonne and I are going to have lunch with Paul and Lynette. Could I have a rain check?"

"Sure, we'll see you later."

Emmy waited until Chase left, then turned to face Tony and

147

smacked his arm. "Why did you do right in front of Chase?"

"Sorry, Em, I forgot where we are."

"Everyone here thinks we're dating. You swatting me doesn't help matters."

"Sorry, Em. I just did it out of habit." Tony looked at Kenny and waved his hands. "I don't swat her butt all the time. I didn't mean to imply that." *Way to stick your size thirteen shoes in your mouth, idiot.*

Kenny raised his eyebrows and shook his head. *I know you guys are just friends and I know Emmy is still trying to keep our relationship a secret.* He followed Emmy and Kristen home. The girls ran upstairs to change into shorts and tops while Kenny hung out downstairs. Tony picked up John Randolph and stopped at the grocery store. He came to the house with more than chicken and potato salad.

Tony set the plastic bags on the table. "There's some cold stuff in here, Em."

"Tony! Why did you get all these groceries?" Emmy asked as she emptied the bags.

"I thought maybe you could make meat loaf and cheesy potatoes for John and me one night this week. Will you?"

"I suppose I could put them together, but you would have to stick them in the oven or else we won't eat until after eight."

"I can use an oven. I make pizzas all the time."

"Tony, why is this in here?" Emmy pulled out a store-bought cake.

"Because your birthday is tomorrow, Em. I didn't want to ask Mama to bake a cake, so I just bought one."

"You know Mama will be really mad at you if she finds out you bought a cake at the store."

"You won't tell her, will you?"

Emmy poked Tony in his side and turned to Kenny. "What am I going to do with this big kid? He and John are always hanging around now that Kristen lives here. I can't get rid of them."

Kenny munched on a taco chip and laughed. "Feed him. You'll have to feed him constantly. Like a shark or something."

148

"Get out of my kitchen, and let me put this taco salad together. We should be ready to eat in a half hour or less."

"I love you, Emmy. You're a great friend. Happy birthday tomorrow," Tony said.

"I love you, too. Now scram," Emmy told them the way Mama would.

Emmy kissed Kenny and grinned at Tony as she chased them out of the kitchen. The guys joined Kristen and John in the living room.

John asked, "When is the new CD coming out?"

"Supposed to be August twentieth. Everything is finished. It just has to be manufactured. We're shipping three million copies the first week."

"Wow! That sounds like a lot."

"Yeah, I guess so. Are you guys ready for training camp?"

"I'm looking forward to it, but I'll miss Kristen. I won't see her for a month," John said.

"What? You never told me that. Why can't she see you?" Emmy walked into the living room after hearing this bit of news.

"Because that's the rule. Coach doesn't want wives or girlfriends around to distract us," Tony replied.

"Are you pulling my leg, Tony Bertucci?" Kristen frowned.

"Maybe I can see you on the weekend for a couple of hours," John told Kristen.

Emmy rolled her eyes. "Do you expect me to believe the married guys go without sex for a whole month? I don't buy that at all."

"It's true, Em. In fact most guys don't have sex throughout the whole season," Tony said with a straight face, and John nodded in agreement.

Emmy shook her head and said, "No way. When I'm married I want to have sex every night—and morning, too." She looked at Kenny for just a split-second.

"How do you know that, Emmy? You might not even like sex," Tony teased.

Emmy blushed as everyone listened to her talking about sex. "I'm pretty sure I'll like sex." Emmy bit her lip as she looked

149

at Kenny again, but they didn't say anything.

Kristen noticed the glance between Emmy and Kenny. *I'm going to pretend I never saw that look.*

"If you guys set the table, I think we can eat." Emmy walked back into the kitchen. *Why did I say that in front of Krissy and the guys? She is going to take it the wrong way.*

The five of them finished the large bowl of taco salad in twenty minutes. Tony and John ate the chicken strips and potato salad, also. Emmy and Kristen stared in awe as the guys devoured everything in sight. Even Kenny had a large appetite. The guys went into the TV room and turned on a baseball game. A few minutes later they were all asleep.

Kristen brought all the plates, dishes and stuff in from the dining room as Emmy filled the sink with hot water. "Did you see how fast those guys made the taco salad disappear?" Kristen asked. "It's like they're machines."

"They must spend a fortune on groceries," Emmy said.

Neither one said anything for a moment, and then Kristen backed Emmy up against the counter and put her hands on Emmy's shoulders. "You know that I would never tell anyone anything you ever tell me in confidence, Em."

"I know, Kristen. I would do the same for you." *Shoot! Here it comes.*

Emmy squirmed to get away, but Kristen held on tightly.

After another pause in the conversation, Kristen said, "I saw how you looked at Kenny when you mentioned you knew you liked sex. Is there anything you want to tell me?"

"Nope," Emmy replied curtly as she pushed Kristen away and turned her back to her. "And I'm still not pregnant."

Emmy stood at the sink washing dishes, and Kristen moved behind her and placed her hands on Emmy's shoulders again.

"Sweetie..."

"I can't tell you anything, Krissy. Please understand."

"You know I love you no matter what and God will, too."

Emmy tensed her muscles as Kristen rubbed her shoulders and her back. "I still feel insecure about that sometimes. I don't feel worthy of His love," Emmy admitted.

150

"None of us are worthy. Even I know that. You know that God has forgiven all your sins and remembers them no more."

"Thank God for that."

They both managed a small chuckle, and Emmy relaxed. Kristen didn't ask Emmy any more questions and let the matter drop. They finished the dishes and checked on the guys.

"Look at them. Fill their bellies, and they fall asleep. Just like babies."

"Huge babies." Emmy giggled.

"Let's go upstairs, and we can take a nap, too," Kristen suggested.

"Wouldn't you rather take a walk or something? Let's play tennis."

"We could do that." Kristen still wanted to talk to Emmy about what happened between her and Kenny.

Emmy looked at Kristen and sensed her desire. "I'm not going to talk about it, Krissy."

"You don't have to, Em. I am here for you if you ever do need to talk."

"I love you, Kristen." *But I'm not talking about my sex life. Not that there's much to talk about.*

Emmy ran downstairs, grabbed two tennis racquets, two packages of new tennis balls and they left the house.

"I love walking past this place, Em." Kristen sniffed the air. "The flowers are beautiful. They make the air smell..."

"The air smells funny." Emmy pointed. "Oooh! Someone didn't clean up after their dog."

Kristen playfully touched the back of Emmy's head with her tennis racquet. "It's so good to see Kenny. I felt awful because I know he avoided coming over to see you because of me. I feel bad that he and Becky broke up."

"At least they're still friends. Kenny will probably always love her in a way. Just like Tony and me. God wants us to love everyone," Emmy said as she swung her tennis racket back and forth.

"You know that's not what I'm talking about. Have you ever been to the college where the Bears have their camp?" Kristen

151

asked to change the subject.

"I've been past it, I think. It's Olivet Nazarene University."

"I think we should go see them on the second weekend they're there."

"What about the rules?" Emmy asked.

"Rules are made to be broken."

"Isn't that records? Records are made to be broken. I've heard that before."

"Look! There's an empty court. Let's grab it."

Kristen and Emmy played tennis for an hour. Even though Emmy was the better athlete, Kristen managed to hold her own and win her share of games. Kristen grew up playing tennis with Derrick, who could probably play professionally if he desired. They headed home, walked in the back door and heard the guys laughing in the TV room.

"At least they're awake," Emmy said.

"Yeah, but that probably means they want to eat," Kristen said and then laughed. "If they're awake, they have to eat."

"I'm going to take a shower. How about you?" Emmy asked.

"I should. I think we were actually sweating while we played tennis." Kristen grinned as she wiped her brow.

"You never sweat, Kristen. You glisten."

The girls took showers and changed into fresh clothes. They came downstairs and cautiously entered the TV room.

"There you guys are. We're hungry. What is there to eat? We're starvin'," Tony said as he patted his stomach.

Kristen and Emmy looked at each other, and Kristen shook her head. "I know. They need a hobby besides eating."

"I can think of one hobby that would keep them occupied, but we should marry them first."

"Emmy! You are being so wicked today," Kristen said and then bumped hips with Emmy.

"I can't help it."

"Well, what about food, Em?" Kenny asked with a smile.

"If you guys want dinner, you either have to take us out, or order something and have it delivered. We are not cooking any

152

more today. We're done."

Tony looked at Kenny and John. "What do you guys wanna do?"

"I haven't been to Darby's for a while. How about that?" Kenny asked.

"Is Darby's all right with you, John?"

"Sure."

"We're going with you guys," Emmy said.

Tony shook his head. "Whoa! Who said anything about taking you and Kristen? This is a guy thing."

"Maybe we should let Emmy and Kristen come with us. They did make lunch for us. Part of lunch anyway," Kenny said.

Tony relented. "Okay, you can come with us."

They piled into Tony's car and headed over to Darby's Dogs.

"Kenny, remember back in high school we would go to Darby's all the time," Emmy said.

"I remember, Em. We lived a lot closer back then. It takes you a little longer now, but it's still worth the trip."

"What kind of car is this?" Emmy asked from the back seat.

"It's a 1995 Chevy Lumina. I picked it up cheap after my good car was totaled. Why?"

"No reason, but don't you think the other players will make fun of it?"

"I'm not going to keep it forever." Tony looked at John who was sitting in the front passenger seat. "Will they get on my case for driving this?"

John shrugged. "It runs all right. Might as well keep it."

They pulled into the parking lot and chatted away as they walked into Darby's. Tony kept teasing Emmy about making meat loaf.

"Well, look who the cat dragged in. Emmy Colasanti, it's sure good to see you."

"Hi, Mr. Darby. It's good to see you. I didn't think you would be here on a Sunday evening."

"Normally, I wouldn't be, but two kids called in sick. It's hard to get good help nowadays. Not like when you were helping

153

me out. What can I get you guys?"

They placed their order and grabbed a booth. Mr. Darby brought their order to them a few minutes later. "I've heard good things about you kids."

"This is John Randolph, Mr. Darby. My roommate at Notre Dame," Tony said as he grabbed a handful of fries.

"And a tight end on the team and now a Bear like you. I follow football."

"It's a pleasure to meet you, Mr. Darby. I've heard about this place for three years, but this is my first chance to eat here. I like all the pictures you have on the wall. There is one of the band with a girl singer. I guess it's Emmy. She looks so young though."

"My son took that one. Danny or Emmy might remember how old she was, but I don't. Anyway, enjoy the food."

"We always do, Mr. Darby," Emmy said enthusiastically.

"Kenny, I still get tourists coming in here and asking about your booth. They take all kinds of pictures." He chuckled and tapped the back of the booth. "Sometimes I think they imagine you guys are still sitting there."

"I hope it helps with business and isn't a nuisance."

"It's never been a bother, and I appreciate the publicity and the extra business. Let me know if you need anything else."

"Thanks, Mr. Darby."

They hung around for an hour, and Kenny even signed some autographs. Tony tossed the trash and placed their trays on the front counter as a Hispanic girl came in and ordered a hot dog and a Coke to go. She looked around nervously. She saw Emmy and the guys and looked like she wanted to ask them something. Kenny noticed her shyness and smiled. Mr. Darby handed her the order. She looked over her shoulder at Kenny and Emmy, hesitated, but then walked over to their booth.

"Hi. Can I do anything for you?" Kenny asked.

"I'm sorry to bother you if you're busy, but you're Emmy Colasanti, right?"

"Yes, I am."

"Hi, I'm Juanita Rosa Garcia. You don't know me, but Yolanda was my little sister."

154

Emmy's heart skipped a beat as she heard the word *was*.

"Is everything all right? Has something happened to Yolanda? I haven't seen her at church for a couple weeks, or more, but I don't always get to see all the teens."

Juanita set her hot dog and Coke on the booth as she stared at the floor. "Yolanda flew home to Mexico City to visit family. A drunk driver hit and killed her on March thirtieth."

"Oh, my God!" Emmy jumped from her seat and hugged Juanita as they both broke down in tears. Kenny closed his eyes and began to pray. Kristen, Tony and John glanced at each other and then sat quietly and respectfully in the booth.

"Is there anything I can do?" Emmy asked a moment later.

Tony handed Emmy his handkerchief, and she wiped Juanita's tears away and then her own.

"I came to the church the night you talked to the teens. That's how I recognized you. Yolanda told me about you and how you talked to her afterward. She told me how you helped her. Yolanda loved going to church after she got saved. I'm sorry if I spoiled your meal."

"You don't need to be sorry. Do you have other family here in SoHam?"

"We have an older brother here, Hector. That's where Yolanda and I live, or lived, I mean. We're going back home though. At least for now. Maybe we will come back again someday."

"Would you mind if I prayed with you, Juanita?" Emmy asked.

"I would like that very much, Emmy." Juanita glanced around. "Where?"

Emmy took Juanita to a booth in the back corner for some privacy. Kristen joined them, and they prayed together.

"Does anyone at the church know what happened?" Emmy asked.

"I didn't want to bother them. They don't know me. Yolanda didn't really have any friends there. I doubt if any of them even know she's gone."

"I will send Pastor Herb an email as soon as I get home. I'm

155

sure the church will want to do something for your family. I remember talking to Yolanda that night, and now I will always remember her. I know it doesn't help with your loss, but I do believe she is in heaven now."

"I believe so, too. That is the only thing that gets me through the day. Thanks for everything, Emmy. I wouldn't have been here tonight except that I craved a hot dog for some reason. I usually don't come here."

"I'm glad for that craving. Otherwise we might have never heard about what happened. Will you be all right? Do you need a ride home or anything?"

"I live just a couple blocks away on East Fifth Street. I can walk."

"I grew up on East Fifth!" Emmy exclaimed. "I lived at 16301. Where do you live?"

"At 16310. At least for a little while longer."

"Are you sure you don't want a ride?" Emmy asked.

"I'll be fine. I'm not afraid in this neighborhood."

Emmy hugged Juanita again and said, "I want to stay in touch. Could you give me an address or something?"

Juanita gave Emmy her address in Mexico City and a phone number. She included her email address, too. Emmy gave Juanita the same information.

Tony handed Juanita her hot dog and Coke. Emmy and Kristen watched Juanita leave and then sat down with the guys again.

"That really sucks," John said as he put an arm around Kristen's shoulders.

Tears poured from Kenny's eyes as he scribbled words on a napkin.

"What are you writing, Kenny?" Emmy asked as she leaned into his shoulder.

"Sssh! Hang on a minute, Em. I think he's writing some lyrics for a song," Tony whispered.

They didn't speak as Kenny wrote on another napkin. Emmy thought about Yolanda Garcia and started to cry. Tony scooted out from his side of the booth, sat beside Emmy and put an

156

arm around her shoulders. Kristen squeezed her hand.

Emmy used Tony's handkerchief again to dry her eyes. "I feel that I should have done more for her. I should have known she wasn't at church."

"It's not your fault, Em. I'm sure you did everything you could. You couldn't have known what would happen. No one did, but God," Kristen said.

Kenny stopped writing and looked at Emmy. "I never met Yolanda, but take a look at this, and tell me what you think, Em."

Emmy read the lyrics and more tears flowed down her face. "This is about her. How could you have written this?"

"I didn't, Em. I wrote the words on the paper, but I didn't write the song."

"I think I understand, Kenny. I think I really understand."

Chapter Seventeen

Emmy went to work on Monday with a heavy heart. The guys in the office wanted to help her celebrate her birthday. They bought a cake and a dozen red roses for her. She tried to put on a happy face for their sake.

She knocked on Mr. Oliver's door. "I appreciate everything you have done for me, but my heart just isn't in it today. I'm sorry." She hung her head as her eyes filled with tears.

"What is it, Emily? Are you all right?" Mr. Oliver stood up, came around from behind his desk and gently touched her shoulder. "Can I help?"

Emmy bit her lip as she looked up at her boss. "Yesterday I learned that a young girl from my church was killed by a drunk driver in Mexico City. I feel so bad because we never knew about it. I feel as though we should have done something for her family."

"Oh, Emmy. I'm so sorry. I didn't know. Maybe we should wait until another day to do this."

They walked out of his office and toward her desk.

"No, Mr. Oliver. I don't mean to spoil the party. Would you let me to tell you about Yolanda?"

"Of course, Emmy. Please tell us," Mr. Oliver said softly. He gathered everyone together in the middle of the office. "Emmy would like to share a story with us."

"Yolanda was fifteen and had just become a part of the youth group at my church. I didn't really know her until I met her after I talked to the teens one Wednesday night. She told me she broke up with her boyfriend because of sex. She wouldn't give in to his demands and something I said touched her heart. She accepted Christ as her Savior and seventeen days later she was taken away. I still can't believe she is gone. It is a reminder that none of us know how long we have on this earth."

Emmy witnessed to the men. They knew Emmy's life changed after she accepted Jesus. Two of the men in her office told her later they used to attend church, but had stopped.

"You know it's not too late to start again. Jesus is always willing to accept someone back into his family."

158

Just before lunch, the phone at her desk rang. Emmy answered absentmindedly. "Hello, how may I help you?"

"Hello, sweetie, I wanted to wish you a happy birthday and ask how you are doing?"

"Oh, Mrs. Colwell, thank you for calling. I guess Kenny told you what happened, huh?"

"Yes, dear. Are you all right?"

"I'm okay. I guess this isn't the happiest birthday I've ever had, but I'm doing fine."

"If you need anything, just let me know."

"I will. Thank you for remembering my birthday."

After work, Emmy listened to the sound of muffled conversations and rhythmic footsteps as she stood off to the side of the lobby while waiting for Kristen. *I sure hope I don't see Richard. I don't want to deal with him today.* She heard the swoosh of the elevator doors opening and spotted Kristen.

Kristen said goodbye to one of her colleagues and walked over to Emmy. "Did the guys have a cake for you, Em?"

"They did, and I thanked them. I told them what I learned about Yolanda. I talked to them about Jesus, and a couple of them came up to me later in the day. They mentioned how they used to go to church, and I told them it was never too late to go back."

"I know you don't want to take advantage of what happened to Yolanda, but maybe God will use her death to bring other people to Him. Maybe you are meant to do that, Em."

On the ride home, as Kristen drove, Emmy thought about how everyone met at Darby's last night.

"Krissy, isn't it so strange that we just happened to be at Darby's at the right moment?"

"I thought it was quite a coincidence."

"I think that God arranged everything. He made sure the guys were hungry, which isn't difficult, and Juanita had a craving for a hot dog. Just think. He used a 'hot dog' of all things to bring us together."

When Emmy got home that evening, Kenny, Tony, John, and Mama were waiting for her. Kenny walked up to Emmy and hugged her. Tony patted her back while John kissed Kristen. Mama

159

hugged Emmy for a moment after Kenny let go.

"Would you guys mind if we don't celebrate tonight? My heart wouldn't be in it."

"Whatever you want to do is fine with us, Em," Kenny said. He rubbed her back as she rested her head against his chest.

"Thanks, guys. We can still eat dinner, but I'm not in the mood for much celebrating."

"We can celebrate the fact that Yolanda is in heaven," Tony said. His heart ached to see Emmy feeling so sad.

The conversation was rather subdued that evening as everyone respected Emmy's wishes. After they finished eating, Mama and Kristen cleaned up. John and Tony turned on the TV. Emmy talked to her mother for a couple of minutes, and then Diane called to wish Emmy a happy birthday. John left to go to his apartment and a while later, Mama told Tony she was ready to go home.

"I'm sorry about Yolanda, dear." Mama kissed the top of her head as she hugged her. "I know how difficult it is to lose someone."

Tony patted her shoulder. "Let me know if you need anything, Emmy."

"Thanks, I don't think I'll go running in the morning. Is that all right?"

"Sure, I understand. You know you can't keep up, so you don't want to be dropped and have to eat our dust," Tony teased.

Emmy laughed for the first time since hearing the sad news about Yolanda. "You're lucky you are such a good friend, or else I would kick your butt and show you guys how fast I can really run."

He whispered, "Happy birthday, Em. I'll talk to you later."

Kristen headed upstairs to her room. Emmy and Kenny went to the basement to practice the song he wrote. Before he went to bed the previous night, Kenny copied the words from the napkins into his computer. He spent part of the day arranging the chord charts and printed several copies. At first Emmy could not make it through the song without breaking into tears.

"Emmy, I know this will be difficult for you, but you can sing this song for Yolanda. I have a feeling that something good will happen out of this tragedy." He paused for a moment. *Should I tell her now and let her think about it? Or should I just spring it on her on Sunday?* He decided to tell her. "Em, I would like you to sing this as the closing song on Sunday."

She bit her lip and shook her head. "No, I can't. I'll bawl like a baby."

He held her close. "I know you will, but that doesn't matter. I think it's very important for the church to hear about her. I've seen you cry during a song before," he said and then grinned. "What is that verse you always claim is your motto?"

"I can do all things with God's help," she answered. "I'll sing it. I will try to do a good job on Sunday for her."

Kenny handed Emmy the two napkins. She held them in her hands as if they were more precious than gold. She walked slowly upstairs to her bedroom and closed the door. She pulled out the bottom drawer of her dresser and removed her music box. She used her key and opened the secret compartment in the bottom. She gingerly placed the napkins on top of her other mementos and closed the box. She replaced the music box and opened her bedroom door. Kenny held out his arms and hugged her.

Emmy took a personal day on Thursday so she could help Kenny and the crew set up for practice. They wanted to record tonight's practice as a trial run. Kenny borrowed the Steward Music Group's remote truck. Luckily, they were able to park the truck close to a door and run the necessary cables without too much trouble or inconvenience.

After the guys got all the gear up and running, Kenny pulled out an acoustic guitar and played the song he wrote for Yolanda. Emmy listened, and after he finished, she hugged Kenny with tears streaming down her face.

"See! I can't even listen to the music without crying."

"You will do fine, Em. Just remember who is helping you."

Practice started promptly at six thirty and Kenny went over the program with everyone. They ran through the songs everyone knew. The tech guys worked out a few minor bugs and glitches. After an hour, they took a short break. When they returned, Kenny

161

played the new song. He passed out charts for all the guys.

"I'd like to keep this simple and mostly acoustic."

"I like that idea," Chase said.

"Em, we might need to run through this a few times. Will you be all right?" Kenny hoped that by doing the song several times, Emmy's emotions would settle down.

"I'll be okay. Just keep playing even if I start to cry."

Kristen sang harmony with Emmy. Chase used his keyboard to add strings. John and Steve played acoustic guitars along with Kenny. Hank added a simple bass line and Skip used a shaker to add a percussive effect. Skip broke down as they played the song. He actually knew Yolanda, the only other band member besides Emmy who did. Chase consoled him until he regained his composure.

"I think that's enough for this song tonight," Kenny said after they ran through it for the third time. "I want it to be fresh for Sunday."

Emmy smiled. "I didn't cry that time, Kenny."

"You did a good job, Em." He put an arm around her shoulders and squeezed. He wanted to kiss her, but didn't. *You may have gotten through it tonight, but on Sunday, you will cry. It will be all right. I want you to show your emotions.*

Kenny played guitar with the band as they ran through all the songs one final time. After they finished, Chase led them in prayer.

Mary Lawson and Yvonne Hillman put together a short video using photos Juanita provided. The worship team sat on the steps of the platform and watched in silence as the four large video screens filled with images of Yolanda and some of the teens from the church. The last picture started off with Yolanda and another girl with their arms wrapped around each other's waist as they smiled for the camera in the teen room. Emmy sobbed when she saw the image.

"I forgot about that picture," Emmy told Kenny.

"You both looked very happy, Em."

Then the image closed in on Yolanda's face with the cross in the background.

Chapter Eighteen

Emmy got out of bed earlier than normal on Sunday morning. She knelt beside the bed and prayed for the worship service that day. She lay her head on the bed and sobbed as she thought about Yolanda. "Please, Jesus, give me the strength to make it through the song," she prayed.

She put on her faded jeans, picked out a dress to wear later, ate a banana and left the house. She picked up Kenny and drove him to the church. They wanted to be there before seven o'clock. Will Consoli and his tech crew arrived at the church shortly after seven to do a final check of the equipment. Kristen and the members of the worship band gathered on the sanctuary platform at seven thirty to rehearse one more time, and then retreated to the music suite for final thoughts and prayers.

"I think we're as ready as we can possibly be. Let's meet back here after Sunday School," Chase said as he sent everyone on their way.

After her Sunday School class, Emmy met with Juanita and her brother Hector.

"I'm glad to see you again, Juanita." Emmy hugged her.

"This is my brother, Hector."

I can see the resemblance between your and your sisters. Emmy shook his hand. "I'm pleased to meet you. I'm so sorry about Yolanda."

"I want to thank you for what you have done. Our family appreciates your kindness."

Emmy bit her lip. "I need to tell you something about today's service..." She explained about the recording and the song Kenny wrote. "I will probably cry. No, I know I will."

Juanita hugged Emmy as they both sobbed.

When they stopped, Emmy asked, "How did you get here today?"

Hector pointed to a man. "He picked us up in a limousine."

Emmy looked at the man and shook her head. "That's my cousin Andy Walker."

"He told us that a limo would take us to the airport later. He

163

told us not to tell, but I have to tell you."

"That sounds like Andy."

"Will you make sure he knows how much we appreciate his kindness?" Juanita whispered.

"I will," Emmy said.

Chase checked the time. "Let's go." He waved the band out of the room.

Andy escorted Juanita and Hector to their seats in the second row. The band walked onto the platform and watched the countdown on the screens. They started playing and the lights came up. Chase got things going with a quick prayer, and then Emmy took over. They would play more songs than normal today because of the recording. Kenny took up a position at the rear of the platform and played his guitar. They played all the songs they had rehearsed and then paused to let the crowd settle. It was finally time for the last one, "Yolanda's Song." Kenny couldn't think of a better title.

Emmy looked back at Kenny and bit her lip.

He smiled and mouthed, "You can do this with Jesus' help. I love you, Em."

Emmy turned to the congregation and began. "I want to tell you about a young girl I knew briefly, Yolanda Garcia. She was saved right here in this church on March thirteenth and seventeen days later, she was killed by a drunk driver in Mexico City..." Emmy paused as she heard the congregation gasp. Then she continued talking about Yolanda.

Most of the people in the congregation had never heard of her and did not know about the accident. The video started and Emmy began to sing. She closed her eyes as she remembered the shy young teenage girl the night she came to talk to her. When Emmy sang the last words of the song, even the most hard-hearted people in the congregation had tears in their eyes. Dr. Ausland came to the platform and led in prayer. He never even got to his shorter-than-normal sermon that morning because so many people came to the altar, including nearly all the teens.

After the service, Kenny and Emmy sat on the piano bench on the side of the platform and talked quietly.

164

"I think they will remember Yolanda now, Em."

"Maybe we will learn not to take anyone for granted. Only God knows how long we will be here."

"I talked to Will, and he told me that song moved him more than anything he's ever heard. He confessed that he cried throughout the whole song."

"Does Will ever go to church?"

"Not really, but maybe he will think about it now."

"We can ask him to join us here."

Emmy leaned against Kenny and he put an arm around her waist. Tony and Kristen found them as they were embracing.

"Oh, Emmy. You sounded beautiful."

Kristen hugged Emmy as Tony shook hands with Kenny.

"I'm hungry. Are we gonna eat soon?" Tony brought them back to reality.

Since they were recording today, Tony and Emmy decided to make it a special occasion by having a picnic at the Bertucci home. They invited the entire worship team and the pastoral staff as well.

Mama cooked all morning to feed the three hungry guys she knew would be there for dinner—Tony, John and Kenny. Mama knew more people were coming, but didn't know the exact number. John helped by running to the store and picking up the food from the caterers. Mama hadn't been thrilled about using caterers, but under pressure from Kristen and Emmy, she eventually relented.

"John, do you think we have enough chairs and tables?" Mama gazed out the kitchen window. "I don t want people to have to stand to eat."

"I took every single chair the rental place could find. Some people will stand around to eat. You shouldn't worry so much. Everything will be all right. Tony called a few minutes ago, and they're on their way. He estimated there might be close to twenty-five to thirty-five people coming. Maybe a few more."

"If you and Tony don't eat everything in sight, we should have enough," Mama said.

165

John smiled. "We will take it easy and make sure the guests get fed first."

Mama put her arm around John's waist and squeezed. "Thank you, John. You've been a big help and thanks for taking me to mass."

"You're welcome, Mama."

Tony pulled into the driveway a few minutes later. He noticed the chairs in the backyard as he opened the back door. He saw Mama by the stove and told her about the service and what happened.

"So Dr. Herb didn't even get to say mass?"

"Yeah, I guess you could say that. He and his wife are coming today. You can meet him."

"Do I look all right?"

"You look beautiful, Mama."

"I don't know if I look good enough to meet Dr. Herb."

Tony smiled and said, "You look good enough to meet the Queen of England."

"You didn't tell me she would be coming," Mama teased.

The back door opened and Emmy bounded inside. "What do you need me and Kristen to do?" Emmy asked as she slid to a stop beside Tony.

"First you need to use proper grammar, young lady."

"Oh, Mama. I can't help it."

Kenny held the door open for Kristen as they calmly entered the kitchen.

"Would you and Kristen grab the guys and have them start taking food out to the tables. Make sure they keep everything covered."

Within a half hour, all the guests milled around the backyard as they waited to eat. Dr. Ausland said a prayer and Emmy looked at Tony.

"Yeah, Mama told me already. John and I are going last."

Emmy grinned as she poked him in the stomach. "I love you, Tony."

"Yeah, I know you're just saying that to keep me away from the food."

166

"Just as long as it works," Emmy teased as she walked away.

Chase was close enough to overhear the conversation and smiled.

Emmy saw Kenny talking to Chase and walked up next to them while Yvonne finished filling plates for their two daughters. "Come on, you guys. Let's get in line."

"What about Tony and John?" Kenny asked. He saw them standing away from the line.

"They have to wait until everyone else has eaten otherwise there wouldn't be anything left," Emmy said and then turned to Yvonne. "Would you and Chase like to sit with us? Maybe Chase and Kenny could talk about the next recording session."

"We'd love to sit with you, Emmy," Yvonne said.

Kenny and Emmy joined Chase and Yvonne in line. After filling their plates, they looked but didn't see any places at the tables for all of them.

"We could sit in the yard," Emmy said. "There's four chairs over there."

They walked over to the chairs and sat down to eat. Chase and Yvonne kept an eye on Anna and Jada as they sat at a table with some of the other kids.

Chase said to Kenny, "I know Emmy said that you guys have known each other for a long time. Do you remember when you first met?"

"I think she was seven when we met, so it's been about five years now."

Emmy poked Kenny in the side. "I'm not twelve anymore." She grabbed a chicken strip from his plate, took a bite and then placed it back. "Too spicy."

"You act like it sometimes, Em." Kenny bumped his shoulder against hers.

"Just because I like to have fun does not mean I'm immature. You should remove that broom from your butt."

Chase sprayed out the pop he just swallowed and coughed.

Yvonne patted his back. "Are you all right?"

"Yeah, I'm not used to the way they act together. We've

167

never seen them together outside of the church," Chase whispered. "Did she really tell him to remove a broom..."

"Ssssh."

A lot of people from the worship team assumed that Tony and Emmy were dating because they were always together at church. Chase knew that Tony possessed some special feelings for Emmy, so it surprised him to see Emmy and Kenny behaving so intimately with each other.

Emmy told Kenny, "Mom wants me to bring you over later this evening. Is that okay with you?"

"Whatever you want to do, sweetheart. Your wish is my command." He touched the tip of her nose.

"What about Tony? Won't he get upset?" Chase asked.

"Hush." Yvonne poked him in the side because she realized Chase didn't know Emmy and Kenny's relationship embodied more than simple friendship.

"He and John will be working out. Kristen is going to see her parents. So I get to hang out with Kenny." She kissed him on the cheek, then pulled on his ear. "Just like old times." *I like your funny ears.*

Chase fumbled his plate and nearly dropped it as he watched Emmy.

"I heard that you used to sing with the band, Emmy. Is that true?" Yvonne asked.

Kenny answered for her as Emmy shoved a mouthful of potato salad into her mouth. "Even before I met my partners, Emmy and I would get together and play and sing. If you want to get technical, Emmy could be called the first singer in the band."

"You couldn't have been very old, Emmy," Yvonne said.

"Fourteen, I think." She tilted her head as she looked at Kenny.

"I think so, Em." Kenny shook his head almost imperceptibly.

Emmy turned back to Chase and Yvonne. "I was fourteen because I was only fifteen when we..." Emmy stopped and covered her mouth with her hand before she let a secret slip out. *I almost told Chase about when we first kissed.* Emmy looked at Kenny,

168

and Chase swore she blushed.

"You were fourteen, Em. I'm pretty sure."

Chase looked at Yvonne, and she smiled. He looked at Emmy and Kenny again. They were feeding each other.

"Oh! I see how it is," Chase whispered to Yvonne.

"Took you long enough."

"If Kenny and Emmy share a history as a couple, it's none of own business," Chase said. *She was really young.*

"I should check on the girls, Chase. I need to talk to Carolyn Ausland, too. I'll be back later."

"Anna and Jada are just gorgeous. I can see the family resemblance," Emmy said as she looked at the girls.

"They look more like Yvonne. Lucky for them."

"You're right about that," Emmy teased. "Do you want more kids?"

"I suppose I would like a son. We aren't really trying for another one now, but then we aren't doing anything to prevent it, either. Do you and Tony think you'll ever have kids?"

Emmy and Kenny looked at Chase with surprise. They both wondered if Kristen had mentioned the pregnancy to him.

"I'm sorry, Emmy, I meant you and Kenny."

"We probably won't ever have any more kids," Emmy answered as she took Kenny's arm in her hands. "But only God knows for sure."

Emmy smiled at Chase, and he couldn't tell if Emmy was teasing him or not. He didn't mention anything more about babies. Emmy knew it would take a miracle for her to ever have a baby.

Kristen came over to talk to Emmy with Tony and John trailing along behind her.

Kristen pointed. "John and I are going to sit by the tree."

"Okay, are you taking John with you later after they work out?" Emmy asked.

Kristen answered, "I'm not letting him out of my sight."

Tony sat next to Emmy and said, "Mama finally let us grab some food. I'm starvin'."

"Is there anything left now?"

"We didn't take everything, Em. There's still a few pieces of

169

chicken and a roll."

Emmy knew Mama had more food in the house that she was saving for after Tony and John went through the line. She took Kenny's empty plate along with her own and dropped them in a trash can. She sang happily as she skipped back to the guys. "I should go see if Mama needs any help."

"Want me to come with you, Em?" Kenny asked.

"Yes, that would be a good idea. You don't want to be too close to Tony when he's eating. He might mistake your arm for a chicken leg." Emmy kissed Tony on the top of his head, giggled, and then stuck out her tongue at him. "You're a doofus."

"Go away, brat," Tony replied.

She took Kenny's hand, and they headed into the house. Tony and Chase turned to watch as Emmy skipped along with Kenny. She seemed so happy and almost like a child with Kenny. Chase wanted to ask Tony a question, but wasn't sure he should pry.

Tony sensed this and answered the question without it even being asked. "They love each other very much, Chase. They always have."

"You mean as friends?"

"No, no, it's much more than that." Tony waved his hand as he swallowed a bite of pasta salad. "It's difficult to explain. They're not like brother and sister, but they kinda grew up together. Kristen and I are very close. She's my cousin if you didn't know that. But we're not as close as Kenny and Emmy. They have been best friends and, to use a cliché, soulmates, forever. I don't know if Emmy has ever said anything, but we used to date."

"I admit that I thought you guys were still dating. So do a bunch of people in the church. Sorry to interrupt. Please continue."

"We broke up because I wouldn't have sex with her... Oh shoot. Please forget I said that. Emmy would kill me."

"Already forgotten," Chase said as he remembered a conversation where Emmy described herself as *naughty and wicked* in high school.

"We tried to get back together, but I screwed up royally. Kenny and Emmy started dating when she was really

170

young—before I even met her in her last year of high school. Then Kenny started touring, then he met someone." Tony paused. "Maybe I shouldn't be telling you all this. Emmy is rather private about some things in her life. I'll just say that the relationship between the three of us could be described as unusual. Wouldn't you agree?"

"You are all still very young. Lots of things will change over the coming years. There's nothing unusual about that."

"There's nothing usual about Emmy. She's one of a kind, and I thank God every day for that. Without her I would not be here today." Tony laughed. "That sounds funny because this is where I live. What I mean is that Emmy led me to Christ. Maybe someday I will tell you about that. There's a bed involved in that story."

Chase gulped.

"Not in that way."

"Is it safe to assume that you and Emmy talked about marriage before you broke up? You were rather young though to consider that."

"I guess we thought about it. I never actually proposed. We used to discuss the future, and I always assumed we would be together. Things have a way of changing though."

"I know you and Emmy have gone through some difficult times, Tony. If you ever need to talk, Dr. Ausland is always available, and I would be willing as well. I know Emmy is close friends with Lynette Jefferson. She has probably talked to her about her... situation."

"Thanks, Chase. We have traveled through some rough water. Since we are both hot-blooded emotional types, I guess that's to be expected. You might not know it, but Emmy can get pretty riled up when her temper gets the best of her. She used to swear like a sailor."

Chase chuckled. "That would be humorous to hear. She is so innocent in most ways."

Tony wondered if Chase knew more than he could divulge.

"I never hear Emmy talk about her family. I know she has a sister, and she has mentioned her, but I never hear her talk about

171

her parents. Are they even still alive?" Chase asked.

"Yes, they are. I should let Emmy tell you about her childhood if she wants. I'll just say that since Emmy became a Christian things have improved, but her parents are not real close to either Emmy or Diane."

Tony paused for a moment and laughed as he watched some kids chasing each other through the backyard. Chase was an ordained minister in the church and not merely a song leader. Tony decided he could trust Chase and continued. "I have never told this to anyone, but you might be able to help her. Emmy used to run away from home because she was afraid of her parents. Her father has a problem with alcohol and used to argue with her mother. I guess they still do. He never became violent as far as I know, but they would argue quite loudly. Emmy has never said a lot about it, but Kenny told me a little bit. Emmy used to run over to his house and stay with him. She would tell him what was happening at home. She would stay overnight at times."

"Maybe that's partly why Emmy shares such a bond with Kenny. She feels safe and protected with him."

"After Emmy graduated from high school, she would crash with friends, or at Kenny's, just so she wouldn't have to go home. She got her own apartment before she turned eighteen, and she's been on her own ever since."

"She does seem to be very determined."

"You can say she's stubborn. I know she is."

Chase and Tony laughed because they had witnessed Emmy's stubbornness at times.

"Her father almost died a while back."

"A heart attack, right? I remember now. I recall praying for him and Emmy's mother. I should have remembered that."

"Then Kristen thought Emmy was pregnant because she was getting sick in the mornings, but she's not." Tony didn't realize how this sounded to Chase. "Her father's doing better now. They were kinda old when they had Em. I don't think they planned to have her if you know what I mean."

"I'm sure her parents love her." Chase didn't mention the possible pregnancy.

"They do, but they both have a difficult time expressing their love for some reason. After Diane moved out, she didn't really speak to her parents for like three years."

"Emmy or Diane?"

"Diane. I meant Diane."

"Are they on better terms now?"

"Diane and her husband and son live in Toledo, so they don't see each other that often. Emmy's parents don't like to travel, and Diane doesn't come home much. It's sad."

"Life is not always easy, Tony. I hope Kenny is prepared to deal with the difficult times with Emmy? There are sure to be some."

"I hate to say this because I still have feelings for her, but I think Kenny is probably a better match for her. He's able to keep her on a more stable level. I don't know if that's the right word." He paused for a moment to collect his thoughts. "Let me put it this way. Kenny and Emmy together are like plastic explosives. They are stable for the most part, but capable of great energy under the right circumstances. But Emmy and I together are like nitroglycerin. A little bump and we explode. Do you get what I'm saying?"

"I think I understand, Tony."

"For better or worse. Isn't that how it goes?"

"Hopefully, there will be a lot more of the better times. If you and Emmy ever need to come in and talk, I am available. You could meet with me together or as individuals."

"Thanks, Chase."

"No problem, Tony. Now I understand Emmy a bit better, and it goes without saying that this is all confidential."

"I never doubted that for a second, Chase."

173

Chapter Nineteen

"Can we take off now, Mama?" Emmy asked as she charged into Mama's sewing room. "We cleaned the kitchen and put everything away."

Mama set down her book, rose from her rocking chair and followed Emmy into the kitchen. She looked at the sink and counters. "Everything looks okay in here. Are the guys finished in the backyard?"

Just then Tony, John and Kenny walked in the back door. "We're all done out back. John and I will take the chairs back in the morning."

"Okay, you guys can take off. Thanks for all your help."

"I need to run home and see my parents," Kristen said.

"We're going to spend two or maybe three hours at the gym," Tony said.

"You can call me after you get home. I'll probably be up late tonight," Emmy said as she stood with her back to Kenny.

He bunched her hair into as ponytail the way she normally wore it.

"Are you going to take Kenny to see your folks?" Tony asked.

"Yeah. He's willing to sacrifice his dignity."

"Come on now, Em. It won't be that bad. Just try not to let your mother get under your skin," Kristen said.

Emmy rolled her eyes. "I hope they don't fight or argue while we're there, but that's a long-shot."

"Maybe they will surprise you. Since your father has been in the hospital, maybe things will be different," Tony said.

"You're such an optimist at times."

"So true. I try to see the silver cloud in every lining."

"You're such a doofus."

Emmy felt better about visiting her parents with Kenny along. Maybe her mother would concentrate on him and not her. She parked in the street, turned and looked at Kenny. "Are you ready for this?"

"I'm always up for a challenge," he replied.

"When are your parents getting home?" Emmy asked.

"Mom said Tuesday afternoon. They're staying with friends in Galena."

"Are they looking for more antiques?"

"They like to look, but they don't always buy something."

They walked up the sidewalk and front steps. Emmy rang the bell and shifted her weight back and forth as they waited.

"Don't you have a key, Em?" Kenny asked

"No, they took our keys away when we moved out. I don't think they wanted us to be able to get in the house if they weren't home, but I know how to sneak in if I have to. I did it a few times in high school."

"After those parties with Rory Porter, right?"

"And a few other times," she said as she grinned.

"Do I want to know about the other times?"

"You might want to know, but maybe I don't want to tell you. Maybe I want to keep some things a secret from you." She liked surprising Kenny with tales of her wilder adventures. *I might tell you someday when we are much older.*

Not having a key seemed normal to Emmy, but Kenny thought it odd. They waited a couple of minutes.

"Maybe we should go. They might not be home." Emmy turned to walk away, but Kenny stopped her.

"Just hang on. You're not getting off so easy. I think I hear someone coming."

Finally, her mother opened the door.

"Hello, Emily. Hi, Kenny. Come on in. We just got up from a nap. Are you hungry? Do you want a sandwich or something?"

"No thanks, Mrs. Colasanti. I'm still stuffed from earlier."

"Come in and have a seat."

Kenny and Emmy sat on the couch in the living room. Her father came into the room and sat in his recliner.

"Hi, Daddy."

"Hello, how are you doing, Kenny?"

"I'm fine, Mr. Colasanti. How are you feeling?"

He picked up the TV remote and hit the power button. "I'm doing a lot better. The doctors tell me I can't go back to work yet.

175

What do they know?"

"You need to rest and regain your strength, Daddy. You shouldn't be in such a hurry to go back to work."

He shook his head. "Your mother is driving me absolutely crazy. She's always around bothering me about this and that. I never get a minute of peace. I can't even take a leak without her waiting by the door."

"Someone has to look after you and take care of this house," Mom said.

"I'm not an invalid, woman. I don't need you hovering around me all the time."

Soon her parents were arguing in loud voices. Kenny looked at Emmy. She slipped her hand into his. He squeezed it to reassure her. She looked up at him and Kenny could feel her trembling. Emmy cringed as her father began to swear at her mother, and her mother yelled back just as loudly.

"Did someone paint the fence?" Kenny had to shout to be heard. "It looks nice." Kenny tried to steer the conversation in a different direction.

"We paid a neighborhood kid to do it. He did a good job—I must admit. Didn't think he would, but it does look nice," Dad said.

"It looks nice because I stood over him and made sure he did a good job. That's what we paid him to do," Mom replied.

"Did you have your whip with you? You probably scared the kid to death."

Emmy and Kenny listened to her parents argue for a few more minutes until Emmy couldn't take any more. She jumped to her feet and stomped her foot.

"If all you're going to do is argue, then we're leaving. Do you ever just have a pleasant conversation with each other? All I ever hear is the two of you arguing. No wonder Dad had a heart attack."

"I did not cause your father's heart attack, Emily Olivia!" Mom yelled.

"I didn't mean to imply that you did, Mother!" Emmy yelled back.

176

"You sure sounded like that's what you meant. I'm doing the best I can with him. He's not easy to live with you know."

Kenny acted as a peacemaker by talking calmly, and eventually everyone lowered their voice. Emmy and Kenny stayed for a few more minutes and then left.

"Where do you want to go, Em? Anything special you want to do?" Kenny asked as they sat in the car.

"Let's go to Windsor Park. I haven't been there for a long time. Would that be all right with you?"

"Whatever you want, Emmy. It's so nice out. Do you want to stop and change clothes first?"

"No, I'm okay. This dress is light and I feel good wearing it. I feel feminine today. Not at all like a tomboy."

"That dress looks good on you, Em."

"Thank you."

Emmy drove to Windsor Park, pulled into a parking space between two minivans and they got out.

"Let's go look at the falls, Kenny." Emmy took off running as Kenny watched. "Come on!"

"The waterfall's not going anywhere, Em. You don't have to run."

Emmy stopped and Kenny walked over to her. "You are acting like a child, Emmy."

"No, I'm not." She frowned and stuck out her lip.

"I didn't mean that as a bad thing. I'm certainly not criticizing you, baby. I think it's because of Yolanda and now your parents arguing. You try to forget the bad things in your life and remember the good things that happen."

"Sometimes I don't want to deal with the bad stuff, so I pretend I'm a little girl again. Maybe I should get some help. See a psychiatrist or a counselor."

"I don't think you need to do that, Em. You face the issues in your life when you need to. Right now you are taking a break from your grown-up life."

Emmy leaned over to smell some wild flowers. "Chase told me that I could talk to him if I ever needed. He's a counselor as well as a minister."

177

"He's a really good person. He would be someone you could trust to keep everything confidential."

"I've thought about it. I don't know if I can, since he's sorta my boss."

"I can understand that. Maybe you could talk to someone else, but I'm sure Chase would keep everything confidential. He could refer you to someone."

"I suppose. Maybe I should talk to him someday. Would it bother you if I told him about my childhood... and us?"

"You can tell him anything you want. Especially if it helps you deal with everything now." Kenny looked into her eyes and saw the sparkle he loved. He held her shoulders and kissed her nose.

She put her arms around him and hugged him close. "What would I do without you, Kenny? You know me and understand me better than anyone—even better than Kristen or Tony. I think that we are both like teenagers. Sure, we have adult responsibilities, but inside we are still kids. You've been my friend, and more, through the good times and bad." She bit her lip as she looked at him. "Remember how I used to run away from home. We would hang out in your bedroom."

"I remember," Kenny whispered.

"Do you remember the times we went camping?"

"Yeah! I remember that. I haven't thought of that in years."

"We would pitch a tent in the backyard, and pretend we were in the jungle or something. There are all those trees in your backyard and those bushes that I would hide under."

"We sure had fun together."

Emmy didn't speak anymore as they walked toward the waterfall. They climbed down the slippery, concrete steps and stood close enough to feel the spray from the roaring falls. Emmy climbed onto the metal railing. She raised her arms and felt the spray on her face and arms. Kenny put his hands on her waist to steady her. "Em, you should get down. You're getting wet."

"It feels good. I remember coming here with Grandpa and feeling the spray on my face. He always held onto me like you're doing. I still miss him."

178

They moved back so they could talk without shouting and where they would not get wet.

Emmy looked up at Kenny. "Can I tell you something without you getting mad?"

"Sure, Em. You know you can tell me anything. What's on your mind?"

"Do you remember when you sent that email about you and Becky breaking up?" Emmy bit her lip.

"I remember." He reached for her hand and held it.

"I talked to Kristen about it, and she asked me if I wanted to get back together with you. I tried to convince her we were just friends like Derrick or Barry, but she didn't believe me for a second."

"Kristen's pretty perceptive," he said. "You and Tony were not together then if I remember correctly."

"Yeah, it was not too long after he confessed to being with that girl. I felt so confused." She took a step away, but he still held onto her hand. "One on hand, I felt guilty because I forced him to go out with other girls at school, but I was so pissed at him, too. He didn't have to sleep with that girl. He could have said no." She turned to face him. "Anyway, Kristen was right. I did think about seeing if you and I could be more than friends again. Like before you met Becky."

"You know you'll always be more to me than just a friend, Emmy." Kenny pulled her closer as his heart beat faster.

She lowered her face and kicked at a rock. "I felt guilty for being happy that you broke up with Becky. I'm sorry. I know you loved her."

"It's okay. It wasn't God's plan for Becky and me to be together."

"What about what I wanted?" She turned around and backed up against him.

He placed his hands on her shoulders. "We are together again." He rested his chin on top of her head.

"Will it be like before?" she whispered. "That's not wrong, is it? What we've done in the past."

"I don't think so. Everyone has things they might regret."

179

She turned to face him. "Do you regret...?"

"No, Em, I don't."

"Neither do I." She looked up at him, pressed against him, and then kissed him. "Let's go for a walk along the trail. I want to see the wildflowers."

"Whatever you want to do is all right with me."

She grinned wickedly at him.

"Emmy! We are supposed to be different now."

"I know," she sounded disappointed. "I want to take some flowers home."

They hiked for an hour; taking their time since they weren't in any hurry to get back. Emmy stopped to check all the different types of wildflowers while Kenny waited patiently. Emmy picked some of the flowers she really liked, and Kenny held them for her. They returned to the car and headed home. Emmy wanted to put the flowers in a vase.

Chapter Twenty

Tony and John finished their workout at the gym, headed home and walked into the kitchen.

"We're back, Mama, but John can't stay. Hey! Something smells good. Did you cook some more food?" Tony asked.

Mama walked into the kitchen and pointed to a cardboard box on the table. "John, I have some food for you to take home. I know you don't cook for yourself. Do you need any furniture for your new apartment?"

"I've got all the necessities. A TV, a bed and an old couch." John bent over. "This smells great. Thanks for thinking of me." He hugged Mama. "I hate to take my food and run, but I want to call Kristen. This will last me for several days. Thanks, Mama."

"You're welcome." She swatted Tony's hand. "Stop it. Those rolls are for John."

"See you later." John carried his food to his truck and left.

Tony called Emmy, but got her voicemail.

"Hi, Em. I'm home. Call me later if you want. If you're still busy with Kenny, then never mind. I don't want to interrupt anything."

At that moment, Emmy and Kenny were sitting at the picnic table on the deck listening to some tunes. She didn't have her phone with her and didn't hear it ringing in the kitchen. She went into the house a few minutes later to grab some water from the fridge and happened to glance at the phone. She saw that someone had called. She listened to Tony's message, but decided to call him later before she went to bed. She took her phone outside in case he called back.

Kristen returned from her visit with her parents. "Hi guys. I talked to Derrick, and he said to say hi."

"Is he coming home at all this summer?" Emmy swung her feet up on the bench and leaned against Kenny.

"He said he might come home for a couple of days before classes start. He's working at a tennis club."

"Probably teaching rich old women how to play tennis," Emmy said.

Kenny watched two blue jays chattering at each other.

"What did you and Kenny do after you left Mama's? Or shouldn't I ask?"

Emmy stuck out her tongue. "We stopped to see my parents. They ended up arguing as usual. We stuck it out for about an hour, and then went to Windsor Park. The flowers on the table are from there."

"You aren't supposed to pick the flowers at the park. If everyone did that, there wouldn't be any left," Kristen said.

"I'm sorry, Krissy. I didn't know."

Kristen winked at Emmy. "It's all right, Em. I just hope the flower police don't show up. They would haul you off to flower jail."

"You're teasing me, you stinker."

"Are either of you girls hungry by any chance?" Kenny asked before Emmy could get after Kristen.

"I knew it wouldn't take too long for you to want to eat again, Kenny Colwell. What would you like?" Emmy asked.

"Nachos. Let's make a big batch of nachos."

"That sounds good to me," Kristen said as she headed for the back door.

"We can do that. I'm pretty sure we have all the stuff we need."

They went inside, and Emmy checked the fridge. "I've got an onion and we have fresh hamburger. There should be a jar of cheese and some diced chilies in the pantry. I've got some sliced jalapenos if you want something with a kick," Emmy said.

"Yes, to all," Kenny said.

Kenny chopped a sweet Vidalia onion as Emmy browned the hamburger. Kristen watched as they worked together in the kitchen and bumped hips. They teased each other, and carried on like teenagers in love.

"I have to get my laundry started," Kristen said. "Emmy is forcing me to do it myself. Don't eat all the nachos."

Emmy and Kenny put together a large platter of nachos, and took it out to the deck to eat. They started eating the warm nachos while the cheese remained nice and gooey. Emmy fed

182

Kenny and got cheese all over his face. She wiped the cheese off with her finger and giggled at him.

"Should we save some nachos for Kristen, or should we eat all of them?" Kenny asked.

"Oh, I guess we should save a few for her, even though she did tease me."

"That would be the proper thing to do."

Emmy put the nachos in the microwave. She came back out to the deck and saw that Kenny had moved. She sat next to him on the lounge chair.

"Why don't you crash here tonight? That way I don't have to run you home."

"I could, but I don't have a toothbrush or anything."

"Hah! You can't use that excuse anymore." She poked his knee. "There are new toothbrushes and stuff in the downstairs bathroom. At least you changed clothes after church."

"Are you sure it's all right, Em? What will Kristen think?"

"She can't object. John spends the night here sometimes. He sleeps in the spare bedroom upstairs. You can crash there."

"What about in the morning? Don't you have to go to work?"

She smiled. "Kristen does, but not me. I'm on vacation."

"Again? How much vacation time do you get?"

"As much as I need—I know the owner of the company. We're tight. And look who's talking. You can take off anytime you want."

Kenny chuckled then said, "Oh, yeah, sure. I can simply tell the guys in the middle of a tour that I want to take a vacation."

"Well, you have time off between tours."

"Which we spend in a recording studio."

She pushed him onto his back, moved her legs and straddled him. "Oh, you poor baby. You've got it so rough." She placed her hands by his shoulders, leaned down and kissed him. "You need a shave."

He grabbed her arms and teased her back, "You'll find out when football season starts. You won't see Tony for months on end, and Kristen won't see John very much."

183

She lifted up. "Why do you think that?"

"They will be so busy during the week with practice. They will be gone half the time on the weekends because of away games. Even when they have a home game the only time you guys will see them is at the game. You'll have to take binoculars to see him."

"It will be like college except he's only a few miles away instead of a few hours. If I want to see him, I can see him at Mama's. I'll just go over there at night, sneak into his room and stare at him while he sleeps. I'll be quiet so I don't wake him up."

"He will think you're a stalker if you do that."

"I'm more worried about how often I get to see you than I am about Tony." Emmy lowered herself onto Kenny and kissed him again. He put his hands on her back.

"I like kissing you like this, and I can tell you're enjoying it, too," she said with a grin.

Kristen came out to the deck and saw them together. "What are you guys doing? Did you forget I am still here?"

Emmy glanced at her.

Kristen shook her head and frowned. "Oh, never mind."

Emmy bit her lip as she looked at Kristen, but she didn't get off of Kenny.

"Did you guys eat all the nachos?" Kristen stood with her hands on her hips. *You had better not let Kenny sleep here tonight, Emmy.*

"I put them in the microwave. We were waiting for you to come upstairs. I'll heat them up and bring them out." She leaned down, kissed Kenny, and then got off of the chair. "Anyone want anything to drink?"

"I'm good, Emmy." Kenny sat up and looked at Kristen. *I'm sorry, but I'm sure you are affectionate with John sometimes.*

"I've got my water," Kristen said. Then she turned back to stare at Kenny. *You're supposed to be different because you're a Christian. Right now you're acting like any other guy.*

Emmy ran into the house. As Emmy heated up the nachos, Kenny asked Kristen, "Emmy wants me to crash here tonight. Is that okay with you?" *She's gonna tell me to go home. I know it.*

184

"Of course. Why would I mind?" *I'll just lock you in the spare room.*

"I wanted to be sure. I wouldn't stay if you objected."

Kristen sighed and then took a few deep breaths while she calmed down. She tried not to frown. "I'll be totally honest with you."

"I would appreciate that, Kristen." He stood up.

"It might not be a good idea if I wasn't here, but since I am, I don't see why you can't." Kristen looked at the back door. "I suppose she told you that John has used the spare room on occasion."

"She did mention that."

Emmy came out with the nachos and forks and napkins and set them on the picnic table. "I brought some salsa, too."

Kristen faced Emmy. "Kenny asked me if I objected to him spending the night, and I told him no."

Emmy stomped her foot. "Why? I want him to stay. Please, Krissy. I let John stay overnight without saying anything."

"I meant that I had no objections, not that he couldn't stay. You don't need to pout."

"I wasn't going to pout. I don't always have to get my way," Emmy insisted.

"Yeah, right. You are so used to having your own way since you moved out of your parents' house."

"It's called being independent, Kristen."

Kenny sat at the table. "While you guys are yapping, I'm eating the nachos."

"Save some for us, Kenny." Emmy sat next to him.

Emmy and Kristen stopped talking and began eating. The nachos soon disappeared. Emmy used a finger to scoop up the last of the cheese. She grinned as she pointed that finger at Kenny. He opened his mouth, and she let him have the last of the melted cheese.

"You guys are so bad," Kristen said. "John and I don't act like two immature teenagers when we're together."

"No, you act like an old couple that's been married for a hundred years," Emmy said.

185

"We have fun in our own way."

Yeah, right. "Are you still hungry, Kenny?" Emmy asked. "I could fix something else."

"I'm full. What are we going to do with the rest of the evening?"

"I want to stay outside since it's not as hot and muggy. We could play tennis if you want, or maybe you have something else in mind," Emmy said.

Kristen rolled her eyes. "I'm still here, Emmy. You guys need to behave."

"I bet I can beat you at tennis." Emmy swung an imaginary racquet back and forth.

"You need to change clothes, Em, if you're going to play tennis." Kristen pointed out.

"I should change anyway. Maybe you guys can think of something to do while I change." Emmy ran upstairs to change out of her dress.

"What's it like living with Emmy?" Kenny asked.

Kristen wondered why he would ask, since he and Emmy spent almost as much time living together. "I love it. She has so much energy. She works all day and takes care of the house. She does all the cooking. It's like she's the energizer bunny—always on the go. She operates at full blast until the juice is gone, and then she crashes."

"I meant as far as getting along?"

"Oh, we never have any trouble getting along. She's the best sister a girl could ever have. Even though she's not really my sister. I wish Emmy could have gone to North Park with me. We would have been roommates the whole time."

"North Park would have been a good experience for Em, but that's water under the bridge. We used to have disagreements over that a lot."

Emmy joined them on the deck. "Did you decide anything?"

"We were just talking about you."

"What about?"

"Kenny asked me how we liked living together, and I lied."

186

Kristen laughed and flipped her hair over her shoulder. "I told him we got along great."

"Oh, yeah. Kenny, you wouldn't believe how hard it is to live with Kristen. She is such a pampered princess. I should kick her out, and have you move in."

"I don't think Jesus would like it if you do that, Em," Kristen said.

"I know, but still..."

"I'm not going to move in, Kristen," Kenny said.

Kristen wasn't convinced. "If I still lived at home, you would and don't try to deny it."

"Diane and Craig lived together for a long time before they got married," Emmy mentioned. "I know that's a bad example."

"Yes, but they fought all the time and Diane either kicked him out or moved out herself." *I wonder if that will ever change even with the baby.*

"Barry and Linda lived together before they got married."

Kristen shook her head. "Lots of people do things that aren't pleasing to God. You and Kenny know better."

"So, if we didn't go to church could we live together?" Emmy put a finger to her mouth.

"You are just being argumentative to tease me."

They kept talking, and before they knew it, it grew dark and really too late to go anywhere.

"I'm going to bed. I have to get up early and go to work," Kristen said. "Unlike some other people I know who are spoiled rotten."

"I can't help it if I have more vacation than you." Emmy grinned and then stuck out her tongue. "I'll see you in the morning. If I get up before noon."

"Such a child!" Kristen said as she marched inside.

Emmy and Kenny stayed up until one o'clock before calling it a night. Kenny slept in the spare bedroom after Emmy put clean sheets on the bed.

Chapter Twenty-One

"Do you want any breakfast, Kristen? I'm going to make something for Kenny and myself." Emmy dug through the fridge for some eggs.

"I'll eat some of whatever you're making, Em. I need to get in the shower. Why are you guys up so early, anyway? You're on vacation, remember."

"I woke up out of habit. So did Kenny. He said he wakes up around six everyday."

"You guys would make a good pair then."

Emmy looked at Kristen with obvious surprise on her face. She knew Kristen would rather see her in a relationship with Tony.

"Oh, I didn't mean it like that, Em." Kristen waved her hand dismissively. "I just meant you both like to get up early."

"I know what you meant."

"Where is Kenny?"

"He went out for a walk so we could get dressed without him around. I'll take my shower after you're done. I'm going to run Kenny home so he can shower, and then we're going to get Tony." She opened the carton of eggs. "We need more eggs. There's only two left. I think I'll make pancakes instead."

"Tony's not home today, Em. Did you forget that he and John are going to Defiance today to pick up some of John's stuff? They're taking John's old truck, spending the night there and coming home late Tuesday."

"Shoot! I forgot all about that, Kristen. That's probably why he called yesterday, and I forgot to call him back. I'll call him this morning before they leave."

"Better call him soon. John said they needed to leave early this morning." Kristen heard the back door open.

"Good morning, ladies. It's a beautiful day in the neighborhood," Kenny said.

Emmy shook her head. "You are the dorkiest rock star of all time."

Kristen nodded in agreement.

Emmy made breakfast for everyone before talking to Tony.

"I'm sorry I didn't call you back last night. I got busy talking to Kristen and Kenny, and I just forgot."

"No big deal. I wanted to remind you that John and I are going to Defiance."

"Kristen reminded me," Emmy said as she poured maple syrup over her pancakes. "I get to hang out with Kenny since he's on vacation."

"Have fun. Maybe I'll call you tonight just to bug you."

Emmy laughed. "I'll make sure I put the phone on do not disturb. Drive safely."

"We'll try. See you later," Tony said.

"I'm serious. I don't want you to get in another accident." Emmy stabbed her pancakes.

"I appreciate the concern, Em."

"Yeah, well, Kristen would be upset." Emmy laughed and took a bite.

A few minutes later, Kristen left for work. Emmy showered and got dressed.

"I'm ready. We can go to your house, and then wherever." Emmy walked into the kitchen and found Kenny doing the dishes. "Thank you, Kenny." She hugged him from behind.

"You're welcome." He put the last plate in the dish rack to dry and turned to face Emmy. "What about Tony? Are we going to pick him up?"

"No, he and John are going to pick up some of John's things from his hometown. They'll be back Tuesday night. Kristen will have to put up with John being gone for a couple days."

"Where is John from?" Kenny asked as he wiped off the counter. "You might have told me before, but I don't remember."

"A place called Defiance, Ohio. It's just across the border, I think. I don't think it's a very big place from what I've heard."

Emmy drove Kenny home. She bit her lip as they passed her parents' house. She waited downstairs in the living room while Kenny showered and packed an overnight bag. Emmy wanted him to stay at her place again tonight.

"Do you want to see your folks since we're so close?" Kenny asked, as he came back downstairs with a duffel bag.

"Not really. They will just fight and argue."

"I'm sorry, Em."

"Have you done anything to the carriage house lately?"

"Not really. I thought about making it into a recording studio, but it's not really big enough. I've still got an old couch if you want to see it." Kenny arched his eyebrows like Groucho Marx.

"You just want to take advantage of me again. I'm not falling for your tricks, mister." She poked him in the stomach.

"What are we going to do today, Em?"

"I thought about something on the way over here."

"And what might that be, pray tell?" Kenny asked.

"There's one thing we haven't done for a while."

Kenny looked at Emmy.

"Besides that!" She tried to jab his stomach again, but he grabbed her hand. "We haven't gone swimming since we got back from Grandma's."

"Hmmmm. I believe you might be correct. I don't recall doing that."

"There's open swimming for adults at the pool at eleven. Interested? It's supposed to be hotter today than yesterday."

"Let me run upstairs and grab some trunks."

"Yeah, grab the ones I like," Emmy joked. "Did you buy some new trunks?"

"I'm not buying one of those Speedo racing briefs. I'd feel too uncomfortable wearing it in front of people." He ran back upstairs and dug through a dresser drawer. He pulled out two swim trunks. *This one is more comfortable, but Emmy will make fun of me if I wear it.* He held up the trunks to compare them. *I don't care if she makes fun of me. I like the longer trunks better.*

They took off and Emmy glanced out the window at her parents' house.

Kenny whispered, "I can understand why you don't want to stop, Em. I know you love your parents, as a Christian should, but it's difficult to be around them."

"There is such a different atmosphere at your parents' house. They get along without fighting or any arguing. Even at

190

Mama's house things are better." Emmy giggled, and then said, "Oh, I guess she doesn't have anyone to argue with, huh?"

"They will always be your parents, Em. You can't change that."

"Yeah, I know. I've looked into being adopted, but I'm too old. No one would want me."

They got back to Emmy's house, and she looked at the kitchen clock. "We still have over an hour to kill before we can use the pool."

"We could read or maybe practice some tunes."

"I need to do laundry, Kenny. Is that all right?"

"Sure. Need help carrying anything downstairs?"

"Yeah. I've got two baskets of dirty clothes."

Kenny followed Emmy upstairs to her room. He glanced at the top shelf of her closet. *I see you still have that stuffed bear holding a football. I gave you that when you were like ten.*

Emmy handed Kenny one of the baskets and said, "If I ever move, I want a house where the washer and dryer aren't in the basement. It gets old carrying the laundry down two flights of stairs."

"I agree with you, Em," he said while looking at the old bear.

"Don't tease me about that. I want to give it to my son if God ever grants me a miracle."

While Emmy worked on her laundry, Kenny grabbed an old acoustic guitar. *I should replace these old strings.* He tuned it as best he could, sat on the couch in the TV room and practiced.

Emmy dashed up the stairs, through the kitchen and stuck her head in the TV room. "I'm going to change into my bathing suit. We should leave in a few minutes."

"Okay, I'll change in the bathroom down here."

"You can leave your wallet here. I've got a season pass that will cover you."

Emmy changed into her suit and put on a long t-shirt and a pair of old denim shorts. She grabbed two large towels, her sunscreen and met Kenny downstairs. They sauntered over to the park and Emmy took care of the admission fee.

191

"I'll meet you by the pool. The guys' locker room is there." She pointed to her right.

"See you in a few minutes."

Emmy went into the locker room and stashed her shorts and her pass. Kenny stood by the deep end of the pool as he waited for her. They claimed a couple of empty lounge chairs by placing their towels over them. Kenny watched Emmy remove her t-shirt. Emmy looked at him and he smiled. He remembered the bikini she wore in Florida at Grandma's.

"I don't ever remember seeing you in a smaller bikini."

"Stop it! You have so."

Kenny shook his head. "Nope. I've never seen you in a bikini that small before, Emmy."

"The one I wore at Grandma's didn't cover much of anything. Should I have worn that one today?" Emmy asked even though she would never wear it to a public pool. "I remember when I went to Colorado with Kristen and a bunch of people. I felt almost too shy to even wear my bikini. I got over it though after I saw Derrick's girlfriend, Amber. She is gorgeous and after seeing her, no one paid any attention to me."

"That's a really nice story, Emmy," Kenny teased.

She stuck out her tongue at him. "Are we going to swim, or are you just going to leer at me like a dirty old man?"

"We can swim if we must, but you are certainly a pleasure to stare at, Em."

"Then I better not catch you staring at anyone else, buster."

After alternately swimming and working on their tans for an hour, they toweled dry, grabbed their gear and headed back to Emmy's.

"We can do that again tomorrow if you want."

"As long as the weather cooperates. You are a pretty good swimmer."

"I learned when I was a little girl. What do you want for lunch?"

"We could make sandwiches and eat on the deck."

"I like that idea. I could work on my tan."

Kenny worked on the sandwiches and Emmy grabbed a bag

of chips and quickly made a dip with some sour cream and a package of dry onion soup mix.

"What do you want to drink?" she asked.

"Water is fine. Have you got any pickles?"

"In the fridge on the bottom left."

"Got 'em. Do you still like mayonnaise on your sandwiches?"

"You remember that?"

"Yeah, why shouldn't I?"

"No reason. I'll meet you on the deck."

Kenny made a plate of sandwiches and brought them outside. Emmy took off her t-shirt but not her shorts.

"Fancy sandwiches, Kenny. I never bother to put lettuce on mine most of the time." Emmy sat at the end of the picnic table bench to be in the sun.

"I saw it in the fridge, so I used it. It wasn't Kristen's by any chance?"

"No, nothing like that. Whatever's in the fridge belongs to both of us. We share everything."

They took their time eating lunch, as Emmy enjoyed feeling the warm rays of the sun on her face.

"I'm going to change out of my bikini. It's still wet."

"Me, too."

Emmy giggled then said, "It will take those baggy old trunks a couple days to dry. They are bigger than your regular shorts."

"They're comfortable," Kenny said as he swatted at her.

"Missed me," Emmy squealed as she ran inside.

Emmy changed into dry shorts and a tank top and met Kenny on the deck. They sat on opposite sides of the picnic table.

"Do you remember the day I skinned my knee during recess, or maybe lunch? I can't remember. You carried me into the school and took me into the nurse's office. She wasn't there so you took care of me."

"I remember it. I also remember you acted so brave and didn't cry."

"I cried when it happened. Maybe I stopped when you put a
193

Bandaid on me." She reached out and grabbed his hands. "Do you remember how I acted in junior high?" *I know I hung out with some wild kids at times.*

"I remember we didn't hang out as much as when you were younger. We were at different schools." Kenny tilted his head. *Where are you going with this, Em?* "Other girls in junior high were only interested in kissing boys, but not you. You behaved like a total tomboy. Sports was your main interest. And your piano lessons."

"Ugh! I used to hate practicing the piano," she said as she pretended the picnic table was a piano and played some imaginary chords.

"I know. You used to complain about it all the time."

"Maybe I would have been 'boy crazy' if the right one wasn't already in high school." She made air quotes.

Kenny looked at Emmy as she smiled at him. "Is that why you always wanted to camp out in the backyard?"

"We didn't do that in junior high, did we? I thought I was in grade school."

"We did it then, but I remember a couple of times in junior high, too."

"You mean when you were in junior high?"

"Nope." He brushed a finger along her cheek. "You were in junior high, and I was in high school."

Emmy laughed. "I wonder what excuse I told my parents. I must have lied to them. I can't believe they would let me stay overnight with you in a tent."

"My parents knew, but they didn't seem overly concerned. I think they trusted me and thought of you as still a tomboy who probably didn't even know about sex."

"I knew about it. Well, sorta." She grinned. "Diane certainly knew about it."

"I didn't know much about it. I knew I wanted to do it sometime. All high school guys are like that."

"Tony wasn't."

"Oh, trust me, Em. He had just as much interest in it as everyone else. He just used his willpower to do the right thing."

194

Kenny took another drink of water.

"He sure did," Emmy mentioned rather sadly. "That's why we broke up the first time."

"Come on. You know better."

"Oh, I know, and now I'm glad we didn't do anything, but it's not easy sometimes," Emmy said and then bit her lip. "Other guys talked about sex all the time. Even in front of the girls."

Kenny nodded. "Sometimes it was all they talked about. If one tenth of the stories I heard in the locker room were true, there weren't very many virgins left in Roosevelt High."

Emmy gazed into Kenny's eyes for a moment. *I wonder if you ever heard rumors about Diane or me?* Emmy wondered. *You never said anything if you did. Of course we were only together at Roosevelt for a semester, and then you graduated early. I know some of the stories about Diane were true, but I never even kissed a boy until you kissed me on the old couch.*

"What are you thinking about, Em?"

She blushed. "I can't tell you."

He smiled and said, "I remember we always slept in our clothes when we camped out."

"I thought I would sleep in my underwear," she said.

"If you did, I never knew it."

"Yes, you did. I know you saw me in my underwear." Emmy looked at Kenny and grinned sheepishly.

"No, I didn't," Kenny insisted. "I think I would remember if I had."

"There's a tent in the garage. Maybe..."

"Yeah, and we could pretend we're in the jungle, too."

"It would be fun."

He saw the serious look on her face. "Emmy, we're not kids anymore."

"I know that. Are you afraid to sleep in a tent with me?" she asked as she twisted her hair into a braid.

"It's not fear that would stop me, Em."

"Kristen could sleep with us."

"Are you hearing what you are saying? We can't sleep together in a tent. With or without Kristen."

"I fell asleep with Barry one night and nothing happened."

"That's not the same, and you know it. What would Kristen say if we slept in the tent?" he asked as he thought about Barry. *Oh, I remember when that happened. It was before you got your apartment.*

"Fine. Spoil all my fun. At least think about it. We can keep our clothes on."

Kenny shook his head.

"Fine! I won't mention it again," Emmy grunted and kicked at his shin.

"Good," Kenny said even as he thought, *It would be fun to do that again, but we're not kids anymore.*

They basked in the sunlight without talking for several minutes, and then Emmy spoke up, "Can I ask you about your money?"

"Go ahead. What do you want to know?"

"Are you investing it wisely? I know you're not wasting it on fancy cars and a huge house. You don't gamble, and you don't do drugs. You must have a few dollars stashed away."

"I live off an allowance, believe it or not. Andy keeps a close grip on all the guys finances. He makes sure it is invested wisely and securely. He uses the same investment company, so we're all in it together. It's called Aberdeen Investments, and they are very secure. You know, Em, if I never make another dollar selling CDs or playing gigs, I would still make music with the guys. We still love being a band."

"Are you ever going to release that live stuff you did in England?"

"I think so. We are thinking we might need to release it in 2003 to fill in a gap before the next CD. It will probably take a couple of years to do the next one because of the tour and all."

"Speaking of fancy cars... when are you going to buy me one? I could use a new car. Maybe a Corvette or a Porsche. I'd settle for a Ferrari if I have to."

"I'd buy you a new Civic if you needed a car. Isn't my old one running all right?"

"It's running like a top. I was kidding... about the Ferrari."

196

"But you'd take a Corvette?"

"Only if it's red," Emmy teased.

Emmy wanted to finish her laundry, so Kenny tagged along as Emmy folded clothes. Not the most exciting thing to do, but life isn't always exciting. After finishing the laundry, they picked up some groceries at the Sainsbury's. To the other shoppers Emmy and Kenny acted like any other young married couple. Wearing a baseball cap and sunglasses as his disguise, Kenny shopped unnoticed—or at least, undisturbed. Emmy planned to make chicken enchiladas for dinner. Kenny requested a salad and promised to make it himself.

"Whoa! Aren't you the gourmet chef? Sure you can handle chopping up some lettuce and maybe a tomato," Emmy teased Kenny, but he didn't take the bait.

"I'll make the salad after you have your dish in the oven. You have to stay out of the kitchen while I chop the lettuce, and we'll see if you like the salad."

"Deal." They shook hands.

Later, after they played a set of tennis at the park, Emmy put her chicken enchiladas together and popped them in the oven.

"The kitchen is all yours, Chef Colwell," she said as she waved a hand and curtsied.

Kenny rose from his comfortable position in the TV room and walked into the kitchen. "No peeking and no snooping in the fridge after it's done. You hear me, young lady?"

"I hear you, oh great one."

"What time to you expect Kristen home?"

"Six. Maybe a little after that. The enchiladas should be ready about then."

Emmy opened the fridge to get a bottle of water.

"You don't really want water. You're just snooping. Now scoot. Skedaddle." Kenny chased Emmy out of the kitchen by threatening to swat her.

"Okay. I'll let you make your salad without anymore snooping."

Chapter Twenty-Two

Kristen made it home a few minutes after six. She walked in the back door and smiled. "Something smells good. Did you make chicken enchiladas again, Em? You know I love those."

"Hi, Kristen. The enchiladas are ready. How did work go?"

"Not bad for a Monday. I saw your boss. He said to say hello."

"Hi, Kristen." Kenny walked into the kitchen and glared at Emmy.

"Hey, Kenny." Kristen waved.

"I didn't peek in the fridge," Emmy said.

"I'll be back in a minute. I want to change into something comfortable." Kristen ran upstairs to her room and returned in a few minutes wearing designer jeans and a Ralph Lauren top.

"Dinner is ready. Kenny made a salad, but he still won't let me see it. He claims it is something spectacular."

"Real and spectacular?"

Emmy and Kristen laughed, but Kenny didn't understand their inside joke.

"If you ladies will have a seat in the dining room, I will serve your salad," Kenny announced formally.

"Do we need to get some dressing from the fridge?" Emmy tried to get past Kenny.

"Not so fast there, young lady. The dressing is already on the salad."

Emmy returned to her seat, and a minute later, Kenny brought out a plate of his salad for Kristen.

"Wow! This looks great, Kenny." Kristen noticed the different colors and the careful arrangement of the different vegetables. "Is this blue cheese sprinkled on top?"

"It is indeed and thank you, Kristen."

He returned to the kitchen and brought out Emmy's salad—a bowl of shredded head lettuce.

Emmy looked at her salad, and then at Kristen's. "Why does she get a fancy salad, and all I get is shredded lettuce?" She held up the bowl in protest.

Kenny grinned and said, "Because she didn't make fun of my culinary expertise."

Emmy looked at Kenny, and her eyes pleaded for forgiveness. "I'm sorry I made fun of you."

"That didn't sound very sincere." Kenny shook his head and shifted his attention to Kristen. "Did it sound sincere to you?"

"Not at all!" Kristen replied with a mouth full of salad. "Oooh! This is divine. Thank you so much for making it, Kenny."

"Could you repeat it, please, Em?" Kenny asked without smiling.

"I'm really, really, really sorry I made fun of you." She batted her eyes. "May I please have a salad like Kristen's?"

"This is delicious, Kenny. What all did you put in here?" Kristen asked as Emmy tried to grab some salad with her fork. "Stop that, Em. Sit back down before you break your chair."

Kenny explained what he tossed in the salad as he brought in a plate of salad for Emmy.

"Thank you, Kenny."

"You're welcome, sweetie." He kissed her cheek.

Kenny sat and ate his salad, too. When they finished their salad, Emmy brought out the chicken enchiladas.

"I wish I could cook like you, Em," Kristen said.

"I've spent more time with Mama in the kitchen than you. You'll learn one of these days." *You better, or else you will poison your husband.*

After they finished dinner, Kenny and Emmy cleaned up the kitchen. Kristen needed to work on a project in her room.

"I'll wash and you can dry. Is that okay with you?"

"Emmy, you do know that this contraption here is a dishwasher. You place the..."

"I know how it works, but we only have a few things to wash."

Kenny grinned. "Just wanted to make sure you realized it was here."

Emmy splashed water on Kenny and giggled.

"Hey! Stop that."

"Ooops! Sorry, that was an accident."

199

"I'm not going to start a water fight in the house, Emily. Of course if you would care to step outside."

"You want to grab the hose and soak me."

"I hadn't thought of that, but there is a hose on the deck."

"No! Please don't. I might melt."

"I doubt it very much, but I won't do anything."

After cleaning the kitchen, Emmy and Kenny sat outside on the deck. Kristen joined them in a few minutes.

"The salad and enchiladas tasted delicious. Thank you, guys."

"You're welcome, Krissy."

They talked on the deck until the house phone rang. Emmy and Kristen jumped up to answer it. "It's probably John or Tony. I don't want to miss his call." Emmy wanted to get to the phone before Kristen simply to tease her.

Emmy got to the phone first and answered just before it went to the machine.

"Hello."

"Hey, Emmy, it's Tony."

"Hi, Tony. Did you have a good day?" Emmy stuck her tongue out at Kristen as they went back to the deck. "Where are you?"

"John's parents' house. Our day was sorta all right. No problems on the drive over here, but when we got to Defiance the transmission self-destructed."

"What?"

"John's truck made a loud grinding noise and stopped working."

"How old is his truck?" Emmy asked.

Tony asked John and then said, "It's a 1987 Ford F-150, and it's got over 200,000 miles on it."

"Can you get it fixed?" Emmy asked. "Is it worth fixing?"

"Yeah, the guy at the garage said it will take a day to get the part, but he can have it done by Wednesday. It looks like we will be here until then. Are you okay?"

"Things are okay here. I made chicken enchiladas for dinner, and Kenny made a salad."

"A salad?"

"Well, I guess it would be unfair to call if just a salad."

They talked a few minutes longer, and then Emmy brought up the tent. She explained how she and Kenny used to camp out.

"Do you think it would be a sin if we set up the tent in the backyard and slept outside?"

"Oh, no you don't." Tony shook his head even though they were talking on the phone. "You're not going to get me to condone something you know is wrong."

"It's not like that. It would be all three of us, not just me and Kenny."

"What have you been drinking? What do you mean all three of you?" Tony turned to look at John. "You don't want to know what Emmy is talking about."

John sat down on the brown leather couch in the family room.

"Can all three of you fit?" Tony asked.

"I think so. We'll see, and if we can't, then Kenny can sleep on that old air mattress thing."

"I know you well enough to realize that you are going to do whatever you want regardless of what anyone thinks. I don't think it would be wrong for the three of you to camp out as long as Kenny isn't in the tent. It sounds like you guys are having fun. Go ahead if you want. Maybe you and I can try that sometime," he added as a joke.

"Maybe we can. You would have to behave though." Emmy knew she would never sleep in a tent with Tony.

"Just make sure you and Kenny behave. You know it would be a sin if you don't."

"Where's a priest when I need one? I could do whatever I want, and then go to confession and do a little bit of penance."

"You know better. I'll get back as soon as I can. I already called home and told Mama. John wants to talk to Kristen."

"Okay, I'll give her the phone. Have a safe trip home."

Emmy grinned as she handed the phone to Kristen. "John wants to talk to you."

While Kristen and John talked, Emmy told Kenny the news

about the truck and the tent.

"They'll be there an extra day, but at least it can be fixed. Tony said we could camp in the backyard."

"What are you talking about, Em? We can't go camping?"

"Yes, we can! We're going to set up the tent in the backyard and sleep outdoors."

"We who?" Kenny asked.

"The three of us." Emmy waved to include Kristen.

They were still talking about camping out when Kristen finished talking to John and returned to the deck. She listened for a moment before asking, "What on earth are you talking about, Em?"

"I think it would be fun to sleep in the tent. It's a beautiful night, and it would be like when we were kids."

"Are you nuts? Have you totally lost your mind? I'm not sleeping outside on the ground and neither are you. I've got a perfectly good bed in my room, and I intend to sleep in it."

"You *have* to go camping with us. If you don't it would be just me and Kenny. Tony said it would be all right."

"Tony actually said that? Is he nuts?" Kristen made circles around her ears with both hands. "Did you keep asking someone until you found one to agree with you? What do you think Pastor Herb would say? Or even Chase?"

"I didn't ask anyone except Tony," Emmy insisted as she frowned. "Kenny and I used to camp in his backyard."

"You were kids! I don't care how many times you slept together back then. You're not a kid anymore, Emmy."

"I was in junior high the last time we did it."

Kristen glared at Emmy. "I don't want to hear about it." She clamped her hands over her ears and began singing.

"Maybe we shouldn't put up the tent, Em," Kenny said, though he suspected he knew what Emmy's answer would be.

"Well, you guys can sleep inside. I'm going to put up the tent and sleep outside tonight." Emmy marched off the deck and over to the garage as Kristen and Kenny looked at each other.

"She can be so stubborn sometimes," Kristen said in exasperation.

"Ain't that the truth," Kenny agreed, and then mentioned. "It would be fun to camp out."

"You're seriously considering this. Why?"

"Emmy wants to have fun like in the old days. I'm going to help her set up the tent at least. She might change her mind later."

Kristen threw her arms up. "Fine! I'll go along with this nonsense, but if I see one bug in the tent, I'm outta there."

Kenny helped Emmy get the tent down from the rafters in the garage. She climbed up the ladder while Kenny kept it steady. Kristen grabbed three sleeping bags from the large storage cabinet. Kenny carried the tent, and Emmy grabbed a tarp to lay on the ground. They picked out a suitable spot and began setting up their camp, as Emmy called it. She was really getting into it, and Kristen thought she was going to suggest they play G.I. Joe. Kristen kept looking for bugs on the sleeping bags, or near the tent. Her heart was definitely not in this adventure. After a few initials struggles, Kenny and Emmy erected the tent. Emmy zipped it open and peered inside.

"It looks clean enough. Take a look, Kristen. I don't see any bugs or spiders or giant centipedes."

"If you're trying to scare me, it's working."

"Let me see if all the bags will fit inside." Emmy tossed the sleeping bags in the tent, and then got in with them. She spread the bags on the floor of the tent. "It might be tight, but we will all fit."

"I'm sleeping in my clothes right in the middle. You have to sleep in the corner, Em, away from Kenny. I can't believe I'm actually thinking about going along with this hare-brained scheme." Kristen threw her hands into the air and frowned at Kenny. *You better hope she changes her mind because I am not sleeping in a tent on the ground.*

Emmy grinned as she climbed out. "Fine by me. We can tell ghost stories."

"Do you want to roast marshmallows and sing Kumbaya, too?" Kristen asked sarcastically.

"I remember Derrick trying to scare me by telling me ghost stories. It didn't work."

"I'm still not sure we can all fit," Kenny said.

"Only one way to find out!" Emmy hollered as she climbed back inside. "Come on, you guys."

They all got in the tent and lay on the bags.

"See. We fit." Emmy turned on her side at the edge of the tent.

Kristen said, "If you kick me like you usually do when we share a bed..."

"I won't be able to kick you. We'll be inside the bags."

"It smells funny in here. Kinda musty." Kristen sat up. "Did she kick you when you did this before, Kenny?"

"I don't remember anything like that. Does she still snore?" Kenny asked Kristen.

"I don't snore," Emmy replied indignantly.

"How do you know? You can't listen to yourself snoring," Kristen said.

"Kenny, tell her that I don't snore."

"I've never heard you snore, Em."

"Is that a bug?" Kristen pointed at the top of the tent. "It is! I'm out of here!" Kristen screamed as she scampered through the tent opening.

"It's just one bug, Kristen. See?" Emmy held up the bug as she climbed out.

"You're gross! Get rid of it!" Kristen shouted.

"It's dead, Kristen," Kenny informed her as he climbed out.

They headed back to the deck.

Emmy said very seriously, "You guys can keep making excuses if you want. I'll sleep out here all alone. I'm not afraid. I'll spray some Febreze in it and it will smell all right."

"I'm not ready to go to bed," Kenny said.

"I'm not, either. I just wanted to get the tent set up, and see if we could all fit. I'm not going to bed until midnight."

"That's okay for you, but I have to get up for work. I need my beauty sleep," Kristen said.

"You are beautiful no matter how much sleep you get, Kristen."

"Not going to change my mind, Em." Kristen frowned at Emmy. *You are absolutely nuts for doing this.*

204

Kenny nodded. "She's right, Kristen."

"Thank you, Kenny," Kristen said as she smiled at him.

They went back in the house, sat on the couch and watched TV until eleven.

"I have to get some sleep, you guys. I can't stay up any longer. I'm going up to my room. Good night, Kenny." Kristen smacked Emmy's foot as she walked past.

Emmy followed Kristen up to her room. "Krissy, I know you don't want to sleep outside. You can sleep in your bed. It's okay."

"Are you still going to sleep outside, Em?"

"Yeah, I want to. Don't worry about me. I'll be fine. Kenny will be with me."

Kristen looked at Emmy. "Duh!"

"No, don't even think that, Kristen Lynn Keasling. That's not why, and you know it."

"Please be careful, Em."

"We will behave and nothing will happen. You know that. Go to sleep, and I'll see you in the morning. Love you, Krissy."

"I love you, Em."

Emmy kissed Kristen's cheek.

"Be good, Em."

"Always am."

Emmy ran down the stairs like a kid.

Kristen lay on her bed and sighed. She wondered about Emmy because something had changed. *Oh, God, Emmy. I hope you aren't doing this to prove your doctor is wrong. You guys can't have a baby now.*

Emmy and Kenny sat on the TV room couch and watched a movie. They tried to be quiet so they wouldn't disturb Kristen. Emmy giggled as she watched the comedy.

"Em! Be quiet, or you'll wake up Kristen."

"I'm trying, but this is too funny. I love romantic comedies like this."

Emmy giggled again, and Kenny put an arm around her. Emmy rested her head on his chest trying to keep quiet. The movie ended shortly after one.

Emmy jumped up and asked, "Ready to go camping?"

"I'm game if you are, Em. You know we don't have to sleep in the tent. I don't want to cause any problems for you and Kristen."

"It won't. I'm going to get ready. It'll only take a few minutes."

"I'll meet you in the kitchen."

Emmy changed into an old t-shirt and gym shorts. She brushed her teeth and grabbed a robe. She slipped on the robe and remembered to take two pillows with her as she went downstairs. Kenny waited in the kitchen for her—still in his clothes. She tossed him the pillows, and they headed out to the backyard.

"Look at that. It's a full moon, Em. Things might get spooky."

"You'll have to protect me if it does. Do you think we should have brought a flashlight with us?"

"We should be okay without one, but if you want me to run back in, I will."

"No, you don't have to. We'll be fine. There is enough moonlight."

Kenny let Emmy get in the tent first. She unzipped the third sleeping bag and opened it up. She placed the other two on top of it for more cushioning between them and the ground. Emmy took off her robe and slipped into her sleeping bag.

"You can come in now, Kenny."

"You're not going to wear that robe, are you? You'll get pretty hot if you do."

"I took it off. I only brought it to wear in the morning in case I get cold."

Kenny got in the tent and tripped over something.

"Ow! That's my leg you just smashed," Emmy hollered.

"Sorry, Em. I couldn't see. Are you okay?"

"I may never walk again."

Kenny slipped off his shorts and maneuvered into his bag without too much trouble. They lay on their sides facing each other.

"Remember how we used to talk until we would fall asleep

206

when we did this before?" Emmy asked as she grinned.

"Yeah, but we were probably in the tent by nine or ten. It's after one now."

"Does that mean you don't want to talk to me?"

"What do you want to talk about, Em?"

"Nothing. I only wanted to make sure you would talk to me."

"You're goofy sometimes, Emmy. You do realize that, right?"

"Do you love me anyway?"

"You know the answer to that."

"I just like to hear it. I'm probably too insecure and need constant reassurance. I never heard it much growing up."

"Now you have friends like Kristen who tell you and mean it."

"And Tony, too."

"I didn't forget about Tony. He loves you very much. You guys fight like brother and sister sometimes, but it's only because of who you are. It doesn't mean you don't love each other."

"I know. Sometimes we get a little frustrated with each other because of... you know."

"I know. You've mentioned it a few times."

Eventually, they ran out of things to talk about, and Emmy fell asleep. Kenny listened to her breathing as she slept peacefully. He remembered the first time they fell asleep in the carriage house. He remembered the reason they didn't date back then—the difference in their ages—even though they both had strong feelings for each other. He recalled that the main reason was Emmy's parents would not let her date until she turned sixteen. He realized the three and a half year difference in their ages would not matter a bit now. He said a quick prayer asking God to be with Emmy. He fell asleep with a sense of peace in his heart.

Chapter Twenty-Three

Kenny woke up to bright sunshine. He figured it must be around eight. He looked at Emmy—still soundly asleep on her back halfway out of her sleeping bag. Kenny knew he got rather warm during the night and wished he slept on top of the sleeping bag. He watched as her chest rose and fell as she breathed. He tried not to wake her, but she began to stir, anyway. She stretched her arms out and touched Kenny. She opened her eyes and smiled.

"Good morning, sleepyhead. How did you sleep?"

"I slept all right. Do you know what time it is?"

"I think it's around eight. Are you ready to get up?"

"I need to pee."

"Thanks for sharing that."

Emmy crawled out of her sleeping bag. She faced Kenny on her hands and knees. She reached down and kissed him.

"Why'd you do that?"

"Just because I could. Will you unzip the tent, please?"

Kenny unzipped the door to the tent, and Emmy got out and ran into the house. Kenny slipped on his shorts and followed. He used the downstairs bathroom while Emmy was upstairs. When she came down, she wore a sweatshirt and a pair of jean shorts.

"Should we leave the tent up for one more night?" Emmy asked as she pulled a carton of orange juice from the fridge.

"We could. Maybe you and Kristen could use it tonight."

"She won't. I know her, and she likes her comfy bed too much to leave it. She's a princess, remember?"

Kenny grabbed two glasses from the cabinet. "Let's leave it up and see what happens. Maybe I will use it by myself."

"I want to sleep out there if you are going to," Emmy said as she poured the OJ.

"I'll close it up, and we'll wait until tonight to decide."

"I'm hungry. Can we go out for breakfast? There's this new place in town. I've got half price coupons," Emmy said.

"That settles it then. How can we pass up such a deal?" Kenny jested.

"You're teasing me. I can tell."

"I would never tease you, Em."

"You always tease me. It proves you love me."

Tony teases you just as much. Does that prove that he loves you too? Kenny wondered as he drank the orange juice.

They showered, got dressed and checked out the new restaurant called Patty's Pancake Palace.

"Did you like your blueberry pancakes?" Kenny asked after they finished eating.

Emmy put her finger to her mouth. "Let's see. The food tasted all right, and the service was even better. I think it deserves another trip. Especially if I have more coupons."

"You're such a goof, Em."

Emmy checked the time when they got back to the house.

"We should leave in a few minutes if we want to go swimming again."

"I can be ready in five."

They changed and walked over to the pool following the same routine as the day before. After they got back to the house, they ate lunch on the deck again.

"I could get used to this, Kenny. Waking up when I feel like it. Going out for breakfast. Taking it easy all day."

"It's called a vacation, Emmy. It's not real life. At least not for people like us. Maybe for the ultra rich. You would get bored soon enough. I know you. You need to be busy."

"You're right. What we are doing isn't the way it would be if we were married. We would have to do all the boring tedious things that go with everyday life."

"We are having fun now without having to deal with all the other stuff. You will have to adjust, if, or when, you get married. Life won't be all peaches and cream."

"Yeah, we'll have to drink some vinegar, too."

After lunch Kenny wanted to take Emmy shopping.

"Let's go shopping, Em. You could use some new outfits for fall."

"Don't you like what I wear?"

"Yes, but you could use some more dresses."

"I think I could afford to buy one dress if it's on sale."

209

Emmy thought about the balance on her Visa card. "Maybe two but no more."

Kenny put his hands on her shoulders. "Don't get mad, but I'm buying whatever you find. You don't have to find something on sale or marked down because it's last year's style. Just for today I'm going to be more stubborn than you. Do you agree?"

She frowned as she looked up at him, but then slowly started to smile. "I suppose so. Won't you be bored watching me try on dresses?"

"Definitely, but I'll give you an hour, and then we'll do something else."

Kenny took Emmy to the mall to a dress shop she liked. He watched patiently for an hour as Emmy tried on different dresses. She chose four, and he bought them for her.

"Thank you, Kenny. I hope it wasn't too boring for you."

"I like looking at you when you are dressed up. Actually, I like to see you no matter how you're dressed to be honest."

"Do those dresses make me look older?" Emmy asked as they headed back to the car.

"I wouldn't say older. Maybe more professional except for that one—the light purple one. I think you look adorable in that one. You look like a teenager. Very innocent, but sorta sexy, too. I don't know why? Maybe you can wear that one, and I'll take you and Kristen out for dinner tonight. What do you think?"

"I'd love it, and Kristen will be happy to go. I'm sure."

They left the mall, and Kenny took Emmy over to DelSasso Sound. This was the shop where the guys bought all their band gear. They walked in, and Emmy headed over to a display of keyboards. Kenny walked toward the sales counter where Gregg DelSasso, the owner, was reading a magazine.

"Hi, Gregg. Andy said to say hi."

Gregg looked up from his magazine. "Hi, Kenny. How are you?

"I'm fine. Did that order come in yet?"

"It came in this morning. I've got it in back. Come on I'll show you." Gregg walked out from behind the counter. "I saw Jeff yesterday. He needed some new strings. You need any?"

"I've got plenty." He waved for Emmy to come over. "This is Emmy Colasanti."

"Hi, Emmy. I've seen you at some of the shows. You've got a good voice."

"Thanks, Mr. DelSasso."

Kenny and Emmy followed Gregg into a back room. Gregg opened a case, picked up a guitar and handed it to Kenny.

"What do you think?"

"It looks great. Can I plug in somewhere?"

"Use practice room three. It's empty, and there's an amp in there that you like."

Kenny took Emmy to the sound-proofed practice room. He plugged in and began playing. Five minutes later he felt satisfied with the new guitar.

"Do you like my new toy, Em?"

"It looks very fancy, and it sounds good to me."

"This guy I know in England custom makes them. He only works when he's in the mood. I persuaded him to make this one for me."

"How much did it cost?"

"Believe me, Em. You don't want to know."

Maybe I shouldn't have bought four dresses. She thought.

They left with the guitar and a new case. Gregg even tossed in several packages of strings.

Kristen returned home from work shortly after five thirty.

"Did you have a good day?" Emmy asked as she met Kristen in the kitchen.

"Not bad. You'll never guess who I saw at lunch."

"Who?"

"Richard Demarco. He stood in line ahead of me."

"Get out!" Emmy put her hands on Kristen's shoulders. "Did he see you?"

"I don't think so, but so what. He doesn't know me."

Kenny listened to the conversation. "Is that the guy you dated a few times, Emmy?"

Kristen answered for her. "That's the guy who made a pass at her the night of Tony's accident. He tried to seduce her, and he

211

almost succeeded. Emmy's lucky he didn't rape her."

Kenny looked at Emmy, "You never told me about that. The part about him making a pass at you."

"I didn't want you to know. I'm sorry I didn't tell you. He didn't come close to succeeding. Kristen is exaggerating."

"Does Tony know?" Kenny asked. "About that night I mean."

"He knows I went out him. I never thought of them as dates."

"He sure did, Em. He wanted to get you in bed. That was the *only* reason he took you anywhere. You were just too naïve to realize it." Kristen leaned against the counter.

Emmy looked at Kenny, "I would have never gone to bed with him. I didn't tell Tony about what happened that night because it's really none of his business. And don't either of you guys tell him. I'll tell him myself one of these days if I think he needs to know. Maybe."

Emmy looked at Kristen and Kenny, and they nodded their heads telling her they would keep her secret.

"Kristen, I told Emmy I would take you both out for dinner. Someplace nice. She bought a new dress today and wants to wear it."

"I didn't buy it. You did." Emmy poked Kenny in the stomach, and then turned to face Kristen. "He took me shopping and bought me some new dresses. He wants me to wear this certain one tonight. I'll show you."

Emmy and Kristen scrambled upstairs to her room. The dress lay on the bed. Kristen picked it up and held it up to Emmy.

"Well? What do you think?"

"This is a perfect color for you, Em. It makes your eyes look almost purple."

"Kenny told me it makes me look like a teenager, but in a sexy way, or something like that. Do you think I will look sexy in this dress?" Emmy asked.

"Sexy, huh? I don't know about that," Kristen said. "You will definitely look younger, though."

"Do you have anywhere you'd like to go? And don't say

212

Darby's." Emmy held up the dress and looked in the mirror.

"Ciao Bella. We can have a bottle of wine and a nice meal."

Kenny took them to Ciao Bella in The Hill section of SoHam. The town originated there along a bend in the Kinmundy River. Art and craft shops, a couple of used book stores and fine restaurants brought tourists, as well as locals, to the area now. The Sabatino family had owned and operated Ciao Bella for its entire existence. Mr. Sabatino greeted Kenny and the girls like members of the family. They ordered their dinner and a bottle of Chianti. Two hours later, Emmy and Kristen kissed Mr. Sabatino on the cheek as they left.

He chuckled and his large belly shook. "My wife will be jealous if she learns that two beautiful ladies kissed me. Please come back soon."

Kenny shook his hand.

"I never get tired of having dinner here. The food is so good, and the Sabatinos are so friendly," Kenny said as they stepped outside.

"I liked that wine. Do you remember the name?" Kristen asked Kenny.

Emmy giggled for a moment. "I remember. It was red."

"We know that, you goof." Kristen laughed at Emmy, and then turned to Kenny. "Do you remember the name of the vineyard?"

"I wrote it down because I knew you girls would forget since you drank most of the bottle yourselves."

"Do you remember where you parked the car?" Emmy began walking in the wrong direction.

"Em, it's this way." Kenny ran over and took her hand.

"Are you sure? Can't we go this way?"

"No, sweetie, we have to go this direction."

"Follow me, Em. If you can, that is." Kristen turned around suddenly and walked right into a man wearing a trench coat and a black fedora. "Ooops! Sorry. I wasn't looking where I was going."

"That's all right, Miss," Detective Thomas Hernandez said as he stepped aside.

"Way to go, Kristen," Emmy said and then giggled.

"Oh, hush. I didn't see him. It's not because I'm tipsy."

Kenny had parked only two blocks away from the restaurant. Not bad for the busy Hill area. Kristen walked ahead as Kenny and Emmy held hands and took their time.

"Did you see all the guys looking at you tonight, Em? They really admired you new dress." Kristen turned around, but continued walking backwards.

"They were not." Emmy giggled as Kristen backed into a bench and sat down.

"Yuh-huh. I watched when you got up to use the restroom, and the guys all looked at you as you went past."

"Did I leave the tags on or something?" Emmy joked.

"Face it, Em. You are a beautiful young lady," Kenny said.

"If you think I'm going to kiss you because of your flattery, you're absolutely right."

Emmy reached up and put her arms around Kenny's neck. She kissed him as he hugged her and Kristen watched.

"All right, you guys. Enough of that. You better sleep in your own room tonight, Emmy. No tent tonight."

"Oh, yeah. I forgot about that. You and I could camp out tonight. How about it?"

"I don't want to sleep outside."

"Maybe tonight I will use the tent by myself. Here's the car. We didn't lose it after all." Kenny opened the rear door for Emmy and Kristen.

"You're a true gentleman, Kenny Colwell." Emmy smiled as she curtsied. "Tony and John should take a tip from you. They don't ever open the car door anymore."

"They open other doors for us, Em. Maybe Tony doesn't open the car door because you don't give him a chance. He opens doors for me."

Back at the house Kristen changed into more casual clothes, but Emmy remained in her new dress. They sat in the living room and talked—no TV tonight. Kristen lasted until eleven. She looked at Emmy, who sat next to Kenny on the couch with her feet tucked under her.

"I'm going to bed. Thanks for dinner, Kenny."

214

"You're welcome, Kristen. It was my pleasure to have two beautiful ladies for dinner companions."

"More sweet talk, huh? Are you angling for another kiss, Kenny Colwell?" Emmy moved to kiss him.

"Come on, Emmy. You need to go to bed, too, and no more kissing." Kristen took Emmy's hand and pulled her up from the couch.

"Oh, well. I'll see you in the morning, Kenny. Thank you for a wonderful day, for dinner and the dresses."

Kristen yanked Emmy away from the couch.

"Ow! Okay, already. I'm coming," Emmy said.

Emmy smiled and waved goodbye at Kenny as Kristen pulled her down the hall toward the stairs.

"You're hurting my arm," Emmy said as Kristen kept pulling her upstairs. "Let go before I get mad at you."

"I'm sorry, but you can't stay downstairs with Kenny any longer tonight."

Kristen pulled Emmy into her bedroom.

"Will you unzip my dress, Kristen? I can't reach it now."

"Turn around, and I'll help you. You do look so pretty in this dress, Em. Did you pick it out, or did Kenny?"

"I don't remember." Emmy pulled the dress off of her shoulders, and then turned to face Kristen. "I'll never look as pretty as you, Krissy. You are the prettiest girl in the world."

"You drank too much wine tonight." Kristen wagged a finger at Emmy. "You don't even realize how pretty you are. That's the amazing thing about you, Emmy. You are absolutely adorable."

"I forgot to tell Kenny something. I need to go back downstairs."

Emmy tried to get away, but Kristen grabbed her arm.

"Oh, no, you don't. You are staying right here if I have to lock you in your room?"

"Okay, if I have to."

Kristen hugged Emmy, and then went to her room. Emmy got ready for bed. She said a quick prayer for the guys to have a safe trip home and fell into bed. Kristen fell asleep easily, but Emmy tossed and turned. Kenny only stayed up a few more minutes before he called it a night. He changed clothes and debated whether or not to use the tent. He decided to camp out again since it was such a pleasant night—not too hot or humid with a cool breeze blowing through the trees in the backyard. He crawled into the tent and fell asleep within five minutes.

After two hours of tossing and turning in bed, Emmy got up. She glanced in the guest bedroom to see if Kenny decided to sleep inside. She didn't see him there, so she went downstairs. She checked the living room and the TV room. No Kenny. She assumed he must be in the tent and decided to go outside. She grabbed a bottle of water from the fridge and walked out the back door. She opened the tent, slipped inside and saw Kenny lying on top of the sleeping bags. She softly called out his name, "Kenny." Emmy hesitated for a moment, and then reached out.

Kenny woke up as she touched his shoulder. "Emmy, are you all right? Is there something wrong?"

"I couldn't sleep. I'm sorry I woke you up."

"It's okay, Em. What's keeping you awake?"

"I don't know. I just couldn't settle down. My mind won't shut off, and I keep thinking about stuff. I kept rolling all over the bed."

"Is it because of the wine you drank for dinner?"

"No, that's not bothering me. I guess I'm just tense for some reason."

"I think you need a back rub, Em. Turn around and let me massage your shoulders for you."

Emmy turned her back to Kenny as she sat in the tent. He moved behind her and began to massage her shoulders and neck.

"You're really tense and all knotted up. Take deep breaths and try to relax."

Emmy relaxed a little as Kenny massaged her.

"How's that? Do you feel better?"

"Yes, thank you, Kenny."

"You're welcome, Em."

She turned to face him. The center of the tent was high enough for them to sit up. Emmy kept her back to the entryway and Kenny sat facing her. Neither one spoke for a moment.

216

"I need to listen to some of the tracks from the CD tomorrow. You wanna go with me?"

"Sure. That would be fun. What time are you going?"

"I need to be at the studio at noon to meet the guys. It shouldn't take too long. Couple of hours, tops."

"Okay, I'll go. Do you want a neck and shoulder rub, too?" Emmy asked. "It sure felt good to me."

"Okay, let me turn around and move back toward you."

"Take off your shirt, too."

"You didn't. Why do I have to?"

Emmy thought, *I would have if you had asked.* But she didn't tell him. "I couldn't because I'm a girl. Remember?"

"I'm teasing, Em. I know you're a girl—a very pretty girl."

Kenny took off his shirt, and Emmy massaged his shoulders and neck.

"How's that? Feel better?"

Kenny turned to face Emmy. "I liked that. Did you ever do that for Tony?"

"I would try, but he's so muscular. My hands aren't strong enough to do much with him. He gets a massage after practice everyday. It helps him recover quicker."

Emmy stopped talking and looked at Kenny.

"What is it, Em? You can tell me."

"Can I stay with you again? It's cooler out here, and I might be able to fall asleep."

"I suppose it's all right. I brought a light blanket out with me because I thought it might be too warm inside the bag. You can use it unless you want to get in the bag."

"You're right. It might be too warm in there. These sleeping bags are more for wintertime. I'll stay on top like you."

They talked for a few more minutes, and then lay down. Kenny covered Emmy with the light blanket.

"Good night, Em. I hope you can sleep now."

"Me, too. Night, Kenny. See you in the morning."

Chapter Twenty-Four

Kristen slapped at her alarm clock when it went off at six thirty. She hit the snooze button for five more minutes in bed. Five minutes later, she hit it again. This time when the alarm sounded, she needed to get up. She dragged herself out of bed and into the bathroom. After that she looked in Emmy's room, but didn't see her in bed. Kristen smiled thinking Emmy got up to fix breakfast for them. Kristen headed downstairs to the kitchen, but there was no sign of Emmy, or any breakfast. She didn't look in the spare bedroom to see if Kenny had slept inside. Kristen grabbed her jacket which hung by the back door. Barefoot with only her jacket on over her nightclothes, she gingerly walked outside. She opened the tent, peeked inside and saw Emmy and Kenny still zonked on top of the sleeping bags. Kenny didn't have on his shirt. Emmy lay under a blanket. Kristen could only see Emmy's head and her bare legs as she slept with a foot and part of her leg on top of Kenny's leg. Kristen quietly closed the tent and slipped back into the house. She started the coffee and grabbed a bowl for cereal. Ten minutes later the back door opened and in walked Kenny.

Kristen stared at him for a moment before speaking, "I made some coffee if you want any."

"Thanks, Kristen. I could use a cup."

"I saw you guys in the tent. Why didn't she sleep in her room?" Kristen asked as she frowned.

"She came outside during the night because she couldn't sleep. She was wound up about something—all tense. I gave her a shoulder and neck rub to relax her and eventually she got to sleep."

"Is she still sleeping?" Kristen poured Kenny a cup.

"I didn't want to wake her, so I tried to be quiet."

"I wonder what was keeping her awake?"

"I don't know for sure. Has she been arguing with her mother again? Did she get mad at Tony for something? I know she still gets mad at him."

"Sometimes I think she worries about..." Kristen paused, not sure if she should continue. "She worries about sex and having a baby. She's afraid no one will like her if she can't have a baby."

218

"She doesn't need to worry about that."

Kristen looked at Kenny.

"She told me what the doctor said. I know all about it."

Kenny and Kristen were sitting at the table drinking their coffee when Emmy walked in the back door wrapped in the blanket.

Kristen saw her first. "You woke up. I thought you would sleep all morning, Em."

"I couldn't sleep last night so I went outside."

"Kenny told me. Do you want some coffee or cereal?"

"No thanks. I need to pee. Then I'm going back to bed for a while longer. What time are you leaving? The usual time?"

"Yeah. You don't have to get up. You can sleep. I'll see you this evening."

"The guys are coming home tonight. Are you anxious to see John?" Emmy asked.

"Who?" Kristen joked.

"Very funny. Maybe they can crash here tonight."

"Where will they sleep?" Kristen looked at Kenny as she asked.

"John can have your room, and you can sleep with me. Tony can stay in the guest room."

"What about Kenny?" Kristen asked.

"I'm going home. I need to sleep in my own bed. Two nights of camping is all I can take," he said.

Kristen went to work. Emmy went upstairs to bed. Kenny got dressed and read until Emmy came downstairs at ten, still in her pajamas with her hair tangled and sticking out in all directions.

"Hi, sleepyhead. Did you get enough sleep?" Kenny asked.

"I guess so. Is there any coffee made?"

"I can make you some if you'd like."

"Thank you, Kenny. Do I look horrible?"

"You look adorable. Your hair is a mess, and you're in your pajamas. Anyone would love seeing you like this every morning. If he's smart enough to marry you, that is."

"You're so sweet. Did I tell you thanks for the massage last night? I needed that."

219

"Yes, you did, and thank you for the returning the favor. It helped my shoulders."

"Can I still go with you to the studio?"

"If you get ready in time. I need to be there at noon."

"It won't take me long to get ready. I'll throw some clothes on over my pj's and put my hair in a ponytail. Maybe I should cut it off. How do you think I would look with short hair?"

"It was curly when you were a kid."

"It would probably still be like that. Maybe one of these days I'll cut it."

Kenny made some fresh coffee, and he and Emmy sat in the kitchen and talked.

"Are you happy that the guys are coming home tonight? Do you think Kristen missed John? Did you miss Tony?"

"You know Kristen misses John when he's not around. She can't wait to see him. I hope they come here first before he goes home. If it's too late at night, he might just go home, and she won't see him until tomorrow."

"I have a feeling he will stop here first, Em. I know I would if I were in his shoes." Kenny asked again, "Did you miss Tony?"

"I miss him, but not the same way Kristen misses John." She waited a second before adding, "And not like I miss you."

Emmy listened to some of the tracks from the new CD at Steward Sound with three of the guys from Fridays At Five. Dave had taken his family on vacation to Montana, but Kenny, Jeff and Jeremy were there. Will Consoli leaned back in his black leather chair behind the mixing console as they listened to the finalized versions of the songs.

"Well, what do you think, Emmy? Sound okay to you?"

"I like it. It has a different feel and sound to it."

"This is the title track. See what you think."

Emmy listened to the title cut "The Ballad Of Johnny March" over and over.

"That's got to be a big hit. I might even buy a copy."

"It must be good if you're going to part with some of your hard earned cash," Jeff teased.

Emmy grinned and then put her hands together as if

praying. "Will you guys autograph it for me if I buy one?"

"That'll cost you, Em. We don't sign autographs for just anyone." Jeremy laughed as he grabbed her hands.

"Please! Pretty please! I'll be ever so grateful."

Emmy teased the guys. She knew they would do about anything for her. They listened to the track "Oh Lonesome Train"—the track where Emmy added background vocals.

"I love that little phrase you add there. It fits perfectly with the feel of the track," Jeff said.

"Thanks. I appreciate you guys letting me sing on your CD. Am I a partner in the group now?" Emmy asked and then giggled.

After the visit to the studio, Kenny and Emmy ate a late lunch at Darby's. They returned to her house, and Emmy began to clean. She made all the beds and cleaned the kitchen. She scrubbed the bathrooms until they gleamed. Kenny watched as she rushed around.

"Relax, Em. The house looks all right. You're going to be a nervous wreck by the time the guys get here."

"I can't sit still and do nothing. I need to burn off this energy somehow."

"Wanna play tennis?" Kenny waved his arm as if hitting a tennis ball. "Go for a run or something?"

"How about both? First some tennis, and then a run. If you think you can keep up with me."

"I'll give it a shot."

They played tennis for an hour, and then decided to go for a run.

"Do you know the loop I usually run? It's just over a mile." Emmy asked as they dropped the tennis racquets off at the house.

"Yeah, I think I remember the way."

"Feel like a bet?"

"What have you got in mind?"

Emmy grinned at Kenny and said, "Loser has to give the winner a massage."

"Okay, deal. I could use a good massage."

"Finish line is the front porch steps. I'll be waiting there."

"Big talk from a little girl. We'll see how it goes."

They took off together, and it soon became apparent to Kenny he would not win. Sure enough, Emmy sat on the front steps as he came huffing and puffing the last few feet. He plopped down beside Emmy and tried to catch his breath.

"You're not even breathing hard," he said. "Did you even break a sweat?"

She patted his back. "Are you going to be all right, old man?"

"I need some oxygen. I didn't realize how out of shape I am. I better start running before the tour starts."

"I'm going to take a shower. Then I'll be wanting that massage."

They both showered and changed clothes. Emmy lay on her stomach reading a book as Kenny knocked on her bedroom door.

"I'm ready, Kenny. You can come in." She marked her place, closed the book and scooted to the edge of the bed. "You can start with my legs. You do know how to do a proper massage, right?"

"I think I might know, but I'm sure you'll correct me if I screw up," Kenny said as he massaged Emmy's legs. "I'm not sure if I lost the bet or not."

She rolled over onto her back and smiled back at him. "I'll rub your shoulders and neck after you finish me."

"What about my legs?"

"That will cost you extra."

They finished the massages and went downstairs. As they reached the kitchen Emmy heard a vehicle pull into the driveway. She looked out the window and screamed, "They're here! They're home early!" She dashed out the back door and waited for Tony to get out of the truck.

"Did you miss me, Emmy?" Tony asked.

She grinned and said, "Oh, were you gone?"

Kenny followed her outside at a more sedate pace, and at that moment, Kristen pulled into the driveway and parked. She saw the guys and came over to see John. He put an arm around her waist and rested his hand on her hip.

"Did you have a good trip?" Kristen asked.

"Yeah, except for the transmission problem."

"Aren't you going to kiss him, Kristen? I know you want him to kiss you," Emmy teased.

John reached down to kiss Kristen.

Tony saw Kenny and shook hands with him. "Hi, Kenny, did she drive you nuts the last couple of days?"

"Not quite, but almost."

"I did not drive you nuts, Kenneth Travis Colwell. You enjoyed being with me. You might not admit it, but you did."

"I'm not afraid to admit it. Kristen and I got along great."

Emmy stuck her tongue out at Kenny.

"I didn't think you would get here until around ten," Emmy told Tony.

"Do you want me to go away? We could go to my house and hang out there until later, and then come over to see you."

"Oh, no you don't. You're not going anywhere," Kristen said as she stopped kissing John.

"Is there anything to eat? We haven't eaten since noon. I could eat a horse."

They went into the house, and Emmy and Kenny whipped up something for dinner. Kristen did her part—she set the table and got the guys something to drink.

"Come and get it, guys. Dinner's ready." Emmy set a pot of spaghetti on the table along with salad and garlic bread.

Emmy prayed for the meal, and the guys dug in.

"So what have you guys been up to while we were gone? Did you go camping in the backyard?" Tony asked between bites of spaghetti.

"Kenny and I did, but Kristen was too afraid there would be bugs."

"I wasn't afraid of bugs. I just happen to like sleeping in my comfortable bed better than on the hard ground."

"She's afraid of bugs," Emmy teased.

"Did she let you get any sleep, Kenny, or did she keep you up all night?" Tony asked. *Shoot! Maybe I shouldn't have asked that. I don't really want to know what they were doing.*

Kenny didn't hesitate to answer. "We stayed up pretty late.

223

Like when we were kids. We talked until she ran out of things to talk about."

"How's your back today?" Tony asked.

"Actually, it wasn't that bad in the tent. Since Kristen wasn't using it, we opened up the third sleeping bag and put the other two on top of it. Not that I want to make a habit of sleeping in a tent, but it brought back some good memories." Kenny smiled at Emmy.

Emmy and Kristen told the guys about their days. Tony told them about the truck, and how they were lucky it happened in town and not out on the highway somewhere. John thought it a little strange that Kenny and Emmy shared a tent overnight. He knew what would happen if he and Kristen shared a tent, or even a bedroom for the night. But it didn't appear to bother Tony at all.

"Are you going to stay here tonight, Tony?" Emmy asked. "The tent is still set up."

"Emmy! You can't sleep in the tent with Tony," Kristen said.

"Why not? I did with Kenny and nothing happened."

Kristen didn't know what to say for a moment. She thought if Emmy and Kenny could share a tent without doing anything, then Emmy and Tony probably could as well. But instead she said, "That's different, Em."

"Duh! I know that," Emmy said.

Kenny stared at Emmy and rolled his eyes.

"Emmy, I can't sleep in the tent with you. I have to help John unload his stuff, and then he's taking me home." He paused for a moment. "I haven't been camping since I was twelve. Derrick and I went fishing with Uncle Daniel and Uncle Carmen in the upper peninsula of Michigan. We might be back in the morning to see you."

"I knew you wouldn't say yes, and I wasn't really going to share the tent with you. I'm not that naive."

"I gotta go," Kenny said after dinner. "Thanks for everything. We'll have to do it again some year." Kenny grabbed his gear, and Emmy walked out with him.

"Oh crap! I forgot you don't have your car here." Emmy

224

slapped her forehead. "Let me grab my keys, and I'll give you a ride home."

"I can walk. It's only a few hundred miles," he joked.

"Very funny. I'll be right back." Emmy ran into the house. "Kristen, can I take your car. I need to run Kenny home. I forgot he doesn't have his car with him."

"You might need to put gas in it, Em. It's kinda low. I was going to fill it up later."

"I'll fill it up for you. Where's Tony?"

"They're in the TV room."

Emmy ran to the TV room and jumped onto the couch between John and Tony.

"I've got to run Kenny home. Will you still be here when I get back? Are you going to spend the night?"

"No, Em, I can't spend the night here. We're gonna leave in a few minutes," Tony said.

"Will you at least call me later if you can?"

"Maybe, but I'm not going to guarantee anything."

She poked Tony in the ribs. "That's all right. You don't have to call me. I've seen enough of you for the day." She jumped up before he could retaliate and ran back outside. "Kristen said I could take her car. I just need to fill it up for her."

"I can do that for you, Em," Kenny offered.

"Don't be silly. We can buy our own gas. It's not like it's three bucks a gallon."

Emmy stopped and filled Kristen's car for her before taking Kenny home. His parents were back, so Emmy went in to see them. She ended up staying later than she planned.

"Let's go get some ice cream, Emmy," Kenny suggested. "I could use a hot fudge sundae."

"Okay, I'll get a strawberry sundae, and we can share."

"Do you want to come with us?" Kenny asked his parents.

Mr. Colwell stood up from his recliner. "I'll go. I have a taste for a turtle sundae."

"I can make sundaes for us here, Carter," Mrs. Colwell said. "Or a milkshake if you'd rather have that."

"How about a chocolate banana shake?" Mr. Colwell took

225

Mrs. Colwell's hand and they walked into the kitchen.

"I guess it's just you and me, Em," Kenny said.

They drove over to the Dairy Queen and placed their order.

"Can I have a taste of yours, Kenny?"

"Of course you can." Kenny gave Emmy a spoonful of his sundae.

"Do you want to taste mine?" Emmy asked.

"If you'll share."

Emmy gave Kenny a taste of hers. They took turns feeding each other like two kids on their first date.

"You've got some fudge on your mouth, Em."

"Can you wipe it off for me, please?"

Kenny wiped the corner of her mouth with his finger, then Emmy grabbed his hand and licked his finger. She giggled, and then put some ice cream on his nose. She looked at Kenny and he smiled. Emmy moved close and licked the ice cream off his nose. Then she kissed him there.

"Are you going to put ice cream on my nose?"

"And waste a bite of good ice cream. No way!"

Emmy stuck out her tongue.

"I'll put some on your tongue if you keep it out."

Emmy stuck out her tongue again and Kenny put some ice cream on it. She swallowed the ice cream and stuck out her tongue again. Kenny looked at Emmy and began to laugh as he imagined Emmy as a young girl.

"More please."

"You're like a baby bird always wanting more food. Should I see if I can find any worms?"

"Yuck! I'm glad I'm not a bird. May I have another bite, please."

"I'm glad I got a large."

"Don't you like sharing with me, Kenny?"

"As long as I don't have to share your tent again tonight."

Emmy looked at Kenny with dismay all over her face. "I thought you liked that."

"You know I did. I'm just teasing you, Em. It was fun to relive old times like that. Even if you did kick me last night."

"Did I really? I'm sorry."

"You move around a lot when you sleep, Em."

"I guess now that I don't have to share my bed with anyone, like I did as a kid, I'm used to spreading out."

"You woke me up once by putting your arm on top of my head."

Emmy laughed.

"And later I lay on my back and you moved up against my side on your back, and you rolled over almost on top of me. You rested your head on my chest and your leg on top of mine. You didn't even wake up so I let you stay there until you moved again."

"What will I do when I get married?" Emmy asked as she grinned.

"Separate bedrooms is the only answer, Em. On opposite ends of the house if at all possible," Kenny said with a straight face.

She smiled but then bit her lip. "Would you want that if we were married?"

Kenny looked at Emmy. For a moment he thought about what she asked. He tried to think of something clever and funny, but couldn't. "Not a chance."

Two hours later, Emmy pulled into the driveway and walked in the back door.

"Where have you been? I was starting to get worried about you, Em." Kristen shouted as she ran from the TV room into the kitchen .

"We stopped by his parents' house and talked to them for a while."

"Yes, and after that?"

"We went out for ice cream and lost track of time. I knew the guys wouldn't be here. Then I dropped Kenny off."

Kristen put her hands on Emmy's shoulders and looked at her. "Are you having sex with Kenny Colwell again? Tell me the truth."

"No! I'm not having sex with him," Emmy answered immediately and with conviction. *What do you mean by again?*

"I know you're in love with him, and you want to have a

baby to prove your doctor wrong."

They looked at each other. Emmy thought about Kristen's question again. "Yes, I still love him," she whispered. "Maybe I do want to prove my doctor is wrong a little."

Kristen hugged Emmy as she began to cry.

"Oh, Em. What are you going to do? You haven't told Kenny have you?"

"No, of course not. I didn't even know until just now. Oh, crap. What have I done, Krissy?"

"Hopefully nothing."

Emmy bit her lip as she remembered what happened at the Dairy Queen.

"Emily Olivia! Did you...?"

"No! We... I'm glad you're so smart, Kristen."

"At least you realize it now, Em. Do you think he is in love with you again?"

"He loves me. I know that."

"But does he want to have a baby right now?"

"No, a baby would change everything. I know I want to be married before I... have a baby."

"Tony might get mad at me for saying this, but he loves you, too."

"I know. When I brought Tony home from Mr. Robertson's office, he told me that he wanted to spend all his nights with me. So I know how Tony feels."

"But you don't feel the same way about him anymore. I know you did at one time. When you first met, you were hopelessly in love with each other."

"I know, and I blew it because of... sex. I mean not having sex..."

"I know all about it. Then when you tried getting back together after Kenny met Becky, Tony blew it by sleeping with that girl at school."

"Did you know about her before I did?"

Kristen looked at Emmy and sighed. "I guess it doesn't matter now, but yeah, I knew about her. Tony confided in me, but he swore me to secrecy."

228

"You knew he was sleeping with her and didn't tell me. Why?" Emmy frowned.

"No! No! No!" Kristen waved her hands. "I knew he was dating Brenda. I didn't know they slept together until you told me." Kristen crossed her heart. "I swear."

"Were they falling in love with each other?"

"I think Tony really liked her, but she just used him."

"Oh, Krissy, what am I gonna do. When I'm with Tony we fight and argue, and he drives me crazy at times. It's like things are great when we're *in love*, but then things start to change. It's like we are either at one end or the other. We either are madly in love, or else we hate each other. With Kenny it's different. We're not just friends. It's more than that. He's like my safe place. A person I can be with and feel safe and secure."

"And loved?"

"Yes! I know he loves me no matter what." Emmy jumped onto the kitchen counter.

"If he was older, I would say he's the father you always wanted."

"Maybe an older brother. That makes more sense to me." Emmy managed a soft laugh.

Kristen put her hands on Emmy's knees. "You have never thought of either of those two as a brother. If it wasn't illegal, you would marry them both."

"Didn't some of the kings in the Bible have more than one wife. I think I read that King David and King Solomon had lots of wives. Maybe I can have two husbands."

"You know you have to choose, right?"

"I want to spend my life with Kenny," Emmy said softly.

"Are you telling me, or are you trying to convince yourself?"

Emmy bit her lip as she looked at Kristen.

Chapter Twenty-Five

"Emmy, would you help me with something?" Kenny asked over the phone on Thursday evening.

"Depends," she said. "I have to leave for rehearsal in a few minutes."

"The tour starts in September, and I need to get in shape. I want to start running in the mornings, and I thought you might run with me. That way we could push each other. You like to treat every run like a race."

"Do you think you can keep up with me? You're not Tony," she said and then laughed. "When do you want to start?"

"Tomorrow."

"Okay, but you have to come over here. I'm not getting up early and driving to your place."

"I thought it would be better to run through your neighborhood. We already have our loop."

"Okay, but you better be able to keep up," she teased.

He arrived at her house at six thirty. Emmy was already waiting in the kitchen.

"Are you ready to go, Em? I'm going to beat you today."

Emmy laughed. "I doubt that very much. Give me two minutes, please." She ran upstairs to Kristen's room.

"Are you going to run with us?" Emmy sat on the edge of Kristen's bed. "Kenny is here, and we're about ready to go."

"Will you wait for me? I need five minutes to be ready."

"We'll be in the kitchen."

"I'll hurry up." Kristen threw off her covers and got out of bed.

Emmy ran back downstairs and into the kitchen. She sat at the table with Kenny. "She will be ready in five, and I need to talk to you."

"Sure, Em. What is it?" He checked the bowl of fruit on the table and grabbed a banana. *I know where this is going. We shouldn't have made out like we did.*

"I had fun at the Dairy Queen last night." She thought

about last night. *Boy, did I.*

"So did I. I'm sorry I kept you out so late."

"That's all right. We weren't out all that late." She bit her lip. *I know you're going to get mad at me.*

Kenny peeled the banana and took a bite. "Tell me, Em."

"Kristen asked me if I wanted to have a baby with you, and I realized that maybe I did." She split off some of the banana and bit into it. "She thinks I want to prove my doctor is wrong."

"But we... Oh, Em. We can't have a baby."

"We would have to do more than we did last night for it to even be possible. I do know how babies are conceived."

"Yeah, tell me. We're lucky we were still at the Dairy Queen and not parked on a dark street somewhere."

"I know where Diane used to park when she wanted to make out," Emmy said. "We could have gone there."

"I know she used to park on Campbell Street, or in the alley behind the carriage house," Kenny said. "I saw her once in a car with someone, and I don't think it was Craig."

"She used to tell me about it," Emmy remembered. "But if we continue... you know... with what we started last night, one of these times we won't stop. We can try to justify it by saying we love each other. Lots of couples do."

"I do love you, Em. More than anyone else I know, but I'm not ready to get married and have a family. Not yet." *I would marry you tomorrow if you wanted.* He wished he had a ring in his pocket. "Maybe in a few years the time will be right to start a family."

"You do love me though?" Emmy asked as she took the rest of the banana. *You better after last night.*

"Ever since you held my hand to cross the street on the way to Roosevelt High. At times it's been just love between friends, but I've always loved you. I think I loved you when we were just kids, but I didn't realize it."

"I don't want to lose your love, Kenny. I don't know what I would do if you weren't there. I understand you have the band and will be gone a lot of the time, but you're only an email away."

"You won't ever lose my love, Emmy. We might not see

231

each other much at times, but I will still love you."

Kristen stood around the corner on the last step of the stairs and heard Emmy and Kenny talking. She came into the kitchen, stood behind Emmy and squeezed her shoulders.

Emmy looked over her shoulder at Kristen. "Did you hear what we were talking about? Are you mad at me?"

"I'm not mad at you, Em. You guys have a special relationship. You are more than just ordinary lovers. You are best friends." Kristen waited for a reaction, but it never came. "I love you like a sister, Emmy, and you need to hear this. If Tony was not still in the picture, things might be different. You and Kenny would be together and that would be great, but since Tony's here and you love him, too, you guys need to cool your jets. I didn't think it was right for you to sleep in the tent together. I mean I really, really didn't think it was right."

"But nothing happened," Emmy said defensively. "Certainly not as much as what happened last night."

"Maybe not this time, but it might in the future. You just admitted that yourself. I don't know just what you guys did last night, but I can imagine."

"We were in the parking lot at the Dairy Queen, Krissy." Emmy held up her hands. "How much could we have done, huh?"

"Well, I'm sure it's happened before."

Emmy looked at Kenny and bit her lip. "You have a bigger back seat than Kenny's car."

Kristen rolled her eyes. "I don't want to hear anymore about last night. Geez, Em! My car? Why?"

Emmy shrugged.

Kristen squeezed Emmy's shoulders harder. "I should have been more forceful and vocal about the tent issue, but I wasn't. You and Kenny have been friends for so many years. He knows you better than anyone. He knows all your secrets, and you probably know his. I'm not saying you shouldn't see each other or anything because that wouldn't be right, either. I know you love each other, but you know neither one of you is ready to get married and start a family. You might want to get married for the sex."

Emmy bit her lip as she looked at Kenny.

232

"I don't blame you for wanting that. If we weren't Christians, who are supposed to know better, I think you guys would be sleeping together all the time. I hope you're not." Kristen paused and stared at Emmy, who didn't change her expression. "Oh, Emmy. This is harder to say than I imagined. I want you to be happy, and I want Kenny to be happy, too. I want Tony to be happy." Kristen started to cry.

"Don't cry, Krissy. I'm not going to run off and get married just so I can have sex without feeling guilty." Emmy bit her lip. *That didn't come out exactly right.*

Kristen let go of Emmy and looked at Kenny. "I want everyone to be happy, but that isn't possible. I think that spending all this time with each other while you're on vacation has turned your heads a little. Do you still love me, Em?"

"Oh, Krissy. I love you more than a sister." Emmy stood up and hugged Kristen. "You're right. I got carried away because Kenny and I were doing all the fun things together."

Kenny watched, and then Emmy and Kristen turned to face him.

"Oh, Kenny, I love you so much. I do want to have your baby, if I'm ever able to have a baby, but not yet. Neither one of us is ready for that." She rested her head against his chest. "I'm sorry I almost ruined things. Will you forgive me?"

"There's nothing to forgive, Em, but just to make you happy, I will. I forgive you. Do you forgive me? I should have known better. I think I was enjoying... being with you, and I didn't realize how much we were flirting with... disaster." He looked at Kristen and wondered what she really thought. *I know you think Emmy and I have already slept together. It's true that we have, but we haven't had sex.*

Emmy hugged Kenny.

He kissed the top of her head and then said, "Since we're all up and ready. I think we should go for that run now. What do you guys say?"

Emmy grinned and said, "I say the last one around the loop buys breakfast."

"You're only saying that because you know you'll win."

Kristen made a face at Emmy. "You should give me a head start."

"I'll give you a ten second lead. How's that?"

"That's not enough," Kristen complained.

"How about I agree to buy breakfast if we all finish the loop without having to walk," Kenny said.

"All right, but you can still have a head start, Krissy."

This time Emmy had to push herself to beat Kenny.

"That was pretty close, Em." Kenny felt better today. "By the end of the week, I'm gonna beat you."

"We'll see about that. Maybe I let you stay close today." Emmy's heart pounded and she had trouble catching her breath.

Kristen struggled at the end. Emmy and Kenny waited on the front steps.

"Come on, Krissy! You can do it! You're almost there." Emmy jumped up and down as she clapped her hands.

Kristen made it to the steps.

"I did it! I ran the whole way." Kristen high-fived Kenny, and then hugged Emmy. "I slowed down a few times, but I never stopped running."

"Good job! Let's get changed so Kenny can take us out for breakfast. Let's go somewhere expensive," Emmy suggested.

"All I can afford is McDonald's." Kenny pulled his pockets inside out. "I don't have much money."

"Why is it that I don't believe you, Mr. Colwell?" Emmy put her hands on her hips and tried to keep a straight face.

"Maybe I can afford Patty's Pancake Palace."

Emmy giggled and then said, "I want boo-berry pancakes. Five of them!"

"You can't eat five pancakes, Emmy." Kristen's heart finally slowed to a normal pace.

"I can now. I'm eating for two, remember?" Emmy joked.

Chapter Twenty-Six

Emmy and Kristen needed to be at church at seven on Sunday morning to go over final preparations for the second recording session. At six forty-five Emmy woke up and looked at the clock.

"Oh, no! Kristen! We gotta get up. We're going to be late. Kenny will kill us. Are you awake?" Emmy hollered as she ran into Kristen's room and woke her up. "We overslept. It's a quarter to seven already."

Kristen jumped out of bed.

"You can shower first. Do you know what you're gonna wear?" Emmy asked.

"That dress on the closet door. I'll hurry, Em."

Somehow Emmy and Kristen managed to get ready and out the door in thirty minutes. Emmy called Kenny's cell phone.

"Emmy, where are you guys?"

"I'm sorry we're running late. My alarm didn't go off, or if it did, I didn't hear it. We'll be there in ten or fifteen minutes."

"Slow down, Em. We will have enough time to go through everything. I don't want you to get a ticket, or have an accident."

"See you as soon as we can." Emmy gunned it through a yellow light.

It's a good thing this is Sunday, and there isn't any traffic, Em. Kristen thought.

Emmy and Kristen made it to the church without being pulled over for speeding. They rushed into the sanctuary and joined the rest of the team. They were out of breath as they sat behind everyone else. Kenny glanced at his watch, frowned at Emmy, but then continued talking to the worship team about today's session.

"If you make a mistake, don't worry about it. Just keep playing. We can fix it in the studio if it needs to be corrected. This is a live session and mistakes happen. Sometimes the CD sounds better and feels more like a live concert. We won't do any overdubbing unless it's absolutely necessary. Any questions?"

"Have you listened to Sunday's session yet?" Chase asked.

Kenny nodded. "Will and I listened to most of it. It actually sounds pretty good even in the rough mix. Once we really mix it, I think you will like the result."

They ran through at least a verse or two of the songs. There were some new songs in today's set. Kenny wanted to do a couple of songs over. He wasn't totally satisfied with the previous Sunday's recording.

Everyone gathered in the music room, and Pastor Chase led them in prayer. As the worship team left the music room, Kenny walked next to Emmy. He grabbed her hand and squeezed it for a moment. She smiled at him.

This recording session ran smoother. The guys in the band relaxed and played just like they would on a normal Sunday. Kenny played guitar to fill in some spots. He stayed in the background except for a guitar solo during one song. He sang background vocals and did a duet with Emmy on "I Will Be True To You." This week Pastor Herb actually got to preach. He prepared a condensed message. The church took another special offering for the Garcia family. Juanita and her brother Hector, had returned to Mexico City, but Emmy gave their address to the church treasurer.

After the service Emmy and Kristen said goodbye to Kenny and Tony.

"Kenny, is it all right if I run over to Mama's to have lunch and see the guys off to camp?" Emmy asked.

"I don't mind. In fact, I needed to tell you that Will and I are going over to the studio to listen to the recordings. Maybe we can have dinner later at my parents' house."

"Okay, I'll call you." Emmy kissed Kenny quickly.

Emmy and Kristen rushed home to change clothes before they headed over to Mama's house. The guys wanted to leave for training camp at two.

"Will you slow down?" Kristen put her hands on the dash. "It's a good thing Kenny never bought you a sports car if this is how you drive a Civic. You'd be getting pulled over all the time."

"I'm only going ten miles over the limit," Emmy said as she took a corner without slowing down much.

Kristen glanced at the speedometer. "I don't think the speed limit is forty miles-an-hour on this street, Em. Or anywhere in the Hampshire Park neighborhood."

Emmy parked in the driveway and jumped out of the car as soon as it stopped. "We made it without getting stopped."

"You're lucky, Em. One of these days your luck will run out." Kristen shook her head.

Emmy ran in the back door and nearly collided with Mama in the kitchen. "Sorry, Mama. Where's Tony?"

"I believe he's in his room finishing up packing."

"Thanks, Mama. Something smells good," Emmy hollered as she ran out of the kitchen and flew up the stairs.

Kristen walked in without being in a big hurry and saw Mama, "Hi, Mama. How are you doing?"

"I'm fine, Kristen. I'm just making lunch. Tony wanted mostaccioli. What's up with Emmy? She ran through here like a tornado."

"She wanted to talk to Tony about something."

John jumped up from the recliner in the living room. He hurried into the kitchen when he heard Kristen.

"Hi, Kristen. How did everything go today? You were recording, right?"

Kristen walked over to John and kissed him. "As far as I know, everything went smoothly. We didn't have much of a chance to talk to Kenny after the service. Emmy practically sprinted out of the church to get over here."

"The little thing almost knocked me over," Mama said. "She really wanted to see Tony for some reason."

"She's like a little kid when she gets excited. You know that, Mama." Kristen wondered. *Why are you in such a hurry to see Tony? You've been kissing and whatever with Kenny, so it can't be that.*

At this moment Emmy was sitting on her knees on Tony's bed watching as he finished packing.

"Kenny made us record a couple of the songs over from last week, but most of the songs were different. We did 'Yolanda's Song' again, but not at the end like last week. I can't wait to listen

237

to the tapes. Kenny said we can listen to them later this week at the studio... and we can..."

Tony moved over and grabbed Emmy's hands and held them. "I was there, Em. You don't have to tell me."

She stopped talking and sat quietly for a moment.

"Did you pack enough socks? What about t-shirts? Did you pack enough..."

"Emmy, this is not my first time away from home. I think I know by now what I need to take with me." Tony put a finger on her mouth to shush her. "I've just about got everything. Will you carry the small case downstairs for me?"

"Okay, I'm sorry."

Tony smiled at her. "I know you are excited, Em."

"I suppose it's because it's finally sinking in that you are really playing for the Bears. I never believed I would actually know a real celebrity."

Tony stared at her and then shook his head. "Duh! You do know that Kenny is a real rock star, right?"

"Oh, yeah, I keep forgetting about that."

"You're goofy, Em." Tony laughed. "Help me get this stuff in the car, please. I think lunch is almost ready."

Emmy helped Tony carry his suitcases to the car. John's and Tony's gear pretty much packed the 1995 Chevy Lumina.

"Tony, I know you recently spent money on this car, but have you ever thought of getting something newer, or bigger?" she asked as she hopped up on the trunk.

"Actually, I thought maybe I could see about a new car when I get back from camp. I bought this because I needed something cheap after the accident that totaled my other car. Do you think it would be all right if I spent some of my signing bonus? I don't want to spend it foolishly."

"I think it would be all right. The other players might make fun of you for driving this old thing. Maybe you could sell it to Barry. He's always buying junky cars."

He tickled her knees. "You're so funny, Emmy."

She swatted his hands away. "Do you have any idea of what kind of car you would like? Maybe you could buy a fancy sports car or a big Cadillac."

"I've been thinking about an SUV. Maybe when I get back we could go shopping together."

"Okay, Kenny and I will do some research while you're gone." She giggled and then said, "I'd love to help you spend your money."

Tony turned to walk back into the house.

"Give me a piggyback ride," she ordered, but then added, "Please."

"No, Em, I can't."

"Why not?"

"Because I just can't."

She teased him, "Are you too weak? Maybe I should carry you instead."

"Fine." He sighed and grabbed her legs as she jumped onto his back. "You are such a brat sometimes."

"I know, but you're still my friend, right?"

"If I have to be." He shook his head.

Mama called everyone into the kitchen. Emmy said a prayer, and they started eating. Thirty minutes later, Tony and John pushed their chairs back from the table. Tony patted his stomach, sighed and said, "I love your mostaccioli, Mama."

"You love everything Mama makes," Emmy said.

Emmy and Kristen had been watching them eat for the last ten minutes—still amazed by how much the guys could put away.

"Do you guys want any dessert? Like a gallon of ice cream, or maybe a couple of apples pies?" Kristen asked facetiously as Emmy giggled.

"No, thanks, Kristen. I'm full," John answered. "Do you want dessert, Tony?"

"What kind of ice cream do we have?" Tony asked.

"How can you possibly have room for anything else?" Emmy asked. "You had three plates of mostaccioli and nearly a whole loaf of bread."

"We're out of ice cream, anyway," Mama said. "You finished it all last night, and I haven't been to the store to buy anymore."

239

"It's okay, Mama. I really don't need any ice cream. I have to be careful about what I eat now anyway."

Kristen and Emmy exploded with laughter. When they were finally able to talk, Kristen asked Emmy. "Can you imagine how much those huge lineman guys must eat? If these two almost-normal-size guys eat this much, those other guys must eat a ton of food a day."

"They probably buy a whole cow every week," Emmy said.

Tony looked at John, and then asked the girls, "Are you finished now? Have you had your laugh?"

"We're sorry, Tony. We're not making fun of you."

"Yes, we are, Kristen." Emmy giggled again.

"You're gonna get it, Emily Colasanti." Tony waved a fist at her as she took off running from the table.

Emmy ran into the living room and sat on the couch, still giggling. Tony chased her. He grabbed her and pushed her down on her belly. He then sat on her butt so she couldn't move. He tickled the back of her knees. She kicked her feet trying to get him to stop.

"Get off of me, you big horse. I can't move," Emmy squealed as everyone else came into the living room.

Tony grinned and started tickling her sides. By this time, Emmy was in tears from laughing so hard.

"Tony, stop tickling her before she has an accident," Mama said.

"Are you sorry for teasing us, Emmy?" Tony asked.

"Yes. I'm sorry. Please let me up."

"Maybe in a minute. I want to be sure you are sincere in your apology."

"I'm really sorry I made fun of... John," Emmy said as she giggled again.

Tony tickled her knees some more, and she started laughing again. "So, you're sorry you made fun of John, but not me, huh? I guess I will have to keep tickling you then."

Kristen looked at John, and they smiled at each other. They were both too mature for such childish behavior.

"You would think Emmy is ten-years-old by the way she acts some of the time," Kristen said.

John nodded. "Tony is not much different. Although I would say he acts more like a fifteen-year-old kid."

"I grant you that. He does act a bit more maturely than Emmy."

Tony stopped tickling Emmy, and he and Emmy both listened to John and Kristen talking.

"You guys are too serious," Tony said as he got off of Emmy. He smacked her butt playfully as he stood up.

She didn't move and asked, "Are you finished, Tony? I was just starting to have fun."

Kristen whispered to John, just loudly enough for everyone to hear, "It's their way of having foreplay."

"It is not, Kristen Keasling!" Emmy shouted as she jumped up from the couch. "We're just playing around. We're not going to have sex. Take that back!"

Kristen stared at Tony. "I'm just teasing you. I know you're not going to do that—not with him."

"Hey! I wasn't doing anything she didn't want me to do," Tony said. *I like goofing around with her, but I didn't really think of it as foreplay. Maybe it was though.*

As Emmy sat up, Kristen sat next to her. "You may not want to, but I know you are going to wait to have sex... again."

Emmy looked at Kristen and bit her lip.

Kristen stared at Emmy. *You aren't ever going to tell me, are you?*

Mama looked at the clock. "It's almost two. The guys need to get going."

The guys made sure they had everything, and then walked out the back door to Tony's car.

"Thanks for driving, Tony," John said. "I'd be embarrassed to drive my old truck to camp. The veterans will harass us enough as it is."

"Like this old heep is any better. The only thing holding it together is the rust."

Both guys gave Mama a hug before facing the girls.

"We will see you in a couple months," Tony said.

"If you wait two months to see me, don't bother. I will have another boyfriend by then," Kristen responded as she looked up at John.

"Maybe we will see you in a couple weeks then. Will that be all right?" John asked.

"Two weeks. And you better call me every night."

"I think we are only allowed one phone call a week, Kristen."

Oh, my God! Did you just make a joke? Is it possible that John Randolph actually has a sense of humor? Emmy thought.

"It's been nice knowin' ya. See you around sometime—not," Kristen answered back.

"Maybe we can break the rules and call more than once," Tony said.

Emmy teased back, "What was your name again? I seem to have forgotten already."

"That's all right. I deleted your number from my phone," Tony teased Emmy.

She stuck out her tongue and made a face.

"Fine. We'll call every night no matter how much Coach fines us."

Kristen looked at Emmy, and they smiled as they both hugged the guys. After a goodbye kiss for Kristen from John, the guys got in the car and pulled out of the driveway. Mama and the girls watched. Mama stood in the middle with her arms around Emmy and Kristen. She hugged the girls and squeezed Emmy tightly as she began to cry a little.

"It's okay, sweetie, they will be all right, and you will see them soon." Mama kissed the top of Emmy's head.

Kristen rolled her eyes. "You are such a baby, Emmy. And I still think you were having foreplay with Tony."

"Am not! Was not! Take that back, Kristen Lynn Keasling," Emmy shouted as she started to chase Kristen around the yard. "I'm not a baby, and I wasn't having foreplay with Tony."

Mama shook her head as she watched and smiled.

Chapter Twenty-Seven

Training, meetings and hours of study learning the playbook occupied much of the first two weeks of training camp for John and Tony. Emmy and Kristen kept busy with work.

"I got a message from John last night. They have three hours of free time this afternoon," Kristen mentioned to Emmy as they got ready for church. "We could go see them if you want."

"Oh, I don't know, Kristen. I really don't miss John all that much. I mean he's okay and all, but..."

"I want to see John. You should visit Tony."

"Who?"

Kristen gave Emmy a dirty look. "Should I tell him that you're no longer his friend?"

"Oh, that Tony. I suppose I would like to see him. This afternoon, huh? Like they are in prison, and we get to visit them when they have time off for good behavior."

"It could be worse. They could be in prison for real."

"Don't be silly. I doubt they would ever do anything to land in prison, Kristen."

"I was being facetious." Kristen rolled her eyes. "Do you and Kenny have plans for today?"

"Not that I know of," Emmy said. "It's definitely quieter around the house without them around. Do you really miss John?"

"I like it when he comes over for dinner. It gives me something to look forward to after work."

"I did enjoy making dinner for all of us. I got to practice my cooking for four or five people instead of just us."

"Don't you miss Tony a little?"

Emmy grinned. "I miss him because now I have to mow the yard and trim stuff. I could always talk him into doing that."

"Yeah, by flirting with him."

Emmy stuck out her tongue.

"John told me that the college clears out all the furniture in the dorm, and they put furniture in the rooms just for them."

"What do you mean, just for them?" Emmy asked.

"King-sized beds, other stuff, and he said the dining room

serves special food just for them. The students don't get the same menu."

"There aren't any students there, are there?"

"I don't think so," Kristen answered. "I think it's just the Bears on campus."

"Are you and John ready to get married?" Emmy asked.

"Where did that come from?" Kristen blushed. "He hasn't proposed. Are you and Kenny ready to get married?" Kristen raised a hand. "Never mind. I know the answer."

After the Sunday morning service, Emmy and Kristen hurried home. They changed clothes and Emmy made a quick call to Kenny to let him know about their plans.

"Kristen and I are going to Bourbonnais to see John and Tony for a couple of hours. You can come if you want." Emmy looked at Kristen. "Is that okay with you?"

Kristen nodded her approval.

"I would, but I need to work at the studio this afternoon."

"Will I see you later tonight?" Emmy whispered because Kristen was still listening.

"I hope so, Em. I missed you this morning."

Emmy turned her back to Kristen. "I missed you, too."

"I heard that, Em," Kristen pulled on Emmy's hair.

"Ow! That hurt."

The girls headed to Bourbonnais to visit the guys. They knew the approximate location of the campus, so they didn't get lost. They arranged to meet the guys in front of the main gate at two o'clock. As Emmy drove, Kristen watched for the guys.

"I think the main entrance is just ahead, Em. I see them. Tony sees us, Em. He's waving his arms."

"At least he can still move his arms. I wonder how hard camp really is?"

Emmy slowed down enough to let the guys jump in, then she took off like the getaway car in a bank heist.

"Why are you in such a hurry, Em? We almost didn't make it into the car. Are you trying to kill us?" Tony struggled with his seatbelt.

Emmy laughed and cut around a slower moving car. "I

thought it would be exciting to pick up some big strong football players and kidnap them."

"So we're your kidnap victims, huh? Are you going to hold us for ransom?" Tony asked. "I'm sure Mama would pay a few bucks to get me back."

"No, we're going to hold you for three hours, then we'll dump your bodies back at Olivet." Emmy gunned the car through a yellow light.

Kristen smacked Emmy's leg. "Be careful! We have professional athletes in the car."

"What do you plan to do with us in the meantime? Torture us perhaps?" Tony looked at John.

"You could say that. I might kiss you both when we get to the place we're going to hold you hostage. That will be my way of torturing you," Kristen answered as she smiled at John.

"Yuck! You can't kiss Tony. He's your cousin," Emmy said and then giggled.

"And where might that be?" Tony asked as he poked Emmy's side.

"Stop that! I'm driving," Emmy ordered Tony as she looked in the mirror. "First we're going to eat lunch at some place close, then we're going to find a place called Cobb Park," Emmy said as she waited at a red light. "It's supposed to be by the river somewhere. Kristen has directions."

They stopped at Chili's for lunch, and then headed out to find Cobb Park. After a couple of wrong turns, Emmy saw the river, and they soon located the park. Emmy parked the car, and they jumped out. Tony walked beside Emmy as they crossed the road and moved closer to the Kankakee River. John and Kristen headed in the opposite direction. They found a bench under a canopy of trees. John kissed Kristen tenderly, and they started talking. Emmy and Tony acted more demonstrative in their reunion. Tony lifted Emmy off her feet as he twirled her around.

"Should I toss you in the river, Em? Do you want to go swimming?"

"You need to put me down and behave." She playfully swatted his butt and took off running.

245

"Hey! You can't do that." Tony waited a few seconds, and then ran after her.

"Why not? I see football players swatting each other all the time." Emmy stopped and turned back to face Tony.

"No we don't," Tony insisted.

"Yes, you do. I think it looks gay." Emmy took off running again.

"You're gonna get it, Emmy." Tony laughed, shook his head, but then chased her.

He caught her but only after sprinting. "Have you been running with Kenny?"

"Yeah, he comes over in the mornings, and we run our loop a couple times."

"Is Kristen still going with you?"

"No, she only ran a few times. She said we were too competitive."

John and Kristen sat and talked to each other. Though Tony and Emmy were just friends, they behaved like two teenagers. They ran around, and Tony tried to tickle her every time they got close enough. Soon Tony hoisted Emmy on his back and gave her a piggyback ride. John and Kristen heard them carrying on and laughed at the sight of Tony carrying Emmy.

"What are you doing, Emmy? Are you ever going to grow up?" Kristen stared incredulously.

"Would you like a ride, Kristen?" John asked.

Kristen shook her head. "No, you don't have to carry me around like that. I would feel silly."

"Do you wish we behaved more like those two? They are having so much fun. They're like little kids."

"We're different than Tony and Emmy. It doesn't mean we don't love each other. I do love you, John, in case in haven't told you lately."

"I love you, too, Kristen. I can think of one way I could show you." John smiled and lifted his bushy eyebrows.

"Are you making a pass at me, John Randolph? I thought you were supposed to catch passes, not throw them."

John grinned as he said, "I would never drop a pass if you

246

threw it to me."

"I bet you used that line a lot back at college."

"I might have."

"Did it ever work?"

John laughed. "I might have gained a few yards, but touchdowns were few and far between." He watched a group of cyclists ride through the park.

"I know you've scored a few touchdowns, John, and I understand," Kristen said seriously.

"None of those touchdowns are really worth six points to me now."

"I bet they were at the time."

Just then Tony and Emmy stopped in front of them. "What are you guys talking about? You both look so serious. Have some fun. Tony will give you a piggyback ride, Kristen," Emmy said as she slid off his back.

"I don't need a ride, Em."

"Neither did I, but I enjoyed it. Come on, it's fun. Get off your butt and go for a ride." Emmy grabbed Kristen's hands and yanked her off of the bench. "John can give me a ride, and we can chase each other."

Emmy convinced John and Kristen to go along with her plan. Tony carried Kristen around while John carried Emmy. Then they switched. John and Kristen laughed like kids as they chased each other around the park. Soon the guys needed to stop, so they sat on the bench. Emmy and Kristen sat next to them.

"What do you think the other players are doing right about now?" Emmy asked. "Are most of the guys married?"

"Are you sure you want to hear the answer to that, Em?" Tony asked.

Emmy looked at him and blushed. "Do you think you're the only players who aren't doing that?"

"There are a few single guys who don't know anyone in the area. They probably aren't." Tony winked at John.

"You're teasing me. I'm not totally naïve," Emmy said.

Kristen snorted. *Oh, yes you are, Em.*

Before they realized it, five o'clock arrived, and the guys

247

had to return to avoid a fine. Since they were both rookies, they didn't want to break the rules. They made it back to Olivet Nazarene University with a few minutes to spare. Emmy parked and Tony, John and Kristen got out.

"Are you coming to the preseason games, Em?" Tony asked as Emmy rolled down her window.

"Kristen and I are planning to come. I know it won't be like a regular season game."

"I don't know how much I'll get to play."

"It will still be fun to see you at Soldier Field." Emmy decided to get out of the car. "Are those guys over there part of the team?"

Tony looked in the direction Emmy pointed. "Yeah, that's Bobby McMullen, Dustin Terrell and Brad Ellington. Why?"

"Can you get their autographs for me, please?" Emmy grinned. "They are real celebrities."

"You're gonna get it, Em." Tony laughed. "We should get back. I'll call you later."

Kristen gave John a kiss as Tony and Emmy watched.

"Hey! We have to get going, Krissy," Emmy teased.

She and Tony looked at each other. He smiled at her and took a step toward her.

She held out her hand. "You can hug me if you want, but I'm not going to kiss you."

"I'll settle for a hug, Em. Say hi to Kenny when you see him."

The girls watched as the guys hurried back to the dorm. They waved goodbye and headed for home.

A few minutes after seven, Emmy heard Kenny pull into the driveway. She ran outside before he could get out of his car.

"Hi, are you hungry?"

"Yeah, I haven't eaten since I ate a sandwich for lunch."

"We're hungry, too. What would you like? Wanna go out, or should we order a pizza? You got any preference?"

"I really don't want to go anywhere, Em. Pizza would be okay. Can we have it delivered?" He checked his wallet for cash.

"Sure, I'll take care of it." Emmy let Kenny get out of the

car and gave him a kiss. She held his hand as they walked in the back door. She left him in the kitchen, stood at the bottom of the stairs and hollered, "Kristen, we're gonna order pizza. Any specials requests?"

"Pepperoni and veggies, please," Kristen hollered from her room.

Emmy placed the order with Kerry Lynn's Pizza and Pasta. "It will be here in about forty-five minutes," Emmy hollered to let Kenny and Kristen know.

Kenny grabbed a bottle of water from the fridge and plopped down on the couch in the TV room. He was mentally tired from his long day. Emmy joined him and told him about their trip to see John and Tony.

"So you let him carry you around on his back, huh?"

"Yeah, I even talked John and Kristen into doing the same thing."

"I can see you and Tony doing that, but I thought Kristen and John were more mature." Kenny realized he was in trouble as soon as the words left his mouth.

"Are you telling me that I'm an immature kid?" Emmy asked as she stood up and put her hands on her hips. "Do you think it's wrong to have a little fun?"

"You know that's not what I meant, Em."

"Are you jealous because I had fun with Tony? Does it bother you that I spent the afternoon with him?"

Kenny closed his eyes. *I'm too tired to get into an argument with you, Em.*

Kristen came downstairs and heard Emmy. "What's going on? Are you guys fighting about something?"

"Kenny thinks I behaved rather immaturely today at the park with Tony."

"You did act like kids..."

"Are you gonna be on his side? You and John did the same thing."

"Oh, for heaven's sake, Emmy. Stop acting like a spoiled brat. I'm sure Kenny didn't mean anything. Sit down and kiss and make up before you guys have a big fight over a mole hill."

Kristen pushed Emmy onto the couch.

Emmy frowned at Kristen, and then at Kenny. He smiled at her. Slowly a smile made its way to her face. "All right, I admit I behaved childishly." She moved next to him. They kissed and made up. Emmy climbed onto his lap and they kept kissing.

Kristen frowned at them. "Come on, you guys. If you're gonna do that, at least go upstairs to your room, Emmy. I want to watch TV, and I don't want to see you kissing and stuff."

Emmy got off of Kenny's lap and pulled him up. "I guess we have to use my room."

He watched Kristen's eyes for a reaction as he followed Emmy out of the room. Emmy stomped up the stairs trying annoy Kristen.

"Cut it out! You're such a spoiled brat sometimes," Kristen yelled.

Kenny quietly made his way up the stairs.

Fifteen minutes later, Kristen heard laughing and giggling from Emmy's bedroom right above the TV room. She heard the floor squeaking, too. After five minutes of listening to them, Kristen jumped off the couch and dashed up the stairs. She placed her hand over her eyes as she entered Emmy's room.

"I don't want to see what you guys are doing, but can you at least keep it down. I can't hear the TV."

"You don't have to cover your eyes. We're still dressed."

Kristen removed her hand. "What are you guys doing?"

"Just having a little fun. We'll try to keep it down, but the bed makes the floor squeak." Emmy stuck out her tongue at Kristen.

"Are you making all this noise because you're mad at me?"

"No!"

"Kenny is she mad at me?"

"Yes, she made me promise not to say anything, but basically, she's mad at you."

Emmy hit Kenny on the head with her pillow. Then she jumped out of bed and marched out of the room.

"I guess she's mad at both of us now."

Kristen followed Kenny downstairs. They heard the back

door open, and then slam shut. Kenny saw Emmy walk into the backyard.

"Emmy, please don't be mad at me."

"Go away and leave me alone. I'm just a spoiled brat."

Kenny caught up with her and wrapped his arms around her. "You're not a brat. You might be spoiled, or stubborn would be a better word, but I still love you."

Emmy turned to face him. "I don't think Kristen can hear us out here. Maybe we can grab a sleeping bag from the garage and lay on top of it. It won't squeak."

"You aren't mad at all, are you? You planned this whole thing just to get me out here."

Emmy grinned as she headed toward the garage.

Chapter Twenty-Eight

Late in the afternoon of Saturday the seventeenth, Tony and John returned home from training camp. Emmy and Kristen waited at Mama's house for their arrival.

Tony pulled into the driveway. "Hey, look. Kristen is sitting on the front porch. I'm surprised to see her waiting out here. I figured Emmy might do something like that."

"They're here!" Kristen hollered inside to Emmy and Mama before she ran to the passenger side of the car. She didn't give Tony or John a chance to get out of the car before she got on their case. "It's about time you got here. Did you guys take the long way home?"

"We needed to stay a little later than expected," Tony said.

"Did coach give you a detention for being naughty?" Kristen teased. "Did you guys make the team?"

Mama and Emmy came outside to meet the guys, but without the excitement Kristen displayed. They walked slowly, not running to the car. Emmy stayed close to Mama as Tony and John got out of the car. Tony walked around the car and hugged Mama as Emmy hung back and watched. John embraced Kristen and kissed her. Tony turned toward Emmy expecting at least a hug, but she stayed away.

"Don't I get a hug?" Tony asked.

"No, not in front of everyone. Maybe I'll give you a little hug later." Emmy twisted her hair and acted bashful for some reason.

Tony thought she was joking. "Aw, come on. Can't I have just one hug, please, Emmy?"

"Maybe later," Emmy answered timidly as she moved behind Mama.

Tony turned to Kristen. "What's going on? Why is Em acting so shy? I thought she would be happy to see me. Is she sick?"

Kristen shrugged as she glanced at Emmy. "I'm not sure, but she's been like this all week. She won't tell me anything."

"Did I do something wrong?" Tony asked. "I haven't talked

to her since the day you guys came to see us. Is she upset about that?"

"I don't think so. She's been really quiet all week ever since she went to visit her parents after church last Sunday. All week long she would get up early and go for a run with Kenny, but she wouldn't talk much about it—not to me anyway. On the rides to work she would hardly say a word."

"Did she and Kenny have a fight?"

"Not that I know of. In fact, he asked me if we had an argument, so I don't think he knows anymore than I do."

"If you open the trunk, I will help bring your suitcases in. At least the small one, I can carry it," Emmy said.

"We can get them later, Em. Let's go inside first." Tony thought about Emmy as he followed her inside. *So you went to see your parents, huh? They were probably arguing about something. But they always argue. That's nothing new, and it has never upset you like this before.*

Everyone gathered in the living room. John and Kristen sat together on the couch with Mama. Tony sat in one of the big leather recliners on the other side of the coffee table facing the couch. He remembered a time when Emmy would have sat on his lap. She didn't though. She stood at the end of the couch next to Mama.

"So how did your training camp go?" Mama asked. "I want to hear all about it."

Tony and John spent the next fifteen minutes talking about camp. Kristen and Mama asked questions, but Emmy was uncharacteristically silent. She moved to the arm of the couch.

"Emmy, aren't you curious about how training camp went? You haven't asked a single question, honey." Mama squeezed her hand.

"I'm okay just listening, Mama."

Eventually John said, "Tony, we should get the luggage out of your car."

Emmy followed along silently. She grabbed Tony's small suitcase and carried it in the house and up to his room.

John grabbed Tony's elbow as soon as Emmy was back in

the house. "I know she can be quiet at times, but this is different. It's kinda spooky."

"Yeah, tell me about it." Tony shrugged. "I've known her for almost five years now, and I've never seen her act like this. Something's bothering her. It might have something to do with her parents."

Emmy hurried back downstairs to the kitchen before Tony and John got upstairs with the rest of his stuff. She stood by the stove. "Do you need any help, Mama?"

"Dinner is almost ready, sweetie. I'm just waiting for the lasagna to finish. Would you help Kristen set the table?"

"Okay," Emmy answered quietly.

A couple of minutes later, Mama pulled the lasagna out of the oven and called everyone to the table. They took their seats, and Mama looked at Emmy about to ask her to say grace.

"I'll say grace tonight, Mama," Kristen said. "Emmy told me her throat hurts." Kristen prayed, and they began to eat.

Mama sat in her usual spot at the end of the table, nearest the kitchen, and passed the food around. In addition to the lasagna, Mama made a special sauce for the broccoli and cauliflower, and put together a garden salad. To save time, she bought the bread from a local bakery.

"Everything looks and smells so good, Mama," Kristen said as she spooned out a helping of broccoli.

"Thank you, honey. I thought the boys would like some home-cooked lasagna tonight. Who knows what they have been eating for the last month?"

Tony cut off a piece of bread. "We ate at the Ludwig Dining Hall most of the time, so we ate healthy stuff."

"Except for the nights we ordered pizzas," John added.

Emmy tried to smile as she listened to everyone, but she remained quiet. She avoided looking at Tony as he passed her the bowls of broccoli and cauliflower. Mama dished out the lasagna as everyone passed their plate to her. She made sure the guys received a large portion. When Emmy passed her plate to Mama, she told her, "I only need about half a portion, please."

Mama scooped out barely enough to feed a small child.

"You can have more if you want, sweetie."

"Thanks, Mama. This will be enough."

The guys inhaled their first plate and loaded up a second helping. Emmy still nibbled away at the food on her plate. The second helping satisfied the guys' hunger.

"That was delicious, Mama." John patted his stomach.

"Thank you, John. I hope you guys have room for dessert. I made two apple pies."

"I've got room for some pie now, and I'll have even more room later," Tony said as he finished the bread.

"Emmy dear, would you bring one of the pies in here, please?"

"Yes, Mama." Emmy went into the kitchen and returned with the first pie along with plates and a knife to cut the pie.

"Thank you, sweetie. Would you like a piece? I know everyone else does."

"No, thanks. May I be excused? I think I will go upstairs and lie down."

"Are you not feeling well? Let me feel your forehead." Mama checked, but she didn't feel warm. "You should lie down on Heather's bed. You are probably just tired. I'll come up to check on you later."

Emmy went upstairs to Heather's room and fell asleep five minutes later.

"Does Emmy need to see a doctor? Is she physically sick or something?" Tony asked. "I'm beginning to worry about her." He looked at Kristen and whispered, "You don't think she's pregnant, do you?"

Kristen glanced at John and Mama. "I don't think so. Kenny would know, and he doesn't have any better idea of what's wrong than I do."

"She's not pregnant," Mama insisted. "I don't think there's anything physically wrong with her, but she looks like she's losing weight and is under a lot of stress. Has she been eating much this week, Kristen?" Mama asked.

"Now that you mention it, she hasn't been eating much. Not that she ever does, but this week she ate even less than normal. I

255

don't think she ate anything at all on Wednesday night. She skipped church and went to her room real early. She even closed the door."

"Well, let's let her rest for now. I'll go check on her after we clean up the kitchen. Will you help me, Kristen?" Mama stood up and was about to gather up the plates. She placed Emmy's on top of her own. *You didn't even finish the little portion of lasagna I gave you, and it doesn't look like you ate any of your veggies. I know you like that sauce.*

"Why don't you let us clean up, Mama? You have done enough work for today. You should rest," Tony said.

Mama looked at Kristen, surprised that the guys would volunteer for kitchen duty. She set down the plates.

Kristen faced the guys and asked, "All right, who are you, and what have you done to the real Tony and John?"

Tony laughed. "I've helped clean up after dinner before."

"Yeah. And exactly what year was that?" Kristen asked.

"He has helped before, Kristen, but it has been a while." Mama chuckled. "Will you keep an eye on them and make sure they don't mess up my kitchen instead of cleaning it up?"

"Okay, I'll keep an eye on them." Kristen glared at the guys. *You must be up to something. You never volunteer for kitchen duty.*

"Good, I'm going to check on Emmy."

Tony and John began the cleanup process under the watchful eye of Kristen. Mama headed upstairs to check on Emmy. She knocked on Heather's bedroom door and entered. Emmy's eyes were closed as she lay on her back. Mama turned to leave, but Emmy whispered, "I'm awake, Mama. You can come in."

Mama walked over to the bed and sat on the edge. "Are you feeling any better, honey? You didn't eat much of anything."

"I'm sorry. I haven't had much of an appetite lately."

"Is your stomach bothering you? Do you feel nauseous or queasy?"

"Not really. I haven't thrown up or anything. I'm not pregnant if that's what Kristen thinks."

"I know you're not." Mama ran a finger along Emmy's cheek. "I know there is something bothering you. Did something

256

happen between you and Kenny, or something at work? Is everything okay between you and Kristen?"

"No, nothing like that." Emmy looked up at Mama and tears began to fill her eyes. Emmy's lip quivered as she reached up to Mama.

Mama reached down and held Emmy close as she began to sob.

"There, there, you just let it go, baby. I'm here for you."

Mama held Emmy tightly as she rocked her back and forth. For over a minute Emmy sobbed softly. Mama let go and Emmy lay on her back again as Mama reached for a tissue to dry her eyes. "You can tell me anything, Emmy. It doesn't matter what it is, I will still love you."

"I know you will." Emmy looked up at Mama, and then closed her eyes for a moment. She opened her eyes and confided, "Last Sunday I went to visit my mom and dad after church. When I got there, Mom let me in even though I could tell she didn't want to see me. She didn't say a word to me. Dad sat in his recliner with his feet on the old ottoman, and Mom sat down in her chair. Mom said, 'Your father has been drinking more than ever and he refuses to go see his doctor again. I'm about ready to throw him out in the street.' Dad just sat in his chair for a moment, and then they started arguing. They yelled at each other. I tried to make them stop, but they screamed at me. They called each other names. Then they stopped for a few seconds, and Mom said something." Emmy stopped and closed her eyes again.

Mama tenderly wiped the tears from Emmy's face. "What did she say, sweetheart? You can tell me if you want."

Emmy bit her lip and didn't say a word for a moment.

"Sometimes it helps to talk about things instead of keeping it all bottled up inside."

Emmy took a deep breath, and then let the words come out in a torrent. "She told Dad she was sorry she ever married him and sorry she ever had his children. Then he said he wished she had never gotten pregnant. He said he never wanted any kids in the first place. Then they looked at me. I was in shock, I guess because I couldn't say anything. I got up and left. They didn't want me,

257

Mama." Emmy started sobbing again.

"Oh, baby, they didn't mean it. Sometimes people say things when they are upset that they don't mean. Your parents love you."

"I think they really meant what they said. They don't love me as much as you or Mrs. Colwell. I wish one of you was my real mother."

Mama patted Emmy's hand. "Oh, baby, I love you just as much as if you were my flesh and blood. I couldn't possibly love you more than I already do."

Emmy stopped sobbing and looked up at Mama. "Do you mean that?"

"Of course, I do. But you know, Emmy, if Mrs. Colwell or I was your real mother then you wouldn't love Kenny and Tony the way you do." Mama smiled at Emmy.

"I never thought about that."

"You lie here and rest for a while. When you feel better you come back downstairs. This will be our secret. No one else needs to know, and I'm sure the next time you see your mom and dad things will be better."

"Okay, Mama, I feel better already. I will rest for a while, then come back downstairs. You won't tell anyone..."

"No, baby, I will say your stomach is upset if they ask. You rest some more." Mama leaned over and kissed Emmy's cheek before she left the room.

Mama closed the door to Heather's room and paused for a moment. She leaned against the wall and raised a hand to her forehead. After a moment, she walked down the hall to her own bedroom and entered. She closed the door behind her and sat in her rocking chair. She began to weep softly and silently as she rocked back and forth. She wondered how two parents could say such mean and cruel things to someone as precious as Emmy. Mama thought about how much she loved her children. She thought about Tony and how proud he made her. She thought about Marco and her heart ached because of the hurt that remained unresolved between them. She loved Marco just as much as always though. She thought about Heather and how she worked so hard to become

258

a doctor. Mama paused in her thoughts for a moment, and then remembered her first child. The baby she lost to a miscarriage. She knew the baby was a girl, and she and Peter even picked out a name for her. She would have been named Dorothy Rose after her grandmother.

After a time Mama got up from her rocker. She dried her eyes and looked at the picture of Peter on the nightstand next to the bed. She picked up the picture, kissed it and sighed. She looked again at the picture of the only man she ever loved. He smiled in the picture and Mama smiled back at him. She set the picture back on the stand and headed downstairs.

Tony, John and Kristen were in the living room again after finishing cleaning the kitchen. Tony and John sat quietly in the recliners, almost falling asleep, while Kristen read a magazine on the couch. Mama sat on the couch with Kristen and Tony sat up—now wide awake.

"Is Emmy sleeping?" Tony asked.

"She is resting for now. I think she will feel better when she comes back downstairs."

"What's wrong with her?"

Mama looked straight in the eye at Tony. "Her stomach is upset."

Tony knew better, and Mama knew he knew.

It must be pretty bad if you have to use that excuse because you can't tell us what Emmy really said. Tony thought. That's okay. I won't pry. I just hope that whatever it is, will be resolved soon. Maybe I should say a prayer for Emmy. She would do that for me.

Emmy rested for another thirty minutes, and then came downstairs.

Tony saw her first. "Are you feeling better now, Em?"

"Yes, I feel better." Emmy sat next to Mama on the couch.

Mama hugged her and held her tight. Mama put her hand on Emmy's side. "You are getting too skinny, child. You need to eat more of my lasagna."

Emmy smiled. "I am a little hungry now that I think about it. Is there any left?"

Mama waved at Kristen. "Will you warm up some lasagna

259

for Emmy, please?"

"Of course I will, Mama."

"Make it a full-sized portion," Mama added. "And give her some of the vegetables with the sauce."

"Can I have more, too?" Tony asked. "I'm hungry again."

"You and John can warm up your own food. Just make sure Emmy gets hers first," Mama warned the guys with a wave.

Tony and John got up and headed to the kitchen. Mama and Emmy were alone on the couch. Mama looked at Emmy, hugged her tightly and kissed her forehead.

Emmy whispered, "I love you."

Mama smiled and answered back, "Not half as much as I love you, baby."

Kenny came over to the house on Monday night after work and made a taco salad for dinner. They sat in the dining room to eat.

"Can I have some more, please?" Emmy asked as she handed her bowl to Kenny.

Kenny and Kristen smiled at her.

"Of course you can, Em." Kenny filled it up again and added some salsa. "You can have as much as you want."

"Does this mean you've got your appetite back?" Kristen asked. *I hope that whatever has been bothering you is all behind you now.*

"I'm starting to get it back." Emmy bit her lip. "I'm sorry that I've been such a mess lately."

"It's all right. I'm still your best friend, and if you ever want to talk about it, I'm here," Kristen assured her.

"Thank you, Krissy."

On Tuesday, August 20, the Steward Music Group released the new Fridays At Five CD *The Ballad Of Johnny March*. The band hosted a release party at the company office. In the evening Kenny took Emmy and Kristen to La Cantina and Emmy ate both tacos and all of the rice and beans on her plate.

"Kenny, look. I cleaned up my plate." She held it up.

260

"Good job, Em. I think you deserve a special treat when we get home," Kenny said.

Emmy bit her lip as she looked at him and then Kristen. "I would like a special treat."

"Should I go visit my parents for the night?" Kristen asked.

"You haven't seen them for a while," Emmy said. "Maybe tonight would be a good time to stop over at the house."

"You don't have to do that, Kristen." Kenny grinned as he waved his hand. "I was thinking more along the lines of ice cream and pie. I thought we could stop at Baker's Choice and pick up a pie to bring home."

Emmy blushed. "Oh, I thought you meant something else."

"Pie and ice cream sounds good to me, Kenny." Kristen grinned at Emmy while flipping her long hair over her shoulder. "Maybe we can have some of that while Emmy takes a cold shower."

"I'd rather take a long warm bubble bath," Emmy replied.

"You can do that, Em."

Emmy grinned at Kristen.

"By yourself!"

"I know. I just wanted to see your reaction." Emmy sighed. *The bubbles would hide me.*

By the end of the week Emmy felt about back to normal. She talked to Tony when he called. He kept very busy with football practice and had not been to Emmy's house all week. He had the sense to know not to ask Emmy about what upset her so much. At least he had the sense after Mama told him not to ask.

"Maybe Emmy will talk to you about it one of these days, but until then, you should just treat her the same as you have before." Mama pointed a finger at him. "She needs to know that you love her and are still her friend."

"Okay, Mama. I will make sure she knows how much she means to me. Should I tickle her, or hang her from the ceiling?"

"Don't you dare. You treat her the same way you do Kristen. She will return to the old Emmy soon. You have to be patient."

261

Emmy did tell Kenny what her parents said to each other about her and Diane. He listened and comforted her the way only he could. He could never understand how her parents could be so unloving, but he never said anything negative about them to Emmy.

"If God performs a miracle, and we ever have a baby, I will cherish her, or him, and love her with all my heart. I will treasure every moment we have together," Emmy insisted.

"I know you will, baby. You will be the greatest mother in the history of the world."

She laughed and opened her arms to hold him. "You will be the best father, too."

"Would it be all right if I let you change most of the messy diapers?"

Chapter Twenty-Nine

On Wednesday the Chicago Bears flew to Miami for the last preseason game. Tony called Emmy when he and John were settled in their hotel room.

Emmy checked the caller ID when the phone rang.

"Hi," she answered quietly as she sat in the computer room in the dark.

"Hi, Emmy, are you feeling better now?" Tony sat with his back up against the headboard of his bed.

"I'm doing better now. How was the flight?"

"Uneventful. Just the way I like. The season starts a week from this Sunday at home against the Vikings."

"I know. How many tickets can you guys get?" Emmy asked. "I might want to go to your first game."

"We each have two, but I suppose we could get more. Just let me know as soon as you can, Emmy."

John turned on the TV. "Are you talking to Emmy?"

"Hang on a sec, Em." Tony nodded to John.

"Should I leave the room?" John grinned as he asked.

Tony shook his head, so John stretched out on his bed. His feet hung over the end of the king-size bed.

"I'm back."

"Say hi to John for me."

"Em says hi and you better not drop any more passes tomorrow or else she will cut you from the roster."

"I did not say that!" Emmy hollered loud enough for John to hear, as Tony held the phone out to him.

"So, let me know about the tickets," Tony said.

"I will." She leaned back in her chair. "Mama told me she was getting calls from people asking for free tickets."

"Yeah, everyone who ever knew me is bothering her. I told her to stop answering the phone unless she checks the caller ID first. At least they don't have my cell number."

"You may have to get her an unlisted number and a cell phone," Emmy suggested.

"I bought her a cell phone, but she doesn't want to get a

new number. It's been the same number since they bought the house back in the dark ages."

"That's like my parents. They still have the same number." Emmy thought about her parents without getting emotional. "I'll talk to Mama, and I'll let you know about the tickets as soon as I can."

"How's Kenny doing?"

Emmy walked out of the computer room and plopped onto the couch in the TV room. "He's been so excited. The new CD came out last week and it's selling like crazy. He told me the record company shipped several million copies. The guys are getting ready to leave on tour in the middle of September."

"Are you gonna be all right when he leaves?" Tony rolled his eyes. "Maybe I shouldn't ask you questions like that. Sorry, Em."

"It's all right. I know you're just concerned and not trying to pry." Emmy rolled over to her belly. "I'll get by somehow."

"We bought a CD so we can listen to it in the locker room. It's probably their best one yet."

"I really like it," Emmy said. She paused and then mentioned, "I miss you. I mean I miss having you come around. The yard needs mowing, and the bushes need to be trimmed."

"Oh, I see how it is. You only want me to do your landscaping. You don't want me for my body anymore, huh?"

John glanced at Tony and raised his eyebrows.

"Ha! Ha!" Emmy faked a laugh. "No, that's not the only reason I miss you. I miss the way you tease me, too."

Tony lowered his voice and asked, "Is it all right if I tease you and maybe even tickle you when I see you again? Mama told me I have to treat you like Kristen until you feel better."

"You can treat me however you want, but don't hang me from the ceiling." She accidentally kicked the end of the couch. "Maybe you shouldn't tickle me, either."

"Okay, I promise to keep my hands off of you," Tony said.

John heard the remark. *Just what have you guys been doing? Maybe Kristen was right about the foreplay.*

Emmy flipped onto her back. "Oh, don't take it like that.

264

I'm just saying, you need to be careful."

"Are you still upset because of what happened after the Ohio State game? You know I didn't mean to touch you... inappropriately."

John sat on the edge of his bed and whispered, "I'll get some ice or something."

Tony waved his hand, so John stayed.

"Oh, too bad. I thought you meant to touch my breast," Emmy teased.

"It wasn't on purpose," Tony said. "But if you liked it."

John raised his eyebrows.

"I might have overreacted that night. I made it into a mountain instead of an anthill."

"A molehill, Em." Tony laughed.

"All right. A molehill instead of an anthill," she said and then giggled.

"It's good to hear you laugh again, Em. I didn't like it when you were upset." Tony laughed and bumped his head against the headboard.

"Did Mama tell you why?" Emmy asked.

Tony rubbed the back of his head. "I can't believe you even asked that."

"Sorry. I know she would never divulge anything I told her in confidence."

"I gotta run. Call me when you know more about the tickets."

"I will. Have a good game and don't get hurt."

Tony hung up and looked at John.

"What's going on with you two?" John stood up next to the bed. "Sometimes you treat her like a kid sister, but then other times, like just now, you flirt with each other."

"I'm not sure. I'm never totally sure when it comes to Emmy." Tony swung his legs around and sat on the edge of the bed.

"You should make up your mind. It's not good for your relationship to keep going back and forth." John picked up a room key from the dresser. "I'm gonna grab a beer at the bar downstairs.

You want one?"

"No, thanks. I'm good."

"Yeah, well, don't call Brenda," John cautioned as he walked out of the room. *Although I wouldn't blame you if you did.*

Emmy lay on her back and thought about Tony for several minutes. *Why can't I ever decide once and for all how I feel about you? My feelings for you change almost as often as the Chicago weather.* She jumped up, dashed up the stairs and barged into Kristen's room.

Kristen looked over her shoulder as she put some clean clothes in her dresser. "What's up? Who was on the phone?"

"Tony, and we need to talk about tickets to the game," Emmy said.

"John told me his family was coming to the game. He's been working on getting enough tickets."

"Can they do that?" Emmy asked. She sat down and bounced on the edge of Kristen's bed. "His whole family?"

"His parents. Both brothers and their wives and kids. Stop bouncing on my bed. It's not a trampoline," Kristen said. "John said Tony could have his regular tickets. We can use them. There will be four seats together. We need to decide who to take."

"Don't you want to sit with John's family?" Emmy asked.

"I'm not sure. I might feel better sitting with you. Oh, those seats are in a section with wives and girlfriends of the players. We might meet some celebrities," Kristen said and then grinned.

"Cool!" Emmy exclaimed. "I'm going to call Mama. She might want to go since this is his first game as a pro."

"Go ahead, but I'll be shocked if she agrees."

Emmy ran downstairs and called. "Mama, do you want to go to the game a week from this Sunday? It's Tony's first regular season game as a pro."

Mama thought about it for a moment. "All right, sweetie, I will go this time, but I don't know how many times I can go. It's too dangerous a sport for me to watch."

"Tony knows what he's doing, Mama."

"Yeah, but do the other guys?" Mama made Emmy laugh without even trying.

They talked for a few minutes before hanging up.

Emmy stood at the bottom of the stairs and yelled, "Mama's going!"

"I'm surprised," Kristen said from the top of the stairs. "That leaves one ticket," Kristen said as she came downstairs.

Emmy wanted to ask Kenny but wasn't sure how Kristen would feel. She bit her lip for a moment. "Would you mind if I ask Kenny to go to the game? He's leaving on the twelfth, and this might be his only chance to see the Bears."

"I wondered if you were going to ask him. Of course I don't mind, Em. I know I got on your case before about all the time you guys spent together."

"So, it's okay?"

"Sure."

"Thank you, Krissy."

Emmy hugged Kristen. "I can't wait for Tony's first game with the Bears. I'm going to call Kenny right away." She called Kenny on her cell phone.

"Hi, I've been listening to the new CD non-stop. I really like it. How do you feel about it? I can hear it in the background."

Kenny turned down his stereo. "I just put it on. You know I don't like to listen to our CDs after they come out. I always think of the different stuff we could have tried."

"You are your own worst critic. I think the whole CD sounds great. Every song could be a hit," Emmy said.

"I don't know about that, but I don't think there's any filler on it. We worked really hard on the lyrics and the arrangements. You even contributed."

"All I did was suggest a word here and there. Nothing too important." Emmy walked upstairs and lay down on her bed.

"Still, you helped."

Emmy crossed her fingers. "Hey, since you are in town, would you like to go to the Bear's opening game?"

"Sure!" he answered without hesitation. "Who else is going?"

"Kristen and I are going, and Mama even agreed to go."

"Really? I didn't think she ever went to his games."

267

"I think she wants to see Soldier Field again. Tony's father took her to a game a long time ago," Emmy said and then explained about all the people asking for tickets.

"I'll go if you let me drive."

"Okay, I hoped you would volunteer," Emmy said. "Are you guys ready for the tour to start? I know you've been rehearsing."

"I'm ready. At least this time we won't be gone for months at a time, and I will be home for the holidays."

"You better be, or I will be pissed at some people," Emmy said.

"I'll talk to you later, Em. It will be fun to go to the game."

Chapter Thirty

Tony got back from Miami and had a couple days off from practice. He seriously thought about buying a new car and talked to a guy he remembered from his class at Roosevelt High. Marc D'Antoni worked as a salesman at the D'Antoni Buick/GMC dealership in South Hampshire owned by his father. On Friday afternoon Tony called Marc and made an appointment to meet him Saturday morning. Tony then called Emmy at work.

"Hi, Emmy, are you and Kenny busy tomorrow morning?"

"Not really. I need to clean the house and do some laundry. Kenny is coming over, but I don't think we have any set plans. Why?" She balanced the phone on her shoulder as she straightened her desk.

"I've got an appointment at nine to see a guy about a horse."

"What are you talking about?" She grabbed the phone before it fell. "Why would you want a horse?"

"It's not really about a horse. I'm going to see Marc D'Antoni about a new car," Tony explained. "You guys wanna go with me?"

"Sure. Are you really gonna buy something new?"

"Yeah, I think it's time. I'm actually looking at a GMC Envoy. It's an SUV, so it's more like a truck than a car."

"Are they expensive? Do you have enough money? Hang on a second. I have to take another call. Be right back." She took the other call. "Okay, I'm back."

"It's kinda expensive, but it should last a long time"

"I'll try to get some of the housework done tonight so we can go with you in the morning. I can help you spend your money."

"Ha! Ha! I'll pick you guys up at eight thirty, Em."

"We'll be ready.

Tony arrived at eight the next morning and walked in the back door. "Anyone home?"

"I'm in the dining room. Keep your voice down. Kristen is

269

still asleep," Emmy whispered.

Tony plopped down casually on a dining room chair. "Is Kenny here? I didn't see his car."

"You're early. If you break that chair, I'm gonna murder you." She kicked his foot and he sat up straight. "Did you have breakfast yet?"

"Not yet. I thought we could stop and get breakfast on the way. Are you ready to go?"

"Kenny isn't here yet."

"Oh," Tony glanced around the room. "I assumed he would be spending the night. We can wait till he gets here."

I should smack you for that remark, but I'll let it slide for now. "Kristen worries if Kenny spends the night too often."

"Why?" Tony knocked over part of the centerpiece on the table.

Emmy glared at him.

"Sorry." Tony straightened up the decoration as best he could.

"She worries about our love life, creep."

"We don't have a love life, brat."

"Not us!" She smacked his shoulder. "Me and Kenny."

Tony grinned.

"You're teasing me. Stop it."

Emmy heard a car pull in the driveway and looked out the window.

"He's here, but he pulled in behind you."

"We'll take care of moving the cars. Are you ready otherwise?"

"Just give me a minute. I need to use the bathroom."

"I thought we could stop at Westfield's since it's right next to the car dealership. They have good food, and it's not too expensive," Tony hollered as Emmy left the room.

"That's okay with me. See if it's all right with Kenny." Emmy ran upstairs and returned in a couple of minutes. "I'm ready."

They took off and made it to the restaurant by eight fifteen.

"I've had the skillets before, and they're really good," Tony

270

said as he studied the menu. "Especially the Irish skillet."

"I'm sure they are. But I can't eat that much. I think I'll have blueberry pancakes. What are you gonna have, Kenny?"

"I'll try a skillet. I feel hungry enough to eat one."

"Are you sure pancakes will be enough, Em?" Tony asked.

"Did Mama tell you to make sure I eat a big breakfast?"

"Yeah, she's worried about how thin you look."

"So am I. I don't want you to get so skinny that a light breeze blows you away," Kenny added.

"I'm not trying to lose weight. Other than when we ate at La Cantina the other night, I just haven't had much of an appetite lately."

"I'm gonna order the special skillet. It has about everything possible on it." Kenny set his menu down. "I'll let you try some of it if you want."

Emmy ate a few bites of Kenny's skillet and managed to finish both of her pancakes. They paid the check and arrived at the dealership just after nine. Tony held the door open for Emmy and Kenny, and then he saw Marc D'Antoni waiting for him.

"Good morning, Tony. It's good to see you again. My dad wants to meet you, but he's running a little late. Did I mention he has season tickets and goes to all the games? I usually get to use the tickets once or twice a year."

"Marc, this is Emmy Colasanti. She graduated from Roosevelt, too."

"Hello, Emmy, it's nice to meet you."

"This is..."

"Hello, Mr. Colwell. I've never met you, but I've been to several of your shows."

"Thank you, but please don't call me Mr. Colwell." Kenny laughed as he shook Marc's hand. "That's my dad. I'm just Kenny."

Marc knew about Kenny, of course, but had never met Emmy at Roosevelt, or heard anything about her. He assumed she still went to college.

"Have you given any more thought to the GMC Envoy, Tony?"

"Yes, I think I would like to see one of those."

271

"Would you like to drive one? We have several in our inventory." Marc looked around the showroom. "I guess they're all outside."

"Sure, I want to drive it before I make my decision."

"Why don't we have a seat in my office, and I can tell you about the ones we have on the lot. Would you like some coffee or anything?"

"No, thanks, I'm good. Do you want anything, Em, Kenny?"

"No, thanks," they both answered. Kenny took a look at the window sticker of a Sierra 2500HD Crew Cab and whistled. "Look at the price of this, Em."

"Holy crap!" Emmy swore. "Don't you ever pay that much for a car or truck."

Marc took Tony, Kenny and Emmy to his office, a desk on the sales floor. He pulled up the inventory on the computer and explained the different styles and trim levels of the Envoy. He didn't push Tony toward any certain one, but allowed Tony to decide for himself.

"I really don't want white or blue, but the silver or the pewter metallic might work," Tony said.

"I've got one pewter metallic, Tony. It's a SLT 4x4 and it's really loaded. You haven't mentioned a price range."

"Can we see that one, Marc, and maybe a silver one?"

"Sure. I can bring them up to the front. They're parked along the side of the building somewhere."

"We can walk, Marc. It's nice out, and we don't mind walking."

Marc took them outside and found Envoys in the two colors Tony mentioned. Tony and Emmy looked at both of the colors as Kenny wandered over to a red Corvette parked next to the building.

"What do you think, Em. Do you like one better than the other? It looks like the sticker price is about the same on both of them."

Emmy saw the sticker price. "Can I talk to Tony for a minute, Marc?"

272

"Of course. I'll get the keys, so we can take one for a drive." Marc headed inside to give Tony and Emmy a chance to talk.

She waited until Marc disappeared into the building. Then she pushed Tony in the chest with both hands. "Did you see the price in the window? That's way too much to spend on a car. You can get a good one for half that much."

"I know, Em. It's a lot of money."

"I don't think my parents house cost that much."

"Emmy, I don't know how much Marc can discount it, but I think it would be worth buying. These are supposed to be really good. They're not great on gas mileage, but they are supposed to be really safe and should last a long time. I'd rather pay more money up front and get something that will last for years than buy something cheaper and have to replace it in a couple of years. The D'Antoni's have been in business for a long time, and they have a reputation for being honest and fair. I like the fact that Marc hasn't pressured me into anything."

"Can you afford it, Tony? Do you have any idea how much the payments will be? You are going to have payments, right?" Emmy realized he had already made up his mind.

"No, Em. I'm not going to make payments. I'll just pay for it. I put some money in the checking account."

"How much did you put into your checking account?" Emmy never usually asked Tony about his money.

"I put fifty thousand into the checking account."

Emmy's jaw dropped. Kenny walked over to Emmy and put his hand on her shoulder. She looked at him. "Tony put enough money in his checking account to pay cash for this. Look at the sticker. Can you believe it?"

"Oh, I believe it all right. Emmy, do you see what's parked over there next to the building?"

"I saw you looking at that Corvette. Is it for sale?"

"There's a sign in the window. Do you want me to buy it for you?"

"Sure!"

"Okay, I will."

273

"No, I'm just kidding. I don't really want a sports car like that. I know I always tease you about getting one, but I don't really want it." *I would get too many speeding tickets.*

"Too bad. I was in the mood to buy a sports car today."

"Now if it was purple," Emmy teased.

Marc came back with the keys to the pewter metallic Envoy. He started it up and got in the back seat. Kenny joined him and let Emmy sit in front with Tony. They took it for a drive, and Tony liked the way it sat up higher than his car. He made up his mind. They got back to the dealership, and Tony parked it back in the same spot. They got out and walked around the vehicle. Marc pointed out some features of the truck without any sales pressure.

"I like it, Marc. Do you like this color, Em?"

"I think I like it better than the silver one."

"It is a 4x4. I know it won't get great gas mileage, but I think it would be safer to drive. I don't know if Mama will ever drive it, but she could."

Marc listened, but didn't say anything as Tony, Emmy and Kenny talked to each other.

"You don't have to make a decision today, Tony. You should take a few days to decide. Maybe go to some other dealerships to see what they have to offer," Emmy said.

"I think that would be wise, Tony. There are other car dealers in town and you might want to see other models," Marc said. "I'm not trying to chase you away, but I want you to feel comfortable with your choice."

"I appreciate that, Marc, but I don't need to go anywhere else. I talked to Uncle Daniel, and he suggested I do business with you. He told me that he and Uncle Carmen have bought several cars from your father over the years, and they're happy with the way you treat your customers. If Uncle Carmen and Uncle Daniel recommend you, that's good enough for me."

"I appreciate that, Tony."

Tony saw a man in a dark suit with a red tie walking toward them. Marc turned and saw his father.

"Dad, this is Tony Bertucci and his friend, Emmy Colasanti. This is Kenny Colwell."

274

"It's good to meet you, Tony and Emmy. How is your father, Kenny? Is he still buying Hondas?" Mr. D'Antoni loosened the tie and popped the top button. "My wife insists I wear a suit to work now. I'd rather wear jeans and an old shirt."

Kenny laughed and nodded his head. *I hate wearing suits, too.*

Tony shook hands with Mr. D'Antoni. "It's nice to meet you, Mr. D'Antoni. Marc told me you are a Bear fan."

"Yes, I am. I've had season tickets for over twenty-five years. I've never met you before, Tony, but I knew your father. I sold him a used car before he and your mother were even married. I hope your mother is in good health."

"She is, thanks."

"Are you interested in this Envoy?"

"Yes, I am."

"Excellent. It's a good vehicle and should last you ten years or more if you take care of it. I'd rather sell you something every ten years that makes you happy than to sell you something which doesn't last more than a few years. I know how expensive vehicles are nowadays. I'll let you guys talk it over. If you think you are ready to decide, come back and see me. I still like to handle most of the deals myself. I like keeping my hands in the mix. I guess it's because I started this place all by myself. I was the only employee in the beginning."

"I'm ready to buy this one today, Mr. D'Antoni."

"Are you sure? There are cheaper ones around here, I think." He looked around the lot full of vehicles.

"I checked the inventory and showed Tony the other Envoys we have in stock," Marc said.

"The maintenance on these Envoys can get a little pricey at times. That's something to keep in mind."

Tony smiled at Mr. D'Antoni. "Are you trying to talk me out of the Envoy, sir?"

"No, but I'm simply trying to make sure you understand the costs that go along with it."

"There are some guys on the team that have these fancy sports cars and all, but those aren't for me. I want a dependable

275

vehicle with some room. I'm not exactly small, you know."

"Miss Colasanti, have you driven this beast, yet?" Mr. D'Antoni looked down at Emmy. *I wonder if you're related to Joe Colasanti.*

"No, but it's Tony's car."

"Yes, but you might need to drive it someday, too," Tony said. "Maybe you should drive it around to make sure you like it."

"Okay, but just a quick drive." Emmy's eyes sparkled.

Emmy took the truck for a drive with Tony and Marc while Kenny talked to Mr. D'Antoni about the red Corvette. The GMC was a lot bigger than Kenny's little Honda Civic, but Emmy liked being up high.

"I can see the other traffic better from up here, Tony. I guess I could get used to it if I ever have to drive it."

You might need to drive it more than you think, Em. Tony thought, but didn't say out loud.

They got back to the dealership, and Marc took them inside to his desk. They didn't see Kenny anywhere.

"What do you think, Tony? If you want to take some time to think about it, I understand."

"I would like to buy it, Marc. I suppose we need to figure out how much it will cost."

"All right." Marc's heart beat faster. *This is the easiest sale I've ever had.* "Let me see if Dad is free. We will use his office, and he will go over the numbers with you. I'll be right back."

Marc returned in a couple of minutes and took them to his father's office. Kenny was already in the office.

"Have a seat, and I will go over the numbers with you. If you have any questions, please, feel free to ask."

Tony and Emmy sat next to Kenny. "I've got a Chevy Lumina now, Mr. D'Antoni. It's a 1995 and it's got over a 100,000 miles on it. I just had some work done."

"Do you want to trade it in, or did you want to try to sell it yourself? You might be able to sell it yourself and get a little more for it that way. You could always keep it as a second car."

"I don't want to try to sell it myself. I'd rather trade it in."

"Okay, I'll have Marc take a look at it. I probably won't be

276

able to give you much for it, but it will reduce the sales tax somewhat. Do you have the keys?"

Tony handed Mr. D'Antoni the keys, and he tossed them to Marc, who left to appraise the car.

"This is the MSRP for that Envoy, that's the price on the sticker in the window..."

Mr. D'Antoni went over the details with Tony and Emmy. He explained exactly what the vehicle cost the dealership, and that he would sell it for five hundred dollars over his cost. He added in all the other costs—taxes, plates, etc.

"What about an extended warranty, Mr. D'Antoni?"

"They're not worth it, Tony. I know other dealers try to sell them to customers, but it's simply a way for the dealerships to make more profit. Most of the time they don't cover what breaks, anyway."

Mr. D'Antoni printed out all the costs in an easy to read and understandable way. He went over everything.

"The final total is $34,137.29. Now if you decide to trade in your car. This number will be reduced. So will the amount of sales tax. These other numbers will stay the same. Did you talk to Marc about financing or anything yet?"

"I want to pay cash, Mr. D'Antoni. I mean I want to write a check, I don't have that much cash lying around."

"Let's hope not."

Marc returned and handed Tony the keys to his car. "We could give you $1500 for the car, Tony. It's got a lot of miles on it, and it's in kinda rough shape."

"I know it's not worth much."

Mr. D'Antoni used his old-fashioned calculator to come up with the new figure for the Envoy.

"Tony, I can sell you the Envoy for $32,500.00 with your car as a trade-in."

"I'll do that, Mr. D'Antoni."

"Great! It will take about an hour to get the Envoy ready. We need to wash it and do an inspection. We will make sure it has a full tank of gas, too. Marc will take you into Roger Alberico's office, and he will take care of all the paperwork. We will try to get

277

you out of here as quick as we can. The lousy paperwork takes so much longer than it used to. At least it's all done with computers now. If you are happy with your Envoy, and the way we treated you, please pass it along. If you aren't happy, come and see me personally, and I will take care of the matter." Mr. D'Antoni stood up and shook Tony's hand.

"Thanks, Mr. D'Antoni."

"It was good to see you. Say hello to your mother for me."

They left the office and walked around looking at the vehicles in the showroom.

Emmy asked Kenny, "What did you and Mr. D'Antoni talk about? Please don't tell me you bought that Corvette. I mean, you could if you want, but I would be afraid to drive it."

"No, I didn't buy it. We talked about family stuff. He went to school with Dad. He thinks it's funny that Dad will only buy Hondas."

Seventy minutes later Tony, Emmy and Kenny drove away in his new GMC Envoy. Marc walked into his father's office and closed the door. "Did we make any money on that deal at all?"

"Not a red cent, Marc. Lost money to be honest, but I think we made a lifelong customer. Besides, did I ever tell you that Howard Lombardi gave me some money to start up this place a long time ago?"

"No, you've never mentioned that before. Who is Howard Lombardi?" Marc sat down to listen to his father's story.

"Tony's grandfather. When I was a kid, I worked for Mr. Lombardi. He was a mean old SOB according to most everyone. I worked my butt off for him for next to nothing, did all kinds of dirty jobs for him, so he treated me with respect. When I told him I wanted to start a used car lot, he gave me the money to get started. Never said a word about paying him back. I did, of course, and I've never forgotten him. He passed away a little over four years ago." Mr. D'Antoni closed his eyes for a moment. Then he slapped his desk and stood up. "Well, let's see if there are any other customers who need a new vehicle. I need to make a little money today."

Tony checked the traffic and pulled out onto Jefferson Boulevard. "Where should we go? Do you guys have any plans for the rest of the day?" He glanced at Emmy, who was sitting in the front passenger seat.

She turned in her seat and looked at Kenny. "Do we?" Then returned her attention to the controls in the middle of the dashboard.

"I don't have any plans," Kenny answered as he rubbed a hand over the leather seats. "I love the smell of a new car."

"What does this do?" Emmy asked.

Tony slowed to a stop at a red light. "Those knobs control the temperature. It's got dual automatic heating and cooling."

"Oh, I see. You just set each side to whatever temperature you want."

When Tony proceeded through the intersection, she turned his side up to eighty-five. A few minutes later, Tony wiped some sweat off of his forehead. "It's getting warm in here. I thought the air conditioner would be cooling off the car, but instead it seems like it's getting hotter."

"Don't tell me you bought a lemon." Emmy poked his arm and then grinned.

"What did you do, Emmy?" Tony frowned. "Are you messing with the dials?" He glanced at the controls and realized what she had done. "Very funny, Em." He turned his side back down to seventy degrees.

She started messing with the radio. "How do you play a CD? Did you bring any CDs to play?"

"No, the Lumina didn't have a CD player."

"Well this does." Emmy began scanning through the FM stations.

"What are you doing now?" Tony sounded irritated. *Are you going to mess up my new ride before I have a chance to check it out?*

"I'm trying to find a station with some Fridays At Five music," Emmy answered. "I don't like this other junk."

"Just find a rock station and leave it there." Tony swatted her hand.

Kenny laughed.

"Well, what should we do?" Tony asked again.

279

"Let's pick up John and go to my house," Emmy suggested. "We can have lunch and decide what to do."

They stopped at John's apartment, and he inspected Tony's new Envoy. "It looks pretty good to me. Maybe in a month or so, if you still like yours, I might buy one. I need something more reliable than my old truck."

"You could always keep the truck. It comes in handy to haul stuff," Tony said as they headed to Emmy's house.

"I probably will. It doesn't cost much to insure."

They arrived at Emmy's, and Kristen came outside.

Emmy jumped out and ran around to the driver's side. "What do you think, Krissy?"

"It looks big." Kristen walked up to John. She put an arm around his waist, and he leaned down and kissed her.

"What do you think about the color?" Emmy asked with a grin.

Kenny thought. *Here it comes. I know you called her to set something up. What will it be?*

Kristen carefully inspected the Envoy. She rubbed some dirt off of the front quarter panel. "It's not too bad. It wouldn't have been my first choice."

"What color would you have picked?" Emmy asked.

Kenny stifled a laugh. *Here comes the punch line.*

"I would have chosen a green one," Kristen said.

"No way!" Tony hollered. "I don't even know if you can buy it in green. I'd never buy a green car or truck. You know this is more like a truck than a car, right?"

"Yeah, whatever." Emmy waved her hand dismissively. "All I know is that a green one would look better."

"You stinker!" Tony took a step toward Emmy.

She giggled and took off for the backyard. Tony ran after her and soon caught her. He picked her up and carried her on his shoulder.

"Put me down!" Emmy hollered as Tony carried her onto the deck. He dumped her onto the picnic table as everyone else laughed. "I still think you should have bought a green one."

Thirty minutes later, Tony drove over to the Nuclear Sub

Station to pick up sandwiches for lunch. Emmy went along for the ride.

"Do you have enough money to pay for lunch, Em?"

"I didn't bring anything." She frowned at him. "Don't you have any cash?"

"I spent all my money on my sweet new ride. Can't you spring for lunch?" Tony grinned.

"Maybe I would have if you had gotten a green one," Emmy said with a giggle.

Tony rolled his eyes. "What's with you and the green routine? It's getting old."

"Sorry. I saw a hideous looking green SUV yesterday, so I thought I would tease you about it. I really think you chose the right color." She turned to look in the back seat. "There's lots of room back there."

After lunch, they sat on the deck and tried to come up with a plan for the afternoon.

"Let's do something," Emmy whined. "It's too boring to just sit around and talk."

"What do you suggest, Em?" Kristen asked. "It's going to be too hot to stay outside all afternoon."

"Let's go swimming at your parents' house," John suggested.

"Yeah!" Tony hollered. "We can toss Emmy in the pool because of the way she made fun of my new Envoy."

"What do you say, Kenny? Do you want to go swimming?" Emmy asked while finishing her tuna sub with jalapenos.

"Sounds all right to me, but I'll have to leave around five, Em. I've got to meet with Andy and Ralph," Kenny said.

"That's okay. Tony will give me and Kristen a ride home," Emmy said.

"I'm sure he will give Kristen a ride, but he might not let you ride in his new car. You teased him a lot."

"He better give me a ride. And don't call it a car. He refers to it as his new truck."

Everyone made it to the Keaslings an hour later. An hour after that, Kenny's phone rang. He talked for several minutes.

281

"Em, that was Andy. I gotta leave now. Will you be all right?"

She climbed out of the pool. "Sure. Kristen will make sure Tony gives me a ride. I'll talk to you later." She kissed him and then jumped back in the pool. She landed right on top of Tony.

"Be careful, Emmy! You could hurt him," Kristen shouted.

Kenny laughed as he took off. "See you guys later."

After a while, Kristen and John went into the house and brought out some bottled water.

Kristen stood at the edge and looked down at Tony and Emmy. "Are you guys going to stay in the pool all afternoon?"

Tony swam over to the side. "We need to get out pretty soon. I'm getting tired."

Emmy swam over and jumped on Tony's back. "You can't be tired already. I'm having fun."

Kristen shook her head as Tony and Emmy goofed around.

"What are those two doing?" John asked as Kristen sat down by him at one of the round tables.

"Do you remember what I said that day at Mama's house?"

John rubbed his chin for a few seconds. "Oh, yeah. I remember now. You're kidding, right?"

Kristen shook her head. "No, it's foreplay."

John grinned. "Would you like to get back in the pool? Maybe we can have some foreplay of our own."

"Not in front of them." Kristen blushed just as her cell phone rang. She checked the called ID. "It's P.J."

"Hi, Kristen, I've got some bad news..."

After being together for over six years, The Notable Exceptions broke up when two of the guys got new jobs out of state. Emmy and Kristen weren't too upset because the band took up more time than they expected, and they planned to quit when school started in the fall for Emmy. At least they had some audio and video memories of their time as stars.

An hour later, Emmy and Kristen were in the back seat of the Envoy.

"That was a blast," Emmy said. "I'm sure glad your parents have a pool."

"Derrick and I would use the pool all the time when we were kids. Now, it's just kinda there. Mom uses it, but Daddy doesn't."

"Hey, Tony, are you upset that I jumped on top of you?" Emmy asked while poking him in the side.

"Was that you? I thought it was a little kid," he teased back. *Are you gonna be mad because of where I touched you? I didn't do it on purpose.*

They got back to Emmy's, and she made sandwiches for a light supper. They sat on the deck to eat.

"Do you need anything else?" Emmy asked as Tony finished his second sandwich.

He grinned. "That will hold me until I get home. I'm sure Mama will have some real food."

"You're a stinker! I don't know why I even bother to try to feed you." Emmy took his plate as she made a face at him.

"Let's go inside, John. It's getting too humid out here," Kristen said.

John followed Kristen into the house, and they sat on the living room couch.

"Now what about that foreplay you mentioned earlier?" John grinned.

"Just be quiet and kiss me," Kristen said.

Emmy sat across the picnic table from Tony. "Do you want a beer or something? There's some left in the fridge from when Diane lived here."

"No, I'm fine with just this." He held up his liter of Ice Mountain water.

"I really should get rid of that beer. No one is ever going to drink it. It's over a year old."

"Geez, Em! Just dump it already," Tony said.

Emmy turned to sit sideways on the bench. She rested her chin on her knee and looked at Tony.

"What?" he asked. *Are you going to yell at me now?*

"I was just thinking about this afternoon."

"I'm sorry that my hand ended up on your butt."

"I'm not upset about that. No big deal." She waved her

283

hand. "We were just having fun, and you tossed me around the pool."

"I was afraid you would be mad." Tony looked toward the back door. "Do you think it's safe to go inside?"

"What do you mean?"

"John and Kristen might be making out."

Emmy jumped up. "Let's go see."

She and Tony walked through the kitchen and into the dining room. Emmy giggled as she peeked into the living room. "Is it safe to come in?"

"Stop being so immature, Emmy." Kristen rolled her eyes. "John and I were just kissing."

John stood up and checked the time. "Are you ready to go?" he asked Tony.

"Yeah, we should get going. See you girls later. It was fun to hang out with you, Kristen." Tony grinned.

"What about me?" Emmy poked him in the stomach.

"I suppose I had fun with you, too... brat."

"Creep!"

John looked at Kristen. She nodded her head and whispered, "Foreplay."

Chapter Thirty-One

Ten minutes after Tony and John had left, the house phone rang, and Emmy hurried into the kitchen to answer it. She glanced at the caller ID. "Hi, Mom. What's up? How are you?"

"I threw your father out of the house today. That's what's up."

"Why? What happened? Are you guys arguing again?" Emmy shook her head in disgust. "I mean still." She opened the fridge and grabbed a bottle of water.

"We're not arguing anymore. I threw his butt out."

"Mom! Tell me what happened." Emmy sighed as she waited for the latest story about her parents' arguing.

"I can't take anymore of his attitude. He is impossible to live with."

"Yeah, yeah, yeah! Like that's something new. Where did he go? You know his heart is bad, Mom."

"I don't care where he went. I never want to see him again."

"You guys are both so impossible," Emmy said as she kicked the refrigerator door shut. "I'll come over and we can talk."

"Don't bother. I'm not changing my mind."

"Do you have any idea where Dad is?"

"He can be in hell for all I care," Mom yelled.

"Don't say that, Mom. You know his heart can't take much stress."

"He's probably down at that bar where he always drinks."

"Which one?" Emmy asked. *He has more than one favorite.*

"Miller's Bar. Do you know where it is?"

"I know where it is, Mom. I'm going to see if he's there. I'll call you later."

"What's going on, Em?" Kristen asked.

Emmy shook her head and explained.

"Do you want me to go with you?" Kristen asked.

"Thanks, but I can handle this myself. I suppose I will have to act as a mediator between them."

Emmy grabbed her purse and keys, got in the car and

285

hurried over to her parents' neighborhood. She stopped at Miller's Bar and parked in the pothole-filled asphalt lot.

"I'd bet they haven't fixed this for twenty years." She walked around a puddle. "That could be ten feet deep."

She looked at the faded paint on the front of the building that was the only way of identifying the business inside. She walked into the old, one-story concrete block building. Miller's had occupied the same location for over fifty years, and her father had been a regular customer for many of those years. Emmy looked around through the smokey haze and saw her father at the end of the bar with a beer in his hand. Emmy walked over and sat on the empty barstool next to him. He looked up to see who had joined him. He took a long swallow of beer, but didn't say a word for a moment.

Emmy touched his shoulder and asked, "Are you gonna say anything?"

"I suppose you have talked to your mother," Dad said.

"Yes, I did."

Another moment of silence passed before her father asked, "Do you want a beer?"

"No thanks, Daddy. You can buy me a Coke."

Her father waved at the bartender. "Ernie, would you get a Coke for my daughter, please?"

"Sure, Ray." He pulled a can from underneath the bar and sat it along with a glass in front of her. "You must be Emmy. Your father is always bragging about you. It's nice to see you again. I remember you coming in here as a little girl."

"I remember coming down here and sitting on the bar. Dad would make me drink milk, and I would eat peanuts."

"I'll bring you another Coke if you want, but your father is cut off. I'm not going to let him have another heart attack in here," Ernie said as he wiped the countertop.

"Thanks, Ernie. I'll take him home."

"I ain't goin' home," Dad yelled.

Emmy sat beside her father and drank her Coke. Neither of them said anything for a few minutes.

"I can't take her anymore, Emily. I've had it up to here." He

286

pointed to the top of his head.

"I know Mom can be hard to live with at times, but you aren't a saint, either. You are both equally to blame."

"I'm not going to argue with you. You can think what you want. All I know is that I'm not going back there."

"Just where am I supposed to take you, Daddy? You need to go home."

"Ain't gonna happen!"

He nursed his beer for a couple of minutes, and then drained it quickly.

"Give me another one, Ernie."

Ernie ignored him.

Emmy coughed twice. "Daddy, I want to leave. I can't take the smoke in here. Where should I take you? I know you never drive over here. Do you want to stay with me and Kristen?"

"Take me to Liam O'Dell's place. The old buzzard will let me stay overnight."

"Why don't you come home with me instead?" Emmy asked. She got down from the barstool and put a hand on her father's shoulder. "We have plenty of room."

"No! I'm not going to stay with you. Just take me to Liam's place. He'll let me stay without pestering me."

"You'll have to give me directions. I don't know where... Do you mean Principal O'Dell?"

"Yeah. He'll let me stay there and crash. I don't ever want to see that woman again." Raymond got down and hollered at Ernie, "Put it on my tab."

Ernie nodded. "Good to see you again, Emmy."

Emmy managed to get her father into her car, but he wouldn't go home. Emmy stopped at the house, but he wouldn't get out no matter how hard she tried to convince him.

"All right, you stubborn old man. Where does Principal O'Dell live?" she asked. *I'm about ready to strangle you.*

"I'll tell you. Just get away from here before that woman comes out and starts screaming again."

Raymond managed to stay awake long enough to give Emmy directions to Liam O'Dell's farmhouse ten miles out of

287

SoHam and then fell asleep. Emmy knew the general area and found the farm after making one wrong turn. She saw the name on the mailbox and pulled into the driveway. She parked, jumped out of the car, ran up the steps, across the porch to the front door and rang the bell. In a couple of minutes the door opened. Emmy saw Principal O'Dell looking at her.

"I'm sorry to bother you but..."

He looked at Emmy, and then at her car. He could see her father in the front seat. "He's been at Miller's again, has he?"

"How do you know?"

"This isn't the first time, Emily."

"You remember who I am."

"I do, child, and I remember now that everyone calls you Emmy. I'll help you bring him in the house. Has he been fighting with Patricia again?"

"Yes. They argue all the time now, and he drinks too much. He suffered a heart attack a few months ago."

"I remember that. The doctors told him to lay off the booze. I see he has ignored them as usual—stubborn old goat. He won't ever learn." Liam shook his head and walked down the steps with Emmy.

Between the two of them, they managed to wake Emmy's father up enough to get him in the house. He fell asleep on the couch as soon as he lay down.

"I'll take care of him, Emmy."

"I take it this isn't the first time you've done that."

"Ray started drinking when we were in school together. I'm sorry, Emmy. I shouldn't say anything. It's not my place to make judgments."

"It's all right. I know he has a problem."

"Will you tell your mother he is staying with me. I'll look after him until he sobers up. Then we'll see what we can do for him."

"Thanks, Mr. O'Dell. Say hi to Annie for me, please."

"I'll do that, Emmy love. Don't worry about your father. I know how to deal with him."

"Thanks, Mr. O'Dell. I'm sorry to trouble you."

288

Emmy drove back to her parents' home and walked up the front sidewalk. She rang the bell, and her mother eventually opened the door.

"Where is he?"

"I took him out to Principal O'Dell's farm," Emmy said as she squeezed past her mother and into the living room.

"Good. He can stay there forever. I never want to see him again as long as I live." Mom sat in her recliner and crossed her arms over her chest.

"You don't mean that, Mom."

"Oh, I most certainly do. That man has been a pain in my butt for over a hundred years. He can rot in hell as far as I'm concerned."

Emmy closed her eyes and prayed silently.

"Saying some prayer is not going to change anything, Emily."

"It changed everything in my life," she answered. "You should try it sometime."

This stunned her mother into silence for a moment.

"He can't come back here. I won't let him in the house."

"You guys need to talk to a marriage counselor," Emmy said.

Mom waved her hands. "That won't do any good. That's just a scam and, besides, your father is too stubborn to change."

"Maybe you both need to make some changes."

"He needs to change more than I do."

"Oh, Mother! You are just as stubborn as he is."

"You're wrong, but I'm not going to argue about it with you."

Emmy rolled her eyes. *Well, I'm going to do something about it.*

289

"Lynette, I'm sorry to bother you, but do you know any marriage counselors? My parents need help. I'm afraid they are kill each other. They are arguing more than ever. Mom threw Daddy out of the house Saturday. Can you help me?"

"Your parents don't go to church, do they?"

"Not for years. They are Catholic, but they don't go to mass."

"There is a doctor I know. She's not a medical doctor. She's a counselor. She would be perfect."

"Does she take new patients or clients? Whatever they're called."

"She does. She works in a clinic with several others. Let me call you back with her information."

"Thanks, Lynette. I appreciate it. I'm at work, but I have my cell phone with me." Emmy ended the call, sat back in her chair and closed her eyes. *Of course, scheduling an appointment is the easy part. I would have to convince them to actually see the doctor.*

Lynette called back thirty minutes later and gave Emmy the information.

"Thanks, I'll call right away."

Emmy called Dr. Tolliver's office and made an appointment for Wednesday morning.

She and Kristen rushed home after work. Emmy prayed and then called her mother.

"What is it, Emily?"

"Don't hang up, Mom. I made an appointment for you and Daddy to see a counselor."

"You're wasting your time. Your father will never agree to see a shrink. I'm not sure our insurance would even cover that, and I'm not wasting money out of my pocket."

"You shouldn't worry about how much it costs. Isn't your marriage worth something?"

"Ha! It's not worth a red cent."

"You guys can't survive without each other. You scream and yell at each other, but you need that chaos in your life. I don't know

290

why, but you do." Emmy put her feet over the arm of the couch in the TV room. "I'm not positive, but your insurance should cover the cost. Will you agree to go to the appointment with Daddy?"

"Sure! If you can work a miracle and get him to agree to go, I'll go along. It could be interesting to hear what a shrink would say."

"Can he come home?"

"Yeah, he can come back. It's not the first time I've tossed him out."

Tell me about it. "Good! I'm going to see if I can reach Daddy."

It took most of the evening, but Emmy finally got through to someone at Liam O'Dell's farm.

"I'm sorry to bother you, Mr. O'Dell, but is my father still there?" Emmy asked.

"He's here and he hasn't had more than one beer a day. Would you like to talk to him?"

"Yes, please."

"Hang on." Mr. O'Dell set the phone down. "Hey, Ray! Your daughter is on the phone. She needs to talk to you."

"I know what she wants. I'm not going back."

"You aren't staying here. You might as well talk to her."

Raymond swore but picked up the phone. "What?"

Nice to talk to you, too. Emmy rolled her eyes. "I talked to Mom and she agreed to let you come home."

"Why would I want to do that?"

"Because that's where you live. What are you going to do? Go from friend to friend and crash until they throw you out?"

"You did that when you left high school."

"I graduated. I didn't drop out."

"Whatever." He rubbed his temples. "Fine. I'll go back home, but I'm not putting up with any crap from her."

"I have more good news."

"Yeah, what?" He sat on the couch and shook his head.

"Mom agreed to go see a counselor with you."

Raymond laughed. "You're dreaming, Emmy. Ain't no way we're going to see some quack shrink who just wants our money.

291

Ain't gonna happen in this lifetime."

"It is if you ever want to see me again," Emmy said.

He froze and stared at the phone for several seconds. "You're going to blackmail me, huh?"

"If I have to. I'll do whatever I can to save your marriage."

"Okay," Raymond said. "I'll go along with this insanity. I know it won't do a bit of good, but I'll listen to this shrink. You know it's all just a load of bull..."

"Daddy!"

"When?"

"Wednesday morning. I'll even pick you guys up."

"Fine! Liam's going into town in the morning. He can drop me off at home."

Emmy drove to her parents' house the morning of the appointment and heard them yelling at each other as she rang the bell and stood on the front porch. Her mother let her in the house after a couple of minutes.

"Will you quit yelling at each other for just an hour? Are you ready to go? I'll take you."

"We're ready, but you don't have to drive us."

"I don't mind." Emmy saw an empty bottle of beer on the table next to her father's recliner. *Really, Daddy? Isn't it a bit early for that?*

"I'm perfectly capable of driving, Emily."

"I know that, Daddy. I just thought I would offer."

"You just want to make sure we actually go see this shrink," Mom yelled.

"She can help you guys."

"We're going to drive ourselves. You don't need to follow us, either." Dad grabbed his keys and cap with the Miller's Bar logo. "Let's go, Patricia." He pointed his finger at Emmy. "This is a total waste of time and money."

"Please, just do it for me, Daddy," Emmy said as she fought to keep from crying.

"That's the only reason we're going," Dad said.

"All right. I have to get to work." Emmy checked the time.

I have to talk to Tony later today. We have to talk about what happened last night. This is going to be a rather hectic day.

Her parents argued in the car on the drive to see the counselor.

"You had better not tell this doctor too much," Patricia warned.

"Hey! I'm not going to tell her squat," Raymond said vehemently. "You better keep your trap shut. She doesn't need to know about our private life."

Patricia stared out the window. "Then why are we going? This will be a complete waste."

"Well, then just don't volunteer too much information," Raymond relented.

They pulled into the parking lot of the three-story yellow brick building just two blocks from St. Bart's hospital.

"Are we gonna go in, or are we gonna sit here?" Raymond asked as he looked up at the top floor of St. Bart's. *I hate that place. I hope I never see the inside of it again.*

"We're here, so we might as well go inside."

They sat on opposite sides of the waiting room and didn't talk to each other. Finally, the doctor came out to see them.

"Hello, I'm Dr. Erica Tolliver. Please come in and have a seat." She carried a folder and her reading glasses were about to fall off of her long thin nose. *I see you chose to sit on opposite sides of the room instead of next to each other on the couch. That tells me something.*

Raymond thought, *At least you aren't wearing one of them white coats. You look more like a lawyer or something in that fancy outfit.*

Neither Raymond nor Patricia Colasanti expected anything to improve in their marriage because of this session. They only agreed to be here because Emmy insisted. They wondered how much it would cost.

"Please, have a seat." Dr. Tolliver pointed to the brown leather couch and then sat down in a matching chair across from them. "I talked to Emily a couple of days ago. She filled me in on your biographical facts. Dates of birth and that kind of information.

293

You have two daughters and one grandson." Dr. Tolliver paused to look at Raymond and Patricia before she continued. "I see you were married in 1959, but your first daughter wasn't born until 1978. Was that a conscious choice not to have children until later in life?"

"No freaking way! She was knocked up when we got married. I had to marry her," Raymond blurted out.

So much for not telling the doctor anything! Patricia threw her hands into the air. "You should keep your big mouth shut, Raymond."

Dr. Tolliver held up her hand. "Please! I should make this rule clear right now. When one of you is talking, the other must not interrupt. You will both have a chance to speak. Do you both understand and agree to this?"

They nodded in agreement.

"Now, who would like to tell me about the reason you got married?" Dr. Tolliver defused the tense situation with a calm authoritative voice.

"I will." Patricia frowned at Raymond. *Since you've already spilled the beans. I might as well go ahead and tell her everything about our messed up lives.*

"Okay, Patricia. Please go ahead, and, Raymond, you will have an opportunity to add anything you might like to say after she is finished."

"Yeah. Whatever." He looked at the plant in the corner and the landscape painting above the desk. *This is such a waste of time. I bet she drives a Cadillac.*

"We met at Roosevelt High School when I was a freshman. Ray was a senior, but he should have already graduated. Do you want to tell her why?" Patricia smirked at Raymond.

"I dropped out for a year."

"Hah! He got sent to reform school for a year."

"I took a couple of cars for joyrides and got caught. It wasn't a big deal," Raymond confessed with a wave of his hand.

There was more to it than that, Patricia recalled.

"We can talk about that later if it's important," Dr. Tolliver said. "Please continue with how you met."

294

"We met at school and started dating when I was fifteen. We got rather serious right away and started sleeping together."

For crying out loud, Patricia. Are you going to tell this stranger everything? Raymond clenched his jaw but held his tongue.

"Our parents had no idea, of course. We would sneak away. Well, anyway, I got pregnant at seventeen. Our parents found out and forced us to get married. A month after the wedding I suffered a miscarriage. By then we were stuck with each other. A divorce was out of the question because of our religion."

Patricia stopped, and Dr. Tolliver looked to Raymond. "Would you like to add anything?"

"My parents forced us to get married more than hers. Her parents didn't want us to get married even though there was a baby coming."

Dr. Tolliver crossed her legs as she said, "You stayed together despite the loss of the baby. Did you try to have another child?"

"Yes. I got pregnant two more times, but I lost both babies very early. After that we gave up. We didn't bother with birth control since we were raised as good Catholics. We assumed we would never have children until I got pregnant with Diane." Patricia paused and blinked away some tears.

Dr. Tolliver checked her notes. "That was 1978, correct?"

"Diane was born in '78. I got pregnant in '77."

Raymond rolled his eyes. *I think the doctor realizes that.*

"That pregnancy went normally. When I got pregnant two years later, it was a different story. I was bedridden for the last three months. I nearly died. Emily was delivered by c-section, and I made sure I wasn't going to have any more babies."

"Were you aware of this, Raymond?"

"Not until later."

"Did you want more children?"

"I wanted a son! I wanted a son!" Raymond shouted as he lost his composure. His shoulders shook and he began to sob quietly.

After a moment, Dr. Tolliver continued, "Emily never

295

mentioned your previous attempts to have children."

"She doesn't know. Neither does Diane. We never told them. We never told anyone. Not even our parents. About the last two, I mean." Patricia pulled on her ear and looked at the wall.

"Why was that?" Dr. Tolliver looked up from her folder.

Raymond and Patricia looked at each other.

Are you going to tell her or should I? Patricia thought.

Raymond waved his hand as if saying, *Go ahead.*

"The second and third pregnancies were not Raymond's babies. I was having an affair with another man. We were separated for almost two years."

"But you got back together," Dr. Tolliver said casually.

"Yes, we did." Patricia nodded.

"We would fight all the time, but we always made up. It's like we weren't happy unless we were fighting about something. Either my drinking or her affairs. There was always something to fight about," Ray explained. "I think my parents were kinda like that, too. But we took it to extremes."

"How did your parents react to this?" Dr. Tolliver wrote some notes in her folder.

"They basically stayed out of it. My parents offered to let me come home, but Ray's father wanted no part of him. We stuck it out because we are both stubborn and..." Patricia looked away.

"The sex was good. You can say it, Patricia. The doctor knows we had sex."

"I'm not talking about our sex life with anyone," Patricia insisted.

You already have, woman. Raymond thought.

"It would be a great help if you were open about it," Dr. Tolliver said softly.

After a minute of silence, Patricia relented. "All right. Sex with him was better than with any other man. Are you happy now?" *And don't you dare ask how many other men there were. That is nobody's business.*

"Did you have relationships with other women during the separation, Raymond?" Dr. Tolliver tilted her head.

"Not at first, but after she got pregnant, and I knew it

296

wasn't my kid, I started seeing other women. I never got serious about any of them."

"They were whores!"

"Please don't interrupt, Patricia," Dr. Tolliver cautioned.

"She's right. They were whores or one-night stands. I didn't really date other women. After she lost the second, no, the third baby, we got together again. I've never cheated since. I drank a lot, I admit that, but I never cheated." He pounded on the couch.

He stopped talking and Patricia started.

"I never cheated again, either. We have been faithful to each other even though we sometimes made each other miserable."

The hour appointment passed quickly.

"I would like to see you both again. I think you each have unresolved issues that stem from the early days of your marriage. You aren't the only couple to have gone through this. There are plenty of other couples with more baggage than the two of you. Will you come back, and we can work through some of these issues?"

"Okay," Raymond agreed reluctantly. *I wonder if our insurance will cover any of this? I'll have to find out. I'm not paying a lot of money out of my own pocket.*

"All right, but I don't want the girls to know about any of this," Patricia warned the doctor as she stood up.

"I will not reveal anything we discuss to either Diane or Emily." Dr. Tolliver closed her folder and stood up. "Maybe at some point, you will feel secure enough to tell them."

"They hate us already. I don't want them to ever know."

"They don't hate us, Patricia. They don't like how we fight. They don't hate us as persons."

"Are you sure?" Patricia asked.

"Yes, I'm sure. You know Emmy would forgive you for anything. She's different now. She's still going through that religious phase."

Dr. Tolliver listened quietly to Raymond and Patricia. *You probably haven't talked to each other like this for a long time.*

"You know Diane has asked you why we never had kids for so long," Ray said. "They will be so disappointed if they learn that

297

we had to get married."

"Have you forgotten the reason Diane got married so quickly?" Patricia asked. "I doubt if she would care."

"She is just like you, Patricia. Strong willed..."

"Stubborn, and she discovered sex at an early age. At least Emmy didn't take after me." *But I think she's making up for lost time.*

"Emmy is just as stubborn. No, she's more stubborn than either of us. She just didn't have sex as early," Raymond said. *At least I don't think she did. I sure don't want to know about it if she did.* He thought about that for a moment. *I know she used to sneak around with that Porter kid. If I ever find out that he touched her, I'll kill the SOB.*

Patricia said, "She's not stubborn, but just independently minded."

"She is something special though," Raymond said as he laughed.

"She is very special. I'm not sorry now that we decided to have her and not have an abortion." *I can't believe we even considered that.*

Dr. Tolliver made a note to learn more about Emmy's birth and early years.

Chapter Thirty-Three

On September eighth, Emmy and Kristen stayed home from church so they could attend the opening game of the season for the Chicago Bears. The Bears faced their division rivals, the Minnesota Vikings, at Soldier Field. Emmy and Kristen got out of bed early—anxious for the game to begin. Kenny decided to drive his parents' Odyssey. He picked up Emmy and Kristen, and they drove over to get Mama. They walked in the back door and found her in the kitchen wringing her hands.

"Mama, you don't have to worry. Tony will be all right."

"I'm his mother. I will always worry about him."

By ten o'clock they were on their way to Soldier Field. They arrived at the stadium and parked in the VIP area. They found their seats and waited. Eventually the players made their way onto the field to warm up. Emmy saw Tony and pointed him out to Mama.

"Look! There he is, number fifty-two. Do you see him?"

"I can see him, Emmy. He doesn't look much bigger than the other players. He looks smaller than those guys." Mama pointed to the huge linemen. "What if he gets hurt?"

"It's always a possibility, but not likely. It will be okay, Mama. You'll have fun."

"If you say so, dear. How soon will they start?" Mama asked as she kept her eyes on Tony.

"Kickoff is around noon."

Emmy smiled at Kenny. "Are you happy I invited you? This is your first game, right?"

He nodded. "Thank you for thinking of me, Em. This is special because it's Tony and John's first game with the Bears. I hope they are ready for the weather. It's pretty hot for football."

Emmy looked around at the rapidly filling stands. "I never thought we would wear shorts to his first game."

"Do you want something to drink, Em?"

"I'd love a Coke and a hot dog. Thanks, Kenny."

Kenny took everyone's order and headed to the concession stand.

"You should go with Kenny. He will need help carrying everything," Mama suggested by patting Emmy's knee.

"Do you want me to go with you?" Emmy stood up.

"That would make things a little easier I suppose."

"Okay, I'll go." Emmy scooted past Mama and Kristen. "Will you be all right?"

"I'm perfectly fine, dear. I have Kristen with me."

Emmy looked at Kristen.

Kristen frowned at her. "Hurry back. You don't want to miss the kickoff."

It took a while for them to return, and, when they did, Kristen gave Emmy a long hard look.

"I'm sorry, Kristen. It just took a while. There were a lot of people in line." She handed Kristen a hot dog. "We weren't doing anything but talking as we waited."

"Okay, I'm sorry. I shouldn't have assumed you and 'Kenny' would do anything."

Emmy stared, as she almost tripped over Kristen's feet. *Oh, God! Do you know what happened? Did Tony tell you? No, you couldn't possibly know what a huge mistake I made.* She bit her lip, and then asked, "Is there something wrong? Are you mad at me? You've been treating me weird the last few days."

Kristen glared at Emmy. "It's nothing I want to talk about here and now."

"All right. Do you know where John's family is sitting?" Emmy handed Mama her hot dog and sat down.

"They are one section over and back about five or six rows." Kristen pointed in the general direction. "I think I see them, but I can't tell for sure."

"We could go over and talk to them later if you want," Kenny said while passing out the Cokes.

"Maybe at halftime, guys."

The Bears won the coin toss to start the game and elected to defer to the second half. They wanted to start the game with their defense on the field. The teams took their positions. The whistle blew, and the Bears kicked off. They hammered the returner at the twenty-five yard line. As the defense trotted onto the field, Emmy stood up and whistled.

"You know he can't hear you, Em," Kenny said as he covered his ears.

"I know, but I told him I would whistle at him."

"Does he know where our seats are?"

Emmy waved at the players even though they weren't looking at the crowd. "He knows the general location."

They were all so proud of Tony as he started at middle linebacker for the Bears in his first game as a professional. The action on the field picked up and before they realized it halftime arrived and the Bears led 14-10. Kristen and Emmy realized it would be futile to attempt to find John's parents in the mass of people. Kenny offered to buy more Cokes and hot dogs.

"Are you sure you don't want anything?" Emmy asked Mama.

"I'm positive. My stomach is too nervous to eat."

"Kristen, do you want to go with Kenny this time?" Emmy asked as a peace offering.

"Don't be silly. You can go with him." Kristen smiled, but Emmy knew it wasn't sincere. Emmy stuck out her tongue at Kristen as she scooted past.

In the third quarter the Bears' defense created a turnover. Tony stripped the runner of the ball and the Bears jumped on it—giving the offense excellent field position. The offense scored another touchdown for a 21-10 lead. The teams traded field goals in the fourth quarter and the Bears won 24-13. Mama said a prayer thanking God that Tony didn't get hurt. The fact that the Bears won was of secondary importance to her. Emmy turned to Kenny and gave him a high-five. Kenny lifted Emmy up and hugged her as she put her arms around his neck and kissed him. Kenny set Emmy down, and she turned to face Kristen. Emmy raised her hand to give Kristen a high-five, but Kristen turned away. Emmy bit her lip and thought. *I think I know why you're mad at me, Krissy, but I can't talk about it yet. And I'm going to murder Tony for telling you.*

They headed home to Mama's house to wait for Tony and John. It would be later in the evening because John planned to

301

meet his family after the game at a nearby restaurant. John's family greeted him like a hero. They spent over an hour together before everyone needed to head back to Ohio. The guys finally arrived at Mama's and were surprised that no one greeted them as they tromped in through the back door.

"Mama! Kristen! Emmy! Is anyone here?" Tony looked at John. "Weren't we supposed to meet them here?"

"I'm sure that's what Kristen told me." John shrugged. "They were all coming back here after the game."

Tony and John walked through the house. They found everyone in the living room reading books.

"Hi, guys. We're back."

Tony expected hugs and kisses from the girls, but they greeted him with a calm indifference. *Oh, crap!* he thought. *Is everyone mad at me and Emmy? Do they know?*

"Oh, hello, son. Did you have a good day at work?"

Tony looked at Mama, then Kenny, then Kristen, and then finally at Emmy. Finally, Emmy and Kristen couldn't keep a straight face any longer. They started giggling, and Emmy got up and ran to Tony.

"We wanted to surprise you somehow, so we thought we would pretend that today was no big deal," Kristen said.

"Did we surprise you?" Emmy asked.

"Yeah, you did. We saw the Odyssey parked in the driveway, so we figured you guys were still here. But then when no one said anything when we walked in, we thought maybe you went out for a walk or something."

Kristen hugged John and kissed his cheek. "You scored a touchdown on your first catch. You should be the starter instead of that other guy."

"Right now he starts because he's a better blocker. Once I become a stronger blocker I might have a shot at starting. I think I'm a better receiver. I know I'm quicker."

"Did you enjoy your first Bears' game, Kenny? Did Emmy behave?" Tony asked. *If Kenny knows, he's sure taking it calmly.*

"I loved it. Usually, when I'm in a stadium like that, I'm playing my guitar and singing. It was nice to be able to just watch.

302

Could you hear Emmy whistling before the game?"

"No, sorry, Em, but we really can't hear much except for the overall noise."

"I whistled as loud as I could. Are you sure you couldn't hear me?"

"That she did. I thought I would go deaf. She can whistle louder than we play at our shows," Kenny said.

"Oh, you guys. It wasn't that loud." Emmy smacked Kenny's arm, and then stood in front of him. Kenny put his hands on her shoulders and held her. "Kenny bought pop and hot dogs for us. Thank you, Kenny," Emmy said as she smiled at him.

"Are you boys hungry?" Mama asked. "I've got some lasagna in the fridge. It won't take too long to heat it up."

"Have they ever refused food?" Emmy asked and then giggled.

Tony looked at John. "You want some lasagna?"

"I suppose I could force myself to eat some. Thanks, Mama."

After they ate, the girls were ready to head home. They had to work in the morning. On the way to Emmy and Kristen's, Kenny dropped John off at his apartment.

"Thanks for the ride, Kenny."

Kristen opened the sliding door and stepped out, so she could give John a good night kiss.

"I'll talk to you tomorrow. I hope you aren't too sore after today's game."

"I feel great. I know it's a long season, but I think we're going to have a good team."

Kristen got back in the van. John closed the door and waved goodbye. Emmy scrambled into the now empty front seat as Kenny pulled away.

"Do you know how to get back to our house?" Emmy asked as she grinned.

"I think I can find my way back."

Kenny pulled into the driveway and Kristen hopped out, but Emmy stayed in the minivan.

"Aren't you coming in, Emmy?"

303

"In a few minutes. I want to talk to Kenny."

Kristen frowned at her. "Don't stay out here too long."

"Yes, Mom."

"Fine. Do whatever you want." Kristen waved her hand dismissively, and then stomped into the house. She slammed the door behind her and muttered, "God! How can you act so innocent with Kenny after what has happened?"

"I've never been to a Bears' game before," Emmy said after Kristen was in the house.

"Neither have I, Em. Will you invite me to another game sometime?"

"As long as you buy the hot dogs and Cokes. Can you believe how much they cost?"

"They cost so much because they have to pay the players so much money," Kenny said. "I heard one of them bought a new GMC and actually paid cash for it. He must make a ton of money."

"Oh, stop it. I know you have more money than you'll ever be able to spend. Unless you marry me. If you do, then Kristen and I will spend it all on new clothes."

"Are you going to be quiet so I can kiss you?"

"Oooh! Are we gonna get in back and fool around?" Emmy grinned as she teased Kenny.

"Have you done that before?"

Why are you asking? Do you know? Emmy bit her lip. "Oh, sure. Lots of times."

"I better go."

"Such a party pooper," she teased. "This is your last week of vacation, right? You guys leave on Thursday. Are you getting excited?"

On Thursday the band would open their new tour in Columbus, Ohio.

"I'm excited about playing in front of people again. Other than the show on the Fourth, we haven't played in front of anyone since last year." He stopped talking and looked at Emmy. He kissed her. "The worst thing about going on tour is that I'll have to be away from you. This has been the best vacation ever. We've spent more time together than ever before."

304

"Tell me. Maybe I should go with you. Do you need someone to take care of you?"

"You mean like a personal assistant or something?"

"You better not have a 'personal assistant' who takes care of what I'm thinking about." Emmy grinned as she touched his thigh.

"Oooh! Just what were you thinking about, you naughty girl?"

"I could show you," Emmy whispered and then bit her lip. She pulled him into the very back of the Odyssey.

"Maybe just one kiss," Kenny said as he leaned closer to her.

Thirty minutes later she kissed him one last time and headed into the house.

Kristen greeted her in the kitchen with her hands on her hips. "What were you guys doing?" Kristen glared at Emmy. "And fix your top."

Emmy checked her top. "What?"

Kristen walked over and fixed it. "This was buttoned before."

Emmy bit her lip. "He just undid that one."

Kristen turned abruptly and began walking away.

"Wait! What's wrong? Why are you mad at me?" Emmy grabbed Kristen's arm and spun her around. "We didn't do anything but kiss."

"So you say. I'm mad at you because you can't decide who is your boyfriend. You're not being fair to either one."

"Kenny is my boyfriend," Emmy insisted.

"Does he know how you and Tony flirted with each other at Cobb Park? How about all the other times when you tease and flirt with Tony? Did you ever tell Kenny about Tony sitting on you and smacking your butt?" She started to say something else but stopped.

Emmy scuffed her foot on the floor and didn't look at Kristen. "No, I haven't exactly mentioned it." *No one will love me if I don't keep some things a secret.*

"Are you going to?"

Emmy took a deep breath. "Yes, I will tell him when the

305

time is right." *Maybe if he tells me more about his relationship with Becky*

"Bull! The time will never be right. I'm getting sick and tired of this... this... whatever. You're supposed to know better."

"Kristen! Just because I'm a Christian doesn't mean I will be perfect. I'm still going to make mistakes and screw up at times."

"That's for sure," Kristen said sarcastically.

"That was uncalled for." Emmy bit her lip. *Or maybe I deserved it.*

Kristen tilted her head back, put a hand to her forehead and sighed. "I'm sorry, Em. That was mean. I know you are trying to lead a good life."

"It's not about leading a good life, Krissy. Anyone can do that." Emmy backed up against the kitchen counter in front of the sink. "It's all about letting Jesus have control of your life."

"I've been mad at you, and I kept it bottled up. I should have talked to you." *But I can't. Tony made me promise.* "I'm sorry that I haven't."

"What else have you been mad at me about?" Emmy twisted her hair. "And Kenny unbuttoned more than..."

Kristen held up her hand. "Stop! I don't want to know all the details. I can understand how you feel." Kristen hung her head. "I have done the same thing with John."

Emmy's eyes brightened. "Have you guys...?"

"We have made out. Nothing else."

"Does he know about your night with Ryan?" Emmy asked. "Did he tell you about his past girlfriends?"

Kristen poked Emmy in the side. "I didn't tell him Ryan's name, and I don't want to know his other girlfriends' names. You are a goof."

Emmy grinned.

Kristen held out her arms. "Will you give me a hug? I'm so glad we are best friends."

I just hope we stay best friends after what has happened. Emmy sighed.

Chapter Thirty-Four

I hope it's just the tour that's occupying your thoughts. Emmy bit her lip as she looked back and forth between Kenny and Tony. *I feel like I'm going to puke.*

Emmy and Kristen stayed home from church on Wednesday night and prepared dinner for the guys.

"This is really good, Emmy. It's gotta be carryout. Where did you get it?" Tony asked as he took another bite of rigatoni. "The sausage has a kick to it."

"Stop teasing her," Mama said. "You know she cooked everything herself." *I doubt if Kristen helped very much.*

Emmy smiled at Mama, who sat at the other end of the table, and then made a face at Tony. "Mama brought the Caesar salad, but Kristen and I made the rest."

"Did you really help make this?" John asked Kristen, who was sitting beside him at the dining room table.

"I chopped the veggies, but Emmy did everything else." Kristen smiled at John.

John kissed Kristen's cheek and whispered, "Everything was chopped into the perfect size."

Emmy rolled her eyes. "Someone is fishing for a few kisses." *Or possibly time to make out.*

"How was practice today?" Kristen asked Tony and John.

They talked about football for a few minutes. Kenny listened but kept a little quieter than usual.

Emmy glanced at Tony. *I know you told Kristen about what happened. I'm not sure if Kenny knows though.*

Mama caught Emmy biting her lip as she kept looking at Tony and Kenny. "How was your class at North Park last night, dear?"

"Okay. I've got another one tomorrow night. They count for three hours apiece, but they shouldn't be too difficult."

"You mean you will only have to study five hours a night in order to get an A," Kristen said. "Heaven forbid you ever get a B."

Kenny grinned. *I know you don't have to study that much, Em. You're so smart.*

Mama noticed that Emmy still didn't eat very much, and her face appeared to be even thinner than ever.

"I'm sorry you didn't like anything I made, Tony," Emmy said as she took his plate. "There's still a spoonful of sauce here. Do you want to lick it clean?"

"It wasn't totally awful, Em. John and I did manage to choke down a few bites." Tony grinned at her and patted her leg.

Emmy stepped back. *Don't look at me like that in front of Kenny and don't touch me, either.*

Kristen joined in and got after Tony and John. "You guys ate every single scrap. You did everything but lick the pots and pans."

"All right. I admit you are a good cook, Emmy. Maybe with enough practice you will learn to cook as well as Mama."

"Thank you, Tony," Emmy said quietly.

Kristen grabbed Tony, pulled him into the kitchen and poked her finger in his chest. "Now you and John clear the dining room and do the dishes. You do know how to work the dishwasher, right?"

"I'm sure we can figure it out. Doesn't Kenny have to help?" Tony complained.

"Keep your voice down." Kristen frowned at him. "No, he and Emmy need some time together."

"What about me? I need to spend some time alone with her, too," Tony said. "You can certainly understand why."

"No way! I'm not letting you near her."

"We'll see about that," Tony stated emphatically. He clenched his jaw. *I never should have told you about that night.*

Kristen knew Tony and John would just ask Mama for help. John entered the kitchen and Kristen continued, "Mama is coming with us. We're taking Kenny and Emmy for a walk. You're on your own and no arguing."

"Okay, we will take care of everything," John said. He assured Kristen with a kiss.

Kristen whispered, "Has Tony mentioned anything special lately? Anything really personal? Something out of the ordinary?"

"Not that I can remember." John grabbed Kristen's hand.

"Why? Is something wrong?" *I'm almost positive he hasn't talked to Brenda lately if that's what you're getting at.*

"I can't tell you. I gotta go."

John rubbed his jaw. *What do you know that you can't talk about? It must be something really important and personal.*

Emmy, Kenny, Kristen and Mama walked outside.

"I just love September nights like this. It must still be in the mid-seventies." Emmy raised her arms and spun around on the driveway.

"How far are we going to walk?" Mama asked. "Should I bring a sweater?"

"You shouldn't need one. Let's walk over to the park. It's not far, Mama, and there are some benches." Kristen led the way. "I just thought you might enjoy the fresh air." *And I can keep Tony away from Emmy.*

Kristen held Mama's arm as they strolled together. Emmy and Kenny moved ahead of them. Kenny leaned down to talk to Emmy, but Kristen couldn't hear what he said though she strained her ears trying. Emmy listened and turned her head to look at Kenny every so often.

Kristen naturally assumed the subject of their conversation involved sex.

"You really should call your mother sometime, Em." Kenny tried to convince her. "I know you don't want to, but she is your mother. You have so many people who love you. Besides Tony, Kristen, Mama and everyone, there are the people at church who love you. You know I will always love you, right?"

Emmy turned her head and smiled at Kenny. "You always know how to reassure me."

"I know I can't force you to talk to your mother, but I would appreciate it if you make an effort to at least try."

Emmy nodded.

They reached the park and Kristen asked Mama, "Is this far enough? Do you want to sit down?" Kristen pointed to a bench.

"I'm not an old lady, Kristen. I'm only fifty-eight, and I'm not an invalid. I do get out and walk around the block at home."

"I'm sorry, Mama. I didn't mean to treat you like an old

lady or anything," Kristen apologized.

"I know you didn't, dear. We can walk to the end of the street, and then turn around. How far are they going to walk?" Mama pointed to Kenny and Emmy whose faster pace propelled them farther ahead.

"They will probably walk around the loop they usually run. It's about a mile all together. We don't have to walk that far."

Kristen and Mama walked to the end of the street and turned around, but Emmy and Kenny kept going. Emmy took Kenny's hand in hers as they walked along without saying anything. He squeezed her hand to reassure her that everything would be all right. Emmy and Kenny walked around the loop and arrived back at the house at the same time as Kristen and Mama.

John and Tony had eventually figured out how to start the dishwasher and plopped down on the couch in the TV room.

Emmy heard the dishwasher running, walked over to the TV room and asked Tony, "How much soap did you put in?"

"I didn't put any soap in, John did."

John looked at Tony. "I didn't put any soap in there. I thought you took care of that."

"You guys are hopeless." Emmy rolled her eyes. "I should have done it myself. Now I'll have to do them all over."

"Sorry, Em," Tony said as he and John stood up.

Mama told the guys, "I'm ready to go home." She hugged Kenny and told him, "You have a good tour. Don't forget the words to your songs and remember to behave."

"I will, Mama. I promise."

"And remember to stay in touch with Emmy. She needs to hear from you more often than usual, right now. I know she told you what her parents said to her. She needs to know you love her. You should tell her everyday."

Kenny realized that Mama knew what Emmy's parents said. "I will make sure I call her more often than normal. I'm glad she has you close by."

Tony shook his hand and gave him a hug. "Be safe, Kenny. I would hate to think how hard it would be for Emmy if anything ever happened to you."

310

"We're not flying anywhere this time, Tony."

Tony made sure Emmy couldn't hear. "I know flying is safer than driving, but I still worry."

No one had ever told Emmy about the emergency landing Kenny and the guys made in Pennsylvania on the last tour. Tony knew how close they came to crashing, but he never mentioned it to anyone—not even John.

"I will pray for you and John when you have to fly to games," Kenny said.

"Thanks, Kenny." Tony glanced at Emmy, as she talked to Mama, and then he looked back at Kenny. "I know how much you mean to each other. I'll try to keep an eye on her while you're gone—not too close an eye, but you know what I mean."

"Thanks, Tony, I appreciate it."

Kristen heard what Tony told Kenny. She shook her head and thought. *How can you say that after what's happened? You flirt with Emmy every chance you get.*

Tony, John and Mama left.

Kenny checked the clock in the kitchen. "I'm going home, guys. Thanks for dinner. Everything tasted delicious."

"Let me give you a hug, Kenny. I might not see you again before you guys leave." Kristen hugged him and asked, "You promise to stay in touch?"

"I will." Kenny walked out to his car with Emmy. They hugged and shared a long kiss as Kristen watched for a moment before going inside.

"I'll call you in the morning, Em. I love you."

"I love you, too. Good night, Kenny. Thanks for coming over and everything else."

"You're welcome, little one." Kenny smiled at her as he got in his car and headed home.

311

Chapter Thirty-Five

"Morning, Emmy. Are you dressed yet?"

"Hi, Kenny. About to jump in the shower," she said and then nearly dropped the phone.

"How soon will you be ready?" Kenny checked the time.

"Give me half an hour, okay."

"I'll be there then."

Today would be Emmy's last chance to see Kenny before he and the band left for Ohio. She took the day off to spend it with Kenny. His tour bus would leave at six that evening. Kenny got to Emmy's house and knocked on the back door. Kristen saw him standing there, as she buttered a piece of toast.

"Come on in, Kenny. She's still upstairs."

"Hi, Kristen. How are you today?" He glanced at the burnt piece of toast. *Poor John. He's going to have to hire a cook if you guys ever get married.*

"Jealous, or maybe envious," Kristen said.

"Why?"

"Because Em has the day off, and I have to work." She made at face at her toast, and then tossed it in the trash.

"You could play hooky and hang out with us."

"I'd love to, but I can't. We've got 'important' things going on in our office, and I have to be there." She used air quotes and then laughed.

Kenny laughed, too. "It must make you feel important to know you are an indispensable part of your team."

"I guess that's one way to look at it." Kristen took the other loaf of bread out of the wicker basket on top of the microwave.

Emmy came flying down the stairs, around the corner and into the kitchen.

"Whoa. Easy there, girl. You don't want to break a leg," Kenny said as he held out his hands to stop her.

"Hi, Kenny. I'm ready to go."

"Emmy, the toaster's broke." Kristen pointed at it. "It ruined my toast... again."

Emmy rolled her eyes and turned the setting lower.

312

"Where are you guys going today?" Kristen put two more slices of bread in the toaster, and then leaned against the counter.

"We're going out to eat now. Then Kenny's going to give me a tour of the new bus. We'll play it by ear and see what happens after that."

Kristen frowned at Emmy. Emmy stuck out her tongue in response. Kenny listened as they bickered while waiting for the toast.

"Well, I've got to get to work. Kenny, I'll see you soon." Kristen grabbed her purse as she ate her toast.

"Have a good day at work, Kristen. Take care of Emmy."

"I always try," Kristen responded and then thought. *But I don't always succeed.*

Kenny smiled at Kristen as she headed toward the back door.

"Bye, Krissy. I love you." Emmy jumped up on the counter.

"Yeah, right. I'll see you tonight."

Kenny watched Kristen as she walked out the door, turned to Emmy and asked, "Are you guys mad at each other?"

"She's upset at me, but I'm not mad at her. It's nothing really." *Actually, I'm afraid she knows about something and it scares me to death.*

He stared into her eyes for a moment before asking, "Where are we going for breakfast?"

"Southern Belles okay with you? I've got a coupon for half off."

"You'll never change, will you?"

"What's wrong with saving a little money?"

"Nothing."

"I can't help it, Kenny. It's how I grew up. You know that. I won't ever get used to anything else."

They ate breakfast at Southern Belles, and Emmy made a big deal about her half price coupon with the waitress to embarrass Kenny. He shook his head. They finished eating and headed over to the Steward Music Group office to see Kenny's new bus. The band leased four new buses for this tour. One for each of the guys. The crew would share three other buses. In addition to the crew buses,

313

ten semi-trailers loaded with gear had already left for Columbus. Coordinating the logistics of a Fridays At Five tour required a staff of several full-time employees now.

"Which one is yours?"

"The one on the end over there."

"So you all have a bus just for yourself. What a waste of space. Not to mention expensive, too."

"Andy will ride with me, and the other guys will sometimes have their families along. It's either this or fly everywhere, and we all decided not to fly unless we were going overseas. Come on, I'll show you the inside."

Kenny didn't mention the reason for not flying. He opened the door, and they stepped inside. Emmy looked around. The front part of the bus looked like the living room in a house. They moved into the kitchen area, and then past a bedroom.

"That's Andy's room. Mine is in the back."

"Where's the bathroom?"

"In here."

Emmy looked inside. "You've got a shower."

"Yeah, and a toilet. There's even running water. Cold and hot!"

"You're teasing me now."

"I'm sorry. I couldn't resist, Em."

Emmy stepped into the shower and pulled Kenny in with her. "There's enough room for two people in here, Kenny."

"Do you want to try it out?"

"Are you suggesting we shower together?" Emmy smiled at Kenny.

"You know that's not what I meant, little girl."

Emmy put her arms around Kenny's neck, moved close to him and whispered, "Show me the bedroom now, please."

"Is it safe to do that?"

"I promise I will behave." *If I absolutely must.*

Kenny showed Emmy his bedroom, and she lay down for a moment, but then sat up. "This is nice! Is it a king-size?"

"It is indeed. You would have all kinds of room to move around in bed."

314

"Oooh! That would be fun."

"I didn't mean it like that, Emmy." Kenny grinned. "I was thinking about how you move all over when you sleep."

"I know. I'm sorry if I'm teasing you too much. Lie down for a moment, Kenny. I want to talk to you." She patted the spot next to her.

He sat on the bed, but left a space between them. "Okay, what are you thinking about?" *I bet I have a good idea what it could be.*

"About when we were kids, and how we shared all our secrets."

"Yeah. We did that, didn't we?"

"You knew more about me that my parents. I told you about everything." She pulled on his belt loops. *I won't bite. Move closer.*

"Believe me, I remember. You told me things I didn't want to know about. Are you going to tell me more secrets today, Emmy?"

"Maybe." Emmy looked at him. She thought about one secret in particular. She didn't have the courage to tell him. "Did I gross you out sometimes?"

"Yes. What kind of secrets do you have now?" He touched her cheek and then the tip of her nose.

She grabbed his finger and bit her lip. "How about a secret about sex?"

"You don't have any secrets about that," he said with a smile. "Not from me, anyway." *At least I hope that's still true.*

Maybe I do, and you just don't know, yet. She pushed him onto his back and closed her eyes for a few seconds.

Kenny turned on his side and looked at Emmy. She lay on her back and smiled at him.

"What is it, Em? I can tell there's something going on in your pretty head."

"Would it be a sin if we made love right now?"

"I think you know the answer to that."

"What about if we were officially engaged, for instance, and we did it then?"

315

"Where are all these questions coming from, Em?"

"I guess I'm just horny. I can't help that."

"I think that's a normal feeling for people our age."

"I know we aren't supposed to do it now that we're Christians, but..."

"I know how you feel, Em," Kenny said as he placed a hand on her belly.

"Sometimes I wish we had done more before we became Christians. Maybe then I wouldn't think about it so much."

"I think it would work just the opposite." He touched the bottom button of her top. "I would think about it even more than I do now." *If that's even possible.*

Emmy bit her lip as she looked at Kenny. She sighed and looked up at the ceiling. "I overheard Tony talking to that girl from school last week. He doesn't know I heard. I couldn't hear what they were talking about, but I know it was her."

"Are you still upset that Tony had a relationship with that girl?"

"Not upset really. I think he should be looking for a girl at church."

"I think there is one girl at church that he really likes."

"Who?"

Kenny poked her in her stomach. "Who do you think?"

"Oh... I thought you meant someone else." She blushed and felt her heart race. "I know he still has some feelings for me, but I think it's more like a cousin or good friend. I still like to be around him. Sometimes we goof around." She looked at him. *Shoot! Should I tell him about what Kristen said? I really need to talk to Tony, but I don't know what to say.*

"I know you do, Em."

I'm not sure you know everything. Kristen doesn't know everything, either. Emmy held her breath for a moment. "I meant like the day of the second recording session. I went over to Mama's, and, after lunch, Tony and I were goofing around. He chased me into the living room and pushed me down on the couch, and then he sat on my butt. He started tickling me everywhere..."

"Everywhere?"

"All the places he knows I'm ticklish but mainly the back of my knees. Kristen told John it was our way of having foreplay. To me it was simply having fun with my friend. Not sexual at all. It would have been different if you were... tickling... me in those places."

"Should I tickle you now?"

"No, because... never mind. I'm just being silly. We should get going before I make a complete fool of myself."

"How would you do that?"

Emmy looked at Kenny. She moved his hand. He knew what she wanted.

"Come on, Em. Let's go have some fun—a different kind of fun."

They stopped in the office to talk to Mr. Kesson for a moment before taking off. They tried to decide where to go, and Emmy suggested Sandusky's. "We haven't been there for a long time. Just the two of us, that is."

"I'll challenge you to a game."

"Should we think of a way to make it interesting?" Emmy asked. *I can think of a few different things that would be fun.*

"You mean a bet of some kind?"

"Yeah. How about this? Loser buys dinner before you have to leave."

"No, I'm buying dinner. Think of something else."

"Loser has to... I can't think of anything, Kenny. Let's just play for the fun of it like when we were kids."

They played two rounds of miniature golf. Then Kenny bought pop, and they sat at one of the outdoor tables. Kenny thought about the first time they came here. He could almost recall their conversation word for word.

"Can I have a taste of your pop, Kenny?"

"Sure, Emmy. Can I try yours?"

Emmy interrupted his thoughts. "What are you thinking about, Kenny? You have a faraway look on your face."

"Just remembering the first time we came here together. You must have been eight or maybe nine at the most."

"I remember. We shared our pop. Do you remember how

317

much I adored you then. I thought you were the best friend in the world. We had so much fun playing together."

"Am I still in the top ten?"

Emmy looked at Kenny and pretended to be thinking. "I'd say you might be number eleven, but if you buy me a Corvette you might move into the top ten," Emmy teased. "You might even be in the top five."

"All right, what color do you want?"

"It's gotta be red."

"Maybe I'll buy a red one for you, and I'll get a blue one for me."

The afternoon passed quickly, and Kenny and Emmy grabbed a quick bite to eat before they ran over to his house. Emmy and Mr. Colwell helped Kenny load his gear into his car.

"Are you sure you don't mind running my car back to my folks house?" Kenny asked.

"It's not a problem. Kristen will pick me up."

"You know you could take it home and use it while I'm gone. That would be better than letting it sit in the garage."

"I'll think about it." *It would be nice to be able to play your CDs in your car. It has a better sound system.*

"All right. It's time to go."

Kenny hugged his parents and said goodbye. They stood on the front porch and watched as he and Emmy took off. Emmy drove him back to his bus. Kenny took his gear into the bus and stashed it in his room—Emmy followed. They looked into each others eyes as they said goodbye. Emmy pulled his face down to hers and kissed him. He responded.

"I'm sorry, Kenny. I know I shouldn't kiss you like that right now because it could lead to other things, and you have to leave soon, but I won't see you for so long. I'll miss you."

"I'll miss you, too, Em. Skyping is just not the same as being able to see you in person. I can't hold you over the computer or smell your perfume."

"I'm not wearing perfume. That's just from my shower."

Kenny took a long deep whiff of her hair. "Whatever it is, you smell good."

Emmy hugged him again, and they held each other close. Emmy didn't want to let go, but she did. Kenny walked her back to the car and gave her a last quick kiss.

"Make sure you stay in touch, Em. I love you."

"I love you, too. I'll send emails everyday if I can."

"Say goodbye to Tony for me."

Kenny watched as Emmy drove away. He stood there for a moment even though he could no longer see the car. Andy Walker walked over to him and placed his hand on Kenny's shoulder.

Kenny jumped. "Geez, Andy, you startled me. I didn't even hear you coming."

"I know how much she means to you, and she feels the same. If you guys weren't Christians, you would still be in your room." Andy pointed to the bus. "And you know I'm right. I don't know how you guys managed not to... you know. Mere mortals would have given in to temptation. When are you going to ask her to marry you?"

"One of these days. I need to buy a ring first."

"You better ask her soon. I thought for sure you would be engaged, or even married, by the time we left for this tour. That's one of the reasons I wanted you guys to have your own bus. I thought you and Emmy would need the privacy."

"I know. So did I." Kenny looked at him and said, "Andy, maybe it's a good thing we don't always get what we want in life."

They looked at each other, laughed for a moment, and then started singing an old Rolling Stones tune.

"You can't always get what you want. You can't always get what you want. But if you try sometimes, you get what you need."

Chapter Thirty-Six

"Kristen! Wake up we need to get ready for church. We don't want to be late," Emmy yelled after looking at the alarm clock on her nightstand.

Kristen groaned and turned over in her bed. Emmy jumped out of bed and ran across the hall to Kristen's room.

"What time is it, Em?"

"It's seven. We need to shower, get dressed, have breakfast. Lots to get done."

"Just ten more minutes."

Emmy lay down next to Kristen in her bed and moved a strand of hair away from Kristen's eyes. "Did you have trouble getting to sleep last night?"

"A little. I was thinking about John."

"Maybe you should take a cold shower," Emmy teased.

"I will if you will, Emmy. You are worse than me."

They lay in bed for a few more minutes before they absolutely needed to get up.

"You can shower first while I make some coffee."

Emmy and Kristen shared the lone upstairs bathroom without any problems. Forty minutes later they headed out the door for church.

Emmy asked, "Do you want me to drive today?"

"It doesn't matter," Kristen said.

"I'll drive. I've got a full tank."

"Should we stop and get some donuts for the guys?" Kristen asked.

"I think we'll need two dozen."

Emmy laughed as she thought about how many donuts the guys ate. They stopped for donuts at the Donut Den and carried them into the music room where the worship team gathered on Sunday mornings.

"Look, donuts," Skip shouted and ran over to Kristen.

"I hope there are enough." Emmy set the boxes on the table next to the coffee pots. "We bought two dozen, and I remembered to get your favorite, Hank, strawberry filled."

320

"Thank you, girls." Hank smiled and grabbed a donut.

The rest of the guys rushed over to pick out their favorite donuts before someone else grabbed them.

Ten minutes later, they moved into the sanctuary and ran through the morning service. Chase kept running through two new songs until everyone knew them forward and backward. They struggled with them at practice on Thursday, but today they knew the songs better. The worship team sang six songs on Sundays now, so they needed to learn more new ones. Chase spent a few hours each week listening to new songs. He was eventually satisfied, so they prayed together and then scattered.

"Please, keep an eye on the countdown," Chase reminded everyone. "I don't want anyone to be late like last week, Skip."

"I won't let it happen again. I was talking to a friend."

Chase chuckled. "You were flirting with some girls and were more interested in them than your job."

The guys laughed and Steve said, "Cut him some slack, Chase. He's just a kid with a normal interest in the opposite sex."

The worship service ran a little long today because of a dozen people being baptized. After the service, Emmy and Kristen said goodbye to a few friends and headed home.

"We'll miss part of the game but not too much."

"That's all right, Kristen. I don't mind missing a few minutes because of church."

They would miss more than a few minutes of the game as a SoHam police officer pulled Emmy over. After the usual request for license, registration and insurance card, the officer returned to his squad car.

"Don't even say it, Krissy." Emmy frowned.

Kristen smirked. "I knew you would eventually get pulled over for speeding. You need to learn to drive slower."

"That's not going to happen. Maybe I should buy a radar detector." Emmy slapped the steering wheel with the heel of her hand.

The officer returned in a few minutes, and Emmy noticed a smile on his face.

"Please watch your speed in the future, Miss Colasanti. By

the way, the game just started. You won't miss too much of it."

Emmy looked at the officer, and she finally recognized him. "Eddie, Eddie Lowery?"

"Yes. How are you, Emmy?"

"I'm okay. I saw your brother a while back. I can't remember how long ago now."

"He told me that he saw you, and you were dating Tony Bertucci. I played ball with him."

Emmy giggled and then said, "I remember the kickoff return. That was so amazing."

"People still call me Crazy Eddie sometimes. I should let you get home so you can watch the game. Please be careful, Emmy, and watch your speed. Not all the guys are football fans."

"I will, Officer Lowery. Tell Eric hello for me, and I'll tell Tony I saw you."

Emmy felt grateful that Officer Lowery didn't give her a ticket.

"Some people have all the luck." Kristen shook her head as she sighed.

Emmy giggled as she floored it.

Emmy didn't bother putting the car in the garage when they got home. She jumped out, sprinted into the house and turned on the TV so she and Kristen could watch the Bears play the Atlanta Falcons in the second game of the year. They sat on the edge of the couch. Emmy jumped up and hollered as Tony made a tackle in the backfield. The runner fumbled and the Bears recovered.

"Did you see that, Kristen? He held that back up with one arm and stripped the ball with the other."

"He's so strong, Emmy."

"And quick, too."

The girls watched the whole game, and the Bears held onto a small lead late in the fourth quarter.

"All they have to do is run out the clock, and they'll win, right?" Kristen asked.

Emmy crossed her fingers. "Atlanta still has two timeouts left. They'll get the ball back unless the Bears get a first down."

The Bears got ultra-conservative on offense. They ran the

ball up the middle for three plays and failed to make a first down. They punted the ball away. Emmy and Kristen watched nervously. The Bears' kicker tried to punt the ball away from the returner for the Falcons, but didn't. The returner caught the ball in the middle of the field and eluded the first two tacklers.

"Oh no! What a lousy punt. Tackle him! Get him!" Emmy bounced on the edge of the couch.

"Come on! That's a penalty." Kristen pointed at the TV. "They can't do that. Isn't that supposed to draw a flag, Emmy?"

"The official missed it. That was definitely a block in the back. He must be blind." Emmy stood and screamed at the TV.

The Bears finally forced the returner out of bounds at the twenty-five yard line. Only five seconds remained on the clock. Kristen pulled Emmy down, and they both sat on the edge of the couch. The Falcons lined up to attempt a field goal. Emmy and Kristen crossed their fingers and held hands as the Falcons snapped the ball. The holder placed the ball down and the kick sailed right down the middle of the uprights. Time expired and the Bears lost.

"Crap!" Emmy swore as she flopped against the back of the couch.

"Well, it's only one loss, Em." Kristen stood up and reached out a hand. "They can snap back next week."

Emmy took Kristen's hand and stood up. "I suppose. I'm glad John got to play a little more today."

"I'm glad neither of them got hurt."

"Are you hungry? We forgot to eat after church," Emmy said as she heard her stomach growl.

"Now that you mention it, I'm starving."

"Do you want to go out?"

"Interested in Mexican?"

"Not really." Emmy shook her head.

"We could always get Chinese."

"What about that new place in the strip mall on Brewster," Emmy suggested. "I hear they have really good food."

"What's it called?"

"I think it's called the Tap House Bar or something like that."

323

"We can give it a try. They probably have TVs turned to the games. We can watch more football." Kristen grinned and clapped her hands. "I like watching football now, Em. I didn't used to like it as much."

"Gee! I wonder what changed."

Kristen smacked Emmy's arm. "You know why."

Kristen drove, and they parked in the last row.

"I bet the place is packed," Emmy said.

They went inside and looked around.

"I guess you were right, Em. Should we go somewhere else?" Kristen asked. "This place is full of guys. I don't see more than two women in here."

Emmy grinned. "Let's stay here."

"I'm going to smack you if you start flirting," Kristen said.

Emmy looked at the TVs tuned to different games. Groups of people waited for tables, but Kristen spotted two empty stools at the bar.

"Wanna sit at the bar, Em? We wouldn't have to wait for a table."

"That's fine. We can still order food, right?"

"Sure."

They grabbed the empty seats and ordered drinks—two Cokes. They looked over the menu and settled on tater skins for a start. The two guys sitting on either side of them started talking.

"Can I buy you girls a drink?" one offered.

Kristen declined with a wave. "Thanks, but we ordered Cokes already."

"I'll buy the next round then." The guy sitting next to Emmy grinned at her.

"Actually, the Cokes have free refills," Kristen said curtly.

Emmy started to say something, but Kristen poked her in the ribs.

"Ow! Stop that. It hurt." Emmy frowned.

The guys sensed that Emmy and Kristen were not interested and soon left. Two more guys sat down after a while. They smiled at the girls but didn't say anything at first. They only watched the games. Emmy didn't pay any attention to the guys, either. The guy sitting next to Emmy left, and a minute later someone took his place. Emmy glanced at him for a second but didn't say anything, and the guy didn't say anything other than to order a beer. Emmy's stomach growled with hunger, so she ordered a burger and fries. Kristen ordered a chicken breast sandwich with a salad. The bartender refilled their Cokes and talked to them. Emmy flirted with him until Kristen made her stop.

"I was just talking to him," Emmy protested.

Kristen said, "You were flirting and leading him on."

"I didn't meant to."

"Don't you realize that anytime you talk to guys in a bar they assume you are flirting?" Kristen said.

"I'm sorry. Will you forgive me?"

"Yes, but please be careful."

Emmy smiled at Kristen and immediately started a conversation with the guy next to her. Kristen groaned at Emmy.

"Have you eaten here before?" she asked and then looked closer. "Wayne! Is that you? When did you grow a beard?"

"Emmy?"

"Wow. Small world, huh? We haven't seen each other since Grady and Maris got married. How are you?"

"I'm doing all right. How are you? Are you still working?"

"Still at Robertson Industries. You?"

"I left the travel agency, and now I'm selling insurance."

Emmy turned to Kristen and asked, "Do you remember Wayne Sanders?"

Kristen looked at Wayne, but didn't recognize him. With his bushy beard Emmy hadn't even recognized him at first.

"Hi, Wayne," Kristen said.

"Where are you living these days?" Emmy asked.

"Right now I'm living with my parents. I'm trying to save up enough for a down payment on a house."

"Kristen and I are renting a place together. We work together for Robertson in the same building."

"Are you still with that same guy, Emmy? My mother heard something from your mom that you guys split up."

"I'm with Kenny Colwell now."

325

"That's nice."

Emmy and Wayne conversed for a few minutes, but then ran out of things to talk about. Wayne paid his bill and stood up to leave.

"It was nice to see you, Wayne. Say hello to your parents for me."

"I will. I'm glad I ran into you and Kristen. Take care, Emmy."

After Wayne left Kristen looked at Emmy.

"What?" Emmy shrugged.

Kristen tilted her head, but didn't speak.

"All right. You don't need to say anything, Krissy. Seeing Wayne made me appreciate Kenny, Tony and John even more."

"Wayne did know how to dance," Kristen said as she took the last bite of her salad.

"I'll give him credit for that at least."

Two more guys sat by them, and Emmy talked to both of them about football until Kristen poked her in the side.

"That's it! We're leaving." Kristen paid their bill and dragged Emmy away from the bar.

"Can't we stay until the games are over?"

"No!" Kristen pushed her way through the crowd.

On the way home Emmy didn't say a word. She stared out the window and pouted.

"Are you going to keep pouting for long?" Kristen asked. "You can if you want. You can pout all day. I'm not going to apologize for what I said."

"I wasn't flirting on purpose. I didn't mean anything," Emmy replied, but she continued to stare out the window.

You are acting like such a baby. Are you ever going to grow up? Kristen glanced over at Emmy. "I know that, but the guys at the bar don't know you. They assume you are flirting with them."

"Why? I don't understand."

"That's because you are too trusting and still a little naïve. You're the total opposite of your sister."

"You make it sound like you are so experienced with men. Having sex one time doesn't make you more experienced than me."

326

"That has nothing to do with it, Em."

Neither one spoke for the rest of the way home. Emmy ran up to her room as soon as they get home and closed the door. Kristen followed, knocked on the door and waited.

Emmy yelled, "Go away! I don't want to talk to you right now."

"Fine! Be that way. I'm going downstairs to read."

"Good! I don't want to talk to you again tonight." Emmy flopped onto the bed. "You're trying to run my life like my mother."

"I am not! I'm only looking out for you," Kristen hollered. Then she smacked the door with the palm of her hand. "You are such a baby sometimes."

For the first time ever, they really quarreled. Kristen went downstairs and read in the living room. Emmy came downstairs an hour later and saw Kristen sitting in the recliner. She walked up with her head hanging down. "I'm sorry I acted like a baby. Will you forgive me?"

Kristen put down her book and opened her arms. "I'm not angry with you, Em."

Emmy sat on the arm of the recliner as Kristen hugged her.

"Sometimes I don't think about my actions."

Yeah, I know all about that, Kristen thought, but she said, "It's okay, sweetie. You think everyone is as honest and kindhearted as you. Remember Richard?"

"Yes. I should have learned a lesson from him."

"I just don't want to see you get hurt."

"I know. I will be more careful from now on," Emmy said as she thought about Tony.

Chapter Thirty-Seven

After work on Monday, Emmy and Kristen rushed home. Emmy changed into jeans and a top, ran downstairs and threw together a sandwich.

"Emmy, slow down and chew your food. You'll choke if you try to stuff the whole sandwich in your mouth." Kristen pulled out a chair. "You should sit down to eat."

Emmy remained standing. "I don't have time. Chase will be here any second. Are you sure you don't want to come with us?"

"No, Chase said Mr. Kesson just needed to talk to you guys."

"I don't know what we should do. I know he would like the worship band to do a little tour, but I don't think the other guys can do it. They have jobs and family responsibilities."

"You can't blame him for wanting to make some money."

"I know." Emmy stuffed the last bite in her mouth as a car pulled into the driveway. "Will you let him in while I brush my teeth?" She ran back up the stairs.

You are still a kid at heart, Em. How will you ever handle being a rock star? Kristen shook her head.

Kristen did a quick check to make sure the living room was uncluttered. Then she let Chase Hillman in the front door.

"Hi, Chase. Emmy will be ready in a minute. Are you excited about the CD release tomorrow?"

"Yeah, I kinda am. I've never recorded a real CD before. I know Emmy has been on some of the Fridays CDs."

"She is concerned about the touring stuff."

"We'll have to discuss that on the way over to the office."

Emmy finished brushing her teeth, raced downstairs, grabbed her jacket, dashed into the living room and said, "I'm ready to go."

"See you later, Kristen." Chase waved.

Emmy stared out the window on the drive to the Steward Music Group office. *What am I going to do? I'm not sure I can handle things like Kenny does. I know the worship band will never be rock stars, but the travel won't be easy.*

328

Chase stopped at a red light and glanced at her. "We have to make some difficult decisions, Emmy."

"That's for sure." She turned to face him. "Are you interested in doing a small tour at all? I understand if you aren't."

"If it only lasted a couple of weeks, I might be interested. I can't see doing long tours like Kenny does. Yvonne has already let me know her opinion."

I'm sure she has in no uncertain terms. "Oh, I totally agree with that. You've got a family and your job at church to consider."

"How do you feel about it, Emmy. You are the reason this is happening. The rest of us could be replaced easy enough."

"I don't know about that."

"Oh, come on, Em. You're the one with the real talent. I'm not trying to be modest. I know I'm pretty decent on the keyboard, and I've got a reasonably good voice."

"You're more talented than you give yourself credit for. The other guys are..."

"They're not pros, and you know it. They're talented guys, but they would never make it as a full-time touring band."

Emmy grinned. *They are kinda old to be a rock band.*

"You might have to consider hiring a real band if you ever decide to concentrate on a career as a singer."

Emmy bit her lip and looked out the window again. Kenny told her the same thing.

Chase pulled into the parking area in the front of the building that housed the Steward Music Group.

"Are you all right?" Chase asked.

"I'm a little scared."

"You don't need to be. Should we pray before we go in?"

Emmy nodded. Chase prayed for direction, and they headed into the building. Mr. Kesson met them in the reception area.

"It's good to see you and thanks for coming out tonight. I know you are both very busy."

Emmy grinned. Mr. Kesson was the owner of the corporation yet he came across as a regular guy. Wearing faded blue jeans and a flannel shirt might have helped with that impression.

Chase shook his hand. "Thank you for taking the time to see us."

After a couple of minutes of small talk, and the offer of something to drink, Mr. Kesson escorted Chase and Emmy into his office. Emmy looked around. She expected the office to be more ostentatious. She looked at the platinum records on one wall. But otherwise the office could have belonged to a college professor. There were bookcases filled haphazardly with assorted books. A stereo system sat on a stand in one corner with a few CDs stacked underneath. Instead of sitting behind his scarred wooden desk, Mr. Kesson directed them to a couch and an old recliner.

"Please sit on the couch. I should throw this recliner away and buy a new one, but it has some sentimental value," he said.

Emmy pictured the old couch in the carriage house and grinned. *No wonder Kenny and Mr. Kesson get along so well. They are both sentimental romantics at heart.*

"The CD will be released tomorrow. I have plenty of copies for you to take with you tonight. I think it sounds great. I know it's a live recording, and there are little... imperfections... shall we say, but that makes it sound better. I think Kenny and Will Consoli did a great job. Of course, he had some talented people who actually played and sang."

Emmy blushed.

"All right, I don't want to waste your time. Let's get right to the point of this meeting. I would like to see if it's at all possible to set up a little tour schedule for the worship band. Maybe a couple of weeks at a time. Nothing like Kenny and the guys do, but just something to let people hear and see you guys in person. You may not realize it, but I think you will find that people will be willing to pay for tickets to see you guys." He waited for a reaction.

Emmy looked at Chase, and then at Mr. Kesson. She lowered her eyes and rubbed her hands together. "I understand you want to make money. I understand that, but that's not my main priority. I believe that God has given me a talent, and He expects me to use it to lead people, mainly teens, to a personal relationship with Him. If it was up to me, I would give the CDs away for free." Emmy bit her lip as she looked up at Mr. Kesson.

330

He smiled. "I thought you might feel that way. I have watched you grow up over the years. I always knew you had a special talent, and I'm grateful you have allowed my company to take advantage of that talent."

"You've always treated Kenny right," she whispered.

"You know we operate a little differently than most record companies. We do like to make money. Don't get me wrong." He waved his hand. "We have to pay the bills like any other business, but we've been fortunate. We can afford to put out some projects that other companies would never release. I think you will be surprised though by how well the public receives your CD."

"Do you think people are just going to buy it because Kenny produced it and plays on it?" she asked.

"I'm certain some people will buy it because of his involvement, but as people listen to it... They will hear it on the radio. The Christian stations will play it. I'm certain of that. But as people hear it and tell their friends about it... word of mouth advertising is the best."

"If we go on a tour, would we be able to use the guys from the worship band, or will we have to use professional musicians?" Emmy asked boldly.

"What? I was under the impression you were professional musicians. Am I mistaken?" He laughed and slapped the arm of his recliner.

Emmy relaxed. "The guys are good enough to be pros, but you know they aren't. They have careers and families—except for Skip, I mean."

"Would you like to use the guys who actually did the recording?" Mr. Kesson asked as he put his foot on his knee and leaned back.

Emmy suppressed a giggle. *He's wearing old tennis shoes just like me.*

Chase spoke up. "We will have to replace John Patterson. He has already informed me that he wouldn't be able to take time away from his job. Skip's parents won't allow him to miss school, but as far as I know Hank and Steve are willing to do a little traveling. Hank is actually going to retire soon. He has a grandson he wants to spoil."

"Stuart Lederer has expressed an interest in working with your group. He works here as an engineer and has done some producing, too," Mr. Kesson said.

Chase added, "We have some men at the church who have volunteered to help us out."

Emmy grinned. "You're talking about the Zawaski brothers, right?"

"Yes," Chase answered.

"They are so adorable. They treat me like a princess, and I just love them."

"We would need to work out the transportation issues and other logistics, but, hey, that's part of what we do here," Mr. Kesson said.

"I'm willing to give it a shot," Emmy said.

"All right!" Mr. Kesson stood up and clapped his hands. "I'll have a meeting with my people and we'll use the Prater-Saylor Agency to handle the booking. I'll get my team working on this right away. Oh, don't leave without these." He grabbed a box full of CDs and handed it to Chase.

Chase smiled as he took two out of the box. "Look, Emmy, a real CD with you on the cover." He handed one to her.

She looked at it and a smile slowly appeared. But then she bit her lip. "You know I wanted all the guys to be on the cover."

"Yeah, but who wants to buy a CD with a bunch of ugly old guys on the front," Chase teased her.

With the backing of the Steward Music Group, the CD was readied for release on September 17, 2002. The CD was available in both Christian bookstores as well as retailers catering to general audiences. Soon it was on the Billboard charts and actually selling rather well. Emmy's voice was heard by thousands of new listeners. The band, which had been named The Crest Ridge Worship Band featuring Emmy Colasanti, was in demand for a tour. Although the music label would have liked for them to tour immediately, they understood that was not possible. However, plans were set in motion for the band to tour in March of 2003.

Chapter Thirty-Eight

"Hi, Kristen, it's Tony."

"Hey, Tony. What's up?"

"I need a favor. A really big one."

"I suppose I could help you out, but it will cost you." She switched the phone to her other ear. "What do you need?"

"Will you help me with some shopping? I need your opinion about something I want to buy," Tony said.

"Could you be a little more specific? You sound like you don't really want to tell me what you want."

"Fine. It's something for Emmy."

"Okay. When do you want to go? Is Emmy going, too? I need to talk to her about my car."

Tony cleared his throat. "Uh, Emmy's not going. I need to buy something for her, and she can't see it."

"Are you buying her some new clothes?" Kristen asked. "She could use some new jeans."

"It's not clothes, Kristen. Can you keep a secret?" Tony asked. "And don't let Emmy hear you talking."

"I've kept some secrets about us for years, so I think I can be trusted." Kristen laughed. "What is it?"

"I'm buying Emmy a ring."

Kristen laughed. "No, really. What are you buying her?"

"I'm serious. I want to buy her a ring."

"A ring? Why? She never wears a ring. Maybe you could buy her a necklace or a new bracelet. She likes those."

Tony took a deep breath, sighed and said, "No, it has to be a ring."

"All right if you insist. Gee! Don't get so bent out of shape," Kristen said. "What kind of ring?"

"THE RING, Kristen!" Tony yelled.

Kristen shook her head and didn't say anything for a few seconds. "Wait a minute. Are you telling me you're going to buy an engagement ring for Emmy?" Kristen sounded totally surprised as she whispered into the phone.

"Yes. I'm going to ask her to marry me."

"What? Have you lost your mind?"

Tony held the phone away from his ear as Kristen screamed into it.

"Don't let Emmy hear! I'm going to ask her to marry me," Tony repeated slowly. *Geez, Kristen, do I have to explain everything?*

"Stay right where you are. I'm coming over. We have to talk," Kristen ordered him. *If this is about what happened that night, you are totally nuts.*

"Okay, I'll be home."

"Don't leave and don't talk to anyone." *This is serious. You've totally lost it.* She grabbed her purse and keys and hollered, "Em, I gotta run out. I'll be back later."

"Is everything all right?" Emmy asked from the living room. "I heard you yelling about something. Are you going to see John? Did you guys fight or something?"

"Don't wait up. I don't know when I'll be back." Kristen ran out the door. *I might be gone for a long time.*

Emmy heard the back door slam and smiled because she assumed Kristen was going over to John's apartment. *Don't do anything I wouldn't.* Then Emmy bit her lip. *Maybe I shouldn't have thought about it like that.*

Kristen made it over to Mama's house in record time. She ran in the back door and saw Mama in the kitchen.

"Hello, Mama. Where is he?"

"He's in his room, I think. Is there something wrong, sweetie?" Mama pulled the last two glasses from the dishwasher and then closed the door.

"Has he told you anything special lately?" Kristen paused in the doorway. "Anything out of the ordinary?"

Mama thought about it for a moment. "Nothing I can think of. Why?"

"It could be nothing, or it could be that he has lost his mind. I'll let you know." Kristen dashed out of the kitchen, sprinted up the stairs and into Tony's room. She slammed the door shut behind her and locked it. Tony lay on his bed reading his Sports Illustrated magazine.

"That was quick."

"Tell me you're joking, and I'll forget this ever happened." Kristen stood at the edge of his bed and crossed her arms over her chest.

"I'm not joking. I want to marry Emmy." He moved and sat up Indian-style.

"Are you sure you don't mean *Brenda*?" Kristen spat out the name like a swear word. "Have you gotten their names confused?"

"I'm not confused, Kristen," Tony replied angrily.

"What makes you think she wants to marry you? You do realize she is, for all practical purposes, engaged to Kenny?"

Tony replied, "Emmy told me she wanted to get married."

"To you?"

"Yes, she said, and I quote, 'Oh, Tony, I want to marry you.' Something like that."

"When did this happen? Five years ago when you first started dating? A lot has changed since then in case you haven't noticed."

"It was... you know... that night I told you about."

"You said you guys kissed and made out. That's bad enough on its own. You never said anything about getting married."

"I didn't tell you everything that happened." Tony tossed his magazine toward the nightstand.

Oh, no! What did you do? No wonder Emmy has been acting so different. "Do I have to beat it out of you? Tell me!"

"All right. It happened a couple of weeks ago."

"I know that." Kristen frowned. "Don't tell me you guys made out more than once." Kristen tried to remember if Tony and Emmy had been together any other nights. "This is the seventeenth. When exactly did this happen? When did she say that?"

"Tuesday. Whatever date that was."

"Emmy had a class that night. If I remember correctly, she stayed at school until after midnight."

"She was at school, but not as late as you think."

"If you don't tell me what happened, I am going to beat you

335

over the head with this pillow until I knock some sense into your brain, which might take forever."

"All right. This might take a while so get comfortable."

Kristen moved onto the bed and sat with her back against the headboard. She put a pillow behind her back and settled in. "I'm waiting." She crossed her arms over her chest.

"I met her after class, and we went out to grab a bite to eat."

"Yeah, you told me about that before."

"Then we drove over to the Riverwalk by the campus and went for a walk. We started holding hands, but then we stopped. I kissed her a couple times..."

"And that was that. She fell head over heels in love with you again, huh? Did you get her drunk? Did you slip some drug into her drink at the restaurant?"

"No, there is more. We went back to the car and got in back."

Kristen's eyes opened as wide as possible. "Don't tell me you did it in the back seat of that monster truck of yours." She reached out and smacked his arm as hard as she could. "Was it like an initiation or something? How could you be such an ass? This is just awful."

"Are you gonna let me finish?" Tony rubbed his arm.

"Please do, and then I'm going to murder you."

"Okay, we kissed and did a little touching..."

"Oh, gross. How could you?"

"... and got a little carried away, but we didn't have sex. Not real sex."

"You creep! How could you? This is awful." Kristen punched Tony's arm several times, but only succeeded in hurting her hand.

Tony grabbed her hand. "Stop hitting me."

"And somewhere in the heat of this *very romantic* encounter she said she wanted to marry you?"

"You make it sound cheap. It wasn't like that."

"You were in the back seat of your truck thing at a parking lot at North Park!" Kristen screamed. "It couldn't be any cheaper than that... unless you were at Roosevelt High."

"We talked while we..."

Kristen waved her hands. "I don't need details of everything you guys did."

"We both realized that we need to be together."

This is totally crazy. Kristen closed her eyes. "Have you talked to her about what happened since that night?"

"I talked to her the next day..."

"And had she regained her senses by then? Did she realize she made a mistake and she felt sorry?" *She probably felt guilty because what you guys did was so wrong.*

"No, she told me she loved me."

Kristen threw her hands in the air and kicked her feet on the bed as she yelled, "Oh, my God! She loves everybody. Don't you know the difference?"

"I know the difference, Kristen. You know she has been going back and forth between me and Kenny."

"No she hasn't! She loves Kenny," Kristen shouted.

"She loves me now," he said.

She hit his arm again. "And you want to ask her to marry you while the momentum is on your side, or what? This isn't a football game, you dork! Men are such idiots!"

"I know that. The part about football, and not all men are idiots." Tony clenched his jaw. "Okay, let's talk about the nights Emmy and Kenny slept in the tent."

"Why? What does that have to do with anything? Nothing happened between them. Although I still think it was wrong for them to sleep together."

"Are you finished?" Tony asked. "Will you just listen?"

"Yes." Kristen stared at him.

"All right. They slept together and nothing happened."

"Are you saying you wish something did happen?" Kristen tilted her head.

"No! The point I'm making is that nothing happened. They didn't have sex because they couldn't do it."

"You've lost me. I think they could have."

"But they didn't because they realize they are best friends,"

337

Tony said as he waved his hands. "Do you understand now?"

"No. All I understand is that you've lost your marbles."

"What do you think would happen if Emmy and I slept together in a tent?" He held out a hand with his palm up.

"You can't sleep together because it wouldn't be right. You guys would fool around."

Tony smiled. "Aha! Now you get it. If Emmy and I slept together... anywhere... a tent... in a bed... wherever... doesn't matter. We would have sex. Emmy and Kenny knew they couldn't have sex, so they didn't. Therefore, she wants to marry me. So I'm going to buy a ring and ask her."

Kristen stared at him without saying a word.

"Are you gonna say something?"

She shook her head slowly.

"You think I'm nuts, huh?"

"Oh, absolutely, without a doubt." She nodded. "You have taken a blow to the head and need to be in the hospital. I'm calling an ambulance." She started to got off of the bed.

Tony grabbed her arm. "I'm going to ask her, so I need a ring."

Kristen stared into his eyes for a moment. "Fine! It's your money. If you want to spend it on a ring and hope she is insane at the time you ask her, it's okay with me."

"You think it's a bad idea, huh?" Tony asked as he looked at her.

"Duh! It's only like the worst idea I have ever heard." Kristen kicked him this time instead of using her hand. "You know I have always wanted to see you guys together, but it just didn't work. Move on!"

"I don't want to move on. I want to marry Emmy."

"Are you sure you don't just want to sleep with her?" Kristen asked sarcastically.

"Yeah, I want to do that, but I want to marry her, too."

"You're a creep! I can't believe you're my favorite cousin."

Kristen spent a half hour trying to talk Tony out of buying a ring.

"I'm not going to let you do this." Kristen again stood by

338

the side of his bed with her arms crossed over her chest.

"I'm gonna do it with or without your help." Tony stood in front of her with his arms crossed over his chest.

For a whole minute they stared at each other without moving or saying another word.

"Why am I surrounded by the most stubborn people in the world?" Kristen threw her hands into the air. "You and Emmy deserve each other." Then she shoved him in the chest. He didn't budge, so she shoved him harder. "You're like a brick wall and about as smart."

"So you'll help me?" Tony grinned.

"I'm gonna regret this, I know, but all right, I'll go with you and we can look for a ring. I'll meet you here tomorrow after work, and we'll go." *Maybe I will wake up and realize this has been a nightmare.*

Tony put his arms around her and squeezed.

"Let go of me, you dumb jock!"

"Kristen, you have to promise not to tell a soul about this until I say you can. Will you promise?"

"Oh, believe me, I'm not going to tell a single person about this. I mean, who would believe me?"

"Promise?"

She shook her head as she looked up at him. "Fine! I promise I won't tell a soul about the dumbest thing you've ever done in your life."

Kristen went downstairs and left without seeing Mama. She returned home and ran into Emmy in the kitchen.

"You're already home?" Emmy asked as she grinned. "I thought you would be gone until late tonight."

"Got finished quicker than I thought I would." Kristen tossed her keys on the table and answered with obvious displeasure. *I am so mad at you that I could spit!*

"Are you all right, Krissy? Do you and John fight about something?" Emmy asked.

Kristen took a deep breath and then spoke in her regular tone of voice. "I'm fine. You? Anything new with you? Have you talked to Kenny lately? Did you guys argue?" She paused and then asked, "Seen Tony around lately?"

Emmy blushed when Kristen mentioned Tony. Kristen saw her reaction and knew something happened between them. She hoped Tony told the truth when he said they didn't have sex.

After work the next day Kristen dropped Emmy at the house.

"Where are you going? Aren't you coming inside?"

"No, I need to talk to Mama about a family matter. Be back later."

"I'll see you later then, Kristen. Say hi to Mama for me."

"Should I say hi to Tony, too?"

"I'll call him myself. Maybe he'll come over after dinner."

Kristen drove straight to Mama's place. She walked in the front door. Tony was already home from practice.

"Are you ready?" Kristen asked.

"Can we stop and get something to eat?"

"I made some mostaccioli if you want some now," Mama said. "You will have to serve yourself because Mrs. McKall is picking me up in a couple of minutes. We're going to play bingo."

"Okay, Mama, I'll see you later." He turned to Kristen. "Mostaccioli sounds good to me. We can grab a bite now, and then go shopping."

"Your stomach still always comes first, huh?"

They sat at the kitchen table to eat. Tony described a ring he saw.

"How many carats?"

Tony tilted his head. "I don't know. Ten or twenty, maybe."

Kristen realized he had no clue and this might not be as easy as she thought. "Do you know where you're going to look?"

"Not really. Do you know of a good place?"

"Watson's Jewelers. It's over by the mall, but not in the mall. It's next to the Burger Bob's."

"Oh yeah. I've seen that building, but I've never been inside.

They finished eating and Tony drove over to Watson's and along the way Kristen explained a little bit about diamonds to him.

340

"There's different shapes and clarity. Diamonds are very complex."

"I don't know anything about that, Kristen. You'll have to make sure I'm getting a good one."

"You should let me lead the way. I *do* know about diamonds."

"Okay, I'll let you do the talking."

They arrived at Watson's and didn't see another customer in the place. The lone salesman greeted them after he hung up the phone.

"Good evening. May I help you find something? I'm Ramon Melendez, by the way."

"Yes, please. We're looking for an engagement ring," Kristen said as she flipped her hair over her shoulder.

"Congratulations! I could tell you were engaged. You look like such an adorable couple."

Tony started to correct the salesman, but Kristen interrupted him.

"I'm Kristen, and this is Tony. I'm looking for a one carat diamond in a yellow gold setting."

Tony stared at Kristen with surprise all over his face. Kristen kissed him on the mouth to keep him from saying anything.

"Just follow my lead."

"Yeah, whatever." Tony looked at Ramon and wondered how much gel he had in his hair.

Kristen described to Ramon what she thought Emmy would like. Tony followed Kristen and Ramon to a display case.

"I'd like to see this one, Ramon, if you please."

"An excellent choice, Kristen."

He pulled it out of the case and showed it to Kristen. She looked at it, but wasn't sold yet. Kristen and Ramon looked at rings for the next fifteen minutes while Tony watched in silence with his hands in his pockets.

Tony checked a clock on the counter. *How much longer is this gonna take? I need to look at game film tonight.*

Kristen kissed him again when it looked like he was going to say something.

341

"Stop that, Krissy," he whispered as he backed away. He walked over to another case and glanced at the rings inside. A certain ring caught his eye.

"Kristen, sweetheart, my precious darling, would you take a look at this ring over here? I think it might be just right."

"Which one, Tony, my sweet love?"

"The one in the corner there. Doesn't it look nice? I think Em..."

"Oh my God! I can't believe it's still here." Kristen slapped her hands to her face.

"What are you talking about?"

She whispered, "Emmy and I were here last month. Just window shopping and we saw this very ring. Emmy absolutely loved it."

"Maybe we should look at it then."

Kristen motioned for Ramon to join them. "May we see that one?"

"But, of course."

Kristen tried it on, and it fit her almost perfectly.

"This is a unique setting designed by Mr. Watson himself. It's one of a kind and therefore is priced accordingly. The diamond is one carat."

"How much is it, Ramon?" Tony asked.

Ramon mentioned the price as if it was a mere pittance. Tony's jaw dropped. It was twice what he expected to pay. He shook his head about to say no when Kristen yanked him away.

"I need to talk to my fiancee for a moment, Ramon."

"I will wait over there. Take all the time you need to discuss it."

Kristen waited as Ramon walked away.

"Emmy loves this ring, Tony. I know it's more than you expected to spend, but I think we can talk him down a bit."

"It is very pretty, Kristen." Tony thought about it for a moment. "Okay if we can get him to come down to..."

Tony whispered a price to Kristen. They waved for Ramon to come back. Kristen began to negotiate with him. They debated for a moment. Then Ramon called Mr. Watson.

"Mr. Watson has agreed to accept your offer."

"Emmy will..."

Kristen immediately stomped on Tony's foot to shut him up.

"Tony, my love, will you write a check for Ramon?"

On the way home Tony sighed as he complained, "I sure didn't think it would take so long to buy a ring."

She stared at Tony for a moment. "You are certifiably insane. Some couples take months to buy a ring. You spent an hour."

"I don't know about these things, Kristen. I saw that ring, and I just knew it would be perfect for Emmy."

"I want to be there when you take it back to have it sized. Ramon will wonder what's going on."

"What if it doesn't fit?" Tony asked as he slowed to a stop at a red light.

"Emmy's fingers are about the same size as mine. It'll fit. They might have to adjust it a little, but that's easily taken care of. When are you going to ask her?"

"Ask her what?"

"To marry you. You goofball. You do have to ask her to marry you, you know."

"I know that."

"Do you really? I seriously wonder about you sometimes. You've been hit in the head a lot over the years. How are you going to ask her?"

"What do you mean?" He accelerated through the intersection.

Kristen rolled her eyes. "Have you given *any* thought to what you might say?"

"I'll say 'Emmy, I love you. Wanna get married sometime?'" Tony knew he had made a mistake immediately. *That didn't even sound right to me. Kristen is going to slug me.*

After being shocked into silence for several seconds, Kristen responded. "Oh! My!! God!!! I'm gonna hit you upside the head with a baseball bat. You are absolutely hopeless. This is what you do. You have to take her out for dinner to a nice place, not

343

Darby's or Burger Bob's. Then you take her home and get on your knee and ask her."

"What should I say?"

Kristen sighed in resignation. "We're gonna have to work on this. Let's get back to the house and show Mama the ring. We can practice what you're going to say."

"Uh. We can't show Mama the ring just yet." Tony looked out the side window.

"Why not?" she asked, and then realized. "You haven't told Mama what you intend to do, have you? Now I know you are totally bonkers."

"I'll tell Mama tonight when the time is right. I promise. Do you think there's a chance Emmy will say no?"

"At this point I have no clue. At least you have a fifty-fifty chance. She will either say yes, or no." Kristen shook her head and sighed. *Lord, give me strength. Please!*

They got back to the house and Kristen made sure Mama wasn't home yet. She pulled Tony into the living room.

"Quit yanking on my arm, Kristen," he said.

"We need to practice what you're going to say and how you're going to ask."

"Okay," he said.

"So, ask me to marry you. Pretend I'm Emmy," she said as she stood in front of the fireplace.

"Do I get to kiss you after I ask?" Tony grinned.

Kristen frowned and didn't speak.

"Okay, no kiss." Tony scratched his jaw. "How's this? Emmy, will you do me the honor of becoming my... love slave," he said and then grinned.

Kristen started to grab the fireplace poker.

Tony waved his hands. "Okay, I'll be serious."

"You need to get on your knee," Kristen said.

"Why? This is just practice."

"You need to practice it the right way. You practice your football plays correctly, right?"

"Yeah," he said.

Kristen pointed to the floor. "On your knee."

344

He rolled his eyes but did what Kristen asked. "I feel silly."

"You should. This is the worst idea ever."

"I think you're totally wrong, Kristen." He cleared his throat. "Krissy, will you..."

"You're proposing to Emmy, you dork."

"Sorry, I feel silly calling you Emmy."

Kristen frowned again.

Tony cleared his throat again and tried his best.

Kristen shook her head and rolled her eyes. "This is going to take all night."

"What is going to take all night?" Mama asked as she walked into the room.

Kristen screamed. Tony lost his balance and fell over. Mama froze with her jacket half off.

"You're home early," Kristen said an eternity later.

"We got bored," Mama said as she watched Tony pretend to be looking for something on the floor.

He looked up at Mama. "I think I lost a... uh... a contact lens."

Kristen kicked his shin and rolled her eyes. "You don't wear contacts, you doofus."

Mama managed to remove her jacket and set her purse on a recliner. "Who is going to tell me what is going on?"

Tony stared at Kristen. She stared back. Tony sighed and stood up. He took a deep breath, closed his eyes for several seconds, opened them, pointed at Kristen and then said, "I was proposing to her."

Kristen smacked his arm.

Mama grabbed the recliner to steady herself.

Tony shook his hands. "No, I mean I was practicing proposing. I'm not going to marry Kristen."

"That's a relief," Kristen said.

"Please take you time and tell me what you are really doing," Mama said slowly.

"You should sit down on the couch with me, Mama," Kristen said. She took Mama's hand and they walked over to the couch and sat down.

345

Tony rubbed his jaw and paced on the other side of the coffee table. He glanced at them and then continued pacing.

Kristen rolled her eyes. "Stop it! Out with it!"

Tony stopped and faced them. "I'm going to ask Emmy to marry me Friday night at Ciao Bella."

Mama put a hand to her mouth. "Oh, my," she whispered.

Tony and John stopped by to see Emmy and Kristen Thursday evening after practice. Tony paced around the living room and couldn't sit still.

John shook his head. "Will you relax? You're driving me nuts."

"I got a lot on my mind." Tony glanced at Emmy, and she smiled at him.

Kristen saw the look. "Anything new going on, Tony? Did you buy anything special lately?"

Tony grimaced and frowned at Kristen.

"I gotta check on dinner. Can you help me, Krissy?" Emmy asked.

Kristen helped Emmy get dinner ready by setting the table.

A few minutes later, Tony pulled Kristen into the computer room. "Have you told anyone about our secret?"

"No, have you changed your mind? Please say you have."

"No, I haven't."

"Have you practiced your... speech... anymore?"

"Kinda..."

They were interrupted by a knock on the door.

"Hey, what are you guys doing in there?" Emmy asked. "It's time to eat."

Kristen opened the door and walked out. Emmy looked at Tony and bit her lip. *How much have you told Kristen about that night? I wish you could have kept your mouth shut.*

After dinner, Kristen was alone with Tony in the living room. "Why are you still waiting?"

"I'm nervous, all right. What if she says no?"

"Then I will have to commit her to a mental hospital. She's not going to say no." Kristen wished she felt as certain as she told

346

Tony. She had been trying to pick up on how Emmy would respond, but without any luck so far.

"Okay. We're taking Mama to Ciao Bella tomorrow night. I'll ask her there."

"Shoot. I hoped I could be there when you propose, but I have to be at my parents' house tomorrow."

"Maybe I should wait until another night."

"No! If you wait any longer she might decide to say no after all."

"I think I know what I'm going to say," Tony said. "I watched an old movie last night and it gave me an idea."

"Which movie?" Kristen asked. "Please don't tell me it was *Animal House*."

"It was called *Love and Other Problems*."

Kristen's shoulders sagged. "You dork," she whispered. "That is a comedy, and his proposal is supposed to be ridiculous."

"Oh," Tony said as he tilted his head and rubbed his jaw. "I thought it was romantic."

Chapter Thirty-Nine

On Friday Tony and Mama drove to Emmy's house. He parked alongside the house, jumped out, ran around the car and opened the door for Mama.

"Thank you, son," she said.

They walked up the steps to the front door, and Tony knocked instead of walking right in.

Emmy ran down the hallway, unlocked the heavy door and opened it. "Too bad Kristen is at her parents," Emmy said as she let them in. "She loves Ciao Bella."

"Yeah, too bad." Tony put a finger under his collar and tried to stretch it out.

"I asked her to come with us, but she couldn't. Do you want to see the kitchen, Mama? We painted it."

"Maybe another time, sweetie," Mama said. "What do you think, son?"

Tony shifted his weight back and forth but didn't say anything.

"I didn't know you were going to wear a sport coat, tie and dress pants," Emmy said. "Did you want me to wear a dress?"

Tony shrugged and stuck his hand into his coat pocket, but he didn't reply.

"You look fine as you are, dear," Mama said with a smile as she noticed Emmy's jeans and white top. "Shall we go?"

"Absolutely! I'm starving." Emmy grabbed her purse and jacket.

Only when Emmy turned around, did Mama notice the braids in her hair and a piece of purple ribbon tied in a bow.

Tony dropped Mama and Emmy off at the door to Ciao Bella and found a parking place only a block away. *That's a miracle.* He locked the car. *I'll take that as a sign of good fortune later. Thank you, Lord.* He sprinted back to the restaurant and stood next to Emmy.

She reached for his hand and squeezed it. "Did you abandon the car?"

"You'd never believe where I parked."

348

Mr. Sabatino walked up to Mama and kissed her hand. "Mrs. Bertucci, it's such a pleasure to see you again. I have a very special table for you tonight."

"Thank you, very much, Enrico. How is Florentina doing?"

"She is very busy, but I will tell her you are here. I'm sure she will want to talk to you."

He escorted them to a table right in the middle of the restaurant. He pulled out a chair for Mama. Emmy pulled out her own chair and sat down.

Tony unbuttoned his sport coat, sat down and felt every eye in the busy restaurant focus on him. Beads of sweat formed on his forehead. He reached into his pocket. He could feel the small gift box containing the engagement ring. His collar tightened until he thought he would choke. Several times he started to pull out the ring, but something always stopped him. First, the waiter came by to take their drink order. Tony used a napkin to wipe the sweat off of his forehead. Another time the server brought their salads. Tony wiped his sweaty hands on his pant legs. Two more times Tony was interrupted as he attempted to pull the gift box out of his pocket. Tony stuck his finger in his collar as it tightened even more.

I never should have worn a tie.

An hour later, they finished eating dinner. Tony waved for the check, and then picked up his water glass.

"Are you all right, Tony? You look like you're about to be sentenced to life in jail," Emmy joked.

Tony nearly choked on a sip of water. "I'm okay. I want to ask you something important, really important."

"Okay. What is it, Tony?"

"Emmy, would you..."

Just then the waiter stopped by to say good night and drop off the check. Emmy smiled at the waiter while Tony cringed.

"What do you want to ask me, Tony?"

Tony asked, "Would you...?" He looked around to spot the waiter.

The waiter walked into the kitchen.

Tony turned back to Emmy. "Would you be...?" He stopped

349

as another waiter collected the empty plates.

"Yes, Tony. Would I what?" Emmy asked softly.

Tony felt the beads of sweat roll down his forehead and face.

Emmy smiled.

Tony's throat became as dry as the Sahara desert.

Mama nodded her head.

Tony's heart raced.

Emmy licked her lips.

Mama closed her eyes and prayed.

Tony blurted out, "Did you like the ravioli tonight?"

Mama sighed. *This isn't going to work.*

"Yes, I love the way they make their ravioli," Emmy answered.

"That's good. I liked the chicken tonight." Tony wiped more sweat off of his forehead.

Mama tapped Tony's arm. She realized what was supposed to happen would not happen in the restaurant. "We should be going, Tony. I want to stop at Emmy's before you take me home. I want to see how the kitchen looks."

"Okay, Mama." Tony sighed with relief as he used his tie to wipe the sweat off of his face.

Tony drove Mama and Emmy back to the house without saying a word.

"Would you like some coffee, Mama?" Emmy asked as they walked into the kitchen.

"No thanks, dear. it will keep me up all night."

"Tony?"

"No, thanks." He squeezed the gift box in his pocket. "I don't think I can drink anything at the moment."

Emmy showed Mama the newly painted kitchen.

"Kristen picked the color," Emmy explained. "I didn't want a yellow kitchen at first, but I kinda like it now."

"It looks very bright and almost like sunshine," Mama said as she touched the wall.

"Should we go sit down?" Emmy asked.

Tony nodded as he tugged at his collar.

350

They went into the living room, and Mama and Emmy sat on the couch. Tony paced back and forth while wringing his hands.

"What is wrong, Tony? You're acting like there's something on your mind. Did you have a bad day at practice?" Emmy asked.

"No, practice went all right, and we actually got out early."

Mama smiled at Tony, nodded her head and whispered, "Go ahead, son."

Tony took a deep breath, looked at Mama, and then reached into his pocket as he dropped to one knee. He pulled out the red velvet gift box and opened it. Emmy gasped, and then held her breath. He looked at Emmy. She looked at the ring, and then at Tony. An image of a three-year-old boy flashed into her mind. Tony gazed into her blue eyes as they glistened and sparkled. Emmy covered her heart with her hands.

"Emily Olivia Colasanti, will you marry me?"